Scars of the Sundering
Book 2

LAMENT

Second Edition

By Hans Cummings

The Foundation of Drak-Anor
Wings of Twilight
Iron Fist of the Oroqs

Scars of the Sundering
Malediction
Lament
Salvation

Summer of Crows

The Zack Jackson Series
Zack Jackson & The Cult of Athos
Zack Jackson & The Cytherean Academy
Zack Jackson & The Hives of Valtra

Sojourn - An Anthology of Speculative Fiction
Forgotten Dreams (Sojourn 1)
The Pleasure Pools of Persiphia (Sojourn 2)
(also available individually on Kindle)

Scars of the Sundering

Book 1 – Malediction
Book 2 – Lament
Book 3 - Salvation

Hans Cummings

This is a work of fiction. All characters and events portrayed in this book are fictional, and any resemblance to real people or incidents is purely coincidental.

ISBN: 978-1-944999-00-1

Electronic edition available through Amazon.com,
Print edition available through Amazon.com and fine booksellers everywhere.

Edited by Cynthia Shepp
Cover design by Eric Hubbel
Cover Art by Lily Yang
Heraldy by Axel Löfving
Cartography by Anna B. Meyer
World of Calliome Logo by Gwyneth Ravenscraft of G-Sharp Productions

Acknowledgements
For Tink, without whom this would not have been possible.

Chapter 1

A chilly blast of air greeted Pancras as he opened the doors that led to the walkway. The waning twin moons of Calliome, the King and Queen, hung low in the sky, their soft light reflecting off the snow-covered Almerian rooftops. The minotaur's eyes scanned to the left and right. Upon seeing the arcade empty, he gave the all clear.

The three draks and the dwarf followed him as they made their way toward the main hall. Sneaking out in the middle of the night was Kali's idea. She assured them she knew the way through the palace's undercroft into the catacombs and from there into the city. By the time Princess Valene and Lady Milena awakened the next morning and noticed their absence, they would be miles away from the city.

Assuming they successfully avoided the Royal Guard.

Almeria should have provided them a safe shelter from the harsh winter. It should have been a place in which to lie low and keep warm for several months. The luck of Dolios had not been with them however, and they found rampant political corruption in the city. Still, they might have ignored it had they not been pulled into the affairs of the prince and learned of noblemen using slave labor in salt mines. While Pancras believed the princess would keep her word and allow them to leave in peace, he didn't want to take any chances.

Delilah took point as they descended the stairs leading to the main hall. She pointed her staff at the floor. As the eyes of the rodent skull atop her focus glowed blue, she whispered an incantation, "*Kalee'steen enoch leetiké goyna.*"

A dozen boggins materialized, then scampered into the main hall, yipping and gnashing their teeth. Were it not for the armored greaves worn by all the Royal Guards, Pancras would not have agreed to loosing the furry balls of hunger in the palace. He hoped their steel armor would be up to the challenge of boggin teeth.

Each downward step sent a new wave of pain into Pancras's leg. Even a day off it would help the wound he incurred the previous morning, but there was no time for healing if they wanted to leave the city before the real fallout from Princess Valene's coup began.

Once the shouts of alarm and clanks of running armored guards receded, the minotaur led the group across the main hall. They crossed without being spotted, and, as usual, found the door to the undercroft unguarded.

Kali chuckled as Kale pulled out his tools and set to work picking the lock. "They never guard the rooms where they store all their junk."

"Dwarves do." Edric grunted as he kept watch around the corner for patrolling guards.

"Dwarves post guards to their privies." Kali snorted. A click from the lock heralded Kale's success.

"Yeah, well, some of those nobles crap gold, you know."

"Enough." The minotaur ushered the draks through the door, snapping his fingers to attract Edric's attention. The dwarf pulled the door closed after hurrying through it.

Kale locked the door behind them. "That should slow them down."

The glow from Delilah's staff illuminated the dusty, crate-filled alcoves. Deep shadows hid the tops of the arches that supported the ceiling, creating the illusion that the room was larger than it was. They heard distant shouts and the sounds of scuffling through the ceiling as guards chased down Delilah's boggins. Vibration from the commotion above them knocked loose a layer of fine dust from the ceiling, which hung in the air like faerie glitter.

"I don't suppose you can banish the boggins you summoned now that we no longer need the distraction?"

Pancras followed the path in the dusty floor left by Kale and Delilah's repeated trips to the catacombs some weeks earlier.

"Oh, probably. I never learned how to do that, though." Shrugging, Delilah pointed out the new wrought-iron barricade bolt crossing the door that led to the catacombs. "'Guess they wanted to be sure undead things couldn't enter the palace."

The minotaur pursed his lips, lifting the bar out of the way. "You might look into that. I'm not keen on leaving a bunch of angry, hungry boggins for others to deal with."

Delilah ducked under his arm when he opened the door. "I won't learn it in time to help here, so don't worry about it. You thought it was a good idea when I suggested it."

"We need to learn some illusions." Pancras waited for Kali, Kale, and Edric to pass before closing the door. He couldn't replace the barricade bar from the catacomb side, a typical limitation of such crude door-barring methods.

"Wait…" Kali held up her hand.

"What?" Kale placed his hand on her shoulder to keep from bumping into her.

"I thought I heard something."

Pancras cocked his head. *As if that's going to help.* He held his breath as he strained to hear anything more than Edric's heavy breathing and the commotion still audible from the palace guards chasing boggins.

He ran his hand down the cold, stone catacomb wall. "Close walls like these cause strange echoes. Could it have been noise from the palace?"

Kali glanced up at him. The orange-scaled drak wrinkled her nose and shrugged. "Yeah, it's probably nothing." She patted Kale's hand. "Let's go. The way I got in should still be open. It'll be tight for the minotaur, but I think he'll make it."

The thought of squeezing into an even tighter space pained Pancras. He stooped to keep his horns from scraping the top of the tunnel. Their packs made the catacomb passageways seem even more cramped. If anyone were down here with them, they would surely be alerted to the presence of Pancras and his companions by the scraping of their packs against the walls.

"All those ghosts and whatnot you draks riled up a few weeks ago are gone, yeah?" Edric gripped the haft of his axe with white-knuckled fingers. He peeked around a corner, jumping as Pancras brushed past him.

"I can handle anything down here, Edric." Pancras held aloft his focus, creating light with the same incantation Delilah used. Pulling Kali to the front of the pack with him, he led the way. He took note of the various twists and turns of the catacombs. One gift bestowed by the gods to his people was the ability to unerringly navigate labyrinths, and the layout of the catacombs was more straightforward than the labyrinths minotaurs occupied in Drak-Anor. He still needed a guide to show him the correct way to their destination; however, he would remember the way back should they need to retreat.

"Shh!" Kali held up a clawed hand to silence the whispered bickering of the drak twins. "I hear it again."

Pancras heard it, too: the sound of voices echoing off the stone walls of the catacombs. It was impossible to pinpoint its origin, but the minotaur was certain what he heard was not the echoes of Kale and Delilah's discussion. The source of the noise drew closer and became more distinct. He turned toward Edric.

"Are dwarves good at locating the sources of sounds underground? I hear three distinct voices."

The dwarf snorted, tugging at his beard. "Maybe some, but not me."

Pancras shook his head and proceeded down the corridor with caution. *It figures I'd travel with the only dwarf who is terrible at being a dwarf.*

***

"Kale and I will scout ahead." Kali took Kale's hand. "Don't follow us too closely."

Kale shuffled along behind her. After withdrawing his hand from her grip, he drew his daggers as they ducked around a corner. He found it difficult to determine the difference between the sounds of his friends behind him and the others in the catacombs. One thing was certain: the sounds from those who were not his friends grew louder.

The stone walls and bone-filled niches of the labyrinthine catacombs couched their secrets in cobwebs and shadow. Kale peered into each alcove as they passed, hoping to see some sort of treasure unneeded by the catacomb's long-dead occupants.

Kali held out a clawed hand. She placed it on his chest when Kale continued to shuffle forward, oblivious to the intent of her gesture. She held a finger up to her lips, before pulling him by the arm into one of the compartments.

The others were close. He heard them clearly now, their voices rising above the scraping of leather on stone and the clink of metal against metal.

"Are you sure this is the way?" The voice sounded familiar to Kale, but he couldn't place it.

"Of course not, Highness. I know the draks used these tunnels to enter my mine, so there's no reason we cannot escape your palace by the same route."

"I shouldn't have to escape from my own damned palace. We're coming back soon, Reznik, to deal with that woman and the rest of the traitors."

Reznik and Gavril! Kale didn't take the time to wonder how the men gained entry to the catacombs. The former mine owner and the former prince didn't seem terribly close during the trial, but Kale was not good at deciphering human body language.

Kali placed her arm across his chest to restrain him as the two men walked past the niche they occupied.

Although they glanced quickly at each alcove, they did not linger long enough to detect the draks hiding in the shadows. Several men garbed in chain shirts and armed with crossbows followed.

Once the humans passed them, Kali released Kale. He crept forward, daggers ready, and peered around the corner. The men stopped at an intersection, whispered, and pointed, clearly disagreeing about which direction they should go.

"They're going to run right into Pancras and the others," Kali hissed in Kale's ear.

Kale nodded, glancing in the direction they had come. It seemed clear. "We should lead them away." He pulled a clay pot out of one of the niches, then let it crash to the floor, sending hundreds of razor-sharp shards into the pathway.

As they heard the cries of alarm from the humans behind them, the two draks took off. Kali shouted directions as they ran. *I hope we don't end up lost down here.*

The draks skidded around a corner, claws scraping on the stone floor, and found themselves facing a door. Kali cursed, and Kale whipped out his tools as he examined the locking mechanism.

"Hurry, Kale!"

Kale poked at the lock with a probe. It was an older-style lock, but it was more complex than most of the mechanisms he encountered in Almeria's palace during their stay there. Furthermore, his initial examination revealed that the lock was corroded and would not be easily coaxed into unlocking.

Behind him, he heard a metallic twang just before a crossbow bolt embedded itself in the door next to his cheek.

"Time's up, little draks."

***

"I heard it that time." Delilah cocked her head toward the commotion.

"The dead could have heard that." Edric picked his teeth with a fingernail as he leaned against the wall.

The drak sorceress eyed Pancras. The minotaur stepped forward, peeked around the corner, and then returned to the group. "The way is clear now, but I don't see Kale or Kali."

"Pah! We'll be wandering down here for days without our guide." Edric spat on the floor.

"We'll not become lost, but I don't know the way out." Pancras crept forward, tracing Kale and Kali's path and motioning for them to follow.

Delilah was confident in the minotaur's ability to keep his bearings in the catacombs, but she did not relish the idea of being surrounded by dead bones for any longer than necessary.

The echoes of the disturbance nearby made it difficult to determine if they were headed toward or away from it. The drak sorceress dragged a claw along the wall as they walked, digging a gouge so she would detect if they doubled-back along the same passageways or became separated from Pancras.

Pancras held up his hand and turned to face his entourage. "I can hear them just up ahead. They've cornered Kale and Kali. Ready yourselves."

The drak sorceress tightened her grip on her staff. Being mindful of her brother's position behind the humans, she contemplated what spell wouldn't endanger him. The humans ahead made no effort to be quiet.

"Where's the minotaur, Drak?"

Delilah recognized the voice of the former Prince of Almeria, Gavril. Pancras slipped his new rod from his belt. It glowed with emerald light as he stepped around the corner.

"Right behind you, Gavril."

"*Kaléste gi stoicheiaki.*" Delilah concentrated on the stone surface behind Pancras as coils of azure aether swirled forth from the top of her staff. A rocky fist punched its way through the floor, and then another. Stepping out from behind the corner, she observed Gavril and his cronies leveling their weapons at Pancras. Kale and Kali crouched behind them, their backs against a door.

The rock creature pulled itself out of the floor, leaving a collapsed, sunken depression of stone and dirt in its wake. Gavril's eyes widened. He stepped backward as the creature advanced. The former prince's lackeys shuffled, glancing at each other. Among them, Delilah spotted the slight man who once controlled Almeria's largest salt mine, Reznik.

"Looks like we're both trying to slink away in the night, Gavril." The minotaur crossed his chest with his arms.

"You see, Reznik?" Gavril glanced over his shoulder at the balding man. "Princess Bitch has turned on him, too." He drew a short, broad-bladed sword. "Fear not. The pain of her betrayal will be over quickly. Kill them all."

Whooping, Gavril's men charged.

Edric moved forward to meet them, axe raised. The dwarf slashed at the legs of the nearest guard as a ray of emerald energy shot over his head. After the ray struck the man in the chest, his face grew ashen, then withered. He collapsed, gasping and howling in pain.

Delilah's rock creature waded into the crowd, its rocky fists smashing men as if pounding wooden pegs into the dirt. She scrambled backward as Pancras moved between her and Gavril.

She directed the creature to clear a path to Kale and Kali, keeping an eye on any humans intent on making her a target. Controlling the rock creature required more concentration than Delilah expected. She was linked to its mind, such as it was, and she understood it wanted nothing more than to pulverize everything and everyone in its vicinity, her friends included. Even a momentary lapse to defend herself might cause it to smash one of her allies.

***

Pancras resisted the urge to marvel at the rock creature pounding its way through Gavril's men. *What else has Delilah learned this winter?* He had heard of such conjurations, of course, but never witnessed them in action. As the former prince approached, Pancras cut his ruminations short.

"I'll gut you this time, Necromancer."

The minotaur ignored the taunt. Raising his rod, he jumped to the side as a flicker of motion in his periphery foretold an attack on his flank by Reznik. He ducked under a guard sent flying over his head by the mighty fists of the rock creature Delilah controlled. The man hit the wall with a crunch and slid down, resting motionless on the floor. Reznik and Gavril lunged at Pancras.

"*Skia veema.*" The multitude of shadows swallowed him, and the minotaur stepped out of an alcove further down the hall. He leveled his rod at Reznik. "*Klepstee dynami tis zois.*"

A verdant ray struck the wiry man in the face. His hair whitened, his eyes became cloudy, and his skin desiccated and withered. He let out a strangled cry, falling backward. Clutching at his aged face, he backed into a guard. Kali seized the opportunity when the two fell prone to leap upon him and Reznik. She stabbed with her daggers until both men lay in pools of blood.

Gavril kicked Reznik's legs out of the way and advanced on Pancras, his eyes burning with rage. The minotaur's wounded leg ached, and he realized he would not be able to evade the murderous human forever. "*Angigma tou tafou!*"

The former prince dove forward, ducking under the green ray. It struck one of the guards instead. The man screamed as ghostly hands grasped at him from the floor and walls, holding him in place. Kale ran by him, slashing at his legs.

Pancras kicked, connecting with Gavril's face as the human rose in front of him. Gavril stumbled back and spat a gobbet of blood onto the floor. He growled, lunging again.

"*Skia—*" Gavril's blade caught the minotaur's side before he finished the spell. Pancras brought his head down and butted the human. Gavril fell backward, reaching out and grabbing the front of Pancras's robe. The human's weight jerked Pancras forward, wrenching his wounded leg.

Pancras gasped in pain. He cried out as a sharp fire bloomed in his gut. Tipping his head, he noticed Gavril's sword protruding from his belly. The human grimaced with bloody teeth as he twisted the blade. Pancras's legs became numb, then buckled under him.

Gavril held his grip on Pancras's robe as the minotaur succumbed. He used the necromancer's weight as a lever to right himself.

Pancras heard Kale cry his name.

From his position over Pancras, Gavril yanked his sword from the minotaur's stomach, spraying the corridor crimson. The former sovereign then plunged the blade between the minotaur's ribs into his chest.

Screaming, Kale and Kali stabbed Gavril, knocking him off Pancras.

The world grew dim as the minotaur's sight failed him. He heard Delilah call his name, and he felt a burst of heat just before the catacombs fell silent.

Darkness took him.

***

"Pancras! Pancras!" Kale tripped over the bloody corpse of Gavril in his haste to reach the minotaur's side. His daggers flew from his hands, clattering across the corridor. Already, the minotaur's limbs were limp, and his blood mingled with dust on the floor. Shaking Pancras, he called his name, but the minotaur did not respond.

"Don't do this. Don't die on us!" Delilah knelt on the other side of Pancras. A bloody gash marred her side.

"Damn you, Drak!" Edric kicked one of the dead guards on his way to them. "Ya nearly incinerated me when ya let off that spell. Oh—" He stopped when he saw Pancras.

Kali probed Pancras's wounds with a claw, then shook her head. Kale's eyes burned with tears he blinked away. His sister stroked the minotaur's hand as she repeated one word again and again. "No."

The nightmare of being alone in a strange city clouded Kale's thoughts. *Without Pancras, we're lost. What do we do? What do we do?* Seizing the minotaur's shoulders, he shook him, as if the violent action would awaken him from the slumber of death. In the recesses of his mind, he heard the clanking of mail and armored boots on the stone floor.

His heart pounded in his ears. Barely aware of Edric's cursing, he didn't react when rough hands grabbed him, then hauled him to his feet. He struggled when they pulled him away from Pancras.

"Stop. Release them!" The voice of Lady Milena broke through his grief. "By the gods, what happened here?"

The Royal Guard Captain's eyes were puffy; she had obviously been roused from sleep. Kale tried to speak, but his words were barely a hoarse croak. He stared at his feet as tears fell from his eyes.

"We grew tired of your hospitality, so we were leaving." Kali took Kale's hand. "Gavril and Reznik had the same idea and attacked us."

Milena stepped over to Gavril's body and prodded it with her toe. "He was supposed to be locked up." She glared at her guards. "Find out who released him and arrest them immediately."

The guards released the draks, then saluted, before they exited through the catacombs. Milena sighed, rubbing her temples, before kneeling in front of the four. "I understand why you might have thought this was your best option. Believe me. I do understand."

"We just wanted to be on our way." Delilah spat the words through sobs.

"Come back to your suite. I'll have my brother tend to your wounds. We'll take care of Pancras. The princess and I bear him no ill will. He deserves a proper burial or whatever you think is appropriate. I'll see to it personally you're given sufficient supplies to last until you arrive at your next destination. You can leave whenever you like."

She glanced over her shoulder at Pancras. "He was a decent man… minotaur. I grieve with you."

"Let's get going, then. I want to walk or sleep." Edric stopped at Pancras. "Go with Aita, Minotaur. You were better than I expected."

They followed Lady Milena through the catacombs and to the undercroft. She locked the undercroft door behind them before they returned to the palace. "I'll have the guards collect Pancras's body and place it in our mausoleum while you decide what is appropriate for him."

In the main hall, Milena instructed guards to clean up the bodies in the catacombs and sent one to fetch her brother Arnost. They did not have to wait long in their chambers before the priest of Apellon arrived. Only Delilah suffered from more than bumps and bruises, the gash in her side superficial, appearing far worse than it actually was. By the time the human finished mending their wounds, the rush of battle and the grief of Pancras's death caught up with Kale, and he fell into a fitful sleep.

Chapter 2

Pancras felt himself falling. He felt the wind roaring and sensed the world around him passing by. There was no light rushing closer, and although it was dark, he sensed the darkness deepening, growing darker, if such a thing were possible.

The wound in his stomach should ache, yet it did not, nor did his knee. The further he fell, the fewer physical sensations he felt, and he was overcome with a sense of disappointment; yet he felt oddly at peace. At last, a creeping shadow engulfed him. He wanted to struggle, to shout, to fight, but he couldn't move. He couldn't feel.

He was dead.

The shadow enveloped him in a cold embrace of total, utter darkness. Yet, even in the stark absence of illumination, he sensed a smile from within it. *You have not evaded me, Necromancer. You will yet serve my queen.*

Pancras wanted to cry out, to deny the dark creature that kept his spirit in thrall. His body was heavy, as though a lead weight pressed down on him. His mind wanted to scream, yet in death, he could not form even one thought.

Your suppositions are wrong. You live and die at the whim of my queen now, Necromancer. Her power grows, and your struggles to deny her, to deny me, are in vain. Feel her glory. Live again, as she desires.

Gasping, he snapped open his eyes to find a white veil obscuring his vision. For a moment, he panicked, unable to move. His body felt as though pins and needles coursed through it. After sliding the veil off his face, he assessed the small, stone-walled room in which he lay on a marble slab. Bolting upright, he screamed. Excruciating pain like that from the fiery heart of a forge lanced through his arm. He pulled it up and across his bare chest, gaping at the limb as it blackened, withering, and his fingers curled into sharp, black talons. As suddenly as it began, the pain stopped. He felt the shadow tickle the back of his mind, but it seemed content to fade into the deep recesses of his memory.

"What in the name of Tinian's lance?" Two guards threw open the door, then dashed into the room. After taking one look at Pancras sitting upright, they fled.

Pancras panted, trying to catch his breath. The air smelled, tasting musty and stale, like the air in the undercroft. He felt as if he had been asleep for days. Darkness hovered at the edge of his vision, a fleeting phantasm that vanished when he tried to focus on it.

A dim light dangled from the ceiling, and he saw a shrouded body lying on another slab next to him. He could just reach it if he stretched, and a quick peek under confirmed it was Prince Gavril. He suppressed a shiver generated by the cold stone and heard approaching footsteps.

Arnost pushed the door open, his hand clutching the symbol of Apellon at his neck. The color drained from his face as he came upon Pancras, and he held the golden lyre before him. "By the light of Apellon, be thou cleansed, foul creature!"

The power of Apellon radiated from the symbol, washing over Pancras. It warmed his body, though the brightness hurt his eyes. He squinted and held up his withered hand to block the light.

"I don't think that's doing what you want it to do. It's quite warm. It feels nice." The absurdity of it struck Pancras, and he laughed. Gathering the shroud around his waist, he swung his legs over the edge of the slab and yawned.

"You are not dead? Or undead?"

Pancras stretched his legs and arched his back. "No. No, I don't think I am. I thought I was." The minotaur flexed his still-bandaged knee. "Huh, it doesn't hurt anymore."

"You were most assuredly dead." Arnost glanced behind him, frowning. "I must report this. Wait here?"

"I have no desire to walk around the palace naked, clutching this burial shroud around my waist."

Pancras remained seated on the slab as Arnost departed. He examined his withered hand. Blackened and leathery, its condition did not seem to impair its function. Colder than his other hand, the nails had lengthened into talons, and it appeared mummified. He ran his good hand over his belly and found no evidence of the wound that claimed his life.

"What sorcery is this?" Princess Valene entered the chamber, Arnost and Milena hot on her heels. The princess wore a black gown of mourning and a lace veil. Pancras noticed the bleak color poorly matched her rich, sepia-toned skin. Milena's armor blazed orange with reflected candlelight.

"Necromancy!" Milena began to draw her sword, but Arnost placed his hand on her arm to stop her.

"By some great fortune, I am not dead. I was, but I am now not." Pancras felt he stated the obvious, but some people needed to hear the obvious when they were in shock.

"Arnost?" Princess Valene addressed Milena's brother.

"The light of Apellon had no effect on him. He appears to be alive and"—Arnost examined Pancras's belly—"unharmed."

"This complicates matters. Arnost, you may leave. Milena?"

Milena nodded to her brother as he ascended the stairs. She turned to the princess. "Yes, Your Highness?"

"Inform the draks and bring them here." She took Milena's hand. "Be discreet."

"It will be done." Milena brought Princess Valene's hand to her lips and bowed. Turning, she left the princess alone with her dead husband and Pancras.

"What now am I to do with you, Minotaur? You have killed the sovereign ruler of Etrunia." Sighing, she crossed her arms over her chest. "Such a crime cannot go unpunished." She regarded him, a slight smile lingering at the corners of her mouth.

"He did kill me first." By Pancras's reckoning, it was a closed-and-shut case. The law, of course, probably would not side with a minotaur, a foreigner at that.

Valene laughed, waving her hand. "Clearly self-defense. Your actions have freed me and this once-great nation from an odious, vile, petty little man. Two of them, actually. I understand Reznik was found amongst the dead. I suspected he would try to save his prince. He probably wanted to retreat with Gavril, regroup, and attempt a coup in the spring. I suppose I'll have to launch an investigation to know for certain.

"You have effected great change here." She paced as she spoke, stopping alongside her husband's body before turning her back to it to regard Pancras.

"That was not my intention when I arrived. My friends and I sought only safety and warmth during the winter."

Princess Valene reached behind, moved her husband's dangling arm out of the way, and then leaned against the stone slab upon which he lay. "I intended to reward your service once things settled down, before you left. I am pleased you're not dead, you know. I enjoyed our shared constitutionals in the mornings. I'm curious how you accomplished this resurrection."

Pancras wanted those answers for himself, as well. He had a suspicion, which lingered at the edges of his memory. A gnawing, twisting feeling deep in his gut indicated he was not free of the shadow creature. He needed more time to research the matter before making any claims, however. "Perhaps the fetish I failed to create properly had some effect after all?"

"Is that possible?"

Pancras shrugged before rolling his neck in an attempt to loosen the muscles. "There are very few impossible things when it comes to the arcane arts. I have heard of ways to cheat death, but I have never tried any of them myself."

"Under the circumstances, I think it best if you keep a low profile. Some of the guards will not understand." Princess Valene circled the slab upon which Pancras rested, her heels clicking on the stone floor. "In a few days, I will have completed my purge of those loyal to Gavril, after which I should think you can move freely again. Besides, there was another snowstorm while you were… away. No one will be able to leave the palace again until tomorrow at the earliest."

"Snow? How long was I… dead?" Intellectually, Pancras realized time must have passed in between the confrontation in the throne room and awakening on a slab, but he had no sense of it.

"You died the day before yesterday. The snow came upon us quickly; otherwise, we might have prepared you for internment in the catacombs by now."

Pancras's head reeled. He swayed, grasping the slab to steady himself. Princess Valene touched his shoulder.

"Easy. Your friends will be here shortly. Rest now."

***

"Firk—blast it, ye scaly—By Adranus's beard!" Edric's sputtering cut through Delilah's concentration like an axe splitting a log. She slammed her grimoire shut and glared over her shoulder at the dwarf. He sat in the center of the parlor with her brother and Kali.

"How am I supposed to get anything done with the three of you making so much noise all the time?" Delilah hopped out of the armchair, then picked up a poker from the side of the hearth. She wanted to wrap it around the dwarf's head but settled on stabbing the smoldering logs in the fireplace.

"Come on, Deli. We're just having some fun."

Her brother, Kale, always wanted to have fun. *How can he think of fun at a time like this? That's why I'm in charge now,*

I guess. I'm the only one who realizes we have serious business to take care of.

"Is that magic book of yours going to teach you how to melt the snow away?" Edric stood, then walked over to the table. He poured himself a goblet of wine.

"No." Delilah pointed the poker at Edric. "But it'll teach me how to burn that beard of yours right off!"

A knock at the doors interrupted his retort. Delilah threw the poker to the floor before crossing the room to find out who disturbed them. Lady Milena bowed as the drak invited her in. The humans had kept their distance since Pancras's death; Delilah waited for the Captain of the Royal Guard to speak first.

She stared at the human. Behind her, Kale coughed. "Deli?"

Delilah raised her eyebrows. She was determined not to extend any niceties.

"Pardon my intrusion. The princess needs to see you and your brother immediately."

Narrowing her eyes, Delilah stepped away from the door. She reached behind her, fumbling at the armchair for her staff. "What for now?"

Lady Milena regarded the dwarf and draks staring at her. "I'm not at liberty to say. It's… it's about Pancras. It's important."

Kali took Kale's arm. "Then we're all going. We're sticking together until we leave this city." She eyed Edric and then Delilah. "Right?"

"Yes." After locating her staff, Delilah tapped the butt of it on the floor. "We all go, or none of us do."

Lady Milena bowed her head. "As you wish." She gestured to the hallway. "If you please?"

The hallway outside their chambers was open to the palace courtyard on one side. From three floors up, one could look out over the city. The fresh, white blanket of snow covering Almeria reflected the sun's light, nearly blinding Delilah as she emerged through the doors. A gust of wind slammed one of the doors shut behind them, and she closed the other one.

Delilah ignored Edric's grumbles about how underground folk should stay underground when the weather turned bad. Her thoughts turned toward Pancras and how he bled out with his head in her lap. When they left Drak-Anor, she thought their excursion would be a fun trip to the far south and then back home. Instead, she ended up involved in a slave revolt and witnessed the only wizard in Drak-Anor murdered by a petty tyrant.

Lady Milena led the draks and the dwarf through the main hall, down the hallway to the undercroft, and through the dusty, cobweb-filled halls to stairs that spiraled down.

Delilah pondered why the knight led them into the bowels of the palace, but all thoughts of betrayal fled when she saw Pancras seated upright on the edge of the marble slab, chatting with Princess Valene.

As Delilah stood frozen, her mouth agape, Kale ran past her and jumped up on the slab to hug Pancras. "I knew you'd find a way to beat them!"

Kali and Edric stared. Edric spat on the floor and stepped backward. "What foul sorcery is this?"

Delilah held up her hand to silence the dwarf. "Not every magical thing you don't understand is 'foul sorcery'!"

She stepped around the slab, touching Pancras as she circled him. Delilah wasn't as confident as her brother, and she viewed Pancras through narrowed eyes. "How did you come back? There was a lot of blood. Are you undead?"

He shifted, covering his right arm. "I feel alive." Pancras rubbed his arm through the sheet. "Mostly."

The drak sorceress examined him. "No cravings for flesh or blood or anything like that?"

Pancras rested his hand on his stomach. "I am a bit hungry now that you mention it, but I think bread and wine would do nicely for a first course. Perhaps some fruit?"

"Sounds like he's okay to me, Deli." Kale released his grip on Pancras long enough to turn and face his sister.

"Indeed." Princess Valene nodded in agreement. "I've never heard of the dead feasting on bread and wine. Lady Milena and I will leave you to your reunion. A guard will be just outside in case you need assistance returning to your chambers."

Delilah tilted her head in acknowledgement. After the two humans departed, Kali and Edric entered the room, then closed the door behind them. The drak sorceress spun on Pancras. "Okay, spill it! How did you do it? You died in our arms."

She joined with her brother in standing before Pancras, stared up at him, and awaited an answer.

"I do not know." The minotaur sighed and shook his head. After uncovering his withered arm, Pancras flexed his fingers. His friends gasped at the skin cracking and creaking like old, dry leather. "It was not without a cost, it seems."

"Is that... are ya diseased?" Edric backpedaled at the sight of Pancras's arm.

"I'm not certain. I suspect whatever force is responsible for my revivification exacted this"—He waved his withered hand—"perhaps as a reminder?" He slid off the slab, knees buckling as his hooves touched the floor.

Clutching the top of the slab to remain upright, Pancras chuckled. "Looks like I might need some help to our chambers."

***

Pancras regained his strength in only a few days, but additional snowstorms further delayed their departure. The minotaur took the opportunity to rest and study the route to Muncifer. Kale was happy to see his friend up and moving around again, though he didn't understand how Pancras was alive. In the end, Kale was satisfied that the mysteries of magic were beyond his understanding. Being alive was better than being dead, in Kale's opinion, and distancing themselves from Almeria and the dangerous political games the humans liked to play was the best way the drak could think of to ensure that all of them remained alive.

As the weeks passed, the snows of winter melted, fading crystal white vistas into dirty slush and muddy streets. The soggy, wet chill soaked into peoples' bones, and he was grateful for the chaos that gave him wings and fire-breath, which kept a warm flame within him.

With the help of Edric and Kali, Kale visited every tavern, alehouse, and gambling den in Almeria while leaving his sister to study her grimoire. Though she didn't say it, he understood she appreciated the solitude. Pancras kept to himself most of the time, poring over scrolls and tomes Lady Milena and her brother brought him as he sought an answer to the question they all wanted answered: why was he alive?

It was a question Kale intended to leave to those smarter than he. In truth, he was eager to return to the road. Of the five of them, only Pancras had been to Muncifer before, and the stories he told at dinner piqued Kale's curiosity.

"Muncifer was once a proud dwarven city."

Edric raised his goblet at the declaration.

"It was until the Sundering, that is. When the world broke, Muncifer was exposed. Great rifts and cracks in the earth opened up. Half of the city fell away into the Maelstrom. When the world was healed, it remained exposed. Most of the dwarves left, seeking solace with their brethren living under the mountains."

This was a familiar story for Kale. It nearly destroyed the world. He wasn't sure what caused it; some said it was the death of one of the gods, Rannos, the Dragon Father. The fae fled, arcane energies infusing the world diffused, and whole nations were destroyed. Since the healing of the world began, magic returned and the fae reappeared, but in every corner of Calliome, evidence of the Sundering remained. The chaos rift through which he was thrown before they left Drak-Anor was one such scar.

"Aye, the dwarves left, and the minotaurs moved in." After draining his goblet, Edric belched.

"Minotaurs and humans." Pancras reached across the table and helped himself to another slab of meat from the roast the kitchen sent up. "There were some draks and a few dwarven traders now and again."

"Draks?" Kali perked up. "What clans?"

"I don't know, Kali. I didn't pay much attention to draks in those days."

Delilah elbowed her brother in the ribs. "And now he can't get enough of us."

"Are we going to be able to make it there by Spring's Dawning, Pancras?" The more the snow melted, the more Kale worried about their timetable. "It's a long way away, and it's getting warmer."

"About six weeks away, by my reckoning." Edric poured himself another goblet of wine.

"Spring's Dawning is marked by the rise of The Plow, Kale." Pancras offered half of the slab of meat he had to Delilah. "Tinian's Eye is still in the sky, and The Plow doesn't appear until that's been gone several weeks." The drak sorceress declined with a shake of her head.

Terrakaptis taught Kale about the constellations of stars in the sky, or tried to. There were so many to remember, each with their own story, and Kale had trouble recalling all of them. "Do you really think the humans will let us leave?"

Pancras glanced at each of them as he considered the question. "Yes, I believe they will. The princess has been very gracious these last few weeks."

Pancras's confidence assuaged Kale's concerns. He couldn't overlook, though, that it was his friendship with Kali that involved them in Almeria's politics to begin with.

Kali cleared her throat. "We should acquire mounts, I think." She eyed Kale from across the table, her burnt-orange scales flashing in the light from the room's candles and lanterns.

Edric grunted. "I hate horses."

Delilah squinted at her brother. "We've never ridden them."

"I have an idea about that." Kali nodded at Pancras. "The Firescale village is a few days west of the city. They have mounts that won't be jittery around draks and minotaurs, and they'll give us a better price than anyone here will. With mounts, we'll easily make up the time it takes to detour."

Pancras scratched his chin, nodding. "All right. I like that idea. Let's spend a few days wrapping up our affairs here and then resume our journey."

Kale raised his goblet. "Hear, hear!" The others joined him in his toast.

After dinner, he walked down to the palace grounds with Kali. Since the gardens were soggy from melting snow, they kept to the paved paths. The two walked arm in arm through the garden. Between the spongy grasses and bare flowerbeds, there wasn't much to see, but it was a diversion from being cooped up within their quarters.

"It'll be nice to get back on the road." As bored as he was hanging around the palace, Kale hoped for an uneventful journey to Muncifer.

"I'm nervous about returning to the village. It's been years." Kali shook her head and kicked a rock off the path. "I fear seeing the damage Reznik did."

Lord Reznik's salt mine under the city enslaved most of the draks from Kali's home village. Disrupting that operation and freeing the slaves were memories Kale could take away from Almeria and be proud of. "I wish we could stay and help rebuild."

"Maybe you and your sister can come back with me when all this business with the wizards is over."

"Yeah, maybe." Kale wondered if his sister would be interested in relocating to a village of draks and leaving behind their friends in Drak-Anor. The thought appealed to him, but he would have preferred for the Firescale village to be farther away from Almeria.

"One thing's for sure: I'll be glad to get away from all these humans."

Kali laughed in agreement.

***

Pancras kept to himself in the weeks following his apparent resurrection. He didn't eschew dining with his friends or socializing when they approached him, but he did not seek out the company of others. Instead, he reflected on his experience, despite having no memory of death itself.

That he had no memory of it troubled him.

His withered right arm and the dark haze at the edges of his vision troubled him as well. While he attended the Arcane University, Pancras learned that rites existed to resurrect the dead, but the specific rituals associated with those rites were lost with the Sundering, and all carried with them terrible costs. Pancras couldn't recall anything in those rituals that resembled what happened to him.

On warmer days, he scoured local book sellers and temple libraries for volumes that might hold the answers he sought. It was clear after a few failures that Almeria was light on resources and those educated about certain arcane matters. There were temples aplenty, but none dedicated to the goddess of magic, Selene.

"They don't have an Arcane University, though, do they?" Delilah glanced up from her grimoire as he groused to her in front of the fire. "Why would they have a temple of Selene?"

"She's not an obscure or dead god, Delilah. She's the daughter of Tinian, sister of Apellon and Anetha. They're well-represented here."

"Yeah, well, they also say they're civilized; yet they had a salt mine under the city staffed by slaves that no one knew about."

"You make a good point." Pancras slumped in his chair and sighed, rubbing his right arm. The warmth of the fire crackling in the hearth did not seem to affect the chill that lingered in his withered limb. He decided to change the subject before she buried her snout in her grimoire.

"I think it's time we return to the road. The worst of the winter's storms should be over."

"Good. The sooner this business is over with, the better. I want to go home, Pancras."

Pancras agreed.

A gust of wind from the opening doors caused the hearth to flicker. Kale and Kali bounded into the room, laughing. Delilah forced a smile onto her face and snapped her grimoire shut. The other two draks took no notice of Delilah and Pancras and helped themselves to some wine from a jug on the dinner table.

Pancras gestured to the grimoire. "Learn anything new lately?"

"As a matter of fact, I've been learning tons of earth magic. Some water magic, too. I don't know how the book decides what to show me." She opened the book to the page she last read. The symbols and writing were still undecipherable to Pancras.

"Perhaps you're just learning techniques in the order in which Gil-Li wrote the book?" That made the most sense to Pancras.

"Maybe." Delilah leaned over to peer around Pancras's chair. "Hey, lovebirds! Pancras says we're leaving soon, so separate yourselves and get to packing!"

"Packing?" Kale brought his goblet of wine over to the chairs in front of the fire. "We're leaving tonight?"

"No, not tonight," Pancras shook his head. "Nor tomorrow. Possibly the day after. I still have a few errands I'd like to run in town." He pointed a withered finger at Kale. "And you still have to pick up my horn tips from that jeweler."

"I forgot!" Kale smacked his forehead. "Things got so crazy with you dying and all. I'll go get them first thing."

Pancras smiled. In truth, he'd forgotten, too. "I'll go with you. I need to find something to cover this arm with. Maybe a leatherworker has a sleeve or something with a glove."

"A black glove?" Kale poked at Pancras's arm with a clawed finger. "You can be mysterious with it."

"That's what I need: to draw attention to myself." Pancras smacked the digit away.

"Will it matter much where we're going?" Kali cocked her head. "Muncifer is more of a minotaur city than human, right?"

Pancras faced her. "About fifty-fifty. Or it was twenty-five years ago. The humans there tend to be more tolerant than they are here." He hoped the situation in Muncifer had not changed drastically since he was last there. *A lot can change in a quarter-century.*

***

The next morning, Delilah busied herself with packing, while Kale and Pancras went into town to take care of last-minute errands. Meanwhile, Kali volunteered to track down Edric. Half of the time, the dwarf didn't return to the palace at night and staggered with a hangover into their quarters in the middle of the following day.

Delilah took the liberty of sending a messenger to fetch Lady Milena so she could inform the humans of their plans. Delilah didn't feel any obligation to be polite to the knight and the princess, but she figured they'd want to be notified Pancras was leaving. To their credit, the humans were true to their word and didn't try to convince Pancras, or any of them for that matter, to undertake any tasks or favors over the last several weeks.

Lady Milena arrived before any of the group returned from their errands. She seemed surprised to find Delilah alone. "Where is everyone else?" Her armor clanked as she entered the room. To Delilah, the thought of having to be clothed in that constrictive, noisy metal all day was incomprehensible. The knight cocked an eyebrow at Delilah, resting one hand on the hilt of her sword.

"They're running errands. We're leaving in the morning. Weather permitting."

Lady Milena blinked, then crossed her arms. "Tomorrow? The princess wanted to have a banquet for all of you before you left. I don't think there's time to prepare now."

A banquet? I wonder if Pancras will delay our departure for a party. "Tomorrow. That's the plan, anyway. I suppose it could change by the time Pancras returns."

"This seems sudden." A frown crept across Lady Milena's face as she listened to Delilah.

"We have until Spring's Dawning to get to Muncifer. We have no mounts, so unless you can magically whisk us away or are going to give us horses or something, we need to get on the road. Plus, it'll be safer the sooner we are out of your hair." As soon as Delilah said it, she realized the implications of her insult. She shook her head, turning toward her bedroom.

"As you wish. I will inform the princess." If Lady Milena took offense from Delilah's words, she gave no indication of it. "I'll see what we can do about arranging mounts for you, though I must caution you not to have high hopes. Almeria's liveries are tight fisted."

Delilah paused, expecting Lady Milena would follow her. The knight left their chambers instead, pulling the doors shut in her wake. Delilah peeked into the parlor to ensure she was really gone. "Well, Deli-girl. Pancras would've dealt with that differently, probably, but he's not here, right?"

Chapter 3

Now that the day of departure was upon them and the chilly breeze served as a grim reminder that winter may yet have a few more statements to make, Pancras wasn't so sure he wanted to return to the road. Guards watched over their possessions at the palace gates while the minotaur, draks, and dwarf said their farewells to the princess.

Princess Valene sat on the throne formerly occupied by her husband. Resplendent in a shimmering, green gown, she observed Pancras leading the draks and Edric across the throne room. A tight braid of her ebony hair fell across her shoulder, dangling between her arm and her body. Lady Milena stood in a relaxed stance to one side, two steps down from the top of the throne's dais. Guards, garbed in the tabards of the new regime, were posted on either side of the platform, flanking each door leading into the throne room.

Flexing his withered hand, Pancras became aware of how loudly his new leather gauntlet creaked in contrast to the relative silence of the throne room. He disliked gloves and other apparel that covered his forearms and hands, but he preferred the gauntlet over having a constant visual reminder that whatever returned him to life exacted a horrible price on his body, a toll he was not entirely certain was paid.

The princess tilted her head toward the group approaching her throne. Pancras stopped and bowed before her, gesturing with his good hand for the draks and Edric to follow suit. "It is time for us to depart and continue our journey, Your Highness. We are eternally grateful for your hospitality and grace." The words felt awkward on the minotaur's tongue. Although Sarvesh disliked such platitudes, despite being the ruler of Drak-Anor, Pancras understood humans tended to appreciate such niceties.

"So Lady Milena tells me." The princess nodded at the knight standing by her side. "Pity we had no time to prepare a farewell feast for you."

Pancras's stomach grumbled at the mention of food. "My apologies, but I fear if we do not depart immediately, I'll lose my nerve and delay our departure until reaching Muncifer on time is impossible."

"I understand." The princess gestured, and Lady Milena stepped forward to present Pancras with a piece of rolled-up parchment. "I have arranged a team of horses and wagon for you. Present this at the livery outside the city gates. If you stick to the roads, it should speed your journey."

Pancras bowed again. "You have our thanks." He turned, stopping to address the princess one final time. "May Anetha grant you the wisdom to enjoy a long, prosperous rule."

"You will be welcome guests any time you come to Almeria. May Dolios watch over your journey."

As Pancras bowed and exited the throne room, he reflected with dismay that Dolios was not only the god of travel, but also of luck, both good and bad.

***

Kale reached under his hat to scratch his head as he circled the wagon and team of horses Princess Valene provided for them. The chestnut-colored horses clomped toward him, stomping and snorting, their breath pluming smoke in the cold morning air. Edric grunted as he climbed onto the bench at the front of the wagon. His stubby legs kicked as he struggled to maintain balance while reaching down to grab the reins.

"You know how to drive one of these?" Pancras regarded Edric who offered Delilah a hand to assist her into the wagon. From the ground Kali boosted Delilah up, even as the sorceress tried to brush away her helping hands. The sorceress reached for one of the wooden rails that arced over the bed of the wagon. A canvas cover was rolled up and secured to one side of the bed, intended for use as protection during foul weather. Kale hoped they'd seen the last of rain or snow for a while, but the puffy, rain-laden clouds drifting overhead threatened to dash those hopes.

"Sure. My sister used to have one, though hers was drawn by a mule instead of two horses. She ditched it when the wheel broke, but she kept the mule. I might be rusty, but I think it'll come back to me."

Pancras offered a hand to help Kali into the wagon. Kale gave her a boost before passing their belongings up to be stowed away. He doubted Edric's ability, given that the dwarf's feet dangled in the air above the floorboard, but he kept his misgivings to himself.

"Up here, Longshanks." Edric patted the bench next to him. "I'm going to need your long arms and legs until we can modify this thing to fit me better."

After Pancras helped Kale up and into the back of the wagon, he took his place up front next to Edric. The wagon lurched forward as Edric cracked his whip. Unprepared for such a jolt, Kale fell backward, grasping at the rails for support. Kali grabbed his arm and helped to right him.

She glanced toward the front of the wagon. "I still think we should detour to my village and see about getting some proper mounts for the rest of us."

Pancras looked over his shoulder at her, nodding. "Agreed. We'll move faster on separate mounts, and we're traveling light enough that this wagon is overkill. What's our route, Kali?"

Kali clambered past the drak twins to stand at the front of the wagon. Her head barely came to Pancras's shoulder as she stuck her snout in between the dwarf and the minotaur. "Turn south where the road splits. There should be a marked trail branching off from that after a ways that leads back toward

Almeria. It cuts through some farms outside the south side of the city. We'll have to stay on the trail overnight, but we should reach Honeywater by tomorrow night."

"Honeywater? That's the name of your village?" Delilah snorted. "Home of the Firescale draks?"

Kali glared at the laughing sorceress. "There's a lake and lots of beehives." She turned to watch the road, lowering her voice. "At least there were before the humans started enslaving us. The lake is still there, but few tend the hives these days."

Kale elbowed his sister in the ribs. She clicked her teeth. "What?"

"Lay off, huh?"

Delilah leaned toward her brother, her voice a hissing whisper. "It's a stupid name!"

"No stupider than 'Twilight Dungeon.' Who lives in a dungeon? You live in a place like that, and you're asking for people to start trouble!" Kale had years to think about it. Drak-Anor was a much more respectable name. It even meant "Home of the Draks." He liked to think he and Delilah contributed to Sarvesh's suggestion of that name.

Delilah huffed and crossed her arms over her chest, scowling at Kale. "Yeah, well, you're not wrong about that, but you're still wrong!" She huffed again, pulling her grimoire from her pack.

Smiling, Kale slapped her knee before shifting in his seat to gaze at Almeria. As the wagon bounced along the road, Kali's voice droned on, regaling Edric and Pancras with stories about Honeywater.

***

Gisella adjusted her grip on her spear as she pushed her prisoner forward. Like most Watchfolk, she possessed a sword, an heirloom from her father, but she preferred to keep her quarry at length. He stumbled, but he remained upright, defiant. With the butt of her spear, she whacked him on the back of his knees, causing him to fall prone. In the Court of Wizardry, defiance was not tolerated from any prisoners when facing the archmage. Gisella sighed. *Archmage. What a pompous git.* The court's guards stood at attention, hands resting on their swords, ready to leap into action if the prisoner showed any signs of aggression.

The Archmage, Vilkan Icebreaker, The Manless, was a hulking man of great girth and vicious temperament. Standing, he tugged at his beard before sweeping the wrinkled folds of his gold-trimmed blue robe to the side with a wide motion of his arms. The high wizards of the court attired in colored robes looked on as he descended the steps, their masked faces concealing their contempt. However, their body language belied their silent approval. Their attitude was a matter of great debate among the lesser peoples of the court. Many said their disapproval was for The Manless himself, though Gisella believed they were disdainful of all who were not high wizards, but especially of The Manless since he ascended to the position of archmage and was not himself a high wizard.

Politics of court did not concern Gisella, however. As one of the court's slayers, she was tasked with glorious purpose: to track down and bring to justice those branded renegades by the court, such as the man she brought before them today. Alik Ironstaff was a mewling worm in the best of times, in her opinion. Nevertheless, seeing him receive his due and likely being the one to carry out his punishment brought no pleasure.

Alik prostrated himself before Archmage Vilkan. "Great merciful one, I beg you. This"—he cast a glance over his shoulder at Gisella—"this golden harpy has accused me unjustly. I've done nothing wrong."

"Nothing? Ha!" The archmage seized Alik by his throat, then lifted the man to his feet. "Who do you think sent her after you? The slayers do nothing without my leave. Especially the Golden Slayer."

Gisella observed in stony silence. *Oh, what you do not know, Manless.*

"I am—innocent—" Alik's protest turned into a choking cough as the archmage tightened his grip.

He threw the squirming man to the floor. "Innocent? Not one among us is innocent. And you"—he thrust his pudgy finger into Alik's face—"you left my sister with a child. A child who killed her from within!"

Alik splayed his hands on the floor, spreading his arms as far as his shackles would allow. "It is no crime to love!"

Gisella's eyes flicked toward the archmage and then down at Alik. She was not aware of Alik's exact crime until this moment, though it made little difference to her. She was bound to obey the court's edicts, regardless of her personal feelings on the matter.

For now.

Eyeing Gisella, Archmage Vilkan drew his finger across his throat. He spun, the hem of his robe sweeping over Alik's prone form. Gisella stepped forward, frowning. She thrust her spear into Alik's back, twisting it as she lunged forward, stopping only when she felt the tip of her spear hit the stone floor. Squirming, Alik cried out, but she held fast, planting her boot on his backside for support. She yanked, and, with a spray of blood, pulled the broad tip out. He twitched for a moment on the floor. Then he lay still.

Taking his seat, the archmage regarded his dour-faced comrades and then nodded at Gisella. "Reliable as always. Have you anything to add to the proceedings?"

Always the same. "Nothing, Archmage. If there is nothing else, I have other business to which I must attend."

Archmage Vilkan's face twisted into a scowl. "Yes, of course. There is nothing further today, then. I may have something for you tomorrow." He gestured for the guards to dispose of Alik.

Gisella wasted no time exiting the court. When she was beyond the chamber doors, she removed her helmet, then tucked it under her arm. She rested her spear in the crook of the same arm as she loosened her hair, allowing her golden tresses freedom to fall around her shoulders. A fellow slayer, Grímar Blackthorne eyed her, fingering the moon pendant around his neck.

"Always a pleasure to see the Golden Slayer release her treasured locks."

Grímar, Gisella, and Archmage Vilkan were all Watchfolk: hardy people from the frozen lands beyond the Iron Gate Mountains to the south of Muncifer, which comprised the Four Watches. Gisella considered Grímar a friend and comrade, however, unlike Archmage Vilkan.

"Vilkan was in a poor state of mind today. Your doing?" She took up her spear and continued her walk. Grímar fell in step beside her. They crossed the courtyard toward a small, half-timbered building from which smoke drifted up its dual chimneys. The Blood Oak stretched its bare arms across the courtyard, winter having stolen its leaves. Soon, it would be alive with new foliage, shading the courtyard with its building-spanning canopy.

"I had nothing to do with it."

She thumped his arm as they continued on. "I find that hard to believe."

They turned into the compound's tavern. After ordering tankards of mead from the barman, they found an unoccupied long table. Grímar smacked his lips after taking a long draft and seated himself. "There are dark rumors flying. Have you heard?"

There were always rumors. They were always dark. They always portended doom and destruction. Folk in Muncifer seemed to have little to gossip about except the Court of Wizardry and their superstitions.

"I try to pay them little mind. What is it this time? An army of giants about to descend from the mountains to pillage Muncifer? A dragon, perhaps? Like the one spotted up north near, where was it? Ironslag?"

"Ironkrag." Grímar laughed. "No, though I have heard the one about the giants. Unrest in the cemeteries up north. Mad Magda says a shadow reaches from the mountains to Vlorey, the shadow of the Lich Queen's withered old hand."

Gisella stopped, mead sloshing against her lips. She peered over the rim of her tankard at Grímar. He continued, heedless of her reaction. "Can you imagine? The Lich Queen? Again? These folks are as cracked as the land around here."

History told of the Lich Queen's ultimate defeat decades ago, and of the Witch Queen's defeat a decade or more before that, even. After the Witch Queen died, from her tomb arose the Lich Queen. At the conclusion of a devastating war, she was said to have been utterly destroyed, and from her ashes, nothing could rise. Of course, Gisella knew better than to take the stories from that war literally, no matter how popular they were. The affairs of wizards contained many mysteries and unexplainable phenomenon.

She set down her tankard. "A new world tree in the Dragon Spine Mountains. More different types of fae folk emerging into the world, dragons, too. The healing of the world has well and truly begun. I could believe almost anything."

Grímar waved over a servant and ordered a plate of sausages. "But the Lich Queen? Again? How many times must someone die before they're truly dead?"

Gisella picked up her tankard and drained the sweet mead before replying, "Some people don't have the sense to stay dead, you know."

**

After a day and a half of bouncing along on a hard wooden bench at the mercy of Edric's driving, Delilah decided she'd walk all the way to Muncifer if need be. She feared her backside might never be the same again and winced when the wagon bounced, dropping from the road onto the stone bridge that led to Honeywater.

On the other side of the bridge, as they made their way to Honeywater's market square, human guards wearing the livery of Almeria's Royal Guard flagged down the wagon, grabbing the horses' reins as Edric brought the team to a halt.

"What's your business here, travelers?" The guard, a tall, lanky human with a weathered face and scraggly beard peered at the draks in the back of the wagon.

Kali poked her head up between Pancras and Edric. "I'm a Firescale from this village. We're heading south and need to trade for supplies."

"All right. No funny business, though. We're watching."

Edric maneuvered the team and wagon toward the location indicated by the guard. As soon as the wagon stopped, Delilah scrambled out to plant her feet in the grass, barely resisting the urge to fall to her knees and kiss the land.

"I guess Princess Valene is serious about fixing this town, huh?" Kale hopped down next to his sister.

"Looks that way." Kali climbed out of the wagon. "I figured she'd send a few guards to clear out the slavers and then leave us alone. But, Royal Guards?"

Yeah, yeah, the princess is great, the princess is grand. Delilah wondered where the princess's grace was when she was dangling by her wrists in the palace dungeon. Grunting, she hobbled her way around the wagon to Pancras, who worked with Edric to secure the horses.

"Are you hurt?" Pancras tossed the lead rope to Edric, then knelt down to examine Delilah.

"My butt hurts! I'm not riding to Muncifer in the back of that wagon, Pancras. I'll walk."

Chuckling, Pancras stood. "I don't think that will be necessary. We should be able to trade this wagon for more suitable mounts." He pointed across the square. "It looks like there are some stables over there."

After Edric finished securing the horses, he joined Pancras and Delilah. "The wagon would be good for the open road, but if I'm remembering right, the road isn't the quickest way to get to Muncifer from here."

"That's my recollection as well. The road skirts the plains and passes by the western edge of the Abbar Moors. It should be faster if we travel cross-country. It's certainly more direct."

"If more direct means we get there faster, I'm all for that." Delilah rubbed her bottom through her cloak, fearing the ache from hours of bouncing on unyielding wood would never abate.

Pancras placed his hand on Delilah's shoulder. "Why don't you take Edric and Kale and find us accommodations for the night? Kali and I will figure out what to do with these horses. We'll meet back here shortly."

"Fine." She gestured for Edric to follow her and walked to the back of the wagon. Kale and Kali spoke in hushed voices, standing closer than Delilah thought was necessary. "Break it up, you two. Kale, we need to go find lodging for the night. Pancras wants to take Kali and trade in these horses."

Kali nodded, then nuzzled Kale. "There should be an inn or two down the road." She pointed toward the far end of the market before she jogged to catch up with Pancras.

The sun hung low in the sky. Long shadows cast by the surrounding buildings stretched across the market like dark, ethereal fingers. Delilah pulled her cloak around her as she led Kale and Edric through the scant crowds. A few vendors vied for their attention, but most ignored them and closed their stalls for the evening.

In contrast to the other inns, shops, and taverns they encountered on their journey, almost every building in this town was drak sized. Most were built from rough-hewn stone, and gentle curves featured prominently on most of the older structures. The hard edges and tall, squared-off doorways of some of the larger buildings marked which ones were built and used by former slavers. She followed the road to the far end of the market. The sign above the edifice that stood near the intersection of the market square and the street proclaimed itself to be Hag's End. From the sounds emanating from within, Delilah took it to be a tavern or inn.

"Looks like the right kind of place." Edric pushed the door open. "I don't reckon the minotaur'll fit, though."

Delilah followed Edric and her brother into the tavern. "Maybe they have a back door." She smelled the aroma of roasting meat on the air within. The din of a dozen conversations paused for a brief moment as the patrons took stock of the newcomers, but it resumed as Delilah shut the door. When her eyes adjusted to the lower levels of light in the tavern, she noted there was no bar, but there were plenty of empty tables.

A dwarf waddled up to them, his wiry, black beard braided and parted to make way for his prodigious gut. He offered a smile and a raised hand to Edric. "Welcome to Hag's End, my friends. I can tell you're not Firescales. Just arrived?"

Edric clapped the dwarf on the shoulder. "I need ale. Good ale."

Delilah ignored Edric. "Do you have rooms? We're four, plus a minotaur."

The dwarf showed Edric and the drak twins to a table. "If the minotaur doesn't mind sleeping in what those human slavers were using, we can accommodate you. There's a door for the longshanks around the side. You draks want anything?"

"Mead!" Kale scooted his chair in as he scanned the room. The tavern was packed with draks, most of whose scales were a similar burnt orange color as Kali's.

Delilah waved a hand in her brother's direction. "What he's having. Got any food? Whatever you're roasting smells good."

"Coming right up!" The rotund dwarf waddled toward the back of the dining room.

"Oh hey, shouldn't we wait for Pancras?" Kale reached over and tapped his sister's arm.

Edric patted his stomach. "He can catch up. That meat they're cookin' is callin' me name!"

Delilah tapped the butt of her staff on the floor. Azure tendrils swirled around the skull atop her staff as she summoned arcane energy. "*Ageliofedros.*" A glowing, fuzzy blue boggin appeared on the table, formed from the strands of aether around her.

"Find Pancras and tell him we're at Hag's End, at the far end of the city market. We got rooms, and we're eating."

The boggin yipped and hopped off the table, darted under tables, and ran straight through the door, leaving a tenuous, fading azure trail in its wake. Delilah realized the entire room had fallen silent, and the assembled draks gawked at her. She heard their hushed whispers.

"They have stripes!"

"Did you see that? Magic!"

"Paz said striped draks were with Kali. The ones that freed the slaves!"

Delilah's eyes flicked, meeting her brother's. "Uh-oh."

***

With Kali's assistance, trading the wagon and horses for more suitable mounts proved to be a quick and easy transaction. The owner of the livery, Chana, was more than happy to acquire a wagon and two draft horses.

For himself, Pancras chose a horse more suited to carrying a rider. Because of his stature, he ended up with a muscular blue roan steed that once belonged to the slavers.

The magnificent creature, standing nearly as tall as he at the withers, was called Stormheart, according to Chana. She threw in a riding saddle, as well. For Kale, Delilah, and Kali, Chana had three nailtooth lizards from the Western Wastes. Green-scaled bipeds, the nailtooths possessed long, muscular tails and strong, clawed feet suited to running. Finally, for Edric, Pancras found a dun-colored pony. Inclusive of tack and saddle bags for all, Pancras paid only twenty silver talons out of pocket.

"We did well." Kali rubbed the neck of her lizard. It hissed and snapped at the air. "We should be able to move overland much quicker with these than in that wagon."

"Do you know this place they're at? Hag's End?" Pancras removed his pack from the wagon and double checked to make sure all their belongings had been unloaded before heading across the market with Kali.

"Sure, but I doubt it's the same as I remember it. The slavers drove most of us from our homes and businesses. The last time I was there, to call it a den of thieves and murderers would have been charitable. I can't imagine the slavers let that stay."

She led Pancras through the now-closed market square to Hag's End. The sign above the door hung level with the minotaur's chin. He coughed and eyed Kali.

The drak shrugged. "I'm sure they checked for a larger door. They must have, right?"

The aroma of roasting meat wafted into the street as a pair of orange draks exited the building. Pancras ducked his head and peeked inside. "They probably forgot." A mass of draks crowded around one table, oblivious to the minotaur sticking his head in through the door. They seemed to be celebrating.

Kali pulled on Pancras's arm to move him out of the way. She clapped her hands as she entered the tavern. "Hey, you lot! I'm back. What's going on here?"

A few of the draks turned to regard Kali. They seemed to recognize her, but through the cacophonous roar of a dozen drak voices shouting at once, Pancras couldn't understand what they said to her. She gestured for Pancras to go around to the alley alongside the tavern.

Pancras located a human-sized door on the alley side of the building. He still had to duck, but he entered with minimal discomfort. Inside, however, was a different matter. Pancras towered over all the patrons and tables, including the one at which Kale, Delilah, and Edric were seated. Kali had dispersed the crowd and joined the dwarf and drak twins by the time Pancras arrived, seating herself next to Edric.

"I don't suppose there's a bigger table?"

Kale drank from a tankard, then wiped his mouth with his arm. "I don't think there are any, but there's a room big enough for you."

Pancras moved one of the chairs to the side with his leg and sat on the floor. His legs barely fit beneath the table. "Have you paid yet? Perhaps after we eat, we can find accommodations that are more… spacious?"

A dwarf approached the table, carrying a platter laden with vegetables and a steaming leg roast. He laughed, slapping Pancras on the back. "Not to worry! There's some human-sized beds in the cellar. Push as many of them as you need together."

After the dwarf left, Pancras leaned over the table. "This is not ideal."

Delilah stabbed a hunk of meat with her fork and waved it at Pancras, sending bits of juice flying toward him. "It's just one night. Besides, this place is close to the road. Did you get different horses?"

Kali nodded as she chewed. "Three lizards, a horse, and a pony for the dwarf."

"Pony?" Edric glanced up from his ale. "Better than a mule."

"Lizards?" The excitement in Kale's voice was obvious. "What kind of lizards?"

"Nailtooth." Kali pantomimed a snapping maw with her hands.

Delilah's eyes narrowed. "What's that?"

Pancras held his hand at about the height of Delilah's head. "You know those big lizards you find on Deep Road? The ones you don't mess with? About that big, but they run around on two legs. Mouths full of teeth."

Kale's wings fluttered, and he scratched the back of his neck. "So why are we messing with these?"

"These are bred for riding." Kali placed her hand on his arm. "There's villages in the Western Wastes that raise them. They're fast, loyal, and good hunters, too. Um yeah… hey Pancras?"

Pancras hadn't thought about food for the lizards, and he was afraid the other hoof would now drop. "We need to buy food for them?"

"Well, we'll be passing through a lot of farmland. We'll probably need to buy some sheep or other livestock from farms along the way for the nailtooths. Otherwise, we might get a mob after us."

Edric snorted in his ale. "That's all we need. Leave a trail of sheep parts from here to Muncifer!" He snorted again, threw back his head, and guffawed.

That was exactly the kind of attention Pancras wanted to avoid. "Maybe Delilah can conjure enough boggins for them to eat."

Kali cocked her head. "Those glowy, blue things? I don't think they can live on stuff that isn't real."

Delilah waved her fork at Kali. "Oh, they're real. Not the glowy, blue ones. Those are just messengers. We got real ones aplenty down under the mountains. Nasty, furry, bitey things." She shrugged, turning her head toward Pancras. "It's worth a try, I guess. Even the golguthrons won't eat them, though. Didn't Gluggon eat a couple of boggins, and they ate their way out of his stomach?"

Kale smacked the table with his palm. "That's right! They chewed their way right out. He died moaning and groaning about how we should always chew our food thoroughly." He shook his head and poked at the meat on his plate. "Poor Gluggon. He was funny."

As he dined, Pancras thought back to the old days in Drak-Anor. He hadn't heard about the particular incident to which Kale and Delilah referred, but he had heard even stranger tales than that one. "We'll give it a try, but if it doesn't work out, I can buy sheep or cows for them. Does anyone need to do anything while we're here in town?"

Only Kali had anything of import. "I wouldn't mind taking an hour or so in the morning to see if there's anyone I know to say farewell to. Do you mind?"

Pancras shook his head. He didn't object to that. "Just be careful, and don't dawdle. I want to arrive in Muncifer as far ahead of Spring's Dawning as we can."

Chapter 4

The next morning, Kale accompanied Kali as she made her way around town. He couldn't help but marvel at the buildings built by drak hands for draks. In Drak-Anor, drak homes were glorified caves, all tunneled out of the lava tubes running underneath Bloodplume. Doors were scavenged wood if the drak was affluent enough, though a curtain of cloth or strips of leather sufficed for most draks.

In Honeywater, however, the buildings were made of stone and wood, like small versions of the buildings he'd seen in Almeria, but with drak touches like the arched doorways and round windows. Humans seemed to like angles, and draks curves. Kale wondered why that was, and Kali had no answers.

"I've never built a house"—she laughed as she took his hand—"or anything, for that matter." They walked along a worn trail on the outskirts of the village, encircling Honeywater Lake. She pointed toward an overgrown island in the center of the lake. "The biggest apiary was over there. Run by a funny old man called Matvei. He was long dead by the time I was hatched, of course. My grandsires told me stories about him. I wonder if someone will clear all that brush away and start raising bees again, now that our draks are free."

Kale's eyes followed her hand. A fringe of frost surrounded the island like a crown of ice. The cold grip of winter seemed reluctant to loose its grasp on the world, and again, he was glad the transformation he underwent kept him warm. Kali seemed to appreciate his warmth, too, wrapping her arms around him as they gazed across the water.

"Come on. We should get going. There are people I want to see before we leave." After freeing herself from Kale's embrace, Kali led him toward the village. Some of the draks to whom she introduced him were familiar faces from the salt mine. Others were strangers, yet they all fawned over him as if he were a hero.

Kale tried to deflect the compliments. "Delilah did most of the work. She's the one with all the magic. I just tried to keep the bad guys from squishing her long enough for her to blast them."

A hunched drak, his orange scales dull and thickened with age, shook a crooked, clawed finger in Kale's face. "Your stripes burden you with glorious purpose. Your wings tell of a draconic heritage unseen in generations. You should be proud. You should embrace your heroism and not be ashamed of it."

Kale doubted his wings connected to a draconic ancestry, especially since they developed because of an accident with a chaos rift. He saw them as a useful aberration and nothing more. Kale kept quiet and let Kali do most of the talking as they made their way to the stables. The anticipation of seeing his nailtooth lizard mount was more than enough to push the old drak's admonishment to the back of his mind.

Pancras assisted Edric with his pony while Delilah directed her lizard in tentative, looping circles around them. The nailtooths' green scales glistened in the morning sun, and their hissing and snapping rose above the din of the busy city market. A smile spread across Kale's face. The nailtooths were unlike any of the cave lizards his sister and he encountered on Deep Road or in any of the other caves and caverns near Drak-Anor.

"They're so small!" Compared to Pancras's horse, they seemed pint-sized, though they were still larger than any of the draks. Leather saddles and saddle bags were strapped to their backs, and a petite drak cooed at them as she held them in check.

Kali took the reins of her lizard, placed a foot in the stirrup, and hoisted herself into the saddle. The lizard hissed and stomped its feet, but it made no move to throw her. She tugged on the reins and spun it in a circle before stopping in front of Kale.

"The trick is to not hesitate and be confident. Show them who's boss. They're less skittish than horses, and despite all their hissing and snapping, they won't eat draks."

Kale took her word for it.

***

As trepidatious as she was earlier to ride a hissing, toothy lizard, Delilah found her backside hurt much less than being at the mercy of the wagon. After a few hours of riding, she became confident it was a superior form of travel to walking.

When Chana first told Delilah the nailtooth was named Fang, she bit her tongue to prevent sarcasm from spilling forth. The lizard had two teeth that had grown together as one, making it appear as if it had one giant fang when the others did not, but Delilah thought it was a mundane name, like a too-obvious one invented by her brother. *At least his lizard has an intimidating name: Blackclaw—just like Kali's alias. That can't be a coincidence.*

Although she was loath to admit it, Kali's instruction in the finer points of lizard riding proved helpful. By the third day, she and Kale appeared as comfortable in the saddle as they did walking. The rolling plains of Etrunia took them through barren farmlands. Patches of hard dirt peeked through the dusting of snow that would soon melt and be replaced by splashes of green as the weather warmed and life returned. As they rode, the isolation of being surrounded by austere fields almost convinced Delilah they were the only people in the world. She distracted herself by conjuring boggins for their lizards to enjoy chasing down and devouring.

An advantage to crossing Etrunia over the open plains instead of following the trade roads meant they encountered no patrols and no brigands. Frankly, Delilah worried more about the patrols than thieves. She could fight a marauder, but Pancras frowned upon blasting random patrols of guards and soldiers, like the ones they encountered at Bramblevale Keep last year.

"As long as we keep the mountains to our right and head toward Greyhawk Point, we won't have to worry about becoming lost." Pancras wheeled his horse about to address the group. They rode abreast for now, though most of the time they proceeded single file. The sun hung past its zenith before slipping behind a bank of wispy clouds high in the sky. Each day was longer than the previous. Even to Delilah, each felt a little warmer than its predecessor.

"What kind of gambling do they have in Muncifer?" Edric shifted in his saddle. For all his earlier protests about how he disliked horses, the dwarf seemed fond of his pony, Yaffa. An "old girl," according to the dwarf, she seemed to doze most of the time if their mounts loped along. Delilah didn't think that was actually possible, but she would be the first to admit she knew nothing about horses.

"The last time I was there, there were no public gambling houses." Pancras shrugged. "Maybe times have changed. Let's all try to stay out of trouble this time, eh?" He spurred his horse and trotted away from the group.

Delilah cast a glance over to her brother. "I think he was talking about you."

"Me?" Kale stuck out his tongue at his sister. "Tell that to any minotaurs who try to kill me."

"No one better try to kill us in Muncifer. It'd be nice for a change."

***

The farther they traveled, the more dread nagged and gnawed at Pancras's stomach. Their long days traveling gave him plenty of time to think about life, death, and not being

48

dead. His memories of the event were still fuzzy, but he was grateful dark dreams did not disrupt his sleep. For that matter, he didn't recall any dreams, however fleeting, since waking up on that slab, and it disturbed him on a different level. It felt unnatural to sleep without dreaming.

The new archmage in Muncifer was a stranger to Pancras, and he considered the possibility the man might be cleaning house, a regular occurrence after a change in power. Pancras hoped by hiding away in a place like Drak-Anor, he might go unnoticed. As it seemed to have been a successful strategy for nearly a quarter century, he speculated there was more to this summons than simply paying his delinquent dues.

Greyhawk Point appeared on the horizon and became the dominant feature of the landscape as they traveled south. Pancras adjusted their course to avoid traveling too far into the foothills where they would be more and more likely to encounter giants who made the mountains their homes. In times of harsh weather and scarce hunting, they were known to leave their mountain dwellings to forage and hunt in the foothills. Sometimes, the various tribes of giants were peaceful, if suspicious. Sometimes, they were not.

The afternoon they passed Greyhawk Point, Pancras spotted a band of travelers in the distance. Haze obscured details of what appeared to be a caravan, though he distinguished wafts of smoke drifting into the sky from the center of its formation. Cautious curiosity got the better of him, and he maneuvered the group to intercept them. As they approached, he noticed a variety of wagons covered in brightly colored cloth.

"A tinker caravan!" Pancras motioned for everyone to slow down and stop with him. "What are they doing way out here?"

"Are there roads?" Kali stood in her saddle and scanned the horizon. "They're not taking those wagons overland, are they? I don't see any roads."

"There weren't any the last time I came this way, but that was a long time ago. Maybe there's a trail."

Delilah stood up in her saddle for a better view. "We should go around, don't you think?"

"When I was a lad, the tinker caravans had a reputation for being open-minded and welcoming of fellow travelers. They'd gladly share their food and fires in exchange for a tale or two. Besides, they might know a little more about the current state of our destination."

Pancras held up his hand, indicating his friends should hold their position, before spurring his horse into a trot and closing the distance. He slowed his pace again as he drew closer, hoping to catch a glimpse of the travelers. The cavalcade was stopped, the wagons set up like makeshift buildings or a mobile village.

One of the caravaners waved to him as he approached. Pancras returned the wave and dropped his hand to the rod kept in a loop on his belt, his arcane focus. The human continued to wave as he approached and was soon joined by several others, but they scattered when Pancras drew close enough to see their faces, leaving the lone man standing.

"Hail travelers! Come to trade?"

"Trade? We were just passing through and saw you. What is this?" Pancras surveyed the area for signs of a road. "We saw no roads; we didn't expect to run into anyone out here."

"No roads, no." The man stepped up to Pancras's horse and offered the minotaur his hand. "We farm the land for miles around here. We meet every spring thaw to swap tools, trade, repair, things like that. We're preparing a feast. Travelers are welcome. Join us?" The man's visage was weathered from years of constant exposure to the elements, and the wind blew his sandy hair into his face with each gust. Pancras saw no deception in his ice-blue eyes, however, and waved for the draks and Edric to approach.

The man crossed his hand over his chest and rocked back on his heels. "Nailtooths! And draks! Goodness, we haven't seen those in a while. The children will be thrilled."

Kali rode up next to Pancras. "Got any livestock with you? Our mounts could do with some variety."

"We might could do a trade." The farmer regarded the three atop the lizards. "What have you been feeding them? Are you fresh out of meat?"

"I've been conjuring boggins for them." Delilah smiled, twirling her staff. It flew out of her hands and landed near the farmer's feet. He skipped back, staring like it was a deadly viper, poised to strike.

"Magic?"

Pancras reached down and touched the man's shoulder. "We can pay with Etrunian talons for any food we eat. We're just passing through to Muncifer, but a night amongst good folk would be welcome."

The farmer nodded at the minotaur. "Put on a show for the kiddies, and we'll feed you for free."

***

"A show for the children? No, no, no, no, no. I'm not a wandering trickster." Delilah shook her head, and she would have stomped her feet in protest were she not sitting atop her lizard. Kale dismounted to retrieve her staff as the farmer rushed off to tell the others about their guests.

"It's no big deal, Deli. Make a few glowy boggins, maybe shoot some fire into the air, and they'll be satisfied, right?" Kale handed Delilah her staff.

"Yeah, putting myself on display like some sideshow." She snatched it from his claws.

Edric laughed. "Maybe Pancras can conjure up some bones to chase the kiddies around."

Kale's eyes widened. Spreading his wings, he bounced on his heels. "Oh yeah! That'd be great."

Pancras nudged Kale with his foot. "I think that would be an extraordinarily bad idea. Animating the dead when you have an intact skeleton prepared is one thing, but doing it to some random dead person who's buried in a forgotten grave in the middle of a field? You never know what you're going to get." He dismounted. "I will not animate a bunch of chickens for mere entertainment."

Kale stared at the dirt and shuffled his feet. "Do you really think there are a bunch of dead people buried under us?" He tried to imagine what kind of war would be fought over a nondescript field in the middle of nowhere.

"Probably not. But I'll bet there's an unmarked grave somewhere around here, or a starving, lost traveler interred within the earth by the passing of time." Pancras led the group into the center of the caravan village.

Kale bowed his head and grieved the lost traveler Pancras described. *What a lonely end.*

In the center of the makeshift village the farmers and tinkers formed with their wagons, there roared a bonfire. Each of the half-dozen wagons possessed a retractable awning and a small cooking fire burning in front of it. The farmer who greeted them showed them where to secure their horses, and a few people helped rope off a separate area to prevent the lizards from eating the livestock. Kale followed Pancras and the farmer as he showed them around.

"I am Vasily." The farmer placed his arm around a stout woman wearing brown leathers. "This is my wife Magda, and over there in that mass of chaos are my children, Alla and Yegor."

Pancras regarded the crowd of children who observed the draks securing their lizards in the makeshift pen. "I'm curious. You don't seem to be alarmed to suddenly have a minotaur and a bunch of draks in your midst. I also haven't seen any farms nearby."

Vasily spread his arms, smiling. "Our farms are small compared to the land that surrounds them. This place is almost in the middle of all of them. We are used to minotaur and drak traders from Muncifer. They're fair to trade with and leave us alone when they're not interested in trading." A scowl overtook his smile. "Not like the soldiers who come through. They take what they want without compensation."

Magda spat on the ground. "Etrunia thinks these lands belong to them. Muncifer says no. A curse on Prince Gavril and the Manless."

Pancras rubbed his right horn. "We've just come from Almeria. You'll be pleased to know Prince Gavril is dead. Princess Valene now rules, alone."

Magda took her husband's hand and gazed toward the heavens. "Then Anetha grant her greater wisdom than her husband had."

After trotting over to them, Delilah tugged on Pancras's sleeve. She recoiled when she brushed against his gloved, withered hand. "We've corralled the lizards in their pen, but someone's going to have to watch them. Edric says he needs your help with your horse. He's too short."

"Oh, we'll take care of that." Magda pushed her husband toward the horse. "Help our guests, Vasily." She tugged Pancras's hand to keep him from following. "Now, you're going to tell me all the news from Almeria."

The minotaur glanced over his shoulder at Kale, silently begging to be rescued. Oblivious, Kale waved at him, smiling, then joined his sister and Kali at the nailtooth pen.

***

Magda brought forth a stool for Pancras and tended the fire while she questioned him about the current events in

Almeria. "You must tell me everything about Gavril's death. He was such a loathsome man. I want every detail."

"It was rather anti-climactic. That is, the people just seemed to go about their business. Of course, there was a lot of snow, so perhaps they celebrated in their homes. Or didn't. I really can't say." Pancras did not intend to reveal that he was directly responsible for the prince's death. Loyalists might enjoy an opportunity for revenge, and one could never ascertain another's political views on sight.

"I imagine a lot of things will change in Etrunia now. Princess Valene is not Etrunian, you know." Magda leaned close to Pancras, then lowered her voice, as if she were sharing state secrets. "She's from Vlorey, to the north. You can always tell them Vloreyans. You know, by their dark skin. Quite striking."

"Yes, so I heard." Pancras decided indulging the woman was probably the best way to deal with her gossip-mongering and bigotry. *Just a humble traveler here. No need to fear a minotaur wizard.* Without regard to veracity in rumors about Etrunian farmer superstition, he suspected most common folk would react poorly to learning he used to create undead for a living.

"The snow was heavy in Almeria, too? Bad winter. Worst in years. Not the worst I've seen, mind you, but not the best either."

Pancras craned his neck to check on the draks. Kali juggled various bits of junk she found lying about, while Kale led the children in clapping to a rhythm. Delilah looked on while leaning on her staff, and Edric conversed with one of the tinkers.

"Why the interest in Almeria? I would think folk like yourselves would be happiest left alone."

Magda tossed the stick she used to stoke the fire into the flame and stretched. "Born and raised just outside the walls of Almeria. When Gavril came into power, my family decided they'd had enough and left. My parents died that first winter out here, but I met my Vasily just after. We've been together ever since. It's a hard life, but it's honest and true."

Pancras respected that. Farms like the one Vasily and Magda worked dotted the plains. They were far enough away from each other that everyone had their privacy but close enough that help was never more than a few days away.

"I'd better go see what's keeping Vasily. He's supposed be bringing back some chickens to cook." Magda wiped her hands on her shirt, then strode toward one of the other wagons.

Pancras stumbled, almost losing his balance as he slid off the stool meant for humans. Delilah straightened when she noticed him approaching.

"So? What's going on?"

"Nothing. Looks like it's about dinner time. Have you done your magic tricks?"

A cheer went up from the children who surrounded the draks. They turned from Kali's juggling and shouted in unison. "We want magic! Magic us!"

Delilah pursed her lips, passing her staff from hand to hand. "Kale, why don't you show them how you can breathe fire?"

Before Pancras protested, the children cheered, and Kale tossed back his head, loosing a gout of flame into the air. The collective oohs and ahs from the children drowned out any cautions Pancras offered. Kale flapped his wings, lifting himself from where he stood, and let loose again, spraying an arc of flames above his head. He landed and bowed to the clapping of tiny hands.

"Fire! Now do magic! Magic, magic, magic!"

Pancras nudged Delilah. "That was a short diversion. Surely, you have something to show them."

"Don't you?"

Pancras shuffled his feet, kicking a small rock. "I'm not sure that's a good idea right now." In truth, he had not attempted any conjurations since returning from the dead. Though he still felt the threads of thaumaturgy woven throughout the world, even the thought of using it caused a tickle in the back of his head. It was not a pleasant sensation and felt fiendish.

"All right, fine. I'll give them something to look at." Delilah stomped over to the makeshift pen where the nailtooths were contained. She swung her staff in an arc in front of her, shooing the children away. Blue tendrils swirled around her head as she spun and pointed her staff into the pen.

"*Kalee'steen enoch leetiké goyna!*"

Dozens of boggins appeared in the pen, accompanied by multiple popping sounds. The children's squeals of delight turned into shrieks of terror as the nailtooths pounced upon the boggins two at a time, rending the furry balls and tearing into them with toothy maws.

Covering his eyes with his hand, Pancras backed away. He heard Delilah chuckling under her breath.

"Aita's bloody bones! What is going on here?"

Pancras noticed a tall, rotund man approaching. His face was drawn together like he'd endured a lifetime of eating sour foods. Firelight glinted off his shiny bald head, and his eyebrows furrowed into angry Vs, a fuzzy wedge splitting his face in two. It was the tinker with whom Edric had been speaking.

"You call this entertainment? What sort of minstrels are you?" He snatched up a screaming boy, patting the lad on the back as he spun on Pancras.

"We're not minstrels, just travelers." Pancras held up his hands and stepped away from the angry human.

"This is what passes for entertainment among you bull-headed, scaly bastards?"

Pancras bit his bottom lip hard enough to draw blood. The last thing he wanted was a confrontation. He felt the crackle of Delilah's sorcery in the air.

"This passes for feeding our mighty steeds, you fat… rock-headed looking…"

Pancras glanced past the man to regard Delilah. Ethereal sapphire swirls danced around her hands and the head of her staff. Pancras narrowed his eyes to glare at her and shook his head. "Everyone, calm down. This is just a misunderstanding."

Edric pushed his way through the crowd. "All right, all right. Look, the drak got carried away, all right? The lizards were hungry, and she conjures the boggins to keep them from eating whatever sheep or cows we might find. Better those boggins than one of your sheep, eh?"

"That's right." Pancras nodded in agreement with Edric, patting the human on the shoulder. "It was an ill-timed feeding, I'll grant you." The crunching of bone and slurping sounds emanating from the nailtooth pen punctuated his point.

"Hey, they got to see some real magic though, right? Not just kiddie tricks."

"Stop helping, Kale." Pancras took the man by the arm. He turned him toward the pen. The nailtooths had finished with their meal and now groomed each other. "See? No harm done."

The tinker shook off Pancras's grip. "No harm? Tell that to our children when they wake up screaming tonight with dreams of torn-up beasties in their heads."

"Oleg!" Magda shooed away the remaining children and observers. "Oleg, your boy needs you. His horse threw a shoe, and he can't handle her alone. Get back to your wagon and leave these folk alone. Their ways are different is all."

Oleg grumbled. With one last, withering glance at Delilah, he stalked toward his wagon. Magda shook her head as he departed. "Always bending his iron, that one. They're going to see sheep slaughtered sooner or later."

She stared at the draks, Edric, and Pancras, placing her hands on her hips. "Well, what are you waiting around for? Dinner's on the fire. You want to eat, you'll help me with these vegetables!"

***

Fire-roasted chicken with root vegetables was a greater meal than Delilah expected to find as they journeyed across the plains of Etrunia. She thought about complimenting Magda, but between the woman's interrogation of Pancras about all things Almerian and Vasily's nonstop stories to Kali and Kale, she couldn't get a word in edgewise.

It was just as well. A smile spread across her face every time she thought about conjuring those boggins for the nailtooths. *I told them I wasn't going to do any parlor tricks. I showed those human spawn some real magic.*

As the night dragged on and the fires died down, the air grew bitter and raw. When she exhaled, her breath created a fog, and she noticed Kali lying practically on top of Kale. Delilah felt a pang of jealousy, not for the attention Kali received from her brother, but rather for her brother's high body heat that allowed him to weather the cold with a thin cloth cloak.

Delilah shivered, drawing her thick wool cloak around her. She scooted closer to the fire, holding her hands toward its warmth. Edric kicked her foot. "Hey, go check on the lizards."

She shot him a glance. "Why don't you?"

The dwarf glanced over his shoulder toward the horses. "Yaffa's fine with the horses. The lizards are drak responsibilities. Scales for scales and all that."

Delilah cursed under her breath and shoved Edric as she stepped past. "You're a pain in my scales."

She stomped her feet all the way to the nailtooth pen. It seemed to keep the chill at arm's length as the warmth of the fire became a distant memory. The Eye of Tinian appeared low in the sky now, marking the inevitable pass of winter into spring, though she guessed it would be several weeks still before it was gone entirely. *Muncifer is still so far away.* The realization of how far she was from the only home she'd ever known caused a shiver to wrack her body. Gritting her teeth, she studied the lizards.

The nailtooths huddled together in a cluster at the center of the pen, sharing body heat and sleeping. After ensuring everything was secure, she turned to find a human child staring at her.

She gasped, jumping backward out of reflex. She recognized the child, who stood almost eye level with her, as the screaming boy Oleg had consoled earlier. It struck her how flat human faces were compared to draks. His greasy, stringy hair fell down around his ears and across his forehead, and the cold air gave his broad nose a red tinge.

"Were those real monsters you made your lizards eat?"

Delilah stared at him, her mouth agape, before she glanced at the nailtooths and back at him. "They were real... they weren't monsters though, not really."

She shifted her weight, desperate for the comfort of her staff, but it was where she left it on the ground near her seat in front of the fire.

"What were they? I ain't never seen things like that before."

"Boggins. They live in the mountains. In caves."

The child continued to stare at her. "Are they nice? Our sheep are nice. I cry when we have to kill one to eat it."

Delilah's lips curled. "They're nasty. They're bitey and stupid."

"Oh." He studied the grass and scratched his leg. "You're a wizard."

Recognizing the boy's statement was not a question, Delilah answered anyway. "Yes. I'm a sorceress."

"What's the difference?"

"Wizards study arcana in schools. I learned it on my own." *I guess since I'm learning from a book now, I'm more wizardly than I used to be.*

"Huh. What's your name?"

"Delilah."

The boy stared at her, his brow creased in thought. "That doesn't sound so wizardy."

"Well, what's your name?"

"Adric."

"Well, Adric"—Delilah offered her hand—"I'm sorry I scared you."

He took her hand, examining it as they shook. "Okay."

Adric turned and ran. He glanced over his shoulder at the sorceress. "Time for sleep."

Delilah watched the boy jog away and then returned to the fire. Vasily continued telling stories, and Magda continued deep in her interrogation of Pancras. Delilah huddled under her cloak with her staff and thought of volcanic fire. *Maybe if I think I'm hot, I won't feel so cold.*

Chapter 5

Cold snaps were not unheard of as the season transitioned to spring, but Pancras had hoped they would not encounter one as they traveled to Muncifer. He shivered as he fell into a fitful sleep, despite having covered himself with numerous blankets and furs.

The tickle in the corner of his mind, which Pancras felt earlier that evening, returned as his dreams resumed and whisked him away to magical places. It started light as a feather's touch and then gripped his mind stronger and tighter like an iron vise. Eyes formed in the darkness, pinpoints like glowing embers in the night.

The glimmering cinder eyes faded to icy blue. A spectral visage formed around the eyes, a mask of death. A woman with sunken cheeks and skin stretched tight as a drum smiled, revealing a mouthful of razor-sharp, pointy teeth.

Seek me out, Necromancer. Your life, your death, belongs to me.

Pancras felt his throat constrict. He tried to awaken but could not. In his dream, he gasped for breath. The grip around his throat tightened.

You can resist. You can fight. You can die. It is useless. Futile. Escape is impossible. Before the end, you will do my bidding.

The grim visage faded before a shadow with glowing ember eyes replaced it, its laugh a chill wind that froze Pancras's blood.

He awoke with a grunt, finding his withered hand locked around his throat and his vision obscured by a dark haze, like a black veil covering his face. Groaning, Pancras rolled over and rubbed his eyes with his unwithered hand. As dawn broke, the haze obscuring his vision faded. The sun's rays backlighted wispy clouds gliding across a rose sky. Edric, already up, stood talking with Vasily by the cooking fire.

Delilah lay huddled next to her brother, who also lent his body heat to Kali.

Vasily saw Pancras stir and raised a hand to him. "Good morning, my friend! Sleep well?"

"Not really. I miss my bed." Pancras rolled his neck, trying to work out the kinks in his muscles. The more he slept on hard-packed, semi-frozen dirt, the more he missed the comforts of Drak-Anor.

"I have helped Edric feed your animals. If you would like to break your fast with us, you're more than welcome to before you resume your journey." Vasily offered Pancras a steaming mug of murky brown liquid.

Pancras sniffed it. "What is this?"

"Beef bro—oh." Vasily snatched the mug out of Pancras's hands. "My apologies. We find it's a good way to start a cold day, but I expect minotaurs... well..." The color drained out of Vasily's face, and he glanced about, as if planning an escape.

"It's all right, an honest mistake." Pancras clapped Vasily on the shoulder. "Do you have any mulled wine? Cider? Anything like that?"

Vasily sipped from the mug he'd taken from Pancras. "Yes, I'm sure someone does. I will find some for you." He ran off, leaving Pancras with Edric and the draks.

"What's the plan for today?" Edric sat at the fireside. "Leave these tinkers behind as soon as possible?"

"Yes, we must continue our journey to Muncifer. We can brook no delay." Pancras nudged the draks with his foot. "Up you get! We must get going. Sleep in the saddle."

The return of the shadow in his dreams worried Pancras. He did not know to whom the shriveled visage belonged, but he was certain it was not that of Aita. The Princess of the Underworld never appeared as a desiccated woman; she either appeared as a bare skull or a dark-haired beauty. Not that Pancras had ever experienced a visitation from the goddess of death. If the shadow and its mistress were malevolent in any way, Pancras wanted to ensure no innocents were within their grasp.

Despite their groans of protest, the draks pulled themselves together. By the time Vasily returned with a carafe of steaming cider, they were breaking their fast together with Magda. Pancras handed Vasily a handful of silver talons for their hospitality.

"This should cover everything, including that sheep you fed to our lizards this morning."

Vasily counted the coins with a smile on his face. "You're too generous. This is far more than that stringy mutton was worth."

Pancras nodded, patting the man's shoulder. "Keep it. Share it with the others. May Cybele watch over your fields."

***

To Delilah's relief, they encountered no other travelers or settlements after leaving the tinkers and farmers behind. As the weeks passed, the sun traversed lazily in its heavenly track during the day, bringing the warmth of spring, though winter's chill remained in the evenings. Her only regret was that she couldn't study her grimoire while riding Fang; the book was too heavy to hold with one hand, and it required too much of her concentration.

The rolling plains of Etrunia grew rockier the farther south they traveled until groves of evergreens dotted the hills. The mountains dominated the western horizon, like a great wall keeping the rest of the world at bay. The rushing waters of the Icymist River awaited them at the bottom of a valley.

Pancras raised his hand to halt their progress. "We have to find a ford. Once we cross, the trade road from Almeria should be over the next ridge. We follow that, turn toward the mountains, and arrive in Muncifer within a day."

Hopefully. Delilah didn't trust the navigation skills of someone who professed he hated travel to give them an exact estimate, but she figured he was probably accurate to within a few days.

"We have to cross that?" Edric pointed at the river. "Don't you surfacers believe in bridges?"

"Who are you calling a surfacer?" Delilah scowled at the dwarf. "Kali's the only one that doesn't live in Drak-Anor, under a mountain, you hairy—"

Pancras silenced Delilah with a glare. "There is a bridge. Probably a week's travel to the west where the trade road crosses the river." He looked up into the sky. The clear blue gave way to dusky rose in the west where the sun was setting. "Tinian's Eye has been gone a week at least. The Plow will be rising soon. I don't doubt the stars of the handle are already visible. We don't have time to backtrack that far."

"But fording means we have to go into the water!"

Delilah snorted. "Afraid of getting wet? You could use a bath, Edric."

"Wadin' through a river ain't like takin' a bath. Dwarves don't swim."

Kali rode her lizard, which she'd taken to calling Taavi, up alongside Edric and his mount. "Yaffa can swim. You just need to not fall off her."

"Bugger that. If I fall, I'll sink like a stone! When we cross, I'm riding with the minotaur. Yaffa can swim herself."

"Fine. You'll ride with me." Pancras turned in his saddle to instruct Kali. "You lead Yaffa across when we arrive there."

Despite Edric's grumblings, the crossing was painless. Kali scouted ahead and found a rocky area through which the river flowed. The water, though crisp, barely reached Stormheart's abdomen. Pancras's steed snorted, tossing his head as he crossed, and even the old girl Yaffa seemed to enjoy the chilly dip, stopping to drink in the middle of the crossing.

When they reached the other side, Pancras waited for Edric to return to Yaffa. "All right, no one died; no one drowned. Let's push on. We're almost there."

Delilah longed to sleep in a bed again and have time to read her grimoire. There was still much to learn.

***

Pancras's estimate proved correct. Shortly after breaking camp the next morning, they rode out of the hills and met the trade road from Almeria. The group let their mounts run on the relatively flat road, stretching their muscles and working out the frustration of picking their way through the rocky foothills of the Iron Gate Mountains.

The minotaur stopped at the crest of a hill. Mountains loomed like impassible walls behind an expanse of cinereous blocks, an abstract field of stone dwellings and towers dotted with tiny blotches of sparse green vegetation. "Finally. Muncifer."

The towers flanking the granite gates of the city reminded Kale of home. From the towers, walls built along the hill surrounded the inner city. Clusters of buildings lined the road leading to the gates, and trails of ashy smoke wafted upward from their chimneys joining the clouds above the city. Where the towers of Drak-Anor felt organic, grown in harmony with the city, the towers, walls, and buildings of Muncifer, cold and rigid, clashed with the mountainous geography. Blocks placed with singular purpose indicated dwarven influences within sharp angles of the natural-colored architecture. A vast, yawning chasm lined with budding trees cleaved the city in twain. Buildings carved into the face of the rock lined the chasm, and bridges crisscrossed the span like threads of a web. Beyond the walls of the city, Kale viewed buildings, all similar shades of grey, though some possessed colorful burgundy, dull sapphire, and auburn roofs, splashes of light in the twilight shades of Muncifer.

Gazing at the city, Kale fluttered his wings for balance when Delilah's mount bumped him as she joined him on the ridge. "It's ugly." Fang hissed, snapping at Kale's mount. He tightened his grip on the reins to keep Blackclaw steady.

"It certainly looks like dwarven architecture." Pancras regarded the draks.

"Aye." Edric nodded in agreement. "That means it's strong. I hope they have good ale." He spurred his pony into a trot, heading down the embankment toward the road that led to Muncifer's gates.

No, it's not like home; it's the opposite. To Kale, the city appeared uninviting. It was as if a child plunked down blocks in the shape of a city. Just slabs with purpose, but no design. Only the roofs of the buildings provided any relief from the monotony of the monolithic architecture.

The wind shifted, bringing a breeze that carried the smells of the city past them. The air seemed sulfurous, and he wondered what burned in the fireplaces of Muncifer to warm its citizens. Kale hoped for more of the exotic spices and herbs he smelled when approaching Almeria. Instead, he inhaled aromas that reminded him not of wonder and a good time, but of work and boredom.

He looked at his sister. "It kind of seems like Drak-Anor's opposite, but not in a good way, you know?"

Delilah took a deep breath. "Let's just get this over with, and then we can go home." She spurred Fang to trot down the road after Pancras and Edric.

"I'm sure we'll find something interesting here, Kale. Together, right?" Kali leaned in close to Kale.

"Right." Kale nodded. He and Kali followed the others toward the gates of Muncifer.

***

Grímar slammed the door to the Court of Wizardry, rousing Gisella from her reading. She looked up as he stomped across the courtyard toward the bench on which she sat under the Blood Oak. After folding the collated reports she had been reading, she greeted him.

"Bad news?"

He sat alongside her, nearly upsetting the bench. Gisella seized his arm for balance.

"I'm being sent after a renegade."

"So?" Gisella guessed that was not likely the cause of his ire. Tracking down renegades was what slayers did.

"In the Southern Watch!" Grímar punched his palm with a mailed fist. "It'll take months to journey there. It never thaws even in the summer. Winters are worse. By the time I find her, I'll probably have to guard her for the entire season before I can bring her back. It's madness!"

Her? Could it be...? "Who is this renegade? Watchfolk don't often become wizards."

"I was told her name is Alysha, though she may be using an alias."

"Alysha?" Gisella laughed. *What have you done this time, sister?* "Alysha is my sister."

Grímar's mouth moved silently. He furrowed his brow. "Sister? There could not be another renegade wizard in the Southern Watch called Alysha?"

Gisella acknowledged the unlikely possibility. Her sister often spoke of going to one of the far reaches of the world to carve out her own kingdom. "I'll wager you five crowns that it's my sister."

"Well, why isn't Manless sending you after her then?" Grímar fiddled with the moon amulet around his neck.

"Perhaps he feels my judgement would be compromised by my relationship to her." Gisella waved one of the court's pages over.

The girl curtsied. "I'm honored, m'lady. What do you require of me?"

"Fetch me parchment, a quill, and ink, please." If Grímar indeed pursued her sister, he might as well deliver some correspondence as well.

The page curtsied again. "Straight away!" She sprinted toward one of the buildings where the scribes worked.

"What do you need that for?"

"I'm sending a letter with you, in case it is my sister you seek." Gisella patted Grímar's knee. "It should make her more cooperative. She can be headstrong and volatile."

"I have other concerns." Grímar stared at his amulet, tracing the shape of the moon with his thumb. "I hear it is often overcast. One could go months without seeing the moons."

Gisella understood why that would be a problem for a man like Grímar. He shared his secret with precious few, and he included Gisella in that number because of their occasional trysts. "There is help. The Circle of the Moon has a counterpart in each of the Watches, you know."

"Yes, I know, but I hear the others are bands of murderers and thugs." Grímar spoke often of his contempt for those who allowed their beast to run wild. He prided himself, as did all members of the Circle, on his control.

Lycanthropes were more accepted in the Four Watches than in the northern lands. The unforgiving living conditions and harsh environment forced folk to be more tolerant of others as long as they contributed to keeping the community fed and warm. Folk able to hunt in near-whiteout conditions unencumbered by heavy furs were a rare breed the communities of the Four Watches could ill afford to turn away.

"I don't think they're as bad as all that. A few bad apples and such."

"Perhaps…"

The page returned with the materials Gisella requested. After handing the girl a silver talon for her troubles, she scrawled a message. She handed the folded paper to Grímar. "Now, before you force a confrontation, see to it she reads this."

Grímar narrowed his eyes, grinning. "A secret note."

"Oh, go ahead and read it." Gisella grimaced, waving her hand toward the letter. "It's not secret. I figured you would, anyway."

He unfolded the parchment. "'Dearest Alysha, I fear Grandmother may be needing you soon. Remember who you are and why you're there. Be kind to Grímar; he is an honorable man. Love, Gisella.'"

Grímar's face blossomed red. "You're too kind."

Gisella kissed Grímar on the cheek. "Be safe, my friend. Try not to eat anyone related to me." She stood and stretched.

Grímar reached for her hand. "Where are you off to?"

"I have to meet with the court." She waved the reports in her hand. "My messengers bring dire tidings."

Grímar laughed. "All tidings are dire. Chasing down those rumors from the north? The Witch Queen or Lich Queen, whichever you prefer."

"Such news is worth investigating. If she has returned, it is no small matter."

"Before you go, tell me, how will I recognize your sister?"

"She's prettier than I, but we both have our mother's eyes." Gisella ran a hand through her hair. "Her hair is as white as pale alabaster." Gisella smiled. "She has voracious appetites. I can only hope her tastes have improved."

"Yes, well… farewell, Gisella."

Gisella kissed his cheek again and left her friend to his preparations. When she entered the court building, she found the seneschal, Lyov, gripping his podium and scowling at a young woman who pranced in front of him. The woman was garbed in tight-fitting, multicolored leather leggings and a garish suede vest. Bells on her tri-pointed hat jingled with each movement of her head. White wisps of hair crowned the thin, elderly man's head. His bushy eyebrows appeared embattled in a sea of tanned wrinkles.

"Lyov! You've got to let me in! It's my job!" The fiendling, a girl who had the misfortune of demonic parentage, had skin the color of lampblack that was almost perfectly matched to the black patches on her clothes. Gisella didn't know her story, but she understood that fiendlings usually resulted from wizards miscalculating the amount of control they had when summoning dark entities best left undisturbed. They were rare in the world, but they were most common in cities where Arcane Universities were located.

"Be gone, Qaliah. The court is not interested in entertainment today." He looked up as Gisella approached. "Slayer, do something about this scamp."

Qaliah spun and skipped around Gisella. "Ooh, the Golden Slayer. Hi ho, dilly doe dump!" She pecked Gisella on the cheek and skipped away.

"She's bound to the court, Lyov." Gisella smiled as her eyes followed Qaliah dancing about the room. "It is not my place to relieve her of duty."

"Bound, bound, bound no more!" Qaliah leaped through the air, landing in front of Lyov. She bent forward and kissed the tip of his nose. "My servitude is finished!"

"Then why are you pestering me, girl?" The old seneschal swatted at Qaliah, but the fiendling proved too quick, giggling as she skipped away, finally hiding behind Gisella.

"Manless must pay my stipend so I can pay for expenses." She stopped prancing and put her hands on her hips. "Being indentured doesn't pay well, you know."

Gisella placed her hands on Qaliah's shoulders. "I have business with the archmage. I will discuss your situation with him."

Qaliah fell to her knees. "The Golden Slayer is the best. Praise to all the gods what control such things. Dolios maybe? Praise Aurora, too, 'cause she's so pretty!"

Laughing, Gisella pulled the fiendling to her feet. "Off you go. We have serious business to discuss today. I'll find you when I have Man—the archmage's answer."

As Qaliah skipped away, Gisella cursed herself in silence for her slip. She understood very well the reason for Archmage Vilkan's moniker, but she tried to minimize the disrespect she showed toward him. Truly she considered him to be contemptuous, but she was the Golden Slayer, and to her, that meant always being dutiful and proper.

Unlike Manless. Grimacing, Gisella steeled herself to answer the archmage's summons.

***

After stabling their mounts, Pancras led the group into the city proper. Muncifer was a walled city, like Almeria, and tall guard houses loomed over the road. Between them an archway stood, constructed of the ubiquitous grey stone, prolific throughout the city. Pancras remembered not liking Muncifer when he lived here, but he forgot the city appeared as if someone leached all the color from it.

Muncifer's populace, however, contrasted its buildings. People scurried about the streets in garments of bright blue, green, orange, and red. Black and brown tones were used as trim or accents, or not at all. Minotaurs towered over the humans. Darting in between the taller folk, as always, was a handful of draks.

Being in the city felt familiar, yet simultaneously alien. The streets were the same as he remembered them, but many of the buildings' occupants had changed. They passed a worn-down building Pancras knew as a bakery, yet now was a tailor. Another shop the minotaur remembered as belonging to one of the magistrates now appeared to be a raucous tavern, judging from the laughter and whoops emanating from within. As they came to one of the bridges that crossed the great chasm, Pancras paused to look down. With much of the undercity cloaked in shadow, flickering lights on the walls were the only evidence of activity. By Pancras's recollection, it bustled with trade, much of it illicit. Many people made the undercity their home, as well, mostly draks and humans too poor to live on the surface.

"If there are any gambling dens here, Edric"—Pancras pointed toward the undercity—"that's where you'll find them."

Edric strained to look over the edge of the bridge. "Wish I'd kept old Yaffa with me."

Pancras took them to an inn he knew by reputation, the Granite Anvil. To his relief, it stood exactly as he remembered. Other than the chiseled sign above the door, the Granite Anvil was indistinguishable from the other buildings on the street. A favored hangout for transient visitors to the Arcane University, the inn was located only one block away from the university's campus.

"I think we should relax for the evening. First thing in the morning, Delilah and I will head over to the Arcane University and clear up these charges. The rest of you will be free to do whatever you want. Just, try to stay out of trouble, all right?"

Despite their assurances, Pancras had the impression the last thing on Edric and Kali's minds was avoiding trouble. He just hoped they didn't drag Kale down with them.

A hot bath and a warm meal completed his evening and began the process of melting away the grime and stress of the long journey. Pancras feared it wouldn't be enough, however. If the new archmage was stickler enough to collect decades'-old debts, there was no telling what other petty tribulations were in store. Pancras tried to put them out of his mind.

Delilah came to his room as he prepared for bed. "What do you think they're going to do to me, Pancras?"

"Probably just make you pay dues and officially join the Mage's Guild. I can't imagine them requiring more than that." Pancras sat on the edge of his bed and removed his belt, looping it around one of the bedposts near his head for safekeeping.

Delilah paced the floor in front of him. "They think I'm a renegade, though, right?"

"Yes, but they've always been lenient on renegades whose only crime is learning magic on their own because they have never been near an Arcane University. If there were teachers in every town, they might come down hard on you, but Maritropa is the closest Arcane University to Drak-Anor, and it's farther away than Almeria. You would hardly be expected to know about such things."

"What about you?" She stopped in front of him and crossed her arms over her chest. "They're just going to make you pay up?"

"I hope that's all they require. Then we can go home."

The drak sorceress shook her head and snorted. "All this way for ten minutes of talk. What a waste of our time."

Pancras didn't disagree with that assessment. "Often, those in power take great delight in wasting the time of their so called lessers."

***

Gisella strode into the Court of Wizardry. Apart from the archmage and his guards, the chamber was empty. Either the business Vilkan wanted to discuss with her was private or deemed not important enough for the whole court to hear. She hoped it was the latter. Vilkan's private discussions always involved a measure of clumsy seduction and machismo. After all the years they'd known each other, he still persisted.

Normally, Gisella appreciated persistence, but coming from Vilkan, it was exhausting.

"You wanted to see me, Archmage?"

Vilkan held up a scroll. "Renegades for you to hunt. Two of them, traveling together."

Gisella bit back a sarcastic retort and took the scroll from him. "You have a great deal of confidence in my abilities if you're sending me after two at once."

"They should be on the road between here and Ironkrag. They're from that city in the mountains, Drak-Anor. One is a minotaur. He's delinquent on his dues and is a necromancer. The other is a drak sorceress who never sought us out. Bring them to me."

Narrowing her eyes, Gisella unrolled the scroll. "How do you know they're on the road?" According to the scroll, their deadline to appear, Spring's Dawning was still three days from today. "They're not late yet."

"I doubt they'll even show. You'll probably have to go to Drak-Anor to get them. You're always interested in events up north. Here's your chance."

"Up north in Vlorey. I have no interest in the mountain cities." Gisella rolled up the scroll, then tucked it under her arm. "Under the provisions of the Covenant of the Slain, they are not renegades until their deadline has passed. I do not have the authorization to hunt them while they are under a travel forbearance."

Archmage Vilkan waved his hand. "You won't make it there in three days, and they'll never know you left early to intercept them."

"Nevertheless, I will wait until Spring's Dawning to depart. They still have three days to arrive."

The archmage heaved his bulk off his chair. He held a finger to Gisella's face and huffed before turning away and throwing up his hands in defeat. "Do as you will, then."

"There's one more matter."

Archmage Vilkan stopped in his tracks. She noticed him tense up before he turned. "What is it?"

"The jester girl, Qaliah. The fiendling? She says her servitude is up and wants the severance stipend you agreed upon." It was a standard clause in most indenture contracts. Gisella assumed Qaliah was guilty of some minor, annoying crimes, and working for the Arcane University was a way to do penance without being thrown in jail.

"Tomorrow. Maybe the next day." Archmage Vilkan sneered. Shaking his head, he resumed his departure. "She's a liar and a thief. You should not concern yourself with such people."

Gisella waited for him to leave before unrolling the scroll again. The minotaur's dues were almost two decades overdue. The charge of necromancy, however, was new. It had only been outlawed when Archmage Vilkan took office. When the minotaur chose to study necromancy, it was perfectly legal, if discouraged.

She sniffed, chuckling as the realization of Vilkan's intent dawned on her. *He's cleaning house. Making sure there is no one out there who can challenge him.* It fit with his ego and his paranoia.

A page ran into the hall. "I must see the archmage. The court, where are they?"

Gisella took the page by the shoulder and marched him out of the court. "They've gone for the evening. You'll have to find Archmage Vilkan in his quarters."

The color drained from the page's face. "The archmage said he is to never be disturbed in his quarters."

"Then you'll have to wait until tomorrow"—Gisella cocked an eyebrow at the page—"or give me the message. I will be reporting to them first thing in the morning."

The page hesitated and then nodded. "Yes, fine. The archduke's emissaries who went to visit the giants, the ones taking the tribute? They've been returned."

News that they returned didn't seem worthy of the page's haste to inform the archmage. Gisella opened her mouth to reply and then paused. "Wait, you said 'they've been returned,' not 'they have returned.'"

"Yes, milady. In pieces."

***

"Do you think your sister will mind having a room to herself?" Kali stretched on the bed as Kale examined his puzzle box. A fire crackling in the hearth, the room's only light at the moment, cast an orange glow across the table, leaving the inner workings of the puzzle box obscured in shadow.

"She's probably happy for the peace and quiet. Can you believe there aren't any lamps in here?"

"Most of the patrons are wizards. They make their own light." Kali rolled over and rested her head on her hands. "Your sister seems jealous of us."

Kale set the puzzle box on the table and looked at Kali. "She is. She's used to it being just us. Me and her against all the tall folk of the world."

"There were other draks in Drak-Anor, though." Kali laughed. "There must have been; the name wouldn't make sense otherwise."

"Yeah, but we were cast out. They didn't include us in any clan events. They tolerated us because we had important jobs." Kale and Delilah started out building traps to keep invaders out of the caves, but years of loyal service earned them the ear of Sarvesh, Drak-Anor's eventual ruler.

"Do you think they'll shun me?"

Kale joined Kali in bed. "Nah, you're not a twin. It might take them a while to warm up to you, but they'll come around. I mean, if we ever get back there."

Kali stroked Kale's arm. "You don't think we're going back?"

"I don't know." Shrugging, Kale leaned back, interlacing his hands behind his head. "To come all this way to pay a fine… then go back? I just can't believe it's going to be that easy."

"Did you hear those humans talking when we were eating?"

"About the giants? Yeah. I think something bad is going to go down around here soon. I hope we leave before that." Kale thought about Kazi and Meriz. He was a two-headed giant and not too bright. He was killed the last time invaders attacked Drak-Anor. Of course, in those days, it wasn't called that. A smile spread across Kale's face. There was a lot more opportunity for mischief in those days. Sarvesh didn't care if Kale and his sister played pranks on the oroqs. He would grumble and complain, but Sarvesh didn't like the oroqs any better than he did.

"Giants aren't all bad. Honeywater used to trade with them. I think they help the draks in the Western Wastes capture nailtooths and other lizards, too." Kali scooted closer to Kale and nuzzled his neck.

He shivered, even though he wasn't cold. "Well, the way these humans were talking, I don't think we want to be anywhere near these giants if they come marching down from the mountains."

As sleep overtook him, Kale fought to keep images of rampaging giants out of his thoughts. He hoped their business with the Arcane University would be resolved sooner rather than later. They would then spend a few days enjoying what the city had to offer and head home.

With luck, they'd be back in Drak-Anor before winter.

Chapter 6

The Arcane University was exactly the way Pancras remembered it. Though the buildings were made from the same stone as the rest of Muncifer, the embellishments made them appear warmer and more inviting. The Blood Oak still stood in the center of the courtyard before the unassuming building that contained the Court of Wizardry. It was a quarter-century taller, but it was the same tree under which he whiled away many hours.

Younger students, in their mousy-brown robes, scurried to and fro, running whatever errands they were assigned by their masters. Older students, wearing robes of various shades of grey accented with the occasional colored sash, stood chatting or walking with their noses buried in books. Only masters and visiting mages wore robes in colors brighter than the surrounding dirt.

Pancras spotted a few people wearing heavy armor and carrying weapons marching the campus. Those with tabards bearing the insignia of the Arcane University—an eye, from which six hands radiated, surrounded by a twelve-point star—were obviously guards. Those moving with purpose, their hawk eyes observing unfamiliar wizards, those Pancras knew to be the slayers.

His eyes lingered on a square-jawed minotaur guard cradling a broad-bladed axe. The tight cords of muscle in the minotaur's arms strained against the weight of the blackened steel blade. He felt his pulse quicken at the sight of the guard's powerful legs when he turned to speak to a colleague. Pancras's eyes lingered even as he pointed toward a pair of armored men walking past the guards.

"Slayers."

"So they're the ones who will hunt us down if we don't pay their... fees?" Sneering, Delilah passed a female slayer wearing scale armor. The slayer cradled a spear in her arms like a precious treasure. Wisps of golden hair peeked out from beneath her helm, like gold thread seeking escape from their metallic prison. Pancras's vision darkened, the haze that lingered at the edge taking over for a moment before it retreated once again. He pressed his knuckles into his eyes and shook his head.

"Is everything all right?" Delilah looked at him, furrowing her brow .

"Fine, just a trick of the light." He waved off her concern. "There was a time when slayers would not be wasted on such trivial matters as collecting delinquent dues." Pancras held open the door to the Court of Wizardry building for Delilah. Benches lined the hall, though no one was currently seated on them. At the far end next to a pair of double doors stood a podium tended by an old man.

"And yet, here we are. It took us months to get here, Pancras. If all we do is pay some money and turn around to go home, I'm going to be upset."

Pancras placed his hand on Delilah's shoulder to reassure her. "You aren't the only one." Part of Pancras hoped it was as minor as that, but another part of him hoped they didn't make this journey just to pay a fine.

The elderly seneschal of the court glanced up from his ledger behind the podium as Pancras and Delilah approached. "Ah, an interesting pair. You have business with the Court of Wizardry?"

"I am Pancras, First Nec—Wizard of Drak-Anor, progeny of the Black Mountain. I was ordered to report by Spring's Dawning to answer charges." The formality of his full introduction felt stiff on the minotaur's lips. His parents were born in Muncifer. Indeed, one would have to trace back several generations before they found any minotaur ancestors of Pancras residing in the villages at the base of Black Mountain. It was the name under which he was enrolled in the Arcane University, though, and if they had records of him, under that name was where they would find them.

"Ah yes." The seneschal flipped through his ledger. He peered over the top of it at Pancras. "Two days early. That is good for you. Who are you?" He pointed a bony finger at Delilah.

"Delilah." The drak straightened her back and stood on tiptoe. "Of Drak-Anor. Those old guys that showed up in Drak-Anor said I had to come because I never went to the Arcane University, and, for some reason, learning magic is illegal without your say so."

Pancras pulled Delilah toward him. She shook him off, snapping at his hand.

"Ah, you wish to be a student."

"I could blast half of these students before they could put down their books!" Delilah tapped the podium with her staff. The eyes of her lizard skull glowed blue.

"Oh. I see." The seneschal closed his ledger, then pointed at a nearby bench. "Have a seat. A slayer has already been assigned to you, so the court will want to wait until she arrives before hearing your case."

Before Pancras and Delilah took the seat offered them, the outer doors opened. The slayer they had passed earlier in the courtyard entered. She adjusted her helm, tucking the stray wisps of golden hair underneath its rim.

"Ah, there she is now." The seneschal gestured toward Pancras and Delilah. "Your quarry showed up early. You may take them into the court at your leisure."

"Thank you, Lyov." The woman approached Pancras and Delilah. She cocked her head as she regarded them. "I'm called the Golden Slayer. The archmage wanted me to hunt you down as renegades. How fortunate that you came to us. Are you prepared to answer for your crimes?"

Delilah huffed, then poked the Golden Slayer in the thigh. "I haven't committed any crime. We lived for years without you people sticking your noses in our business, and we're only here to deal with this extortion."

Pancras cleared his throat. "We are prepared to clear up any misunderstandings." He pulled Delilah away from the slayer.

The Golden Slayer rubbed a mark Delilah's claw made on her polished armor. The hint of a smirk appeared on her lips before she gestured toward the doors. "Very well, then. Let us proceed."

For the first time in his life, Pancras stepped hoof into the Court of Wizardry. Most students, if they behaved, had no need to enter these halls. Disappointed, he noticed a lack of ornamentation in the nondescript rectangular room. Opposite the entry doors, a wide dais with thirteen high-back chairs of the Court of Wizardry arranged around it stood before him. Apart from the center chair occupied by the archmage and the ones on either side of him, the other chairs remained empty. The wizards flanking the archmage kept their faces covered, according to tradition. A tradition whose origins Pancras had long suspected kept students on their best behavior because they never knew whether their instructors served on the Court of Wizardry.

"A minotaur." The archmage stood. "This must be Pancras, lately of Drak-Anor."

The wizard to the archmage's right, presumably a man, wore head-to-toe orange robes and looked at his counterpart, who wore violet robes not unlike the ones Pancras often wore. "And the drak we were told about."

The violet-robed wizard nodded. "You are expected. You are early. Good."

The archmage slashed the air with his hand. "Silence. I am Vilkan Icebreaker, Archmage of the Arcane University, highest of the high wizards." He returned to his seat, tossing back his head before clutching the arms of his chair. "I am surprised you answered the summons."

Pancras placed his hand on his chest and bowed. He warned Delilah with a glance to remain silent. "It was never my intention to dishonor the university."

"Yet you practice a forbidden art."

Pancras blinked. "Forbidden?"

"Necromancy was declared a forbidden art five years ago. Had you maintained a proper relationship with the Arcane University, you would know this."

Pancras felt a bead of sweat drip down his back. Practicing forbidden arts was usually punished by death, and the Court of Wizardry laughed at those claiming ignorance as a defense.

"Ignorance is no excuse." The orange-robed wizard intoned, as if he'd read Pancras's mind.

"He was trained under the law." The Violet Wizard raised his hand in reply.

"Yes, yes." The archmage glared at the Violet Wizard, irritation etched on his furrowed brow. "That is why I am not ordering his death."

Pancras let out a breath he did not realize he had been holding. He heard the armor of the Golden Slayer rattle as she shifted her weight behind him. Delilah tugged at his sleeve. Pancras shook her hand away and gave her a short, crisp shake of his head in reply.

"I am thankful for that, Masters. May I speak?"

The archmage rubbed his nose and sniffed. "I suppose."

"I am prepared to make payment for all my lapsed guild dues, as well as any future dues I will accrue for the remaining years of my life… to your best estimates, of course." Pancras hoped the lure of gold would be enough to put an end to this archmage's machinations.

"He seeks to make restitution."

"As an honorable wizard should."

The archmage cut them off with the wave of his hand. "Yes, fine. That is what you owe, but there is a matter of punishment for the forbidden arts."

"In my defense, I have not actively practiced necromancy in at least five years"—he gestured at Delilah—"as my friend here will attest."

The archmage laughed. "I will not accept the testimony of a renegade in this matter. It's never even been trained in the arts."

Pancras sensed Delilah bristle and placed a hand on her shoulder to keep her in check. "She is a skilled sorcerer. She has acquitted herself well in battle in the defense of others."

"Whatever." Archmage Vilkan rubbed his knees and leaned forward. "Defense against wizards like you is a skill so many of our kind neglect to learn. Indeed, reports from the north indicate even teachers who know how to defend against your type are in short supply."

The fur at the back of Pancras's neck stood on end, and his stomach knotted. He dreaded where the archmage was headed with his tirade, and he suspected it would end with a conclusion he would find unpleasant.

"You"—the archmage drew his wand and pointed it at Pancras—"will go to Vlorey and assume the mantle of defenses master there. *Yepakououn katanankasmo sas mechri thanto.*" The blast of azure energy smashed into Pancras before he parsed the words spoken by Archmage Vilkan. He'd never heard a spell recited so quickly.

Pancras wanted nothing more than to go home. *No, that's not it.* He shook his head and squeezed his eyes shut. *I want to go to Vlorey. They need a teacher.* The icy fingers of the shadow crept through his mind, and his head filled with hollow laughter.

Yes, Necromancer. You will go to Vlorey. You will join us.

"Pancras? Pancras, are you all right?"

He was on his knees now. Delilah shook him. Pancras opened his eyes to see the Golden Slayer looming over him, her hand outstretched.

He brushed them off. "I'm all right. I'm fine. It was just… it's nothing. Fine. I'm fine." Pancras stood, unsure if he worked more to convince them or himself that he was fine.

"You will serve in that capacity for no fewer than five years, Pancras. Beginning from the time you take office, of course. Gisella"—the archmage stowed his wand—"take the minotaur away. Assign a slayer to accompany him to Vlorey to ensure he meets his obligation."

"Surely the geas you placed upon him—"

"Do as I say, Slayer."

The Golden Slayer bowed before taking Pancras by the arm. The minotaur allowed her to lead him out, all thoughts of standing by Delilah replaced by a desire to journey to Vlorey as soon as possible.

**

As the Golden Slayer took Pancras's arm to lead him away, Delilah moved to follow.

"Hold, Drak. I'm not through with you, yet."

Damn it. Delilah bit her bottom lip and turned to face the archmage. She took a deep breath and walked toward him, chin held high.

"You're guilty of practicing the arcane arts with no training, no master, and no authorization."

Delilah snorted. "Says you. Until last year, your kind didn't care what we did in Drak-Anor, as long as you didn't have to deal with us. Now, you decide you want to stick your nose in our business and make us conform to your ways? Rannos craps bigger than you lot."

Archmage Vilkan rose from his seat. "Rannos is dead. Killed by 'my lot,' as you say." He stared at her for a moment before he laughed. "You have fire. So few draks seek us out, because so many are executed as renegades."

Delilah clenched her fists. She wondered if she could take all three wizards staring her down before they killed her. *Maybe it's time to try out some of that new magic Gil-Li taught me.*

The archmage took his seat. "You'll pay your dues, and I will teach you wizardry. You've learned enough of those hedge-wizard tricks the peasants call magic to fool many, but under my tutelage, you'll learn true power." He turned to the Orange Wizard. "Let the record show that I am taking this drak as my apprentice."

"That is most improper."

"The drak has not passed the Initiate Trials."

"Even the archmage has not the authority to advance prospective students past the ranks of initiate and novice."

Scowling, Vilkan held up his hand. "Fine! I don't have time for this squabbling right now. Enter her into the rolls as an initiate."

The Violet Wizard tilted his head toward Delilah. "What is your name, Drak?"

Delilah opened her mouth to reply, but Archmage Vilkan held up his hand. "She has no name here. She is 'Drak' until she passes the Initiate Trials. Arrange for her quarters and her beige robes."

"It shall be done." The Violet Wizard bowed his head.

"Be gone, Drak. Your instruction will begin tomorrow."

Delilah stared at the three wizards, her mouth moving in silent protest. *I could do it. I could destroy them all.* In the periphery of her vision, she saw the eyes of the lizard skull topping her staff glow blue, and she tensed her legs.

Then, she relaxed. Her shoulders slumped. Delilah released the well of arcane energy she gathered, spun on her heels, and ran out of the Court of Wizardry. She ran past the old seneschal and into the courtyard. Pancras and the Golden Slayer stood beneath the Blood Oak.

"He made me an initiate, Pancras!" Delilah spat the words, as if expelling them from her body would undo the archmage's decree. "Me? An initiate? It's an outrage!"

Pancras rubbed his forehead. "She should go with me, you know. She and her brother. We left from Drak-Anor together, and we should stay together."

The Golden Slayer touched Pancras's arm and looked up at him. "She can't. If she leaves now, she'll be branded a renegade."

Delilah wanted to blast all of them into oblivion. She refrained from flinging her staff into the grass, but the throbbing in her head made her want to break something, anything. "I didn't ask for this. I learned my magic on my own. I don't need you. I don't need him! I know more than most of the people in this damned school."

"Delilah—" Pancras reached for her.

The drak sorceress batted his hand away. "I'm talking about her, the golden smoothskin, and that bastard in there. Not you, Pancras." She dropped her staff and hugged his leg.

Pancras pulled her away, kneeling to return her hug. "We'll figure something out."

The human cleared her throat. "There is a solution, if you're patient."

Delilah didn't want to hear from the Golden Slayer.

"I don't think she'll want to suffer his instruction long enough to earn autonomy."

"Not that. You are the defenses master at the Arcane University in Vlorey. You can request her as your apprentice. Or as your assistant. Anything, really. She surely will have passed the Initiate Trials by the time we reach Vlorey, Possibly even the Novice Trials."

"That's great."

Delilah pulled herself away from Pancras and turned her head toward the tall human. "It can't be that easy."

The Golden Slayer knelt to bring herself closer to Delilah's eye level. "As I said, it requires patience. Pancras cannot make such a request until he has taken up his office."

"Hey do dilly, a minotaur and a drak! Can it be? Might it be the mages are under attack?" A human with skin like a moonless night danced by, her untold dangling bells jingling.

Not a human... a fiendling. Delilah glowered at the annoying creature as she danced around the Golden Slayer.

"What say you, Slayer? Doth this pair need slaying?"

"Not now, Qaliah." Gisella glared at the fiendling.

"Oh, shhh." The fiendling crouched down. "Serious business. Look, am I getting paid so I can leave this hellhole?"

Gisella swallowed, closed her eyes for a moment, and then smiled. "Yes, Qaliah. Probably tomorrow. You, of all people, should know no one can force the archmage to do anything. Now, please."

"I know you forced him once." Qaliah laid her finger alongside her nose and winked. "Or should I say, kept him from forcing you, eh?" The fiendling giggled, leapt up, and danced off to annoy a passing group of older students.

Delilah retrieved her staff. "Can I blast her? I'm pretty sure I can make it look like an accident."

"We're staying at the Granite Anvil. Her brother is there, as are a few of our friends. May we go put our affairs in order?" Pancras stood, brushing the dirt off his robes.

"Certainly. Someone will be along with instructions for the drak. Delilah, right?"

Delilah snorted. "Not according to Manless. He's calling me 'Drak' until I pass the Initiate Trials."

Pancras chuckled. "I remember those. Don't worry. You can do those in your sleep."

The Golden Slayer remained at Delilah's level. "I will give you some advice regarding Archmage Vilkan: don't be too eager to please him. He will take advantage of it, but neither should you ignore him or argue with his requests. He's busy and will likely not notice if you take your time to do things properly. Also, do not call him Manless. If he hears you..." Gisella drew her finger across her throat.

Delilah's lips curled, and she tugged on Pancras's sleeve. "Let's go. We need to come up with a plan." She wasn't going to stand for this. Between her and Pancras, they would figure out a solution and flee Muncifer—never to return.

***

Gisella returned to her quarters after seeing the minotaur and drak to the Arcane University's gate. She shuffled through the papers on her desk, reports from various messengers. Up north from Maritropa and Celtangate, they submitted similar tales: dread omens, restless dead, and a sense of foreboding. She found it curious the dead didn't attack anyone in the same cities in which they had been buried, but rather, they arose and left their eternal resting places, as if they decided they no longer wanted to be buried there.

Most narratives did not specify in which direction the dead marched, but those that did all pointed to the same location: Badon Hill, the site of the last and final defeat of the Lich Queen.

Gisella sat back in her chair and sighed. She needed to investigate things in Vlorey for herself. She smiled. Archmage Vilkan had just given her the perfect excuse to leave Muncifer and travel there. The minotaur's reaction to the archmage's spell was odd. He seemed injured by it, and that was not normal. *You want a slayer to ensure a geas works on this minotaur? I thought you'd never ask.*

Archmage Vilkan rarely allowed Gisella to venture far from Muncifer. He strongly believed in keeping those close who, at some point, had opposed him. Gisella's reasons for wanting to go to Vlorey to investigate these Lich Queen rumors were personal and unrelated to her slayer duties.

Although, if the Lich Queen has returned, she will be a renegade by default.

After straightening the stack of reports, she picked up her spear. If her timing was right, she would catch the Court of Wizardry before it adjourned for the morning. After turning into the courtyard, she dashed toward the court building. Upon spotting Qaliah pestering some novices, Gisella tilted her head toward the walkway and hoped the fiendling wouldn't notice her. She didn't dislike Qaliah, but it was not her responsibility to solve the indentured servant's problems.

Dolios is with me. The archmage and the two high wizards were still in session. Seneschal Lyov shook his head as she passed. "They're adjourned. They're not going to like this."

Gisella grinned as she threw open the door. "It's their fault for not leaving immediately."

She let the door shut before crossing the room to stand before Archmage Vilkan. The drawn lips and steel gaze were enough to make his feelings on last-minute business obvious. "I found a slayer to accompany the minotaur Pancras to Vlorey."

He lifted his hand, palm up. "So? Assign them."

Gisella allowed a slight smile to crease her lips. "The Golden Slayer will accompany him."

Archmage Vilkan's face fell. "What?"

"I have business in Vlorey. Slayer business. It doesn't concern the university."

The Orange and Violet Wizards regarded each other. "Unusual."

"All slayer business is university business."

Gisella held up her stack of reports. "According to the Covenant of the Slain—"

The archmage waved his hand. "Yes, yes. I'm sure you have everything figured out. However, I forbid it. You serve me… us. This branch of the Arcane University."

"Slayers are not bound to specific branches, only the guild itself." Gisella cocked her head. "You lack the authority to keep me here if I have legitimate business elsewhere."

Archmage Vilkan stood, his lip quivering. "I am the archmage. I have the ultimate authority in all guild matters."

"Archmage authority cannot supersede the Covenant of the Slain."

"Archmage duties with respect to slayers are clearly defined in the *Rose Concordat*."

The two high wizards eyed Archmage Vilkan and spoke as one. "She is correct. You do not have the authority to keep her here."

"Fine!" The archmage stepped down from the dais and pushed past Gisella. "Be gone then. Leave with the necromancer. I will be glad to finally be rid of you."

He slammed the door, leaving Gisella alone with the two high wizards. They studied her face.

"He can assign you permanent duties here." The Orange Wizard cocked his head.

"But we are not obliged to indulge his power plays." The Violet Wizard bowed to her.

"I'll keep the council informed of what I find, of course." Gisella smiled and bowed to the two high wizards. She hadn't expected them to take her side, but there were many who felt Archmage Vilkan was a powder keg and wanted him gone. Helping her leave was a passive-aggressive show of rebellion she supposed, but she took it. Until his tirade, she considered passing on the messenger's report regarding the archduke's emissaries. Now, however, she would just pen a quick note to the Archduke and leave Vilkan out of it.

***

"You're staying?" Kale didn't believe his ears. After almost dropping the puzzle box, he placed it on the table and sat on the bed. Delilah leaned on her staff, her tail thrashing in frustration.

"I don't have much of a choice, Kale. They'll hunt me down if I leave, and I'm not going to be able to get much of a head start on them."

When Kale heard the news that Pancras had to go to Vlorey, he assumed they would all go together. *But if Deli's staying here—*

The choice was simple in Kale's mind. "Then I'm staying too."

Delilah's slumped shoulders conveyed her relief. She pulled her brother into a hug. "I knew you would."

"You'll have to be okay with Kali staying, too, Deli." Kale pulled away from his sister's embrace. He gritted his teeth. Delivering news Delilah didn't want to hear was always nerve-racking, and what he was about to say next would likely set her off.

"Fine, whatever, as long as…" Delilah narrowed her eyes and sniffed the air. "Something's… different. What is that?"

Kale swallowed. The butterflies in his stomach threatened to escape and bring his breakfast with them. "Kali is my mate, Deli."

Delilah clutched for the bedpost as she found the edge of the mattress before she crashed to the floor. "What? When did—?" Her eyes blinked several times in succession, and her breathing became fast and ragged.

"Last night… well, this morning?" In Kale's defense, it was dark and he wasn't really looking at the stars to determine the time.

Delilah pushed him away and stood. She threw up her hands, pacing the room. "I'm standing before the executioner, and meanwhile, my brother's mounting this—"

"Don't say anything you'll regret, Deli." Kale faced his sister. "She's family now." Delilah was always jealous when anyone paid the least bit of attention to anyone other than her. He loved his sister, but he wasn't going to let her bad-mouth his mate.

"Great." Delilah raised her hand and then let it drop. "So you'll be brooding a clutch of eggs while I'm scrubbing this human's floor like a beggar desperate for coin. I should've stayed in Drak-Anor."

Kale wasn't privy to what transpired at the Arcane University, but he was familiar with his sister's propensity for exaggeration. "Deli, we'll be here to help you. So what if we have a clutch of eggs? You know I'll never abandon you."

It was true. Kale would give his life for his sister. He just hoped she would not ask him to choose between her and Kali. At the moment Kali entered the room, Delilah's eyes narrowed, and Kale detected smoldering she normally reserved for enemies she was about to destroy. It was a fleeting moment, gone as quickly as it appeared.

"Kale and I have something to tell you, Delilah." Kali opened her arms.

Scoffing, Delilah shoved Kali out of the way. "Yeah, congratulations." She slammed the door behind her.

Kali let her arms drop. Kale wrapped her in a hug from behind. "Don't worry about her. I told you she wouldn't be happy, but she'll get over it. I think she had kind of a bad morning, you know?" He didn't much blame Delilah for her jealousy. He wasn't the nicest drak when he thought she gave Zarach Stoneclaw too much attention back home. Maybe he'd be waiting there for her still… if they ever returned to Drak-Anor.

"She hates me, Kale. She always has."

"No, she doesn't. She's just—"

Kali turned to face him and nuzzled his neck. "Shh… it doesn't matter. I only care what you think about me."

Kale grinned. "Well, I think we established that earlier, huh?"

"Mm. So, what happened with her at the Arcane University? Did she have a chance to tell you before you blurted out the news? 'Cause I can imagine her spending that entire time berating you for slumming with someone like me."

Kale pulled back, holding Kali at arm's length. "Slumming?"

"You're a Child of Destiny. Clearly, you're too good for the likes of me, she thinks."

Pressing his lips together, Kale narrowed his eyes. "You said you didn't care what she thinks. Besides, I know for a fact that neither one of us buys into that special destiny stuff."

"Yeah, why not?"

"A dragon told me it was nonsense." Kale had a fuzzy memory of Terrakaptis telling him prophecies were just vague stories invented by old sages and had no bearing on the real world. He had been recovering from falling into a chasm and was half-dead at the time, but Kale was fairly certain he recalled a real conversation.

"Am I ever going to meet this dragon of yours?" Smiling, Kali ran a clawed finger down to the tip of his snout.

"Of course—" He'd been about to tell Kali he would introduce them when they returned home, but he realized he didn't know when that would be. "I mean, eventually. We're going to be here a while now, I think."

"Why?"

"Delilah has to stay here. The archmage made her an initiate. If she leaves, he'll make her a renegade, and those slayer people will hunt her down. I'm not leaving her, Kali."

Kali wrapped her arms around him and nibbled at his ear. "I understand. I wouldn't ask you to. I wanted to explore this city, anyway. Now we'll have plenty of time for that."

***

Pancras swirled the mead in his goblet before drinking the last gulp. "So, Edric. Are you coming with me, or staying?"

After the dwarf slurped the foam from his mug of ale, he consulted his money pouch. "I don't fancy staying with the draks, so I reckon I'll come with you. Ain't had no luck here anyway."

"You're under no obligation."

Edric shrugged. "One city's much like the next, but this one"—he glanced at his surroundings—"reminds me too much of home, but without my kinfolk. Maybe I'll find someplace better along the way. Until then, I'll tag along, I reckon."

Pancras traced his finger along a stain on the table. Now that his head felt clearer than when he stood before Vilkan Icebreaker, he realized the archmage placed a spell of compulsion on him. Waves of nausea assaulted him every time he thought of going anywhere except Vlorey. Even if there was a way to defeat Vilkan's charm, in his heart, he wasn't sure he should even try.

He regretted having to abandon Delilah. The draks, Kale and Delilah, at least, were like family. He felt responsible for their well-being, even though they were fully capable of caring for themselves.

"Well, I guess I should figure out the best way to get there."

"What's to figure?" Edric took a swig of his ale. "Follow the trade roads north until you run out of road and into the ocean. That's where Vlorey will be, right?"

"So it seems. Back through Etrunia, past Almeria and Maritropa to Cardoba, then Vlorey." He blew out a long breath. "It's a long way."

"I have a suggestion." Gisella, the Golden Slayer, pulled up a chair. Edric gave her a sidelong glance before returning his attention to his ale.

"By all means, have a seat." Pancras regarded the Golden Slayer in the common room of the Granite Anvil. *What does the archmage want now?* "Do you always keep your helmet on when walking around town?"

"There are men foolish enough to assume all women are prey in this part of town, particularly if they appear to be foreigners." After adjusting her helm, she placed her hands before her on the table. "I have assigned myself as the slayer who will accompany you to Vlorey, and I know a faster way than taking the roads."

Pancras rubbed his right horn and held his goblet up for a refill. "You? Why?"

"I have business there, so it is a matter of convenience."

"So what's this other way?" After draining his mug, Edric slammed it on the table.

"Due east... well, east and slightly south." She traced a route with her finger on the map she unrolled onto the table. "Past Curton, to Cliffport. Buy passage on a trading vessel and sail up the coast. Much faster than horses."

Pancras noticed the color drain from Edric's face.

"I ain't getting on no ship."

With the trouble they had convincing him to ford a river on horseback, Pancras didn't want to contemplate how they'd coax the dwarf onto a ship. That, however, was a challenge they would address later.

"I don't really need an escort. The spell—"

"The archmage has issued a decree. It's not your place to challenge it." Gisella rolled up her map. "Besides, what I said was true. I have business in Vlorey. There's no reason not to travel together."

The dwarf pointed at the map marker for Curton. "Dwegerthon's near there, I reckon. Have you heard anything about the dwarf-folk there?"

Gisella tore her eyes away from Pancras for a moment to shake her head. "Little of import—"

"What if I don't like you?" He had no real opinion about the woman, but he disliked being under control of a compulsory enchantment. He liked it even less that the archmage added insult to injury and employed the slayer as escort to guarantee he'd arrive at his end destination.

Gisella reached over and patted his hand. "You're only saying that because you don't know me."

Sighing, Pancras rubbed his eyes, resigning himself to travel with Gisella as his escort. *Things always become worse before they improve.*

Chapter 7

Delilah stomped into the common room of the inn, stopping short when she saw the Golden Slayer sitting with Pancras and Edric. She hoped to catch Pancras alone. He perked up when he saw her, then gestured for her to join them. Delilah girded herself before pulling up a chair.

"I'm glad you're here. I have a list of things you need to bring with you tomorrow when you report to the archmage." Gisella withdrew a scrap of parchment from her pouch, then passed it to Delilah.

She looked it over, thankful Pancras helped her learn to read the common trade language while the lexicon she studied bettered her vocabulary. The list seemed innocuous enough: a quill pen and ink, a codex of blank pages, a small cauldron, a mortar and pestle, a sharp knife suitable for chopping, and an object to be attuned into an arcane focus. The list provided quite a lot of detail on the last item. Either a staff or stick to be used as a wand, a trinket to be made into an amulet or affixed to a larger object.

"I already have an arcane focus. Where am I supposed to get this stuff?" She handed the list to Pancras. Delilah had no money; to this point, Pancras handled all the expenses.

"I'm sure there are shops that sell these things. I'll leave my mortar and pestle with you, if you like. I can replace it when we arrive in Vlorey." He passed the list back to Delilah.

"She should buy her own. She'll make a better impression on the potions master with new equipment. She can be very finicky."

Edric pushed himself away from the table. "I'm going to see what's around. Don't leave without me."

Pancras looked up. "Not to worry."

"So, he's going with you?" Delilah figured the dwarf would stay in Muncifer, since it used to be a dwarven city.

"Yes, he says it reminds him too much of home to stay here."

Delilah looked over the list again. Furrowing her brow, she tried to guess how much each item might cost. The worry must have shown on her face.

"It's just for a little while, Delilah. Don't worry. I'll make sure you have enough money to get you started." He looked at Gisella. "Students still receive a stipend, yes?"

"It's not much, but if you take your meals at the university and live there, it'll be enough to get by."

It was not an ideal situation. *At least if I live alone, I won't have to put up with that other drak.* Her thoughts turned to ways of evading slayers like Gisella. *If I flee into the mountains, they might not follow, not with all the local trouble with giants. Maybe Kale and I can find a drak village on the other side. I'll bet they don't send slayers into the Western Wastes.*

"Delilah?"

Upon hearing his finger tapping on the table to gain her attention, Delilah met his gaze. "Go retrieve your things, and we'll see about shopping for those items on the list. You will have a busy day tomorrow."

Gisella nodded in agreement. "The first few days will be constant, but they should slow down a bit after your Initiate Trials."

Delilah's lip curled. "If he ever lets me take them." She had no expectation of fair treatment. She perceived Manless would hold her back and have her perform meaningless, pointless, degrading tasks until she escaped or died doing them.

"All trials are scheduled and frequent. He won't be able to stop you, not with the whole university watching a new drak student. Once you earn your novice's robes, you'll have a bit of autonomy."

"He's going to be watching me like a hawk!"

"He's the archmage." Gisella offered her a smile. "He'll be too busy to give you that kind of personal attention all the time."

"If he does, he's neglecting his duties as archmage." Pancras scratched his chin. "And once you're a novice, you'll be out and about frequently."

"The masters take perverse delight in sending novices all over the place on pointless errands. You'll be sent all over the city, possibly to some of the nearby villages as well. The archmage will be too busy running the guild to worry about where you are."

Delilah doubted that. Nevertheless, she didn't have a lot of choice in the matter. She returned to her room, creeping past Kale's room. The last thing she wanted was a confrontation with her brother and that other drak. After grabbing her staff and her pouches, she returned to the common area where Pancras waited for her, alone.

Together, they ventured into the heart of the city and down into the undercity. "Gisella says the best prices on the items you need can be found here."

Delilah didn't care what Gisella thought and almost told Pancras that before remembering he planned to pay for her supplies. The undercity was even more like Ironkrag than the rest of Muncifer. Avenues and streets were completely encased in stone, a legacy of their dwarven architecture. Stairs cut from rock led deeper into the chasm bisecting the city, and bridges allowed access to shops on both sides of the rift.

The people of Muncifer paid no mind to Pancras or Delilah as they made their way down, looking for shops that sold the supplies she needed. She noticed more draks and fewer minotaurs the deeper they went. Most of the archways separating plazas and streets were low enough that Pancras had to duck underneath them, though most of the humans did not. The smell of soot from the myriad of open flames providing light hung in the air.

"You'd think the wizards would create lanterns or something, like we did in Drak-Anor." She stopped in front of a stall that sold a variety of tankards and mugs.

"Most people up top don't care much for what goes on down here. Certainly not enough to enchant street lights for them." Pancras pointed to a shop across the way. "That place looks like it has cauldrons."

The shop not only sold potion brewing supplies, but was, in fact, also a fully stocked apothecary. Despite the ever-present tang of soot, the shop had a warm, spicy fragrance layered on top of the undercurrent of unpleasantness. The proprietor, an older minotaur who had black fur streaked with white and a part of her left horn missing, smiled when Pancras entered.

"Ah, a strapping male entering my shop. Not looking for virility potions, I hope? You're far too young for that."

Pancras cleared his throat. "No, we need a cauldron. A sharp knife too, for reagent chopping?" He patted Delilah's shoulders before nudging her toward the minotaur.

"Sounds like an initiate's getting ready to start at the Arcane University." She shuffled around behind her counter and pulled out a short-bladed knife and sheath. After laying it on the counter, she stepped over to a rack of shelves containing various cauldrons.

"That one. I want that one." Delilah pointed to a silvery-grey cauldron with three clawed feet on the bottom. *If I'm going to be forced to listen to wizards prattle on and on about magic, I might as well have the nicest equipment.*

"A fine choice, but it's not really a beginner's cauldron. How about this one?" The minotaur held up a plain black cauldron with a ring base.

"I want the other one. I'm only an initiate because that Manless bastard is making me start at the bottom because he hates draks."

"Oh, ho, ho, someone is a little bitter. Not my business, no, it isn't." She brought the cauldron Delilah selected over to the counter and leaned, letting her tunic fall forward a bit to give Pancras a view. She smiled at him.

"Are you one of the masters there? A new one, maybe? I've not seen you around."

Pancras made a point of looking away from her. "No. No, I'm just passing through. Delilah here is the student, and I'm just helping with expenses. How much?"

The proprietor reached over to stroke the back of Pancras's hand. "So rare to see an intelligent male in these parts. How long are you passing through for? Maybe looking for some company, hm?"

Delilah pushed Pancras's hand out of the way and stood on tiptoes to peer across the counter. "Don't get out much, do you? How much? We have other shops to hit before they close for the night."

"Two crowns for all this. I'll take six and a half talons if you want the other cauldron instead."

Pancras fumbled in his pouch. "Two crowns is fine." He tossed two gold coins on the counter, turned, and left Delilah to gather her new cauldron and knife.

"If he changes his mind, I'm Alecta, little drak." The proprietor grabbed Delilah's hand, pulling her up against the counter. "And take care who you mouth off to about the archmage, hm? He has ears everywhere and very long arms."

Delilah took her purchases, exited the shop, and joined Pancras in the street. He stood at a railing overlooking the chasm. "Geez, what was her problem?"

Pancras chuckled. "She's lonely, I guess."

"Her name's Alecta if you change your mind. I didn't have the heart to tell her you won't."

"Thanks." Pancras rubbed the back of his neck. "I never have the heart to tell females I'm just not interested in them, and the older they are, the more aggressive they become."

Talk of courtship brought back feelings Delilah didn't want to think about at the moment. She pushed images of her brother and his mate out of her head. "Where to now? I still need paper and ink."

Pancras led her down another flight of stairs and across a wooden bridge. "I think I saw a place over this way."

Despite Delilah's expectations, this shop contained no books and seemed to offer no merchandise at all. In one back corner of the shop alongside some sort of machine that made rhythmic pounding noises, she observed a drak reclined in his chair with his feet propped up on a desk. When Pancras and Delilah approached, he nearly fell out of his chair in his haste to sit properly.

"Oh, hey, customers. I'm Jairo. What can I do for you?" He stumbled out of his chair, wiping his hands on a dirty apron. "Jairo's Printing, for all your"—he stared at Delilah—"umm…desti… umm… printing needs."

"We need a blank codex, quill, and ink." Pancras fished within his pouch for money.

"Right. Scribes?"

"Student." Pancras sorted through a handful of coins.

Delilah cringed to hear herself described as a student. The drak fumbled as he searched for the items Pancras mentioned while he stared almost entirely at Delilah.

"I didn't… I didn't know there were… umm… Children of Destiny here. In Muncifer, I mean. I hadn't heard. That's umm… that's something. And you're learning magic, huh? Yeah…"

Delilah cleared her throat and thumped the butt of her staff against the floor. "I already know magic, and I'm not from Muncifer. We're from Drak-Anor."

Jairo stopped and stared, his body a statue as the candlelight flickered on his dusty-grey scales. Finally, he regained his wits. "I've heard of that." He pointed a shaking finger at Delilah. "You, the draks, drove out the dwarves and oroqs and claimed a whole mountain kingdom for yourselves!"

Pancras glanced at Delilah. "Our legend grows."

"That's not how it happened."

Jairo ran to his desk. He dipped a quill pen in ink and pulled out a fresh sheet of parchment. "Oh, I must hear all about this."

Delilah tapped the butt of her staff against the floor again. "Supplies. Customers. We're buying or walking."

Pancras pursed his lips and shook his head as he laid a hand on Delilah's shoulders. "I'm sure there will be another time Delilah can set the record straight. Jairo, is it? We have a busy afternoon, so if you would, please gather ink, a quill, and a black codex?"

"Oh, yes, of course." He laid down his pen. After gathering the supplies, he offered them to Delilah. "If, if you would promise to spend some time with me, set the record straight, you can have these, no charge. The draks here need to know about Drak-Anor. The true story." He looked up at Pancras and then back at Delilah. "There are so many humans, oroqs, even minotaurs, who treat us like vermin, some draks are starting to believe it of themselves. We need good news."

"What are you going to do with the story of Drak-Anor?" Pancras helped Delilah stow her supplies.

"I print a weekly broadsheet. A penny for all the goings on in Muncifer and more." He chuckled. "Well, when I can find more. Advertise for services, that sort of thing. I would print the stories in the broadsheet. Most of my customers are draks, some minotaurs. They're generally nicer to us than humans. It's important for them to hear these things."

Delilah thought of the stories she could tell Jairo. The story of how she and Kale were trapped in a cave-in. How he found the Earth Dragon, Terrakaptis, while she traveled to break the ice between the dwarves of Ironkrag and the residents of Drak-Anor. How Drak-Anor won its freedom from the oroqs, and how she and Kale freed the slaves in Almeria. A grin appeared on her face, unbidden, and she nodded.

"Yeah, I have lots of stories to tell you. Let me get through these stupid Initiate Trials. Then I'll come find you."

Jairo's smile almost split his head in half. "You will? That's fantastic! You have no idea how big this is!"

***

Excitable draks aside, his shopping trip with Delilah went well. It was a bittersweet afternoon for Pancras, for it would be many months, if not years, before he saw her again. He wished to have spent as much time with Kale, too, but he felt it was more important to help settle Delilah. The drak sorceress was often volatile, and she needed last-minute guidance, or Pancras feared her temper would lead her to a bad end.

After ensuring Delilah returned safely to the Granite Anvil, Pancras headed out again to acquire the provisions he needed for the trip to Cliffport. He wasn't sure how long the journey would take, but according to the map the slayer showed him, the distance appeared to be at least twice as long as the trip from Almeria to Muncifer. He assumed there would be settlements along the way from which to purchase supplies. The minotaur felt a pang of nostalgia for his old haunts and decided to pay a visit to Gisella at the Arcane University. Surely, a few extra days in Muncifer wouldn't hurt.

As he entered the university campus, he passed a group of novices and initiates practicing illusions. One young man attempted to create an image of a beautiful woman and failed. Proper illusions were supposed to be indistinguishable from reality at a quick glance, and if they were exceptional, they held up under scrutiny. This man's illusion appeared more like a spectral painting, translucent and flat. The woman's movements were stiff, like an automaton's.

Pancras had never mastered that type of conjuration, and as the novices poked fun at the young initiate's efforts, he felt a pang of sympathy for him. A female novice stood by, glancing up from her book in irritation as the fiendling jester swatted at her with a long feather and danced around her.

"Put up the book and have a look! Don't be dull. Don't be droll. All the boys think you're a troll!"

The novice snapped shut her book and stormed off. Giggling, Qaliah danced toward Pancras, despite his purposeful gait and efforts to avoid eye contact.

"The slayer's minotaur has returned! Got any butter I can churn?"

Pancras spun on her. She halted, raising her hands to her mouth and widening her eyes. "Terribly sorry! I—sometimes when I'm throwing out random rhymes, things don't come out quite right."

Comparison to cows or other four-legged bovine was a sure path to a minotaur's bad side. Pancras tried to ignore such insults, but they still upset him enough that he had difficulty masking his reaction when he heard them. Minotaurs might resemble bovine animals, but they were not in any way related. The insults served as a reminder that facts did little to eradicate bigotry.

She pressed her hands together in front of her and bowed her head, her singsong tone replaced by a deeper, sultrier voice. "I beg forgiveness, Master. No insult was intended. Honestly, I do know better than to make such comparisons."

Qaliah's demeanor became sober compared to the lighthearted dancing, singing jester, and Pancras puzzled over how both personalities existed within the same person. "Apology accepted." He decided to use her newfound seriousness to his advantage. "Tell me where the Golden Slayer is, and all will be forgiven."

"The last I saw, Master, she was in the tavern." Qaliah gestured in the direction of a squat building along the compound's east wall. "I did not notice whether or not she left it yet."

"Thank you. Carry on."

A grin overtook Qaliah's face, and she snapped her fingers and danced. "Hi ho, tummy rum! Drink some dummy rum! Have enough rummy rum and your tummy will be having fun!"

Pancras cringed at the horrible rhyme as he turned away from the jester and proceeded in the direction Qaliah indicated. The tavern itself was small enough that it took only a quick scan for Pancras to determine Gisella was not there.

The barkeep, a tall woman with chiseled features, confirmed having seen Gisella. "She stopped in, bought a couple of casks of mead, and then left. Didn't stay long enough to say what she was doing or where she was going."

"Where does she live? Nearby?"

"I never asked." The barkeep offered Pancras a shrug and a smile. "Not my business."

Pancras left the barkeep to tend to her customers and returned to the courtyard. He noticed the jester turning cartwheels near some initiates, who watched her intently. The initiates bowed their heads in deference as the minotaur approached.

"Hey ho, dilly doe, it's the tall minotaur wizard! Ring-a-ding, ring-a-ding, what happened to your lizard?"

The initiates laughed and applauded when she somersaulted and rolled into a bow in front of Pancras. She looked up at him, cocking her head before a wry and slanted grin crossed her face.

"Can you tell me where the Golden Slayer lives?"

"Hey-day dilly! Information don't come cheap! Cross my palm with coin, or I'll not say a peep!"

Pancras fished in his pouch for a copper penny, but he pulled out a silver talon, instead. Sighing, he tossed it to her. Qaliah snatched it out of the air, allowing it to roll down the back of her hand before flipping it into the air and catching it again. She spun around, then pointed toward a square tower behind the Court of Wizardry.

"In the Guardian Tower, she makes her dwelling be. You have my thanks for flipping this coin to me!" Qaliah laughed, skipping away before Pancras could ask a follow-up question. His hand dropped to his rod unbidden.

"I really need to learn some sort of restraining spells."

Upon seeing the initiates' raised eyebrows and furtive glances, Pancras realized he had spoken aloud. Coughing, he rubbed the back of his neck. "My specialty didn't cover those… and she's quite flighty; I wasn't finished asking her questions."

He felt their eyes upon him. "You should return to your studies."

Pancras exited the courtyard, suspecting the students probably made all manner of unsubstantiated judgements and suppositions about him. He didn't care. The Guardian Tower was a four-story, square, crenelated structure connected to the rear wall of the Arcane University. In Pancras's day, the tower was used for student housing. No new buildings had been added since Pancras was a student, and he was certain the building across the courtyard contained classrooms. *Perhaps they've cleared out all the old underground storage vaults and students live there.*

Guardian Tower was built to surround a small courtyard. Balconies on each level ran the circumference of the interior, and each apartment faced inward toward the courtyard. He heard stories of similar towers at other Arcane Universities, but those towers had no stairs; students were required to learn levitation to access the upper levels. That was never a requirement at the Muncifer university.

A couple of quick inquiries of the guards he saw relaxing provided him the information he needed, and he proceeded to the far side of the inner courtyard. Gisella's apartment was the center one. As it contained no marker or distinguishing features, Pancras hoped he knocked on the correct door.

He heard thumping from within before it opened. A fully armored Gisella greeted him. "Oh, it's you. I was expecting my sparring partner."

"Sorry to disturb you." Pancras held up his hand and bowed his head. "I was buying supplies for Delilah and our upcoming trip, and I realized it's been a long while since I've been home. I don't suppose we could delay our start a few days?"

"No, that's not going to be possible." Gisella vanished for a moment before she reappeared holding her spear. "Anything else?"

Pancras looked away. "No, I suppose not." The minotaur hoped there would be room for negotiation. He wanted to help Delilah through her first few days at the university, and perhaps visit a few of his old haunts. "No matter, I apologize for the intrusion."

"It's no trouble. I have a few things I need to finish before leaving tomorrow. I'll see you then, at your inn. Yes?"

"I shall be ready." Pancras wasn't sure how he could ever be ready to abandon his friends and travel to what felt like the other side of the world, but saying the words felt right. *That's the spell the archmage put on me talking.*

He left Gisella to her tasks. His thoughts turned to the preparations for another long journey and his former lover, Thanos. Following his lover's ill-fated expedition to the Western Wastes, so many years ago, Pancras left the Arcane University and Muncifer. *At last, it is time to close that chapter fully.* He headed into the undercity.

The mercenary company Thanos joined, the Band of the Griffon, still had an office in the undercity. Carved into the bedrock, three levels below the upper city, the Band's office was little more than an antechamber and a series of rooms in which the mercenaries bunked.

A corpulent minotaur with black horns wider than his shoulders and a gnarled scar covering half his face greeted Pancras when he entered. "Ho there, brethren. What business have you with us today? Looking for work, or someone to work? How can old Reko help you?"

"Looking for information, actually, about an old expedition. Well, about one of your members who went on that expedition."

"I've been with the company most of my life, gave as much blood, sweat, and flesh as one can without dying. But, I don't know that I can help you. Why do you want this information?"

"A minotaur, called Thanos of the Black Mountain minotaurs, went on an expedition to the Western Wastes over twenty-five years ago. He was my lover. I'd heard that the entire expedition was wiped out, killed by giants in the Dragon Spine Mountains." Pancras scanned the room. Apart from a couple of tables and chairs in front of the hearth, a tapestry covering one wall was the only ornamentation in it. The tapestry depicted a variety of battles and the minotaurs who fought in them. "I was passing through and thinking about him. Information about what happened back then was spotty, and I was hoping someone could tell me something more specific."

"Thanos?" The old minotaur pulled two chairs over to the hearth. He gestured for Pancras to join him. "I've known many minotaurs called Thanos, but we haven't crossed those mountains in twenty years. Too much to do on this side of them."

The way the old minotaur spoke gave Pancras hope. "Do you remember him? He was about my size, more muscular, but similar height. His horns turned up at the tips."

"I remember." Reko crossed his arms over his chest and stared into the fire. "It wasn't giants. They dwell in the mountains in vast numbers, but that day, it was something else. A few of us made it out." Reko ran his hand down the scar that covered the left side of his face. "Most didn't. Now, I've never seen a dragon, but that's what some of us thought this thing was. It was savage, bestial. Skin like armor plates, not scales. Fought us with tooth and claw. Thanos fought well. He dragged many of his brothers to safety before the beast split him open."

Pancras took a moment to absorb what the old minotaur told him. *Thanos is as dead as he was when I thought giants killed him.* "Thank you. It changes nothing, but it's good to know he earned his place in the Halls of the Valiant."

"He did indeed." Reko slapped Pancras's knee. "Come, I want to show you something."

He guided Pancras into the barracks. A handful of the bunks were occupied with sleeping minotaurs. Reko pointed toward a head mounted on the wall. "We avenged them all a year later."

The creature's angular, insect-like head was large enough to swallow a human whole, or bite a minotaur's head clean off, but it lacked the elegant and organic curves characteristic of the one dragon he knew: Terrakaptis, who lived in the caldera of Drak-Anor. It appeared to be some mad wizard's idea of a dragon mated with a beetle.

"Did it have a lair?"

Reko rubbed the mounted head's chin. "Yes. It was deep in a cave, filled with blood, slime, and all manner of vermin and things I still see in my nightmares. We had some of the sages at the Arcane University come examine it, but no one could identify it. I'd always heard dragons were graceful, beautiful, but this… this is the ugliest damned thing I've ever seen."

Pancras decided it also topped his own list of ugly things as well. He thanked Reko for his time and stopped by a provisioner's shop on his way back to the Granite Anvil. He arranged for the supplies he needed to be delivered to the livery where Stormheart was stabled.

Time for one last meal—no—feast with my friends before we part ways.

Chapter 8

Pancras described the parting as a bitter, sad moment. Delilah would have chosen stronger words. The rough-spun beige robes the university forced her to wear chafed against her scales, and more than ever, she wanted to make a break for it with Pancras.

"It'll never work, Delilah." Pancras looked over his shoulder at Gisella. "There's a slayer right here. It's time for us to go our separate ways, no matter how miserable that option seems."

The drak sorceress was ambivalent about Edric's departure, but when it came time to say goodbye to Pancras, tears fell no matter how much she tried to control her emotions. The last thing she wanted to do in front of the dwarf, Kali, and the Golden Slayer was collapse into a blubbering mess, and it was only her own pride and vanity that kept her from clinging to Pancras's legs to attempt to prevent him from leaving.

Pancras knelt before her after saying his goodbyes to Kale and Kali. "Brave heart, Delilah. You are strong and clever, and you'll be fine. I know you and Kale can handle anything this city can throw at you, and, with Kali, you'll be even stronger."

"Sure, you're just saying that to make me feel better." Delilah sniffled, refusing to meet his eyes.

"I know it. I will send for you as soon as I'm able, but it could be the better part of a year before I am settled in Vlorey. Try to understand that these humans are frightened of you, and that's why they sometimes say things that offend you. Try to rein in your anger with them. They don't mean to offend most of the time."

"I'm pretty sure the Manless offends on purpose." She didn't care if he had spies listening to her right now. She was willing to risk the confrontation.

"Yes, probably. Now look, your skills are far beyond those of any of the students. If you participate in any duels, go easy on them. But, keep an open mind. You might learn a new way to approach a technique you think you've mastered or perhaps some kind of utility you never thought of. This is an opportunity for you to refine and further develop your power. There is an extensive library at the university. Use it."

Delilah nodded, then wiped her nose. "I will... remember what you said. I'll try to be good."

Pancras looked over at Kale and Kali. "Your brother and his mate are both here for you. Help each other. Make some friends. We'll be together again before you know it."

The drak sorceress didn't believe that, but Pancras seemed to, so she accepted his word. She stood apart from Kale and his mate as they watched Pancras, Edric, and the Golden Slayer ride out of the city. Delilah's eyes followed them until the three were out of sight. The sun was already creeping toward its zenith. Her guts churned and knotted as she contemplated reporting in at the Arcane University.

"Deli?" Her brother reached for her.

"I'm fine. I have to go to the wizard place." She turned to face Kale and his mate. Kali, her face devoid of expression, regarded the sorceress. Delilah sighed. "We're all each other has for now. Why don't the two of you take that money Pancras left us and try to find a more permanent place to stay? I'll probably be stuck at the university for a couple of days. I'll send a message to you when I can and keep you apprised of my situation."

"Deli, I—"

She held up her hand. "It's fine, Kale. I've not been nice to either of you. It'll be different the next time we see each other. I promise. Just have a place for us to live, all right? Don't make me live alone, by myself."

Hugging her, Kali caught Delilah off guard. "You'll be welcome with us, as long as you want to stay. We'll find a home while you're doing your duties. It'll be fun. You'll see."

Kale accompanied Delilah to the gates of the Arcane University. He made no attempt at conversation, and Delilah seemed quite content to stew in her thoughts. Her promise to try to treat Kali better made him feel a bit more confident about the future. Kale didn't know how long they'd be stuck in Muncifer and suspected they'd have ridden alongside Pancras toward the coast if the wizards had not coerced Delilah to remain behind

While he escorted his sister, Kali checked on their mounts. They would have to exercise them periodically in the countryside to keep them fit and content, and Kale saw this as an opportunity to explore the area rather than as a chore.

Delilah neither waved nor bade him farewell before she disappeared within the university property. He watched her until the guards shut the towering gates, sequestering the wizards and their students from the rest of the city.

He decided to explore the undercity and become familiar with its configuration. *I wonder what I can find to do around here. If I keep myself busy, I won't get into trouble and I won't miss Pancras too much.*

Usually shops of like purpose clumped together in cities or, at least, tended to be grouped by the socioeconomic status of their patrons. The funds Pancras left them were generous; more than the common folk saw in their entire lives, many of whom had no choice but to dwell in the deep, dark spaces of the undercity.

Kale tried not to brood on that as he navigated the crowds. Draks and minotaurs were most prevalent here, and though the minotaurs paid him no mind, every drak's head turned as he passed by.

They stared.

Folding his wings as tightly as he could against his body, Kale wished he had brought a cloak. Although accustomed to his wings now, he suddenly realized that with all the legends and stories about striped draks and winged draks passed down through the generations, seeing his wings and stripes might give other draks pause.

He ducked into a glassblower's shop. The heat of the crucible comforted Kale until he heard the crash of shattering glass behind him. The drak gaffer regarded Kale and fell to his knees. "Great Rannos! A sign!" The gaffer prostrated himself in the jagged shards before Kale.

"Don't do that." Kale took the gaffer by the arm and pulled him to his feet. "It's embarrassing."

"My arm! You touched me!" The drak cradled his appendage, staring at it, his eyes wide in awe. "Oh, blessed arm, what wonders will you now be capable of? Touch my lips that I might blow mighty, magical bottles!"

Kale ran out of the shop and into a minotaur pushing a cart full of potatoes. The minotaur's tree trunk-like leg was sufficient to halt Kale's forward motion, causing him to fall backward onto his butt.

"Watch where you're going, Drak."

The minotaur was mobbed by draks rushing to defend and assist their fallen idol.

"Hey, get off! Let go! Clear off!" The minotaur hopped, flinging draks left and right and shaking his legs to dislodge those clinging to him.

"Stop! Leave him alone!" Kale jumped into the air, hovering as high as he was able. He was still working on the endurance to fly under his own power, rather than just glide, but he managed a good five seconds of air time before exhaustion from the exertion forced him to land.

"The Child of Destiny speaks!"

"He has come to lead us!"

"No, no, I haven't!" Kale held up his hands and backed into a wall. The draks surrounded him, forgetting about the minotaur and giving the potato-pusher the opportunity to flee with his cart of tubers.

"Show us the way, O Great One!"

Kale realized he was in over his head. *Deli or Pancras would know how to get out of this.* He blurted out the first thing that came to mind. "I'm not great. I'm cursed!"

"No, you are the one of the prophecies!"

"Child of Destiny!"

"You will lead us away from the longshanks!"

"I'm a twin! I have a sister, hatched from the same egg! She's even a wizard!"

The collective gasps sucked all the air out of the area. The crowd backed away from Kale, making gestures intended to ward off evil. Kale took a step forward, and the mob of draks stepped away.

That's not quite what I wanted. He decided to go with it, though, and ran.

***

Delilah flipped through the pages of her common language lexicon as she sat in the antechamber of the Court of Wizardry. The archmage was occupied with guild business, according to the seneschal, so she was instructed to wait until he was ready for her. She thought about studying her grimoire, but figured as soon as she was able to relax and concentrate enough to make sense of the arcane pages, she'd be interrupted.

So, she brushed up on her language skills. The seneschal clucked his tongue. "That's not a book of magic, is it?"

"Do you think I'm stupid? I know if I read that one, I'll be interrupted." Delilah held up the lexicon. "It's a language book. We speak Drak and Minotaur in Drak-Anor, not your language."

"Apologies, Initiate." The seneschal bowed his head. "I just didn't want to see you reprimanded. Initiates are not permitted to peruse tomes of arcana."

"That's stupid. How are they supposed to learn?" Delilah closed her book and put it away in her pack. "I'm only an initiate because Man... the archmage said so. I've been practicing magic for most of my life." She wagged a finger at the seneschal. "And I'm older than I look!"

"I wouldn't presume to make assumptions about your age, Initiate. Your scales still carry the shine of youth, or they do to my old eyes."

"Oh, well, thank you." The edges of Delilah's mouth curled up in a smile at the unexpected compliment. She scratched her belly where the robes chafed. "Are novice robes better? These itch."

The seneschal stepped around his podium and knelt down in front of Delilah. He rubbed the hems of her robes between his fingers. "Hm. The cheapest of the initiates' robes. If you want something more comfortable, you'll have to buy it yourself. If you rely on what the university provides, you'll always get the cheapest."

"I'd rather just wear my cloak. Robes are for humans." The robe the Golden Slayer dropped off for her was made for a tall human and even if she stood on Kale's shoulders, it would have dragged on the ground. She'd been forced to make alterations with a knife. As a result, it looked less like a robe and more like a sack with sleeves.

"You'll have to talk to the archmage about a cultural exception of some sort." The seneschal stood, then returned to his podium. He glanced down at his book, then nodded. "He's ready for you now. Go on in."

She wondered how he could possibly determine that; she did not hear the archmage beckon from the court chamber. The seneschal held open the door for Delilah. She strained to see the top of his podium as she passed, but she was too short.

The archmage was not alone on the dais. The dozen wizards flanking him were each garbed in a uniquely colored robe. All the colors in a rainbow and beyond, including black and white, were represented. Their faces were expressionless masks, but then Delilah realized their faces were covered by actual masks.

And they all eyed her.

How did I not notice their masks the last time? She chalked it up to nerves.

She walked toward the archmage, using her staff as one would a walking stick. When she was a few paces from the bottom step, she inclined her head in a bow. "Well, I'm here. I guess it's time to teach me."

"Such disrespect."

"Foolish drak."

"A striped drak. Interesting."

"Or foolhardy."

The archmage slashed through the air with his hand, silencing the chorus of comments from the assembled high wizards. "You should show deference to your superiors, Initiate Drak. Disrespect is punishable. However"—Archmage Vilkan sniffed and looked at his fellow wizards—"I will allow you to try that again."

Delilah's lip curled. She bit back several choice comments of which she knew Pancras would not approve and bowed deeply, using her staff to keep herself from falling forward. "O Great Archmage, I present myself, a lowly drak, to your mighty tutelage."

Among the gasps of the high wizards, Delilah heard a lone chuckle. When she raised her head as she awaited his response, she noticed Archmage Vilkan's face flush first light pink, deepening until it became the blood red color of aged wine, and she thought she saw pulsing in his temple. He drew a shaky breath before speaking. "You will learn respect, Drak."

He snapped his fingers, then gestured toward Delilah. Guards rushed forward and seized her arms. One took her staff, and the other took her pack. "Take this initiate to Master Agata. Tell her this initiate is hers to punish. You will show us respect, Initiate Drak, in the end. Our resolve will prove superior."

Delilah spat on the floor as the guards dragged her away. She dug in her heels as they hauled her through the courtyard. She couldn't overpower them, but she would be damned if she would make things easy for them. The guards took her into a nearby building and down a set of stairs. After opening a door, they tossed her in.

"Hey! You can't take my staff and my pack!"

The guard smiled, raising Delilah's staff up over his head beyond her reach. "Yeah? Watch us. You'll get it back when your punishment is done." He kicked the door closed.

Cauldrons of all sizes and in great piles filled the room, some rusty, others covered with solidified gunk. A short human woman sat on the floor, scraping at one of the cauldrons with what resembled a chisel. Blowing a lock of raven hair out of her eyes, she continued working.

Delilah picked herself up and brushed off her robes. "I suppose you're Agata?"

The woman snorted. "Not hardly. Got yourself cauldron cleaning duty, huh? I didn't know we had any draks enrolled."

The woman's robes, beige and rough-spun like Delilah's, were covered with a network of patches that didn't quite match the original color. She groaned as her chisel became stuck, and she swore when it flew out of her hand and the cauldron clattered to the floor.

"Damn it!" She brought her hand up to her mouth and sucked on it.

Delilah sat back against the wall, bringing her knees up to her chest. "So what? I have to clean these now? Where's Agata?"

"If they sent you down here for her, she'll be along in a minute. The masters are always busy, but they always seem to find the time to punish us. Who are you anyway?"

"Delilah."

"Katka. What did you do?"

The drak sorceress knitted her hands together as she considered where to start. "I was born, lived a life away from all these humans, and learned magic on my own. Stupid archmage."

"Wow." Katka grunted, chipping away at gunk coating the interior of the cauldron.

"How about you?"

"Master Bruncvik had a cat, right?"

Delilah didn't recognize the name, but she nodded for Katka to continue her story.

"Well, I might have accidentally exploded it."

Despite herself, Delilah chuckled. She never managed to explode something by accident. Her eyes scanned the room, settling on a nearby cauldron similar to the one she purchased. The inside was filled with a solid mass of red and green swirls. When she scratched the sludge with a claw, it rippled like the wake of a stone skipping across it. The mass remained at the bottom of the cauldron, however, even when Delilah tipped it past the point where it should have spilled out.

"What is this gunk?"

Katka swore, jamming her chisel into the bottom of the cauldron she was working on. "Whenever a student messes up in Alchemy, their cauldron needs to be cleaned. Most of the time, you can just dump it out, give it a rinse, and start over." She gestured to the pile of cauldrons. "These are what happen when you really mess up."

"Why don't they just melt them down and buy new ones?" Delilah turned the cauldron upside down, then shook it. When not so much as a drip or a drizzle exited the pot, she dared to look up into it. The mass wobbled, but it remained affixed to the bottom.

"Most students can't afford to buy a new cauldron every time they mess up a potion. The good news is, once you mess up this badly three times, they kick you out of Alchemy. Some people just aren't cut out for it, you know?"

"I guess." Delilah never dabbled in alchemy. She and her brother used to work together to create enchanted siege weapons for the defense of Drak-Anor, but since the establishment of a treaty with Ironkrag, they hadn't needed to use them.

The door opened again. An older woman wearing mossy robes entered. Her silver hair hung in braids, framing a face lined with age. She shut the door behind her and leaned against it, tapping a slender finger against her chin.

"So, you're the drak initiate. I am Master Agata. I teach Alchemy here. What is your real name? The archmage insists your name is 'Drak,' but I'm not foolish enough to believe that."

"Delilah."

"A pretty name and unusual for a drak." Master Agata cocked her head, peering at Delilah. "Hm. Stripes, also unusual."

Delilah stood, balling her hands into fists as she stood before the alchemist. Master Agata knelt, lowering herself to eye level. "You're mouthy but not unskilled from what I've been told. I can't really blame you if you're resentful toward all these rules that have never meant a pint of rat's piss to you before. But, you're here now, so make the best of things, eh?"

Master Agata handed Delilah a scraper. "Clean these cauldrons as best you can. Somewhere in that pile is a tub you can dump the worst of the gunk into, if you find anything that's still squishy."

The older woman stood, bracing her back with her hands. "I'll tell you both what I tell everyone who has this duty: it's hard work, even horrible at times, but there are far worse masters under whom you could be punished. Be thankful, and tell everyone"—she pointed alternately at Katka and Delilah—"how I'm a horrible old witch and you'd rather gnaw your own fingers off than work for me again."

Delilah looked over at Katka, who, wide-eyed, regarded Master Agata.

"Now, what are you two going to tell the other initiates?"

"That you're horrible?"

Delilah understood. "You're a horrible, old, wrinkled, withered witch. I'll chew my and my brother's fingers off before I do a damned thing for you again."

Master Agata tipped her head, then winked. "Just so. I'll be back when it's time for your midday meal." The older woman exited.

Katka picked up her chisel, then jabbed at her cauldron. Delilah dug into the multi-colored goo as well. *So, not everyone here bows and scrapes before the archmage. I can work with this.*

***

As he shifted in his saddle and attempted to find a comfortable position, Pancras reflected that one night in a warm, soft bed was insufficient. Even his worst guesses about what awaited him at the Arcane University didn't include being sent away as soon as he arrived. As if it weren't exhausting enough having to travel several months to Muncifer for only a few minutes with the archmage, he was now required to travel back all that way and then some.

At least winter is over.

The setting sun warmed his back as they rode away from Muncifer, the clip-clop of Stormheart's hooves muffled by the damp earth of the trade road. Edric rode ahead of him, and by the way the dwarf's head bobbed, it appeared as though he was asleep in the saddle. The rattle of Gisella's armor and gear behind him served as a constant reminder of the penalty should he not fulfill his obligation. Although the enchantment cast upon him by the archmage made it difficult for him to desire anything but arriving in Vlorey as soon as possible.

They rode until dusk and then moved off the road to set up camp. As Pancras tied up Stormheart for the night, he caught a flash on the horizon, a glint of light at the point at which the setting sun touched the earth. It winked and jounced before disappearing as the last bit of sun dipped out of sight. He'd heard of perfect situations over water where the setting sun caused a green flash at the horizon, but not over land.

"See something?" After walking her horse over to Pancras and Stormheart and securing her, Gisella unbuckled her saddle.

"A burst of light. A glimmer, really. It's probably nothing, just a trick."

Gisella strained to focus on the horizon. "Light reflecting off armor perhaps? By the road?"

"Possibly. Do you think someone is following us?"

Gisella studied the sky for a moment. The King waned overhead, but the Queen had not yet risen, and all the stars which composed the Plow constellation were fully visible.

"I doubt it. I can't imagine who, unless your draks have decided to follow. That would be very unwise on your sorcerer friend's part."

Pancras felt confident Delilah would do the right thing, despite her grumbling. Still, he kept silent on the subject. "Soldiers on patrol, perhaps?"

Gisella rubbed her horse's nose and fed him an apple. "That seems likely. Nothing to be concerned about."

Pancras agreed. He wouldn't have brought it up if she hadn't broached the subject first. Stormheart nickered before nuzzling Gisella for a treat. Pancras hadn't thought to buy anything of that nature. Fortunately for Stormheart, Gisella had another apple she fed to him.

Pancras joined Edric in building a fire. Scattered clouds blowing overhead blocked some of the stars, but the fine spring evening was otherwise unmarred by poor weather. The next morning, clouds rolled in on the wind chasing them from the mountains in the west. Rumbling thunder in the distance threatened a downpour. The three travelers rode on, aware that outrunning the rain was a futile task, but making the effort nonetheless.

***

Between being chased out of the undercity by a mob of crazed draks and worrying about his sister, Kale didn't have much of an appetite. Kali eyed him over their plates of food, furrowing her brow in worry.

"What am I going to do? I can't just stay inside the rest of my life. You should have seen them. They thought I was some god or something." Kale pushed the meat around on his plate with his fork.

"Maybe if they see you doing mundane things enough, they'll start to leave you alone." Kali gestured for the barkeep to bring another bottle of wine. "Today is the Spring's Dawning Festival. Maybe it'll be busy enough people won't pay attention to you."

"I guess I could get a really big cloak. Maybe wear… clothes." The thought churned in his stomach. He was warm enough without draping rags on himself like humans did. He would be miserable bundled up like that.

Kali rubbed the top of his snout. "Won't cover up the stripes on your head."

"I'll only go out at night. If anyone asks, I'll just say it's a trick of the light." Kale didn't like the idea of slinking in the shadows. If anything, it might draw more attention to him.

She rubbed his hand as he played with his food. "I don't think you're going to be happy with that."

"Maybe I'll just stay up here for now."

Kali nodded and smiled. "There's plenty we can explore up here. Maybe we can spy on your sister a bit while she practices her magic."

Kale perked up. "Yeah, maybe." A grin appeared on his face just before he slapped his hand on the table. "We can snoop around there tomorrow and see what we can find out."

Kale's appetite returned swiftly at the thought of sneaking to spy on his sister. Humans and minotaurs weren't impressed by his stripes, and though they regarded his wings with curiosity, none of them ever mobbed him the way the draks in Honeywater or in the undercity did. The night passed more slowly than Kale imagined it could, and when it was time to break their fasts, he wolfed down his meal and dragged Kali away from the table even as she reached for the final scraps.

Retracing his steps to the Arcane University proved to be the easiest part of Kale's day. Everyone knew where it was located. While most of Muncifer was built on, down, and around cliffs and crags, the Arcane University was located in a newer area that encompassed relatively flat land near the south side of the city. Taller than some of the nearby buildings, it was surrounded by a smooth, grey stone wall. Frowning men wearing tabards emblazoned with the Arcane University's sigil guarded the wrought iron and ornately decorated gates. Wearing perpetual scowls, the guards watched passersby and occasionally commented to each other. They shooed away folks dressed in tattered rags who jingled coin-filled cups at anyone who made eye contact.

"Do you think they'll let us in the front gate to watch them practice?" Kali leaned against a wall as she eyed the guards.

"Probably not. I guess we can ask, though." Kale had observed his sister perform sorcery most of his life, but he was curious as to how the Arcane University would teach a drak who believed she already knew everything.

As soon as he approached the gate, the guards snapped to attention. "What's your business here?"

Kale peered around them, searching for any sign of Delilah. "My sister is a student here. I wanted to watch her practice."

The guard dismissed him with a wave. "Get out of here, Drak. No visitors and no spectators. Find your entertainment elsewhere."

Kali pulled him away from the gate. "That figures. Let's go this way."

She led him around the side of the compound where they found sparser crowds than at the front of the university, but no one paid any mind to the two draks. None of the nearby buildings were as tall as the surrounding wall, and all the trees were carefully trimmed to keep branches away from the top of the fortification. Kale ran his hand along the stones as they walked. They were as smooth as glass, yet opaque.

"It's almost like they don't want anyone seeing what goes on in there."

"Secretive lot, wizards." Kali gazed up toward the top of the barrier. She tried to gain a foothold, but her claws slid down the façade. They continued to circle the campus, seeking some flaw in construction they could exploit. At the rear of the compound, they found many structures built right up against the barrier, but they were too short to reach the top, even if Kale and Kali climbed onto their roofs.

When they reached the front of the compound, they reversed and retraced their path. Kale thought he heard a scraping sound behind him. When his eyes scanned the area, he saw only citizens of Muncifer going about their business. He smacked the wall with his palm.

"Hey!" The voice was a whisper. For a moment, Kale wasn't sure he even heard it over the din of the crowd. Then he spotted a cloaked and hooded man waving from the shadows of an alley. He gestured again when Kale brought the man to Kali's attention.

Kale fingered one of the daggers on his bandolier as he approached the hooded man. His face was hidden in the shadows of his cloak, but he appeared unkempt and dirty, like other street dwellers he encountered.

"You lookin' for a way in? To see the wizards?" The man took a step backward, further obscuring himself in the shadows.

"Maybe." Kale wasn't sure what to think of this human. He smelled of moldy cheese, dung, and stale sweat. Kale supposed hygiene was not one of the man's priorities in life.

"No way in, unless you're a wizard yourself. But, I knows a secret way."

Kali scoffed. "I'll bet you do. And all we have to do is follow you, right? We weren't hatched yesterday."

"No, no." The man shook his head. He produced a small bag from inside his cloak and bounced it in his hand. Kale heard the jingle of coins. "I tells you the way, and you sneaks inside. Grabs something for me. Then you gets paid. Get you in, get me thing, and we all happy, yes?"

"Sounds easy enough." Kali stepped closer to the man, resting her hand on the hilt of her blade. "What thing? What is it?"

"Kali, I don't know if we should steal anything from wizards. They might turn us into something unnatural."

Kali shot him a look. "Says the only drak with wings in Muncifer."

"Oh, yeah. Wings on drak. You jump over wall to escape. Fast, quiet. They not catch you."

The smelly man sparked an idea in Kale. He pulled Kali away from him, toward the main street. "Hey, he's got a point. If we can climb just to the top of one of the nearby tall buildings, I can glide us to the top of the wall."

"Oh, I'm sure the wizards will never see us coming." Kali pointed to the sky above the Arcane University. "There's not a lot of cover there."

Kale considered her point. "So? Why would they even be looking up? They're safe, deep in a city, teaching. They don't have to worry about invaders from above. Who'd be crazy enough to rob a wizard school anyway?"

They both looked at the hooded man. He flashed a smile before he turned and ran down the alley. Kali took Kale's arm. "Well, there goes our chance."

"He was probably crazy anyway. I don't want to rob wizards. Seriously, you know how easily upset Delilah can be, and how powerful she is. Imagine making a whole school full of Delilah's angry?"

Kali leaned her head on Kale's shoulder. "I kind of like the idea of taking a glide with you. Maybe we should try that. What's the worst that could happen?"

Kale envisioned plenty of negative possibilities. They could crash into a building. They could crash into an ill-tempered wizard. The wizards might have some sort of enchanted shield over the university. Maybe they executed trespassers. He told her as much.

"That seems extreme."

"Let's go find me a cloak and look around the undercity. Now that I've had time to think about this, I'd rather risk a mob of admirers than the anger of a wizard."

Chapter 9

After spending all the first day scrubbing cauldrons with Katka, Delilah decided to try a different approach with the archmage on the second day: feigning respect. In keeping with their word, the guards returned her possessions to her before taking her to the barracks. After a bit of haggling with some of the other initiates, she managed to take a bunk next to Katka. She wasn't sure what she thought about the human yet, but she was, at least, someone Delilah knew.

When she reported for her studies the next morning, Delilah bowed and demurred. Huffing, the archmage narrowed his eyes, but since she kept her tone even and avoided his gaze, he couldn't rightly accuse her of disrespect. True to what Pancras and Gisella predicted, he was unable to give her his full attention. In between requiring her to sit quietly and observe court business, he paced and lectured her on the proper method in which to attune an arcane focus. She tried to explain she already knew how to do that, but he ignored her protests. Interruptions were constant the first several days, but Archmage Vilkan seemed to regard them as a matter of course.

As the week neared its end, Delilah shuffled about the student barracks in a dejected state. So far, she'd been lectured many times, but the archmage had refused to actually teach her anything. Each of his lectures covered subjects she learned on her own back home. Her heart sank when she saw Katka approach, almost bouncing with energy. Her eyes flashed with excitement. "They're going to hold Initiate Trials tomorrow! The Black and White Wizards will be presiding while the archmage is meeting with the archduke."

"Great. He'll probably make me hold his cloak while he talks. I'll miss my chance." She shook her head. "Doesn't matter anyway; he hasn't taught me a damn thing."

Another student, a novice, overheard and joined them. "The archmage can't do that. All initiates are required to attend the trials, even if they don't participate." He offered a hand to Delilah. "I'm Conner, by the way."

His appearance and accent reminded Delilah of Princess Valene in Almeria. "Are you from Vlorey?" Delilah shook Conner's hand.

He sat on the edge of her bed. "My parents are. Were. They were merchants and brought me down here when I was small. They died a few years back."

Delilah rubbed her snout. "I can't tell how old you humans are."

Katka laughed. "That's okay. We can't tell how old you are, either. Old draks have dull scales, right?"

"Yeah, they dull with age, right?" Conner looked at Katka and then Delilah. "It's not like all draks are shiny, and then, bam! They're old and dull."

The drak sorceress shifted, kicking her legs against the side of her bed, uncomfortable discussing drak aging with two humans. "It's gradual. I spent a lot of time underground, so I can't be exact. There's really only two seasons worth tracking: when snow blocks us in and when it doesn't. I think it's at least thirty winters or so, but in Drak-Anor, it's easy to lose track of time."

"Wow! I've only seen sixteen. And you're only an initiate?"

"She learned a bunch on her own, before she came here." Katka sat on her bed and looked at Delilah. "Right?"

"That's right." Delilah pulled her pack up onto the bed with her. "My brother and I helped defend Drak-Anor for years before I came to this pit. They said I was a renegade and I had to start here, as an initiate, or they'd kill me." She didn't want to talk about the Court of Wizardry, the archmage, or guild business, so she changed the subject. "How old are you, Katka?"

"Fourteen. My parents sold our best horses to pay for my enrollment. They said I was a natural." She chuckled. "So far, I've only managed to fail three trials and melt two cauldrons."

Conner slapped her knee. "Well, tomorrow's trials will be different. Black and White are always more lenient. They think the other masters spend too much time proving to initiates that they're better than them and too little time teaching magic."

Delilah snorted. "They must teach from the same plans as the archmage."

He stood and shook their hands again. "Good luck, both of you. Hopefully, this time tomorrow, you'll be in grey robes."

***

Throughout the next few days, Pancras kept checking behind them to determine if they were being followed. When he wasn't searching for their elusive pursuer, he wracked his brain, pondering who would follow them. And why?

He concluded it was no one from Muncifer, and he figured anyone from Almeria would have long ago been noticed. *Perhaps it is an agent of that shadow demon in my head?* Pancras thought he heard a chuckle somewhere in the deep recesses of his mind. *It's probably nothing.*

Pancras's paranoid diligence did not go unnoticed by Gisella. Not only did she agree that someone was following them, but also their mysterious companion behaved like a lone traveler, staying close enough to observe where they were headed in order to follow, rather than someone who coincidentally traveled the same route. After cresting a hill, she halted her horse and dismounted.

She handed the reins to Pancras. "Slow your pace, but keep going. I'm going to lie in wait for our companion and ascertain whether they're a threat to us. I'll catch up in a bit."

Pancras and Edric slowed their pace. The dwarf looked back as Gisella hunkered down in some scrub near the road. "This is our chance, you know."

"Chance for what?" Pancras played dumb.

"Leave her behind. We could divert off the road, and you could head back home. She'd be none the wiser."

The very thought turned Pancras's stomach, the enchantment the archmage placed on him causing the reaction. "She'd notice by the end of the day. Slayers are legendary for their ability to track their quarry."

Edric scoffed. "They say a dwarf could find ale in the Western Wastes, too. Doesn't matter to me, anyway. You wanna do what they say, that's up to you."

Of course, it didn't matter what he wanted. Not anymore. The archmage made sure of that, sending a slayer along to ensure the outcome of his decree as insurance. Pancras wanted to be angry, to rage at the heavens at being forced into the journey against his will. But he wanted to go to Vlorey. He needed to. That the shadow in his head was pleased about this worried him.

Whomever the shadow demon in his mind served, Pancras felt its malevolent touch whenever he thought about magic. He suspected the haze in his vision was the shadow's doing, as well. For that reason, he kept his hands away from his arcane focus as much as possible.

Edric made small talk as they rode, but Pancras, absorbed in his own thoughts about their follower, the shadow demon, and traveling to Vlorey, barely noticed the dwarf's voice. The morning became afternoon, and as they stretched their legs and walked their horses, Gisella caught up to them.

With her was a figure familiar to Pancras: a black-skinned fiendling with flaming red hair. He recognized her even without her garish outfit.

"This scamp has been following us since we left the city. Good eyes, Wizard."

Pancras acknowledged the compliment with a nod.

Qaliah's hands were bound in front of her. She held them up. "Gonna cut me loose, Slayer? I'm not going to run away. I was coming after you."

"So you say." Gisella took her horse's reins from Pancras. "And no one sent you. You're not after me, or the minotaur, or the dwarf?"

"That's right. I wanted out of Muncifer, and I didn't want to travel alone."

Pancras looked over at Gisella. "Why did you bind her?"

"I wanted to keep control of her until I caught up with you."

The minotaur unsheathed his knife and cut her bonds. He didn't understand why she would follow them at all. "Surely, there were other people leaving Muncifer with whom you could travel."

Qaliah rubbed her wrists. "Surely. Didn't know them, though."

Gisella's horse nickered and placed her head over the slayer's shoulder. Gisella looked back at Qaliah. "I tried to send her home. She fought me."

"I wasn't trying to beat you." Qaliah laughed. "I don't think I can. I'm not letting you send me back, though. My debt to the Arcane University is paid, and I'm a free woman now. I can go where I want, and right now, I want to go where you all are going."

"Why?" Pancras couldn't imagine anyone wanting to go with them, except Kale, his mate, and Delilah. Especially someone who was not aware of their destination.

"Why not? I don't want to stay in Muncifer, and you're going away from Muncifer. Good enough for me." She held up her hands. "I'm not a complete fool, no matter how well I play at being one. Traveling alone is dangerous. I won't get in the way, and I'll pull my weight. Don't have a horse, though."

"Bah, girl's lucky we kept a slow pace." Edric climbed onto his pony. "Let's get some more road under us before nightfall."

"Indeed." Gisella mounted her steed. She nodded toward Qaliah. "We can't keep you from following us, I guess, but you'll have to keep up." She spurred her horse into a trot, passing Edric. The dwarf followed suit.

Pancras mounted Stormheart and contemplated following before he sighed, offering a hand to the fiendling. "Come on, then. Stormheart can carry us both for a bit."

***

The Initiate Trials took place in the practice area at the side of the courtyard, between the tavern and the Court of Wizardry. A covered pavilion stood at one end, in which the Black Wizard, the White Wizard, and various masters sat. Practice dummies lined the back wall of the compound. Students of all ranks stood on the sidelines, some waiting for their turn to demonstrate proficiency, others observing. A tall, thin older woman with greying hair woven in a tight braid that hung down her back stood before the reviewing stand as the proctor of the trials. Delilah recognized her from Katka's gossip as Master Galina, one of the students' favorite defensive magic teachers..

The drak sorceress and Katka stood on the sidelines with Conner, observing some of the other initiates perform required spells. Delilah lost track of their names. That the archmage kept her separated from most of the other students, except at night, didn't help.

Initiates were called one at a time to stand before Black and White, as the students referred to them. The first student called was an older initiate. At least, he looked older to Delilah. She still found it unreliable to determine the age of students based on their appearance. He was taller than Conner, but his face was just as smooth, though lighter. The smooth skin of humans unnerved Delilah. She didn't like the way it felt under her fingers, either. It reminded her of dwarf flesh, but it felt a bit more squishy and warm.

"Initiate Ludek, can you produce for us, a ball of light?" Master Galina paced in front of him, her hands clasped behind her back.

"Certainly, Master." Ludek held aloft his wand. "*Fos.*" Emerald swirls of aether spun around the tip of his wand, coalescing into a ball of light.

"Now, Initiate Ludek, I will cast a spell at you." Master Galina stepped back, fingering an amulet around her neck. "If it hits you, it will harm you. Do you understand?"

Ludek extinguished the light and nodded. "I understand."

Master Galina held up her amulet and pointed at Ludek. "*Dynami velos!*" Wisps of azure formed a sphere and hurtled at Ludek.

He twisted, raising his wand. "*Aspida tou ravematos.*" A shield of glittering energy the color of grass reflected the attack.

The gathered initiates applauded his quick reflexes. Delilah looked on with growing impatience as they tested his ability to levitate an object out of the Blood Oak and cast his own bolt of energy at one of the training dummies.

"That is sufficient, Initiate. You may trade in your beige robes for grey ones and join the ranks of the novices." Master Galina bowed to Ludek. The initiates offered him another round of applause.

One by one, Master Galina called the initiates. Some passed, some failed, and some failed painfully in the case of those unable to erect a shield in time to avoid Master Galina's spell. When it was Katka's turn, Delilah wished her good luck. The girl was able to create light, defend herself, and retrieve the object from the tree, but when it came time to attack the training dummy, her bolt fizzled before it splashed against the wood-and-straw target like a snowball.

Master Galina cocked an eyebrow, then glanced at the two high wizards. They shook their heads.

"You will remain an initiate, Katka."

Katka hung her head and nodded. She returned to Delilah and Conner, offering them a weak smile. "Here I stay. I just need more practice with that one, I guess."

Delilah smacked her lips. Her mouth was dry from anticipation. There remained one untested initiate: her. Some of what the students had been asked to do was unlike anything she'd learned in all her years of practicing magic. There wasn't much call for grabbing boxes out of trees while fighting oroqs underground.

"Initiate Dra—" Master Galina frowned at her list of initiates and turned to the reviewing stand. "Really? Initiate Drak? Isn't that a bit demeaning?"

The crowd murmured. Black held up his hand to silence them. "It is as it was entered by the archmage himself."

"What utter nonsense." Master Galina faced Delilah. "Initiate, what is your name?"

The drak sorceress, holding her head up high, stepped forward. "Delilah Windsinger, of Drak-Anor."

"Enter that into the record. Very well." Master Galina rolled up her list before stowing it under her robes. "Can you produce light?"

Delilah tilted her staff forward. "*Fos.*" Azure mist gathered around the top of her staff and burst into a ball of light.

"Initiate Delilah, I am going to cast a spell at you. If it hits you, it will harm you. Do you understand?"

Delilah gulped and nodded. Pancras knew shielding spells, but that was one area of magic she hadn't learned.

Master Galina pointed at Delilah. "*Dynami velos!*"

The drak twisted and dove forward. She felt the magical bolt pass over her back as she rolled and came to her knees with her staff pointed at Master Galina. "*Oph—*"

A blast of energy from the reviewing stands knocked Delilah off her feet, sending her skidding across the yard.

White stood, his staff pointed at Delilah. "Initiates are not permitted to retaliate against masters."

Delilah leaned on her staff as she rose to her feet. "Apologies. It was a reflex." That much, at least, was true. Combat was second nature to the drak sorceress after years of dodging and fighting dwarfs, oroqs, and the other hostile denizens of the underworld.

"You did not shield yourself." Black was standing now.

"Nevertheless, she was not struck by Master Galina's spell." White lowered his staff.

"Proceed," they intoned as one.

"Initiate Delilah." Master Galina gestured toward the Blood Oak. "There is one box remaining in the tree. Use your magic to retrieve it, please."

Yeah, sure. I'll just wish it over here. She tapped the butt of her staff on the grass and gathered the threads of magic to her as she thought. She had an idea, but she didn't know if it would be accepted. *Better to fail trying then to not try at all, I suppose.*

"*Ageliofedros.*" A glowing blue boggin popped into existence at Delilah's feet. As she knelt before it, she heard murmuring and giggling from the crowd. "Tell Conner I need his help. Ask if he'll come to me, please."

The boggin yipped, running into the crowd, then stopped in front of the dark-skinned boy. Master Galina cleared her throat and turned to the reviewing stand. "I do not see how this is relevant to the test."

Black eyed White and then addressed Master Galina. "Let it play out."

"She has not failed yet." White nodded in agreement.

Furrowing his brow, Conner approached Delilah. His eyes darted from Delilah to Master Galina, to the reviewing stand, and back. "I'm here. Master Galina?"

"Well? Proceed, Initiate Delilah."

Delilah chuckled, looking at Conner. "I can't quite reach it. Can you retrieve that box for me? Please? I'll owe you an ale or something."

The novice stammered and stared at the tree.

"Get on with it, Novice."

Conner withdrew a wand from his robes. Emerald energy swirled around him. "*Dynami antikeimeno kalesei.*" The wooden box in the tree shuddered before it flew through the air toward him in a lazy arc. He put his wand in his pocket and caught the box. Then, he passed it to Delilah. He bowed to the reviewing stand and returned to his place in the crowd.

Delilah placed the box at Master Galina's feet. The wizard drew her lips tight and shook her head. "I do not believe that is the correct solution to this part of the trial."

Tapping from the reviewing stand drew their attention. Black and White again stood, and, in succession, addressed Master Galina.

"An improper solution. Unintended."

"A clever use of resources."

"Explain yourself."

Delilah licked her lips. Master Galina nudged her. "Well? The high wizards have addressed you."

"I was not taught levitation or telekinesis. I don't know how to work that kind of magic."

White looked at Black. "Did not learn?"

"Who taught you what you know and not that?"

"I taught myself. The archmage sure hasn't cared to teach me anything."

The crowd gasped, murmuring until Black's upraised hand silenced them. "Proceed with the final test."

Master Galina sighed and shook her head. She pointed at the training dummies. "You've seen what the other students did. Can you do that, at least?"

I'll show her. Delilah snorted and stepped toward the targets. She reached deep within her and concentrated. Normally, she didn't focus the type of magic she prepared to perform too tightly, but she desired both precision and effect. The azure tendrils near the top of her staff swirled and coiled around her head. "*Synnefotone shifone!*"

A cloud of whirling blades appeared around the training dummy. Wood splintered as they tore into it, sending great clumps of hay into the air and shredding the stand to which the dummy was attached. When Delilah dismissed the effect, nothing remained where the dummy stood, save a ragged stump.

The crowd stood in stunned silence. In the distance, a lone bird chirped. Then, applause and cheers erupted from the assembled students. Delilah turned to the crowd and bowed. When she faced Master Galina once more, the older woman regarded Delilah with a sour expression.

"Not exactly what we were looking for, but I cannot argue with the results."

"Impressive conjuration."

"Not in our curriculum for initiates. Well done."

Master Galina quieted the crowd. She reviewed her checklist. "You are lacking several key skills, yet seem to excel in other, more advanced areas. You will remain an initiate until you can pass the trials in the intended fashion."

"What? Pacha's blue balls, you smooth-skinned—" Delilah bit her tongue to avoid issuing curses some of the younger initiates probably shouldn't hear until they were older. Master Galina's sour face tightened. Delilah wasn't sure if it was possible for a human to frown hard enough to split the skin and slough it off their skulls, but she had a feeling she was about to find out.

"The drak's knowledge is incomplete."

"Her time studying this week has been wasted."

"What studying?" Delilah stepped past Master Galina and addressed the Black and White Wizards directly. "Archmage Ma—the archmage has done nothing but lecture me about the history of the university and arcane focus creation for the past week. The only time I've spent with any of the masters was the first day when I scrubbed cauldrons for Master Agata. No one has even tried to teach me—"

The Black Wizard stood, then raised his hand. "That will be remedied."

The White Wizard nodded his assent. "You will be remanded to a master for private instruction to bring your basic skills up to the level needed to pass the Initiate Trials."

"I volunteer!" A melodious voice rose above the buzz of the crowd. A slender, nut-brown-skinned man stepped forward. His pointed ears swept upward, poking through his dark, mossy hair.

An elf? Oh, fantastic. Delilah rubbed her snout, sighing. *This gets better and better.* Despite warming relations with Celtangate, Delilah never cared much for the elven traders who came to Drak-Anor. They all seemed very aloof and self-important to her.

"Master Valyrian." Master Galina bowed. "Good to see you back safely."

"Indeed! I will teach this drak what she needs to learn. Her skills are quite advanced from what I've seen here today, but she is lacking in some appalling ways." He stepped around Delilah as he spoke, ogling her in a way that made her feel like a piece of meat in a shop window.

"Very well." Master Galina faced the crowd. "Congratulations to our new novices. Those of you who failed, study hard and do not be discouraged. The arcane arts require practice and skill. We will hold more trials one week from today. Be ready!"

Master Valyrian patted Delilah on the shoulder and gestured for her to follow him. She rolled her eyes at the elf and caught Katka's reassuring gaze as she passed. The elf's tone was too cheerful for Delilah's taste as he walked alongside her. "Come, Initiate Delilah! You have a week left as an initiate, so let's make the most of it."

***

As stars appeared in the moonless sky, Gisella squatted by a pot hanging over the crackling fire, then stirred the stew within. After removing the gilded tips of his horns, Pancras polished them with a rag. Smiling, Qaliah leaned against a tree, observing the dwarf's struggles to wrangle their horses.

Gisella's blonde locks, unbound now, fell past her shoulders, glowing like molten gold in the reflected firelight, and Pancras understood the reason for her nickname. The same light danced across the scales of her armor. He found it mesmerizing in a way. Upon catching Pancras staring, she flashed him a lopsided grin.

"Admiring the view?" She tossed her hair over her shoulder before banging the spoon on the edge of the pot. Gisella sat alongside Pancras, then leaned back against her saddle.

"I was contemplating the Golden Slayer, yes." Pancras held the gold tip up to the light. Satisfied it was as clean as it could be, he fitted it over the tip of his horn. "You're not what I expected."

"Thank you." Gisella tilted her head in gratitude. "I pride myself on defying expectations. I do my job well, make no mistake. I'm a Watchmaiden. I know how to fight, but that doesn't mean I cannot enjoy life as well. There's no need to be dour all the time, especially if one has a reputation as a fierce warrior."

Dwarvish cursing filled the air as Edric tethered the horses. Pancras glanced his way to make sure the dwarf wasn't in over his head. As Edric worked to secure them for the night, he seemed to be frustrated rather than actually in trouble. Qaliah offered suggestions that seemed to compound Edric's difficulties.

Deciding he would be a hindrance if he offered to help Edric, Pancras returned his attention to Gisella. "One could mistake you for two different people."

"One face I wear when dealing with The Manless and the other slayers"—Gisella's eyes narrowed—"or when I'm hunting renegades." Her smile returned. "The other is for everyone else. Only my enemies need fear me, and thus far, I do not count you among them. You've been pleasantly cooperative. For that, I thank you."

"Well, that's a relief." Pancras fitted the second tip over his horn.

"So"—Gisella wrapped her arms around her legs and leaned forward—"what gods do you pray to?"

The question took Pancras by surprise. The last thing he expected from this warrior was a discussion on theology. "Aita." He shook his head. "But I seldom pray to her. She doesn't listen. The goddess of death and the underworld has little time for the concerns of the living."

Edric stepped over to the stew pot and stirred the contents before sitting down. "Damned horses, and damn that fiendling."

As if on cue, Qaliah joined them at the fire. Laughing, she slapped the dwarf's shoulder. "Most people think I'm damned already, Edric."

Gisella glanced over at Edric. "How about you, Dwarf? What gods' ears do you bend?"

Edric looked up. "Eh? Oh, I sometimes visit shrines to Aurora and Pacha. When I'm tense."

"Indeed." Gisella raised an eyebrow. "I'll bet you're the life of the party."

"Oh, aye. I've been ejected from me clan and banished from me home."

"Aurora and Pacha, eh? Sex and spirits! Good choices." Qaliah laughed, nudging Edric. He scowled, then moved away from her. "I like them when I need to unwind, too. Nothing like grabbing a bottle of Pacha's finest and seeking 'enlightenment' from a comely lad or lass of Aurora."

"There's more to the worship of Aurora than carnal pleasures, Qaliah. I would gladly expound on that later for you." Gisella returned her gaze to the minotaur. "I would have expected you to revere Selene, Pancras. Any particular reason you do not?"

Pancras cleared his throat. He respected the goddess of magic, but truth be told, he gave little more than lip service to any of the gods and goddesses watching over Calliome. "No reason in particular. My studies drew me to Aita."

"What exactly drew you to follow the dark path of necromancy?" Gisella drew her legs closer to her. "Is that a tale you're willing to share?"

The minotaur chuckled. "It is not much of a tale. I was angry at first. My ostracism at my choice of lovers and his subsequent death… I suppose I wanted revenge on the world. When I realized what was actually required of me, I adjusted my goals."

"How so?"

"A friend once told me I had too much heart to be a proper necromancer, so I dedicated my studies instead to learning how best to thwart them. It was necessary to learn their ways. Plus, our ruler at the time demanded expendable soldiers. Animated skeletons filled that demand perfectly. Eventually, I chose to limit my animations only to those who gave their consent prior to death. Many minotaurs in Drak-Anor were all too eager to continue to serve beyond their demise.

"Drak-Anor's current ruler finds undead distasteful, so once again I shifted my focus, now to alchemy. And what about you, Slayer?" Pancras decided to determine how much of Gisella's pleasant act was a mask hiding her true self. "To whom do you dedicate your kills?"

That radiant smile fell, and Gisella eyed her feet. "I don't dedicate my kills. I don't revel in the victory. I pray to Adranus for the strength to see my tasks through and to Anetha for the wisdom to know when I must let my spear speak instead of my mouth. But... I seem to be in good company. Aurora is my patron." She looked up at Pancras, a glint in her eye. "I know many archmages used the slayers for vendettas, their own personal murder squads. I believe The Manless thinks of us as assassins, but there is good to be had in the hunting of renegades. Most of them are malevolent; yet I have still given every one I have hunted a second chance."

Pancras swallowed and fought to keep from revealing his guilt on his face. "My apologies. My previous encounters with slayers were all with men of dubious ethics and more than a little bloodlust." He crossed his hand over his chest and bowed as deeply as he could from a seated position.

"There are many such men in our ranks. Women, too. They probably outnumber slayers like me, who kill only to save the lives the renegades would otherwise take." Gisella sighed. "It can be a harsh world."

"The strong are always preying on the weak and unfortunate." Qaliah spat into the fire. "Pick the wrong pocket, and you end up dancing for a wizard's amusement."

"I, for one, am relieved you can speak in more than just rhymes." Pancras smiled at Qaliah.

The fiendling stuck out her tongue at Pancras. "Do you know how difficult that was? I slipped a few times in front of the archmage, and he tried to have me turned into a frog."

"He is a petty, vindictive man." Gisella rose to check on the stew again before returning to her seat.

Pancras decided to satisfy his curiosity. "Why is he called 'Manless'?"

"I can guess." Edric snorted.

"There are several stories about that." Gisella stretched and yawned. "The most popular one is that he tried to have his way with me and I un-manned him." She snapped her fingers. "A flick of my wrist and away went his ability to sire children or enjoy the company of a woman."

From the corner of his eye, Pancras noticed Edric cringe and cross his legs. Qaliah sneered and then giggled. "A king's rod isn't the only thing making a man a man, though. I hear one of the other masters was born a woman and lives as a man, searching for the transmutation spell that will make his transformation complete."

"True enough." Gisella placed her hand on her chest. "I cannot say which, of course, he entrusted me in confidence."

The fiendling shrugged. "Doesn't matter to me. I heard the same story about Manless. I have to applaud you for that."

Pancras eyed Gisella who shook her head at Qaliah's response. "That's not the truth, though. It's only partly true. He did proposition me a few times, but he never tried to force himself on me. The girl he forced himself on caught him off guard. Then he throttled her. By the time we responded to her screams, she was dead, and it was his word against that of a corpse. He claimed she mutilated him out of hate, spite, and/or jealousy. Pick one."

The Golden Slayer sighed. "We all suspected the truth, but we couldn't prove it. So, one girl died, and her killer went on to become archmage, albeit one with a nickname he loathes."

"Sad though it is, not everyone gets justice." Pancras sympathized with the girl. Gisella's story and candid contempt for the archmage redoubled his fears about leaving Delilah under Archmage Vilkan's tutelage. *I hope she's all right.*

Chapter 10

Kale missed his sister. He'd been separated from her before but never in such close proximity without a means of contacting her. He tried to pass a note to the guards for her, but they refused him, and, thus far, he'd been unable to convince the owners of the taller buildings to let him onto their roofs. He propped up his head with one hand as he stirred his bowl of porridge with the other.

The tavern down the street from The Granite Anvil felt like a second home to him and Kali. Sitting in front of the crackling hearth, he flapped his wings to cool his back, the din of patrons in the tavern providing a pleasant background to his musings.

He glanced up when he noticed the conversations around him ceased, unsure of how long the glowing, blue sphere of fuzz with feet had been yipping at him from the center of the table. It yipped once more. "Mistress Delilah would like to inform you that she expects to be stuck with the stuffy human wizardlings for at least another week before she'll be permitted to leave the compound. She hopes you're doing well."

It disappeared in a puff of azure smoke. Kale slumped in his chair. He shoved the porridge around in his bowl while he contemplated Delilah's message. The din of conversation in the tavern resumed as the other patrons realized the show was over.

"Look at this!" Kali slapped a large piece of paper onto the table in front of him. He pushed it toward her.

"I never learned to read that language. Everything we have in Drak-Anor is written in Drak or Minotaur." He brought the spoon to his mouth. Stirring the porridge for half an hour did not improve its flavor, and now it was cold, as well.

Kali pulled a chair close to Kale. "It's a broadsheet. I got it in the undercity. It talks about the miracle of the winged, striped drak, and, get this: it mentions another striped drak, a sorceress. The drak who wrote it says she's going to give him the scoop on Drak-Anor."

"When did he talk to Deli?" Kale examined the paper in Kali's hands and wished he'd taken the time to learn the written trade language.

"Probably when she was down there with Pancras, shopping. Look, I had an idea." Kali set aside the broadsheet. "The undercity runs under the whole city, right?"

"I guess?"

"I'll bet we can enter the Arcane University from below. Like we snuck around in Almeria."

"Oh, speaking of that, Deli sent me a message." Kale related the information from the boggin. "It arrived right before you got back."

"So, do you still want to try to sneak into their compound to visit?" Kali took Kale's hand.

"It's only another week, right?" Kale pushed away the bowl of cold, goopy porridge. "It's probably better to wait a week than risking making the wizards angry. Delilah used to threaten to turn people into toads or cave lizards, but I bet there are wizards there who could actually do it."

"Fine. Speaking of lizards, we should go check on ours. They probably need to be ridden, if they haven't eaten all the other animals in the stable."

Kali had a point. Kale was so wrapped up in wanting to see his sister, he'd forgotten about their mounts. "I'm glad you're around to remember things like that for me."

His mate enwrapped him in a hug. "Someone has to keep you in line."

***

As Gisella tightened the straps on her saddle, Qaliah approached. "I have a question, and a request."

She did not meet the fiendling's eyes. Gisella had no quarrel with Qaliah, but she found herself annoyed the fiendling had followed them and insisted on tagging along. Unexpected changes in her plans exasperated Gisella almost more than any other type of interruption.

Gisella's lack of acknowledgement did not deter Qaliah. "You know the route we're taking pretty well, right? Is there a town or village we're going to pass so I can get a mighty steed of my own?" She held out her hand for Moonsilver, but the mare shied away from it.

"Yes." Gisella saw no reason to lie. "I doubt you'll be able to afford it, though. The farmers around here hold their horses in high regard."

"I've scrimped and saved my pennies. I have more than that parting stipend."

"Was that your request or your question?"

"That was the request. My question is for you: what's a Watchmaiden got love for Aurora for? I thought you people were all swords and bearskins, mead halls, and singing bawdy songs about your conquests."

"Just like all fiendlings are seducers and murderers, bathing in the blood of virgins at the altar of Maris, right?" Gisella didn't believe that, of course, but she was acquainted with many people who did. The sight of horns, black or red skin, and a tail was enough to send many villages into total panic, even if the fiendling was an innocent traveler passing through. She understood their trepidation: one born from the union of something evil, must, itself, be evil. Experience taught her the truth often did not match common folk's expectations.

"I've never done that. Sure, I've stolen to survive, but I've never murdered. I don't even like Maris. War gods are so grim and have no sense of humor or fun."

Gisella mounted Moonsilver. She held a hand out to Qaliah. "You can ride with me today. We might reach Rock Ridge by nightfall. You can buy a horse there, I think."

She pulled Qaliah up to sit behind her. "Hold tight. I don't want you to fall off." Gisella pulled Qaliah's arms around her waist, and the fiendling rested her head on the slayer's back.

"You sure? You don't seem thrilled I'm here at all."

Gisella patted the fiendling's hands around her waist. "Another woman's company is most welcome. I was disconcerted at the change in plans, that's all." She looked toward the minotaur and dwarf. Pancras and Edric were already mounted and ready to go.

"Truth be told, I'm glad you were able to get away from Muncifer. It pained me to see you play the fool. I always suspected you could be more than that."

The fiendling squeezed her. "I appreciate that."

The riders spurred their horses and rode toward the road. Clouds rolled in overnight, casting a grey pallor over the day and hiding the warmth of the sun. The damp morning air made the chill of early spring even more pronounced.

By midmorning, the heavens opened. Wind blew torrential rain across the hills and road. Gisella contemplated stopping but decided huddling together under a blanket on the soggy ground was no better than traveling forward on a wet horse. She figured if they continued moving, there was a chance of outrunning the storm.

The day grew dark, and the downpour continued unabated until, at last, through the haze of rain, Gisella noticed the lights of a village ahead. The deluge threated to quench the torches at the village gate, and Gisella strained to read the sign above the entrance: Rock Ridge.

After dismounting, she approached the gate. It was shut tight, with no guards in sight. That, in itself, was not unusual at night and in periods of bad weather for small villages and towns along the trade road. She pounded on the wicket.

"Hopefully, the guards are nearby."

Pancras hopped off Stormheart. The horse tossed his head, spraying them with water. "If they've any sense, they're inside."

The wicket opened, revealing a frowning guard holding his torch aloft. Rain dripped down his face, causing his ample moustache to droop like a drowned rat. "Ain't you got sense to get in out of the rain?"

"If you'll notice"—Gisella gestured toward the rest of her group—"that's precisely what we're trying to do."

The guard grunted. After closing the wicket, he opened the main gate. "All right then, come ahead. Toma's place has stables and beds. It's just up the road on the right, across from the Lord's Tower. There's a shrine of Dolios next to Toma's, if you want to leave an offering."

He waited until after they trekked past him and then shut and latched the gate. Gisella heard him grumbling about the weather and the late hour as he shuffled back to the guard house. She led the group down the main street in search of the place the guard described. Streams of water ran down the street, creating rivulets of mud and muck that coated their horses' feet.

She found the place, seemingly a private home. Upon finding no one attending the attached stable, Gisella tied up her horse and signaled for the others to wait while she investigated the building.

Pancras tossed his reins to Qaliah and joined Gisella. "It's dangerous to go alone."

"In Rock Ridge?" Gisella laughed. "Maybe if I slip in the mud and crack my head on a rock." She stepped around the building, holding the hood of her cloak to keep the wind from blowing it off her head. Her helmet provided some relief from the deluge, but the early spring rain ricocheting into her face from her metal armor, reminded her how cold water became before it froze.

She climbed the stoop that led to the front door. She rapped the attached knocker against the door and waited. Through the windows, Gisella noticed a dim light moving within the dwelling. The clickety-clack of turning locks preceded the whoosh of the door opening. A one-eyed, bearded man squinted at them through the rain. "Yes? Travelers? Come in! Come in! This weather is not fit for fine folk to be out in it."

Gisella let Pancras pass her and enter the building. She placed two fingers to her lips, then whistled, hoping Qaliah and Edric would hear her. Rendering her concern unfounded, they dashed into sight from behind the building. When they were all inside, the older man helped them remove their cloaks.

"Aren't you a motley bunch? Minotaur, dwarf, human"— he eyed Qaliah—"well, that's something. Reminds me of a joke. You'll be needing lodging for the night?"

"Yes, please." Gisella bowed her head to the man.

Pancras fished in his pouch, jingling the coins. "Beds, baths if possible, food if you have any."

"Only two rooms left. Plenty of food, as always." The man counted on his fingers. "Four talons?"

"It would be best if Qaliah and I shared a room. You and Edric can make do, yes?" Gisella passed a couple of talons to Pancras."

The minotaur nodded, handing the coins to the man. "No baths?"

"There's a tub. Not big enough for a minotaur. We don't have any more hot water tonight though." He led them through the foyer into a dining room containing a long table set with plates and food. Several people, humans all, were already seated and eating.

"I'm Egor. I'll bring up some more wine for everyone. Sit, eat. We'll work out the rooms when you've food in your bellies."

Gisella helped herself to bread and meat. She noticed the other guests staring at Qaliah and then coughing and looking away when the fiend noticed and winked at them. The attention seemed to please rather than bother her, even though they regarded her, not with lust or curiosity, but with fear.

During dinner, they discussed their plans for the next day. By the time they retired to their beds, they all agreed to stay in town until the rain let up, giving their horses a rest and themselves a chance to clean and dry their mud-soaked clothes.

The Golden Slayer retired to the room she shared with Qaliah. The fiendling slipped out of her clothes and into bed, patting the mattress next to her with a smile. "Let's keep each other warm and celebrate Aurora together, eh?"

Gisella felt her face flush. Turning away, she cursed in silence that the fiendling managed to embarrass her. She sat on the opposite side of the bed from Qaliah. The fiendling scooted over, grabbed Gisella's shoulders, and tried to pull her into the bed.

"Stop it."

Qaliah ran a hand through Gisella's hair. "You're very beautiful, and it's been a long time since I didn't have to settle."

Gisella held the fiendling's hand, noting her flesh was warm, almost hot to the touch. "I will not deny that you have an allure I'm sure men find irresistible, however"—she placed Qaliah's hand on the bed and patted it—"I am not interested." Gisella decided upon leaving Muncifer she'd enjoyed her last night of carnal pleasure until this task was done.

"What?" Qaliah scooted over farther, so her head hung off Gisella's side of the bed, looking up at her.

"I like men, and only men. I'm sorry." Gisella hoped Qaliah wasn't too upset. Fiendlings could be volatile, and she had not expected the young woman to proposition her. They shared a room out of necessity. Gisella assumed Pancras and the dwarf would be more comfortable together.

"Men are fine, but the dwarf is too stout and hairy for my taste and the minotaur is, well, a minotaur." Qaliah stared up at Gisella with doe eyes, clear and blue, like ice from a deep lake in the heart of the Southern Watch.

"I can go sleep in the stable with the horses if it's easier for you." She flipped the covers over Qaliah to conceal her nakedness.

The fiendling flipped off the covers and repositioned herself on her side of the bed before drawing them up to her chin. "I can behave myself. If you're not interested, you're not interested. I'm sad for you."

Gisella slid off the bed and picked up her belongings. Qaliah gasped. "You were serious? Don't go!"

The Golden Slayer looked over her shoulder to ease Qaliah's concern. "It's no trouble, really."

"Look, I'm sorry if I made you uncomfortable just now, but those men downstairs? They weren't looking at me like they wanted to have some fun, all right? I noticed. I really do not want to be alone in here. I'll go sleep with the dwarf and minotaur if I have to. In fact, I will." She slid out of bed and pulled on her clothes. Gisella remained silent as she gathered her things and left.

Gisella sighed, dropped her pack, and then crawled under the covers. It was not the outcome she intended, but she wasn't going to squander the opportunity of a peaceful night's rest.

***

By the end of her first day under the tutelage of Master Valyrian, Delilah understood the breadth of the gaps in her knowledge. There were whole schools of magic about which she'd never heard. Both she and Pancras were fairly specialized in their knowledge of wizardry, and though they performed a smattering of the arcane arts outside their areas of expertise, Delilah realized she should have worked alongside him to learn as much as possible. Instead, her own pride in her abilities convinced her she knew as much as he did, albeit in a different discipline.

Master Valyrian was more patient than the archmage was with her, and she was grateful official guild business kept Archmage Vilkan from bothering to find her over the next couple of days. She said as much to Katka one night as they prepared for bed.

"I don't know why he thinks he needs to watch me constantly. I'm here now, I'm learning, and I'm not going anywhere."

Katka brushed her boots, trying to knock as much dirt and mud from them as possible. "I've heard other masters say he likes to control everything. They don't like him much, I don't think."

"Why'd they let him become archmage, then?" Delilah didn't understand why someone didn't just kick him out if they disliked him that much.

"Maybe they didn't have a choice." Katka blew dust off her boot. "How's Master Valyrian? He's so pretty. I could watch him all day."

Delilah chuckled and shook her head. "His skin is too smooth, and he's foppish. I have to admit, though, he knows his magic. I'm going to pass the next trial." She was sure of it. Delilah suspected the only reason she failed the first time was because she didn't know how to create a magical shield. She'd heard students utter the words to create the effect, but knowing the words was not the same as understanding how to use them effectively. Without practice, she had no hope of executing one of those spells in the heat of the moment.

Dropping her boots onto the floor, Katka lay across her bed and interlaced her fingers behind her head. "I hope I pass this next time. I'm not the oldest initiate by any stretch, but I've been here the longest."

"You have to really focus for attack magic." Delilah wanted to see the girl advance. She enjoyed the young human's company, and she wanted them to be able to continue helping each other. "Everything you've got, you know? In the heat of battle, you don't have time to finesse a spell with the idea that you can add more power the next time. There might not be a next time."

"I guess. I've never even been in a fight." Darkness crept in around them as the other students extinguished their lights. After Delilah blew out her candle, Katka followed suit.

She crawled into bed and faced the other student's bunk. "Maybe we can practice tomorrow. I'll help if I can."

"Thanks, Delilah."

Sleep came quickly to Delilah. She dreamt of her brother and her friends, and also Sarvesh and Bargle back in Drak-Anor. When morning came, she was refreshed, but upon hearing the archmage's summons, she wanted nothing more than to crawl back in bed. She pulled herself together and gave a weak smile to Katka before she ran to meet with the archmage.

Archmage Vilkan paced the floor of the Court of Wizardry. Other high wizards in attendance stood conversing, and they paid no mind to the archmage. He stopped pacing when he saw Delilah.

"It's about time, Initiate Drak. Where have you been?"

Delilah wanted to bash him in the face with her staff. "I ran over here as soon as I heard the summons."

He stroked his beard. "No matter. You will attend me today. The archduke is paying us a visit. I'll give you both a demonstration of true power."

Delilah wanted neither to entertain the Archduke of Muncifer, nor witness the archmage's exhibition. She smoothed her robes, bowing her head and nodding. "As you wish, Archmage."

***

Kale stroked the side of Kali's head as she reclined in his lap. She held the broadsheet above her head, reading it for the third or fourth time. "You know, I think we can use this sacred drak thing to our advantage."

He looked down at his mate. "How do you mean?"

"If he's excited about Delilah telling him about Drak-Anor, he should be even more excited to get a second perspective, right?"

Draks generally viewed their striped brethren as sacred. When the draks from Kale and Delilah's clan learned they were hatched from the same egg, their attitudes changed. They viewed twins as just one step above abominations. Having stripes was the only thing that saved Kale and Delilah from having been abandoned at birth because the elders couldn't decide which took priority: that they had stripes or that they were twins.

"I don't know. Is this a good idea? Maybe if you can convince him to come up here to talk. I don't want to get mobbed in the undercity again." Kale didn't mind being the center of attention when he did something that deserved it, but the adoration of the draks in the undercity made his skin crawl.

"I'll go ask." Kali let the paper fall to the floor. "You should get them used to seeing you walking around, though. We can't stay cooped up in here all the time. The weather is becoming warmer, and it would be a shame to stay inside. There will be enough of that in the winter."

Kale conceded the point. "Maybe if I cough some fire on them, they'll keep their distance."

"Ooh, we might be able to use that, too." Kali sat up and spun to face him. "You'd be a great distraction for an enterprising pickpocket."

"I thought we wanted to stay out of trouble." Kale did not fancy seeing the inside of this city's jail. The one in Almeria was enough.

"Trouble sure, but I wouldn't mind having a little fun, you know?" She reached over and stroked Kale's cheek. "I'll be honest, I don't want to stay cooped up in here, but I don't want to go all over town without you. You're my mate. We're in this together. That's what we said, right?"

"Right." Kale took her hand and closed his eyes. Despite having his mate alongside him, he felt alone without Delilah nearby. So many things remained unsaid between them when she entered the Arcane University compound. Since she was sequestered there, he feared there might not be a chance to clear the air. He understood her resentment of Kali, but they had often discussed how they would eventually have to follow their own paths. He realized now that neither one of them ever really believed the time would come to pass.

Kali's right about one thing: we can't stay cooped up in here. As he fell asleep, he ruled out ideas one by one of how best to handle unruly crowds. A feeling of hopelessness followed him into his dreams and fitful sleep. The next morning, Kale awoke with no fresh ideas and no clue how to discourage the crowds.

Later that same morning, he and Kali left the Granite Anvil and headed into the undercity. The stairs that led from the streets of the upper city were slick from overnight rain. Humans and minotaurs in the upper city eyed the winged, striped drak in their midst, but Kale had become accustomed to their curious glances. Entering the undercity, however, was like opening the floodgates. Every drak who saw him stopped and stared or followed and cried out for his attention.

Kale saw a familiar minotaur pushing a cart of potatoes. He nodded as he passed, but the minotaur's face dropped when his eyes met Kale's. He swung the cart around and pushed it away at an ever-increasing speed. Kali pointed toward a platform ahead at the edge of the walkway. It was used by town criers to spread news and announcements.

"That platform gives me an idea!" She pulled Kale over to it, then gestured for him to step up. "Attention, draks of Muncifer!"

Kale removed his hat and held it before him, tucking in his wings as they waited for a crowd to gather. Kali maneuvered him in front of her.

"This is Kale Windsinger of Drak-Anor," Kali called from behind him.

Shouts arose from the crowd.

"He is Chosen!"

"A gift from Rannos!"

"Can you cure my scale itch?"

"He will save us!"

Kale raised his head and spat a gout of flame into the air. The draks shrank back and became silent.

"He has stripes, yes. Wings, too." Kali patted his arm. "Tell them how you got them."

"I wasn't born with the wings." The crowd gasped when Kale unfurled them. "They weren't a gift from Rannos or any other dead god either." Kale didn't want to tell them the whole truth. Telling an unruly mob about a chaos mutation would require too much explanation. "The wings are… are… uhh… a wizard did it! He was trying to turn me into a bird, but I stabbed him and messed up his magic! He was an evil wiz—warlock, yeah, and me and the minotaurs helped free Drak-Anor from his evil spell so we could be free and—"

Kali smacked him in the shoulder. "Freeing Drak-Anor was Kale's destiny. His purpose is already fulfilled. He can do nothing for you, and we ask you to please, just let him live his life."

"No, he is blessed!"

"He can help us, too!"

Kale stepped up onto the platform, put an arm around Kali, and spread his wings. "I've seen oppression. I've seen drak slavery. I don't see it here."

A dusty-grey drak pushed his way to the front of the crowd. "I can help you tell your tale!"

Kale looked at Kali; she nodded. He extended a hand to the other drak and helped him climb onto the platform. The grey drak turned to the crowd.

"You all know me—"

"Jairo!"

"He prints truth!"

"Bah, it's a rag!"

The dissenting voice was shouted into silence. Jairo held up his hands to calm the crowd. "I'll get this drak's story. We'll all hear it. We'll take it to the upper city. The humans and the minotaurs will hear us."

Kale stomach tightened. He did not want to become involved in a revolution, but neither did he want to endure undue adoration of an oppressed lower class every time he stepped out of his shop, if indeed, that was the case with these draks. The sound of metal banging on metal interrupted his thoughts. A squad of guards pushed through the crowds, smacking their cudgels against their shields.

"Clear out, you lot! You're clogging the streets! Clear out!" The guards stopped in front of the platform. "Causing trouble again, Jairo?"

Though the crowd of draks moved away, they still watched Kale. He stepped in front of Jairo. "He was just trying to help convince them to ignore me."

The guard grunted. "So you're the troublemaker, eh? What manner of drak are you anyway?"

Kali took Kale's hand. "He's my mate, and he's not causing trouble. These draks all seem to think he's some savior come to free them from oppression."

The guards laughed. The one who spoke to Kale gestured to his fellows. "Hear that? He's come to free them from their oppression!"

"No! No, I haven't." Kale folded in his wings and tried to shrink away from the guards. Even standing on the platform he had to look up at them to meet their eyes. "My sister is at the Arcane University. I just wanted to look at some shops! I don't want trouble."

The guard gestured to one of the other guards. "Go break up that lot. Get them moving." He turned to Kale, and poked him in the stomach with his cudgel. "You're packing a lot of blades on that bandolier for someone who doesn't want trouble."

Kale fingered the hilts of his daggers as he counted them. "I don't want trouble. It doesn't mean I'm just going to let it happen to me."

"Stop stirring the pot, Jairo." The guard poked the grey drak. "We all have to abide by the archduke's edicts."

"Even when they're unfair? It's like he doesn't want us in town. We were here first!"

"Enough!" The guard slammed his cudgel on the platform next to Jairo. "I don't make laws, I just enforce them. Make your case in that broadsheet of yours." He leaned in. "I know for a fact several councilors read it. You'll have better luck with your silent voice in that than stirring up mobs in the undercity."

The rest of the guards ushered people away, uncluttering the streets enough that Kale considered dashing to a nearby shop to move away from the crowd. The carved angular design of the sign gave no clues about the type of merchandise inside. *With my luck, it'll be a dress shop.*

"Let's go, Kale." Kali stepped down off the platform. "Maybe they'll let us go about our business for a bit."

The guard grabbed Kale's arm and leaned down, his breath stinking of beef and cheese. "Don't encourage the mob. They're angry and bored. They don't need more instigators. You're not inconspicuous, so don't think you can hide in the shadows and stir up trouble."

Kale tilted his head upward toward the guard and shook his head. "I don't want trouble. I just want to mind my own business."

He released Kale and nodded. "Fine then. Go on your way."

The crowds kept their distance the remainder of the morning, though he still overheard their whispers of awe and adulation. It was only a matter of time before the guard's admonishment was forgotten and they mobbed him again.

He pulled Kali aside as they ate some spit-roasted squab from a stand in the undercity market. "I don't know what's going on in this town between the minotaurs, humans, and draks, but I really don't want anything to do with it. Maybe we can go visit some of the nearby villages after Deli passes her trials."

Kali nodded in agreement. "As much as I don't want to be bored, I don't want to deal with Almeria all over again."

***

Once the weather broke, Pancras anxiously wanted to return to the road and continue their journey. Part of it was his compulsion to arrive in Vlorey as soon as possible, but a more immediate incentive was his desire to leave Toma's house. The bed was too small, Edric too noisy, and having the fiendling share with them because of some unspoken disagreement with Gisella was awkward.

Fortunately, one of the farmers had a gelding, Comet, she was willing to sell Qaliah. Pancras felt it was more out of a desire for the fiendling to leave than to make money. Nevertheless, after they acquired a young piebald of gentle disposition, they left Rock Ridge behind.

As they rode under a clear blue sky, Pancras's thoughts wandered to the draks he left behind in Muncifer. He felt responsible for their welfare, even though Kale and Delilah were both adults and capable of caring for themselves. In addition, Kale seemed well on his way to settling down.

A whoop from Qaliah shattered the peace of his thoughts as she raced past him with Edric hot on her heels. The dwarf swore continuously, calling down the wrath of the gods on her head, but her spirited young horse outpaced his pony.

Gisella nudged Moonsilver next to Stormheart. "Those two are going to kill each other, I think."

"If Edric would just ignore her jibes and baiting, she'd grow bored quickly enough." Pancras knew Qaliah's type. In every place he had visited or lived, there was always someone who enjoyed provoking others. Qaliah knew exactly which of Edric's buttons to push, as if by instinct.

"She's quite the instigator."

"What happened between you? What sent her to our room?"

Gisella coughed, looking away. After a moment, she sighed. "She propositioned me. When I told her I was not interested, things became awkward between us."

"Ah. Yes, I understand." Pancras acknowledged that both Gisella and Qaliah were attractive by most standards, but he held no interest for either of them. Several minotaur females propositioned him in Drak-Anor over the years, and revealing to them why he wasn't interested always yielded an uncomfortable moment.

The fiendling let the dwarf chase her for most of the morning. When they finally settled down, the sun shone high in the sky and their steeds needed rest. After dismounting, they all walked their horses.

Were it not for the road they followed, Pancras understood how one could ride in circles for days, traveling nowhere. The rolling terrain dotted with groves and fields appeared largely the same from hill to hill, their subtle variations lost on city-dwellers like Pancras. He wished there was a quicker way to travel to Vlorey and cursed the archmage for sending him so far away.

"I'm bored." Qaliah broke the silence. "Hey Wizard, don't you have some magic that can make this trip go faster? Or be less boring?"

"Not really, no." Pancras knew no conjurations or spells that would speed their journey, although he remembered hearing stories of a time from before the Sundering in which magic enabled wizards to cross vast distances quickly. If that type of magic ever actually existed, it was long ago lost to the world.

"So much for all-powerful wizardry."

"Wizards only want you to think magic is all-powerful." Gisella looked back at Pancras. "Isn't that right, Pancras?"

"I never tried to convince anyone of any such thing. I just wanted to be left alone with my books and alchemy equipment."

Qaliah leaned in close to Edric, but she made no effort to lower her voice. "It's always the quiet loners you have to watch out for, eh?"

Edric chuckled. "Especially the ones that make your bones jump up and dance out of your body."

"Ohh, he's one of those wizards." Qaliah regarded Pancras with a sly grin and winked.

He sighed and stared into the sun, shielding his eyes as he tilted his head upward. *Maybe if I wish hard enough, time will speed up.*

Chapter 11

Archduke Fyodar was a more imposing man than Archmage Vilkan, a feat Delilah thought impossible. His velvet cloak hung from broad shoulders, and though his belly protruded like a round pot at his waist, she sensed he could hold his own in a fight. Piercing grey eyes sat above prominent cheekbones covered by a salt-and-pepper beard that bounced as he paced.

From his spot at the end of the table, Archmage Vilkan stabbed the map laid upon it with a crooked finger. "Fallow Gulch and Oakcreek will be the first to fall if the giants attack."

Delilah stifled a yawn and leaned on her staff. For the past three hours, the two men argued about the giants. Without the context of their prior conversations, she found it difficult to follow their conversation at first, but after three hours of them retreading the same ground, each convinced of the other's fault and incompetence, her understanding grew.

"The giants have kept the peace for decades." The archduke stopped and slammed his fist on the table. "Why now?"

"Why not? It was a harsh winter. Even the giants need food, and I'll wager they burned through their stockpiles faster than they planned. Now, what we trade is insufficient, and they want more."

The archduke shook his head. "No. No, I cannot ascribe to that interpretation. We've had bad winters before. This wasn't even the worst of the last decade."

Archmage Vilkan spread his hands. "Something has them riled up. Perhaps your emissaries insulted them. We don't know what occurred during their last meeting."

"It was your plan! I sent them with your instructions!" Archduke Fyodar spoke through clenched teeth.

"They obviously failed. Let me send my own emissaries. They fear magic. My people can calm them down."

"I don't want them to fear us!" The archduke resumed his pacing. The floorboards under his feet creaked as he strode the length of the table. "I want the peace to continue. They've been good allies and a great deterrent for whatever is in the Western Wastes."

"Cathar, fiendlings, and savage elves who've turned their backs on the trees and survive on the flesh of men."

Delilah encountered the cathar, a race of ill-tempered, vulture-like creatures, but it was the first she'd heard of feral elves. The way the archmage's eyes followed the archduke's every move, she guessed he embellished a bit.

"Everything was fine until after your visit this spring, Vilkan. Perhaps they blame you for those tremors." Pursing his lips, the archduke stared at the archmage.

"Preposterous." Archmage Vilkan crossed his hands over his chest, glaring at the archduke. "I know nothing of earth magic."

The two men continued their debate, addressing the same issues as they had during the previous three hours of their meeting. Delilah didn't see what the archmage hoped to accomplish by bringing her along with him. She sighed, wishing once again that she could have snuck in her grimoire.

Bolting into the room, a page interrupted their discussion. Fighting to catch his breath, the page waited as the archduke poured a glass of wine. After gulping it down, the page slowed his breathing. "A band of giants have come down from the mountains. They're in the gulley leading to the old watergate!"

"What? How did they avoid our scouts?"

The archmage slapped the map near where the page indicated the giants were. "Now their scouts are probing us! I will handle them, Archduke. Come, Initiate!"

Archmage Vilkan spun, whipping his cloak behind him, and stalked out of the room. Delilah scrambled after him as he ignored the protests of the archduke. She followed him through the dimly lit corridors of Grimstone Keep and up onto the battlements.

Located at the edge of the city, Grimstone Keep overlooked the western gate. A dry riverbed south of the gate handled overflow water, which cascaded from the mountains. Much of the water was still locked in snow, but from what Delilah had heard, the riverbed would be close to spilling over within the next month.

A band of five giants armed with clubs that appeared to have once been trees marched into the gully. The two giants at the rear dragged a cart covered in furs of some sort. All five resembled humans, albeit three times the height of the archmage, with wider noses and more muscular bodies and skin the color of wet stone. They were clad in patchwork animal skins and furs, and even at this distance, Delilah noticed short tusks protruding from their lips.

"Vilkan! Wait just a damn minute!" The archduke sprinted up the steps onto the battlements. Delilah clicked her teeth and nodded, impressed that a man with a belly that vast could move so quickly.

The archduke was too late. Already, smoky swirls of red aether writhed around the archmage. He held aloft his focus, a bejeweled vial, in his right hand as he chanted, "*Astrapes kataigida!*"

Dark clouds swirled overhead, roiling in the sky and flashing with energy. Forks of lightning sought ground, the booming thunder that accompanied them seeming to rattle the very stones of the keep. Archduke Fyodar moved to grab the archmage, but Delilah raised her staff, laying it across his chest as she stepped between them.

"Bad idea, Your Grace. It's too dangerous," she shouted over the crashing thunder and howling wind. To his credit, the archduke heeded her warning, glaring at the archmage instead of interrupting his spell. The giants raised their clubs over their heads. They turned and ran but found no cover in the open fields and gullies.

Delilah realized from the glowing wisps of red smoke surrounding Archmage Vilkan he was far from finished. *"Elenchomeni anemostrovilos!"*

The dark clouds covering the western sky swirled. Dirt and debris flew through the air. The howling wind became a roaring animal in Delilah's ears. She clutched her staff, fighting to remain upright while it buffeted her. As she stumbled toward the crenellations, her staff flew from her trembling fingers and clattered across the battlements. Daring to raise her head, she peeked over the wall.

A whirling funnel descended from the clouds above the giants. It scoured the land clean where it touched down, carving a line of destruction toward the giants. They split up, fleeing in different directions, as did the tornado. One by one, the funnels of death found them, pulled them into the air, and flung them away as bolts of lightning stabbed them from the heavens. Delilah observed one of their smoldering corpses bounce over the earth near a farm, breaking through a fence before coming to rest.

The drak sorceress ducked behind the crenellation as the magical storm raged at the whim of the archmage. Archduke Fyodar crouched next to her, his face a mix of fury and fear.

When the storm abated, the archmage kicked Delilah's staff to her and stood in front of the drak and the archduke. "That is how we will handle the giants, Your Grace."

***

Kale's hat flew off his head. Struggling against the sudden wind, he held fast to Kali's hand as they sought shelter in the undercity corridors. He observed draks and minotaurs on the walkways doing the same, all running toward the nearest shops or covered side streets. The sky above turned angry;

dark, swirling clouds barreled in like an avalanche from the heavens, transforming the clear blue sky into a roiling mass of inky blackness within minutes.

A minotaur pulled two draks behind him as he ran into the corridor behind Kale. He crouched over the draks to protect them. "I've never seen anything like it! Where did it come from?"

Kale had no answer for him. In the distance, he heard the roaring howl of what sounded like a great beast descending from the heavens to devour the city. The lack of rain perplexed Kale most as he watched the dust and debris blowing past the now empty walkways and bridges. A crack of thunder reverberated through the chasm, its sound amplified by the rock walls.

More thunder rattled the huddled masses, and though it seemed impossible, the wind intensified. Kale heard a deep, primal scream just before a man-shaped mass fell past the entrance and into the chasm that bisected the undercity. He strained to gain a closer look, clutching his mate to keep from being blown away. Pulling in his wings, he shrouded Kali within them.

The howling stopped, and the wind subsided. The dark, roiling clouds slid away and dissipated like a pinch of sand dropped in a swift river. For a moment, all was still, and then a bird chirped, as if to say, "All clear!"

Kale stepped onto the walkway from the side street, still holding his mate's hand. He looked up, the clear blue sky showing no sign of the storm that drove them all to shelter.

"What in the name of Tinian's lance was that?" A minotaur shielded his eyes, glancing skyward. He stepped over to the railing before he saw the body in the chasm. "By Anetha's Shield!"

Kale peered into the crevasse. He felt his head swim when he tried to focus on the shape at the bottom. A human shape lay twisted and broken on the rocks far below. *That can't be… a human wouldn't look that big from way up here.*

"It's a giant!" The minotaur reeled backward, squinting. "Giants, falling from the sky! What does it mean?"

"It's a sign! An omen!" A drak with dark-green scales ducked under the minotaur's arm and scowled as he inspected the cavern. "Adranus is displeased! He will rain giants upon us and destroy us all!"

"What sense does that make?" Kali pulled the drak away from the edge. "That giant is dead, smashed to bits! Not much of a plan if all the giants he throws at us end up like that one."

The drak squirmed, unable to free himself from Kali's grip. "Not all of them will fall into the chasm. I'll bet some of them will land on the walkway. Right now, there could be giants rampaging through the upper city! Our doom is at hand!"

Kali released the ranting drak. He bolted, screaming about the end times, an apocalypse of giant men.

"He's cracked his nut, that one has." The minotaur eyed Kali and then Kale. "You! I can't get my potatoes to market because of you!"

Kale recognized the potato-pushing minotaur. He held up his hands, backpedaling. "Hey, I can't help it if these draks go crazy when I'm around. They think these stripes actually mean something."

Gritting his teeth, the minotaur clenched his fist. He advanced upon Kale. "They mean something all right: trouble for me. I ought to throw you to the giant down there."

Kale fluttered his wings before drawing them close to his body. "Yeah? Go ahead."

"Kale!" Kali reached for him. The minotaur darted forward, then seized him. Kale heard Kali's shriek of despair as the potato merchant flung him over the railing.

Despite Pancras's most fervent wishes, time did not speed up. In fact, it seemed to slow to a crawl. The land east of Muncifer was mostly farmland and grew flatter the farther from the city they traveled. Unlike the farmland south of Almeria, ample forests and groves dotted the landscape. Every few days, they left the comfort of the road and traveled through rougher terrain in order to avoid contact with, and pass, slow-moving trade caravans. They had nothing to trade and no desire to court trouble if any of the caravans harbored unfounded fear of fiendlings.

"Somewhere along this road, we left Muncifer's area of influence and entered the extended reach of Etrunia." Gisella attempted to stave off the party's mutual boredom by engaging them in conversation once Qaliah grew tired of antagonizing Edric.

"I didn't realize Etrunia had lands this far south. Is not the Icymist River the southern border of Etrunia?"

"The land between the Granite Tributary and the Greatbear Run are in dispute. Prince Gavril annexed the area east of the Greatbear a few years ago, including the Shadowfen Marsh. Gods know why."

Now a sunken swamp and the castle in ruins, the grandeur and splendor of Abbar Castle once stood at the center of Shadowfen Marsh. Pancras scratched his head. "Of what value are those lands to nobles in Almeria?"

"Only the gods know." Gisella continued. "Now Etrunia controls almost everything up to the Iron Gate Mountains, except the city of Muncifer. Of course, the mudders of Curton and the people in Cliffport don't really see it that way."

"I wonder if Princess Valene will enforce those claims." Despite his time amid Almerian court, Pancras learned little about the political landscape. "She seemed to oppose many of her late husband's policies."

"Time will tell. If she's smart, she'll send soldiers to garrison the forts and reinforce the fact that Etrunia controls the lands."

Pancras could vouch for Princess Valene's intelligence. If there was strategic value to Almeria enforcing the Etrunia rule of these lands, she would figure out a way to make her intent clear to the population.

A tower appeared on the horizon. Gisella spurred her horse. "Speaking of the forts—"

With the sun creeping toward the western horizon, Pancras guessed Gisella's purpose. An abandoned fort would not be the worst place to seek shelter for the night. If it was garrisoned, it would be even better.

***

Panic gripped Kale's heart as he fell. The last time he experienced this sensation, Bloodplume erupted and he thought he was falling to his death. That was years ago, before he encountered a chaos rift.

Wings! I have wings! When Kale spread his wings, their leathery flesh caught the air, and he lurched into flight. Piercing pain tore through his back and shoulders as he swooped up and rolled. For a brief moment, he considered descending to investigate the bottom of the crevasse and the fallen giant but decided it would be better to reunite with Kali as soon as possible.

When he pulled up and came about, he realized he was below the lowest level of the undercity. Kale flapped his wings, straining to ascend, but his muscles weren't strong enough. He resigned himself to gliding, maintaining altitude while he searched for a place to land. *Maybe if I find a perch, I can climb up.*

Kale spotted a dark area on one of the walls. His eyes had not yet adjusted to the shadows of the chasm, but it appeared to be an outcropping of some sort. As he glided closer, the ledge seemed like a safe place to land.

Once he firmly planted his feet on the rock, a quick glance revealed the shadow he noticed while flying was a tunnel, which led from the ledge into the cliff. Kale folded his wings and ducked inside. The passage was tight and black like a starless night, but his eyes soon became accustomed to the absence of light.

The tops of his wings scraped on the roof of the tunnel, and in several places, he was forced to crouch as he followed its level path farther into the rock. Ahead, he spotted a clearing where the tunnel widened. Once upon it, he noticed the junction was not of nature, rather, the very rock had been scooped out to create the chamber.

The sigil placed on his chest by Terrakaptis throbbed when he crossed the threshold. Though he could not see his chest in the dark, he traced each line, each curve of the symbol with a claw, noting it felt warm, warmer even than his skin ran normally these days. The discomfort faded after a few moments, his attention to it waning quickly as the workmanship of the walls caught his eye.

The drak was not an expert in underground construction, but it was obvious to his eyes some kind of claw created the chamber. Fine striations in the texture of the walls resembled the kind of gouges his claws made in dirt, but these were in solid rock. Sconces, each containing a gem, lined the hollow, set into the wall high above his head. He jumped to reach, but they were secured well enough that Kale could not dislodge them.

He observed a stone circle in the center of the room. Without better lighting, he couldn't determine whether its construction matched that of the surrounding floor, but it appeared the stones lay atop the floor of the chamber, almost like a dais. Upon his approach, he noticed the center of the circle appeared smooth, like the obsidian walls of Drak-

Anor, or perhaps black glass, or a pool of perfectly still ink. Even though he could see in the dark, he saw nothing in the center of the circle. *It's like that hole I jumped into under Ironkrag. I wonder where it goes?* He reached out to touch it, but changing his mind, he retracted his hand.

Better not touch what I can't see.

Raised runes of the sort he and his sister had seen in Ancient Drak writings encircled the perimeter of the stone circle. Kale recognized some of the words as magic, but he did not understand them. Other words were plainer: gateway and moon. He recognized sigils of Selene, goddess of magic and the moon, and one Terrakaptis taught him: Rannos Dragonsire.

Kale whistled. "Deli should see this."

His eyes searched the room again. Other than the stone circle in the floor, the sconces on the wall, dust, and cobwebs, he saw nothing. *No, not nothing!*

Kale raced over to an area of one wall where the claw marks adjoined in an odd way. He ran his hand along the marks and felt a seam. Following the pattern of unmatched marks with his eyes, he discovered a door. The mechanism, elegant and complex, reminded him of the puzzle box Terrakaptis gave him. He found the hidden catch and flipped it with one of his claws. The door swung open with a loud clack, revealing a small antechamber dominated by a spiral stone staircase. It led upward.

Bookshelves lined the walls of the stairwell, each tome covered with a thick layer of dust. Kale wanted to open a volume and explore memories of the ancient past entombed within but didn't want to risk destroying an important historical or arcane text. At least, not before he shared this place with his sister.

"Pancras and Delilah would both get lost in here. I'd never see them again!" He ran his finger along the spines of the books, the bindings crackling under his touch. A cool breeze sent a shiver down his spine, and he spun. Kale felt eyes on him, but he saw no one.

He quickened his climb.

He felt an unseen hand brush the back of his neck. Around and around and up and up he sped. Finally, at the top of the stairs, he found another door. After easily deciphering how to unlock the mechanism, he passed through into a storage room filled with broken furniture and dusty, moldy linens. Kale shut the door behind him, taking note of its location as the door joined seamlessly with the wall, leaving a smudge in the dusty floor as the only trace of its existence.

More stairs led up, such as those from a cellar. He found himself in what looked like an abandoned home. Upon further exploration, he discovered a storefront ahead of the living quarters. Long abandoned, the shop gave no clues to its original purpose. Dust, cobwebs, and the distant squeaking of rodents were its only stock now.

A door allowed egress onto one of the deep streets of the undercity. Kale followed his nose to fresh air, taking note of the abandoned shop's location. The street upon which he stepped led him to one of the walkways in the chasm. He worked his way up, eager to reunite with Kali.

He encountered her two-thirds of the way back to the spot where the minotaur threw him.

"Kale!" Kali enveloped him in a hug. They nuzzled each other for several minutes in relief.

At last, Kale broke their embrace. "You won't believe what I saw down there!"

* * *

Delilah was still trembling when she left Grimstone Keep. Archmage Vilkan bade her to return to the Arcane University while he engaged in a private discussion with Archduke Fyodar. She understood he meant for her to board the carriage that brought them, but she waved the driver off when he opened the door for her. The drak sorceress walked through the keep's gatehouse and onto the streets of Muncifer. While in the shadows of the gatehouse, she pulled off the itchy beige robe and discarded it.

She made her way through the twisting streets, trying to remember the route, but in the end, she had to ask a guard for directions. Once he put her on the right path, she doubled her pace and didn't slow until she arrived at the Granite Anvil.

The innkeeper looked up when she walked in. "No rooms; we're all full."

"I'm looking for my brother. He looks like me, but opposite colored with wings. Hangs around with a rusty-colored drak."

The innkeeper shook his head. "Nah, haven't seen them today. They go to The Stone Maiden a lot, you might check there. Up the street. Can't miss it."

Delilah didn't usually trust the word of humans, but in this case, the innkeeper was correct. The Stone Maiden was impossible to miss. A pristine marble statue stood between two entry doors; over one shoulder, the figure stared down disapprovingly at whoever might choose to enter the tavern. The din from within indicated the building was packed.

She pushed her way through the crowd, scanning the seated customers for Kale or Kali. His face was obscured, but her brother's wings were unmistakable. Though part of his table was hidden from view, she assumed Kali was with him. Delilah slinked toward them, ducking behind the humans to conceal her approach.

Kale yelped when Delilah caught him from behind by surprise, hugging him against the chair. "That's what you get for sitting with your back to the door."

"Deli!" Kale laughed, squirming to look at his sister, but she held him too tightly. She released him, moved to his side, and stood between him and Kali.

He pointed past her. "Back's to the door, but my front's to the bar." He waved at the barkeep and pointed at his sister. Kali inclined her head to Delilah.

The drak sorceress pulled the other drak into a hug. "I haven't been fair to you. I'm sorry."

Kali's mouth moved in silence before turning into a smile. "Thanks."

"Deli! Did you see that freak storm? Did you pass your trial?"

Delilah pulled over a chair to sit alongside her brother. She waited until the barmaid brought her ale, gulped it down, and wiped her lips. "Yes and no."

Kali cocked her head. "Which?"

"I saw the storm. Oh, did I see it! I was right there in front. Whoosh! Giants flying left and right when they weren't being fried by lightning."

"Giants? Ha!" Kale slapped the table. "I knew they weren't falling out of the sky just because Adranus wanted to kill us with them."

"No, but they were marching toward the west gate. The archmage blew them away with a magic storm, whirlwinds, and lightning! It was…" Delilah searched for the right word to describe both the exhilaration and terror. "Awesome."

Kali leaned forward, taking her mate's hand. "Giants were marching on the city?"

Delilah flagged down the barmaid and ordered another round of ale. She intended to drown her fears in a deluge of alcohol. "It was only six of them. I don't know what they hoped to accomplish. They're big and strong"—she shook her head—"but six against the city gates and all the guards?"

"That doesn't seem like an invasion or even an attack." Kali furrowed her brow and nodded at her mate.

"No, it doesn't." Delilah shook her head. "Maybe if they were just attacking one of the villages between here and the mountains, but not Muncifer. They'd have to be crazy to attack the city with just six."

"Sounds to me like the archmage overreacted." Kale scratched his chin. "Hey, how long are you here for? I have to show you something!"

Delilah took the mug of ale the barmaid brought, then raised it to her lips. "Not long. I need to buy some comfortable robes and go back. I'm not supposed to be out here to begin with."

"Oh, well, maybe I can take you there on the way. I found this really, well, old place in the undercity. You have to see it."

Delilah swigged her ale. "What kind of old place?" She didn't want to play guessing games with her brother. Part of her was tempted to stay with Kale and Kali, and if she didn't drown that part of her with booze soon, it might have its way with her.

"I don't really know how to describe it. It's in an old, abandoned shop on the very lowest level of the undercity."

Delilah did not doubt Kale found whatever it was he discovered fascinating, but a decrepit storefront did not appeal to her in the least. Not now, not with all the other matters she was dealing with at the Arcane University.

The ale made Delilah lightheaded. The room tilted a bit when she stood up. "I can't go look at it right now. I have to get back. The archmage will probably be looking for me when he returns."

Kale stood up, tapping his sister's arm. "Want us to come with you?"

"If you don't have anything better to do. I have to buy a new robe and then head straight back."

"It's no trouble, as long as Kale can avoid taunting any more minotaurs." Kali tossed a few coins for the drinks onto the table.

Delilah decided she didn't want to hear about her brother's aggravating antics. *He should have learned his lesson with the minotaurs in Almeria.*

Together, the three draks left The Stone Maiden and strode to the undercity. Throughout their trek, Delilah overheard people discussing the freak storm. In the undercity, the railings to the chasm were crowded with people gawking at the giant Kale told her about. Delilah managed to sneak a quick enough peek. Her curiosity sated, she left the dead-giant watching to people with nothing better to do with their time.

Kali led them to a clothier who sold a variety of cloaks and robes. Merchants in the undercity catered to either minotaurs or draks almost exclusively, and this particular merchant specialized in drak clothing. Though most draks eschewed full-body clothing, they set aside their pride during the bitter, raw Muncifer winters. Fortunately, the merchant still had stock leftover from winter, and Delilah spotted a beige robe with dark brown trim that suited her taste and fit her well enough. Because it was made from lightweight wool, it didn't itch her like the one provided by the Arcane University. On a whim, she rummaged for a similar robe in a larger size and one of each size in grey similar to what novices wore.

"I'll wear the small beige one. Can you wrap the others for me?" She presented several talons to the merchant. It was the last of her portion of the funds Pancras left them.

As the merchant folded and packaged the robes, Delilah donned the small beige one and cinched the belt at her waist. She turned to Kale. "Do you still have any of the money Pancras left? That was the last of mine."

Kale reached into his pouch and passed her a handful of gold crowns and silver talons. "This won't last forever."

"I know." Delilah dropped the money into her pouch. "You might have to find work."

"We'll figure something out. We're going to look for a place more permanent to live other than that inn." Kali took Kale's arm as the three draks left the shop. "Someplace down here in the undercity will surely be less expensive."

"Good. Fine." Delilah hugged her brother with one arm, while struggling to keep hold of her parcels. "I need to be going." She moved to hug Kali, but stopped short and offered a weak wave instead.

"Don't you want us to come with you to the Arcane University?" Kale followed his sister.

"No, they won't let you in anyway. I have to go!" Delilah broke into a run. She didn't see any point in Kale accompanying her, except maybe to carry her packages. Although, now that the ale had taken effect, she felt antisocial.

She dodged the minotaurs and draks going about their business in the undercity. The hem of her robe caught between her legs and she stumbled, flinging her packages down the walkway. After righting herself, she collected them, thankful none tumbled off the walkway into the chasm.

Delilah strode with more care the rest of the way to the Arcane University. When she arrived, she let out a sigh of relief as she noticed the archmage's carriage had not yet returned. Delilah entered the student barracks and sought out Katka.

"I have something for you." She handed the human girl one of the parcels. "No, wait, I don't think that's the right one." Delilah examined the remaining two packages. They were all unmarked, though one was smaller and lighter. "Oh, well, it's one of these two. I guess both of them."

Katka smiled and took the parcels. "But why? Have you been drinking? You're slurring your words."

"I might have stopped off for a few since the archmage sent me off by myself."

"Hey, are you wearing new robes?"

Delilah nodded. "Got me a new one and a new grey one for when I'm a novice. Got you one of each, too, though I had to guess at the size."

Katka squealed and tore open the wrapping. She held the robe up. It was a bit long, but seemed to be the correct size otherwise. "This is wonderful, but why? What's the occasion?"

Delilah flopped onto her bed. "Just happy to be alive, I guess. The archmage made that freak storm. He killed a bunch of giants with it who were approaching the city."

"The archmage did that?" Katka sat on the edge of her bed, clutching her new robe. "He killed giants with bad weather? Such power—"

"Yeah, just to make a point, I think." Delilah stared at the ceiling. Her fervent hope was for the archmage to be thoroughly engaged with other tasks and not pester her before her next trial. She wanted nothing to do with him.

Chapter 12

As much as Pancras hoped the fort toward which they rode would provide good shelter for the evening, it was obvious, as they approached, it would not. Tattered flags flying the Etrunian crest and the hammer and anvil of Adranus flapped in the wind. Even at a distance, Pancras recognized the blackened wood and shattered stone that told a tale of woe, a tale worsened by the desiccated and rotten bodies staked to the dirt alongside the road.

Gisella called for everyone to halt. "I feel I must investigate this. It's possible whatever happened here has long since passed, but I must know."

"Bah!" Edric fought to control Yaffa. The pony snorted and whinnied in protest of the dwarf's efforts to force her to stop downwind of the odor of death. "You said yourself these are Etrunian lands. I don't see you wearing their colors."

"I don't expect you to understand. Nevertheless, I am going." Spurring Moonsilver, she rode toward the fort.

"I'm going with her. You can stay here if you like." Pancras did not wait for Edric's response before putting the spurs to Stormheart and following after her. He heard Qaliah argue briefly with Edric before following with Comet.

Dread crept upon Pancras. The closer they approached the fort, the more acutely he felt it. The way the bodies had been staked out, and now, piles of bones flanking the battered gates, engendered apprehension he would recognize the culprits. The wind carried on it the sickly sweet stench of decaying flesh.

Gisella stopped Moonsilver by a hitching post just outside the gates. She secured him before picking up her spear, then waited for Pancras and Qaliah. To Pancras's surprise, Edric lagged not far behind, though he still complained as he dismounted Yaffa.

"Look." Gisella pointed to faded markings on the walls of the gatehouse. Anxiety gripped Pancras's chest as he examined them. The crudely rendered markings made with dried blood appeared as skulls—the symbol of Aita.

"Death cultists did this." Pancras couldn't be certain, of course, until he found the culprits, but he felt confident enough to make the pronouncement. Death cults dedicated to Aita cropped up from time to time. The priesthood denounced them, stating that death came naturally to all, and the church's official position was that the Princess of the Underworld didn't need help from mortals. Death cultists disagreed, believing they served the goddess of death best by killing as many people as possible.

"What would death cultists want with an Etrunian fort?" Qaliah drew a thin, short-bladed sword as they walked through the gatehouse.

"Did you see the other flag? There was a priest of Adranus here." Edric referred to the flag flying the stylized hammer and anvil. It was not uncommon for small settlements that featured a priest-operated forge to fly a banner of some sort proclaiming allegiance to the god of smiths and craftsmen.

Pancras removed his rod from his belt. Since he stopped wearing his focus on the tips of his horns, animating the dead in his sleep ceased to be a problem. "Death cultists kill indiscriminately, without reason."

They stepped into the courtyard of the fort. Several burned-out buildings stood on the perimeter, but save for a murder of crows pecking at the bodies strewn throughout, there appeared to be no sign of life.

"We should stay together." Taking point, Gisella led them toward the smithy. "It's unlikely anyone is still here, but we'll be stronger together."

A body hung from the hearth of the forge. Its upper half, little more than charred bones, lay fully within the firebox. The rest dangled, partially eaten and rotten. What clothes remained were blackened, burnt beyond recognition. Above the body and affixed to the bricks of the hearth, they found the symbol of Adranus had been smeared with blood.

"Maris take 'em." Edric spat on the floor. "They desecrated the forge."

Pancras moved closer to the body. The man had been dead for weeks. "I hate death cultists." The last time he heard rumors of a death cult was shortly after he left Muncifer as a youth, years before he even took up residence in Drak-Anor.

"They're all gone by now, right?" Qaliah kicked the corpse's legs. "This guy's been dead a while. Why would they stick around?"

Gisella inspected some of the broken and half-forged weapons scattered about the smithy. "They might stick around to lure in unsuspecting travelers, but you're right, this place seems abandoned. Still, we should make sure."

Edric picked up an axe-head that had been rusted by the elements. "What's the point? We can't do anything for these poor bastards." Shaking his head, he flung the axe.

"If the cult is still here, we can give them justice." Gisella motioned for them to follow.

"And if they aren't"—Pancras glanced over his shoulder at Edric as he stepped past—"perhaps we can put their spirits to rest."

Two major buildings comprised the majority of the area they needed to search. A cursory inspection of the stables revealed what the odor suggested. All the horses were slaughtered and left to rot. Thick clouds of flies swarmed the carcasses like miniature storms.

They followed Gisella into the two-story building adjacent to the stables that contained the living quarters. The entry doors were little more than burnt remains clinging to the remnants of rusty hinges. Bodies littered the rooms within. Guards and death cultists alike, frozen in a grim diorama of death, lay where they were slain, fodder for scavengers and carrion-eaters.

"At least they put up a fight." Qaliah rolled one of the cultists, still clad in a woolen kilt, over with her foot. His wounds and the toll of time and decay marred the bone-white paint, now cracked and flaking, covering his body.

By all indicators, the soldiers of the fort did indeed defend themselves. All the cultists suffered multiple wounds from spears, swords, and maces. Every dead soldier was surrounded by multiple cultists. In every room of the living quarters the story was the same. Handfuls of guards held out against dozens of cultists, overwhelmed by the sheer numbers of their suicidal opponents.

Not suicidal, Pancras reminded himself. *They just don't care whether they live or die.* Their recklessness was what made such men so dangerous. He concentrated on his rod to gather the magical energy he hoped he would not need. Something about the fort and its fate did not sit right with him. He suppressed a shudder as magical energy coursed through him. At the edge of his memory, he felt shadowy claws. When he tried to concentrate on them, they disappeared.

Besides rats and maggots, they found nothing alive in the living quarters. Gisella stopped in the courtyard for fresh air.

"There's no point in going in the main keep." Edric sheathed his sword. "Everything in there is as dead as everything else has been."

Gisella glared at him. "Then stay out here. I'm going into the keep. Watch the horses." Without waiting for his reply, she picked up her spear, then entered the tower. Pancras noticed the charred remains of a ballista behind the crenellations on top of the building, indicating the battle reached the roof, as well. Qaliah followed the Golden Slayer, leaving the minotaur with Edric.

"There's something more here, Edric. We need to find out what." Pancras didn't like Gisella's righteous curiosity, but he acknowledged investigating this slaughter was the right thing to do.

"Bah! You're as bad as she is." Edric threw up his hands and stormed away. Shaking his head, Pancras followed behind Qaliah.

Gisella and Qaliah stood before a crude altar erected in front of the hearth in the main room. Flesh hung off the bones used in its construction. Pancras swore and kicked it, scattering the bones. "They defiled the forge shrine of Adranus and replaced it with this crude, hastily erected mockery. Aita take them all."

"That's the idea, isn't it?" Gisella scattered the remaining bits of the altar with the butt of her spear.

"Yes, I suppose it is. Still, she would not approve." Pancras examined the room. Doorways flanking the hearth led to other rooms on the ground floor. Stairs on either side led alternately up and down.

"You sound like a priest of Aita." Qaliah climbed onto the hearth and looked up the chimney before tapping the bricks inside with her sword. "What do they call them? Bonelords?"

More than just priests of Aita, bonelords were wandering agents of Aita herself. They sought out and destroyed those who did evil in Aita's name, as well as assisted those who suffered in crossing over to find release in death's embrace. Pancras encountered one once when he was a practicing necromancer. He and the bonelord didn't see eye to eye at first, but in the end, they parted allies.

"I'm not, but I have worshipped Aita most of my life."

"Worshiped, but seldom prayed?" Gisella smacked Pancras on the shoulder as she passed him. "We'll check out the lower level first and then work our way up."

All the torches and lanterns in the keep had long since exhausted their fuel, leaving their descent to the lower level in pitch black. Pancras held up his rod. "*Fos.*"

His magical torch sufficiently lighted their way. The stairs, extending deep under the keep, angled toward the courtyard. The odor of moldy, rotten food greeted them, the remaining stores of the fort unneeded by the dead.

"My sense of smell is never going to be the same." Qaliah wrinkled her nose at the olfactory assault. The odor of death reminded Pancras why, when he was a necromancer, he worked only with skeletons. The fleshless dead had no odor. The acrid odor of rotting dead, on the other hand, possessed a tinge of just enough sweetness to turn the stomach.

After leaving the larder, the group found several dead soldiers strewn in pieces about the armory, torn limb from limb by their assailants. Pancras stooped to examine one, noting the remaining flesh was ragged, and the joints on the limbs were exposed.

"If humans did this, something granted them unnatural strength." He stood and dusted off his robe.

"What else could have done this?" After sheathing her sword, Qaliah helped herself to a crossbow from the weapons rack. She cocked the weapon and nocked a bolt before looping a quiver around her shoulder and hefting the crossbow. "If whatever did this is still around, I don't want it getting close."

Pancras's heart skipped a beat at a clatter in the distance. Spinning, his breath caught in his throat. In the darkness beyond the reach of his light, there was nothing.

He jumped when Gisella placed a hand on his arm. "It came from upstairs."

"Edric." Pancras nodded and let out his breath.

"Are you always this jumpy? I thought you were this great wizard." Qaliah followed Gisella as they left the armory.

"I'm extremely uneasy in this place. Besides, being a great wizard doesn't mean I like danger and adventure. Quite the contrary, in fact."

Gisella waved him forward. "You'd better come up there with me. I need your light, remember?"

Pancras gritted his teeth and walked ahead of her. *I wish one of the draks were here right now. They'd be joking about all this.*

* * *

Gisella's eyes scanned ahead of Pancras as they climbed the steps to the ground floor. She wasn't entirely comfortable with a loaded crossbow at her back. Although she doubted Qaliah was an experienced fighter, she noticed the fiendling had loaded the crossbow as if she knew what to do.

Upon seeing no sign of the dwarf in the main room of the keep, Gisella peeked outside. Her heart sank when she saw him tending his horse. Gripping her spear, she gestured toward the left doorway. "That wasn't Edric we heard. Be on your guard."

She remembered Pancras's tension when she touched his arm in the armory. Even now, she saw his hand shaking as he held the rod aloft to provide them with light. "Are you all right?"

"Yes, fine. Let's complete our task here."

Pancras did not sound fine, but Gisella did not feel she should question his courage. They entered the keep's bakery. Ashes in the ovens told of baking interrupted, as if the slain bakers lying across their worktables were not enough. When Qaliah passed her to examine the larder, Gisella heard the scrap of a boot on the floor behind her.

A scream of primal rage caught her by surprise as a painted man rushed at them. She leveled her spear, but he leapt to the side, raising an axe and slashing at Qaliah. The fiendling fired her crossbow, sinking the bolt deep into the man's shoulder.

He snarled and slashed the air as she backpedaled. Qaliah thrust her crossbow forward, jabbing him in the face and smashing his nose with the cocking stirrup. As he stumbled backward, she reloaded her weapon,

Gisella thrust, but the man grabbed the haft of her spear. He threw his weight against it, pulling her around the table. She saw a flash of green from Pancras's direction before an emerald ray struck the cultist's chest.

The cultist gasped for breath as his chest sank, outlining his ribs in parchment-like flesh. "Aita take you but not until the Queen has her way!" He flung the axe at Pancras.

The minotaur ducked under the flying blade. After Gisella pulled her spear out of the cultist's grasp, she thrust it forward, impaling the man under the chin. Loosing a battle cry, she drove him backward until the tip of her spear burst from the back of his neck and sprayed the wall with blood.

Gisella planted her boot on the cultist's chest and pushed him as she withdrew her spear. He collapsed onto the floor.

Qaliah approached him, aiming her crossbow.

"He's dead." Gisella regarded the minotaur. He stood, brushing the dirt and flour off his robes.

"Just making sure." Qaliah fired the bolt into the cultist's head.

"I guess they didn't all leave or kill themselves." Pancras knelt alongside the cultist. The man, clad in only a kilt, possessed sharp, elongated fingernails. Pancras noted the man's teeth had been filed into points.

"Think he's the only one?" Qaliah cocked her crossbow and fitted another bolt.

Gisella wiped the tip of her spear on the cultist's kilt. "Let's make sure." She led the fiendling and Pancras, whose eyes had become unfocused, into the main room, into the sunlight. There she noted the whites of the minotaur's eyes were fully black, his fur seemed darker, and the whispers of white on his chin had disappeared.

"You look different, Pancras. Are you sure you're all right?"

"I… am…" Pancras's eyes rolled back in his head, but he remained upright. A shadow enveloped him, spreading its smoky wings. Red-tinged emerald tendrils swirled around him. "*Seeko osta sto choma kai na—*"

"Pacha's blue balls, I see it!" Qaliah jumped backward and raised her crossbow.

"No wait!" Gisella lunged for the fiendling. She didn't yet understand the powers at work, but was certain shooting the minotaur was not the solution.

"*Ipakousoun tis entoles mo!*"

The tendrils of energy, now more fiery crimson than emerald, shot from his body in every direction. Qaliah loosed her bolt. The missile impacted Pancras's chest, dead center, burying itself to the fletching. He fell to his knees, laughing, a choking, gurgling sound, and then collapsed.

"Bugger this." Qaliah threw the crossbow to the ground and drew her sword. Gisella heard Edric shout from outside. She ran into the courtyard, spear held at the ready. Bodies lashed to stakes thrashed and groaned, and those that weren't tied down lurched to life, staggering toward the dwarf. When they noticed Gisella and Qaliah, some turned toward them as well.

"Aita, take him." Gisella smashed the butt of her spear into the nearest decaying face. The undead cultist grabbed the haft. Writhing like a fish, it pulled its way, hand over hand, toward her. Gisella shoved her assailant, then drew her sword. She faced the garrison of undead advancing on her and the fiendling.

Qaliah slashed at the nearest undead face. "Do you think swords will do any good? How do you kill the dead?"

The Golden Slayer, experienced at fighting wizards, and sometimes oroqs, goblins, and other foes, had never encountered undead before. "I don't know."

With a backhanded swing, Gisella severed the head of an advancing soldier. It tumbled to the ground before the body collapsed. The slayer's lips drew a tight line on her face. "Cut them to pieces."

***

Kale pulled the strongbox out of his pack. Ever since Pancras left, he'd kept the money the minotaur left them hidden and out of sight. He never took the time to count it before, but he needed to know how much money remained. From the weight and sound of coins, there was quite a bit. He dumped it out on the bed.

But will it be enough?

He counted it twice by the time Kali returned. In addition to the gold crowns, silver talons, and copper pennies, there were a handful of gems taken from Drak-Anor's treasury.

"What did you find out?" Kale shut the strongbox after Kali sat on the bed beside him.

"The owner died fifty years ago, and the last of her kin died five years ago. Technically, the city owns that building."

Kale chewed on his finger. "So, can we buy it from the city?" He wanted the shop that led down to the runic circle, and one way or another, Kale would find a way to acquire it.

"We need to speak to one of the magistrates at the Hall of Records."

Kale shoved the strongbox in his pack, placed his puzzle box on top of it, and hopped off the bed. "Great! Let's go."

Kali seized his hand. "Why is this so important? It's just a moldy old shop."

"It's not the shop." Kale took Kali's other hand and pressed his forehead against hers. "It's that rune-covered circle I found. It's important. I know it, Kali. Deli can figure out what it all means, but I don't want to risk someone else getting to it first."

Kali slid off the bed. "If we hurry, we can probably see the magistrate today." Kale followed her down the stairs and out of the Granite Anvil. The Council District of Muncifer was in the shadow of Grimstone Keep. All governmental functions: the courts, the Council of Elders, the various trade guild halls, the Hall of Records, were all in the Council District. This part of the city was crowded, though it contained fewer draks and minotaurs than Kale saw in the undercity and many more humans. He spied a couple of elves and a dwarf or two, likely visiting dignitaries.

The two draks passed a temple of Anetha on their way to the Hall of Records. Most cities featured a splendid temple to the goddess of wisdom and civilization, and a lesser one to Hon, the god of marriage, family, and pacts. Anetha's Hall soared above the surrounding buildings, a gleaming white monument that stood in contrast to the rest of the grey buildings around it.

Hon's Temple stood behind Anetha's Hall and next door to the Hall of Records. Kale noted how diminutive it appeared next to the goddess's temple. Were it not for the twin hearths flanking its double doors, Kale would have mistaken it for an ordinary building, perhaps a government office.

Groups of citizens entered and exited the Hall of Records in steady streams. Busts of former rulers of Muncifer, a mix of humans and minotaurs, flanked the stairs leading to the doors. Inside, clerks rushed to and fro, moving with precise purpose, unlike Kale and Kali.

Holding up a hand, Kale flagged down a clerk. "Excuse me, we need help." The man shook his head and rushed past. The next person ignored him entirely, seeming oblivious to Kale's cue.

Kali nudged him. "Spit some fire at the ceiling. That'll get their attention."

Looking up, Kale took in the beauty of the colorful fresco that decorated the ceiling. He didn't want to damage it and suspected doing so would land him in jail. He stopped the next clerk who walked by, spreading his wings in front of the man to block his path.

The clerk tilted his head up and clenched his jaw. "Yes? What is it? What do you want?" His arms full of scrolls, his red-rimmed eyes, and unkempt beard suggested he was overworked.

"We need to speak to the magistrate in charge of abandoned property." Kali peeked over one of Kale's wings. "Can you tell us where to find him?"

"He's… let's see, I don't have time for this." The clerk's eyes flicked to the ceiling, before gesturing with his head to a spiral staircase in the far corner of the room. "I think he's in the archives right now. Magistrate Yulian Bukhgalter." He shook himself free of Kale's grasp, then continued on his way.

They found the archives located on the top floor of the Hall of Records. A balding man with a close-cropped beard shuffled through a rack of scrolls. He glanced over when Kale and Kali entered the room, but he made no other sign of acknowledgement.

"Are you Magistrate Yulian Bukhgalter?" Kale raised his hand in greeting.

"Yes. Two draks." He pulled a scroll from the rack, then approached a desk. "What do you want? Do you have business here?"

Kale shook his pack, hoping the jingling of coins within would catch the magistrate's attention. "We're interested in one of the abandoned shops in the undercity."

"We were told we had to speak to you about it." Kali stood on her tiptoes and rested her chin on the top of the desk.

"Where did you obtain the money?" Narrowing his eyes, he pushed Kali's head off the desk. "Most of your kind just squat in abandoned shops down there."

Kale dropped his pack on the floor with a resounding thud. "We brought it with us. Maybe you didn't notice, but we're not from around here."

The magistrate grunted. "You all look the same to me."

Holding out her hand, Kali lifted Kale's and held it next to hers. "Really? Black and red stripes look the same as orange and look the same as all the grey and blue draks you have around here? Are humans colorblind?"

"No." After crossing the room, the magistrate opened a ledger. "Which property is it?"

Kale chewed his lip. "It's under... a, umm, rocks? Undercity near, umm... there's another shop nearby. I don't know what they sell; I didn't look..."

Kali shook her head, sighing. "It's at the bottom of the undercity, on a street just off the main thoroughfare by the Shadow Bridge. The shop itself is a storefront, a storage room, and living quarters. The owner died fifty years ago; the last of her kin, five. The guards couldn't give me names."

Magistrate Bukhgalter flipped through the register. After stopping near the front, he scanned the pages with his finger. "Ah, yes. Belen's Candles. Fifty crowns and you'll be expected to clean it up and keep it maintained. Someone will inspect it regularly until we're satisfied that you are doing so."

Fifty crowns was far less than Kale expected. He dug through his pack until he found the strongbox. He opened, then searched through it. A quick count showed there were nowhere near that many gold coins. He picked up a small ruby and held it up to the light between two claws. The magistrate watched him, frowning.

"I don't have that many crowns. I have this." He offered the ruby to the magistrate.

Yulian examined the gem. "Where did you acquire this?"

"I brought it from home, from Drak-Anor."

Kali hissed at him and put away the rest of the money when a scribe entered. The man crossed the room to pick up a scroll, then left without looking up.

"That's near Ironkrag, yes? It will be sufficient. I'll have a clerk meet you at the shop with the deed." After pocketing the gem, he tapped the edge of his desk. "Don't flaunt that wealth so openly. No one will admit it, but there is a guild of thieves operating in the undercity."

"Oh yes, of course." Kale rearranged his pack to conceal the strongbox. "We'll be careful."

As they exited, Kali took Kale by the arm. "Did that seem too easy to you?"

Now that his mate mentioned it, the transaction seemed to go a bit too smoothly to Kale. Thus far, he'd seen nothing to suggest the humans in town possessed any sort of concern for draks. He was always willing to give the benefit of the doubt, however, and there were always exceptions to every rule.

"Maybe he's one of the nice ones?"

"A bureaucrat?" Kali laughed and squeezed his arm. "You're one of the nice ones."

They made their way back to the Granite Anvil and gathered their possessions and Delilah's. Then they told the innkeeper where they were headed in case Delilah came looking for them. When they arrived at the shop, Kale carried their packs to the living quarters. Together, they began the process of cleaning up their new home.

***

"You must concentrate!" Master Valyrian snapped his fingers. The box Delilah attempted to retrieve telekinetically flew at her head after the snap of the elf's fingers broke her focus.

She ducked and glared at him. "I was concentrating until you interrupted me."

Master Valyrian clucked his tongue. "The real world is full of distractions. You must learn to block out such things."

Delilah leaned on her staff. "I've been using my magic in battles since I first figured out how to use it. Using magic in a fight is nothing like trying to learn a new technique while a tree-hugging elf snaps his fingers in your face."

"Fair enough." After picking up the box, the elf returned it to the empty spot on the shelf where it once sat. His chambers comprised wall-to-wall shelves and bookcases filled with more bric-a-brac than Delilah had ever seen in one location, outside of a junk shop.

"You know the words. You can work the magic. You just need to practice your control. As long as you don't break the box during the trial, you should pass." He turned to face her, wand at the ready. "Shall we practice your abjurations?"

He taught her a more advanced shielding spell than the ones she had seen the other initiates use. Azure tendrils gathered near the top of her staff as Delilah readied herself.

"*Dynami velos!*"

Before he finished speaking, Delilah chanted, "*Apokryfess kelyfos prostasais!*"

The bolt of energy streaked toward Delilah, vanishing when it slammed into the invisible shell she erected around herself. According to Master Valyrian, no magic would pass the shield she created. *This one I must figure out how to cast without speaking.* She recalled the lessons Gil-Li's grimoire tried to teach her about voiceless magic. It was her fervent hope that once this initiate business was finished, she could resume studying her tome.

"Excellent!" Master Valyrian twirled his wand in his fingers and slid it up into his sleeve. "You're going to be wearing grey robes any day now. I noticed you're no longer using the robes provided by the university. Are you sure that was a wise purchase?" He narrowed his eyes. "Or did you expect to linger as an initiate for a long time?"

Delilah fingered the trim on her robe. "I bought a grey one, too. Just in case. I figure the archmage will figure out some way to keep me down. It's his new hobby, I think."

"I cannot fathom why the archmage has taken such personal interest in you." Master Valyrian rubbed his chin.

That was a question Delilah wanted answered as well. "I came all this way just to pay dues so I wouldn't be branded a renegade. I never had anything to do with the guild, the university, or anything. I was just minding my own business in Drak-Anor."

"Well, I avoid guild politics and the Court of Wizardry as much as possible. Frankly, I think it's just another layer of control humans try to exert over that which cannot be controlled. They like to delude themselves, you know? Control is the greatest illusion of which one can convince one's self." Master Valyrian uncorked a bottle of wine, then offered a glass to Delilah.

The drak sorceress accepted the proffered glass and drank it down. After sipping a few more glasses for good measure, they parted for the evening. Delilah was sure she would pass her Initiate Trials. The only real question was whether or not the archmage would allow it.

Chapter 13

Pancras found himself in an endless expanse of uniform grey. For a moment, he thought he was blind but realized he could see his extremities. There was, quite literally, nothing else to see. Somehow, he perceived the difference between sky and land, despite the absence of delineation or horizon.

In the distance, a speck appeared. It closed in, growing in size, as it approached. He wanted to run, to hide, but there was no cover in sight. It grew larger than he before it shrank to match his size. A skull atop robes of black and red stared at him. Its eyes were black and glistened like pools of still water on a moonless night. Pancras felt his muscles seize, and his mind screamed as he failed to draw breath.

Paralyzed, unable to breathe, blink, or move in any fashion, Pancras was utterly helpless as the skull creature circled him. He felt its presence behind him. When it moved into sight, the skull disappeared, revealing in its place the pale face of a woman. Her short, raven hair framed her alabaster face, falling to either side of her eyes, the same eyes that had regarded Pancras from within the skull. In the back of his mind, Pancras recognized the irony that at this particular moment he appreciated the beauty of her robes, finer quality than any he ever owned.

A dark presence battered away his fleeting bemusement. The shadow that lurked within wrapped its cold claws around his mind and squeezed. The woman scowled before placing a hand on his chest.

Through his robes, Pancras felt her icy touch. It traveled through him, as if freezing his very soul. Eternity sparkled in the woman's eyes, and when she withdrew her hand, a writhing ball of shadowy tendrils wrapped itself around her palm and fingers. She made a fist, crushing it until nothing remained but wisps of smoke, blown away on an unseen wind.

The woman's expression softened. She reached up and caressed his face with her icy fingers. Pancras wanted to shiver beneath her touch but still he could not move. He noted without emotion that the shadowy presence was gone.

Pancras. The woman neither moved her lips, nor changed expression, yet the voice was hers.

Pancras, son of Acrisius and Voleta of Black Mountain. Faithless, yet devoted. Twice killed. Twice alive. Tainted.

The minotaur tried to speak. He wanted to defend himself. Still, he could not move. He could only think. He needed to cry out, to rage against the forces that conspired to separate him from his friends and granted him only death in exchange for his attempts to atone for the mistakes of his youth.

Look upon me and know me.

The paralysis faded. The minotaur felt control return to his muscles, yet, he was compelled to look only at the woman. The woman beneath whose face lay a skull. A skull with eternity in its eyes. Aita.

He fell to his knees before the visage of the goddess to whom he had devoted his work. She caught Pancras's arm and pulled him to his feet.

The Lich Queen works through you.

"What? No! I have only ever served you." Pancras despised necromancers who used their power to conquer and destroy. Even when he practiced the dark art, he limited himself to animating only volunteers and created mindless automatons, never intelligent or free-willed undead.

I know. What you have done. I see all. From my faithful. And devoted. The cadence of her speech in his head was odd, stilted, as though communication of any type was unfamiliar to her.

"I tried to fight the shadow demon. It was within me. It used me."

Aita took Pancras's withered hand. The chill in her touch spread up his arm. *You. Are strong. The Lich Queen is stronger. Her power grows. She seeks to return.*

"I don't know—"

Silence. Listen. Understand. Aurora was first to act. The love goddess shames us all. Cultists defile. The shadow waits and strikes at opportunities. You served. As one agent. Among many. I have destroyed the shadow. You will serve me again. Still. As always.

Pancras's mind raced to parse the words. She continued, unabated.

Twice, you have died. Twice, you have lived. I will return you for a third life. A final life. A hint of a smile crept upon her face. *Do not. Fall again.*

"I have never broken your faith. You have always been my patron."

Aita placed a finger on his lips. *You speak when you should listen. You listen when you should speak. You served well. You lack faith. You ignored the knock of opportunity.*

Pancras clutched at his head as a flood of images flashed before him. Growing up in Black Mountain. Moving to Muncifer with his family. Learning magic at the Arcane University. Choosing necromancy but rebuffing a priest's suggestion to formalize his relationship with Aita. Falling in love with Thanos. Losing Thanos. Every milestone of his life raced through his mind, yet Pancras still knew not of what Aita spoke.

Bonelord.

Realization hit Pancras like a runaway potato cart. Aita, ever present. Although he venerated her, she offered him so much more than he was willing to admit in his youth. In his ignorance, he turned away from his calling.

He fell to his knees, and again, she caught him. He looked up into eternity. "I will serve in any way you wish. Faithfully. Until my last breath leaves my body." He chuckled. "Again."

After steadying him on his hooves, Aita placed a hand on his brow. He bowed his head. *Return to Calliome, Bonelord. The faithful servant of Aurora will guide you. She harbors a secret, but it will aid your struggle. She is with you now. She will believe. You must convince her. Listen, and remember: Bekkhildr's blood, blood of Vibeke.*

More images engulfed Pancras's mind as the grey expanse fell away. The visage of Aita faded until the skull with eyes of eternity was all that remained, and finally, it, too, faded away. In an instant, the goddess's purpose became as clear as the crystals in the caverns beneath Drak-Anor. He understood his task. His purpose. Why he was given another chance. He recognized what tools he needed to be successful and how to obtain them. Clarity conquered his doubt.

Pancras lived once more.

***

A one-armed cultist lunged at Gisella, his mouth torn open from the trauma that killed him. She slashed at him with her sword, then rammed her armored elbow into his face. He staggered backward, leaving enough space for her to remove his head with one well-placed swing.

The most unnerving thing about the creatures they fought was their silence. No cries of pain at the horrible wounds Gisella, Qaliah, and Edric inflicted, no sound issued from their screaming maws as they attacked. Qaliah ducked and slashed, serving more as a distraction. The fiendling's blade was effective against most living opponents, just not against the walking dead.

From his position near the entrance, Edric fought off zombies intent on killing their mounts. With one swing of his axe, he cut the legs out from under one of the rotting corpses and then buried his axe in its head. Once it was down, he severed its head from its body and kicked it away like a ball.

As Qaliah slashed open a dead cultist's belly, an undead soldier grabbed her shoulders from behind. Gisella stabbed her sword upward, impaling him through the back. The Golden Slayer swept his legs out from under him as she withdrew her sword, ichor following her blade in an arcing spray. When he fell prone, the fiendling stabbed him through the head.

With hunger for flesh of the living and their faces locked in screams of silent rage, more zombies advanced on them. Two more seized Qaliah. The fiendling slashed at them, her small blade ineffective against the remnants of the armor that still covered them. They pulled her down.

Edric roared, racing across to her as fast as his stubby legs allowed. He dove toward Qaliah, rolling under the zombies and bowling them to the ground. In a flash, he rocked to his feet, then hacked at their heads.

The Golden Slayer slashed at the legs of a zombie that reached for Edric, severing a leg at the knee. After the zombie fell onto Qaliah, Gisella gripped the back of his tunic to yank him off her. She stabbed him through the mouth while Edric helped the fiendling to her feet.

"Where's the minotaur?"

"He did this! He's dead." She yanked her sword out of the corpse and slashed at another zombie, sending it backward.

"What? Again?"

Furrowing her brow, Gisella stared at the dwarf. Qaliah shrieked, punching a soldier's corpse in the nose. It went down staggering. "It's true. He raised an army. Then I killed him!"

"There's too many of them! We have to find a defensible position." Gisella's eyes scanned the area as she fended off another one. More poured from the keep with every passing minute. Soon, the entire garrison would surround them.

Edric pointed toward the gate. "Get to the horses!" He cut down another zombie and then ran.

A half-skeletal creature blocked their path. The blacksmith. His blackened arms held a massive sword. He raised it as Edric charged.

Gisella heard a voice behind her.

"*Aita pairnei piso tee dyaenamee pou eiche klapei. Ypoloipo nekrees psychees. Peegainete sto aionio yeapno sas!*"

Turning to face the voice, she viewed Pancras holding his bejeweled rod aloft. Green tendrils writhed around him like serpents before they exploded in a flash of emerald light. As she felt the energy wash over her like a blast of warm wind, Gisella shielded her eyes against the glare.

Wet, sticky liquid splashed her, and when she opened her eyes, Gisella stared in shock at the carnage. Only she, Edric, Qaliah, and Pancras remained standing. All the undead and severed remnants were obliterated, reduced to bloody mounds of decaying flesh, bones, and clothing, as if the hammer of the gods pounded them into the earth.

Gisella leveled her sword at Pancras. After securing his rod in the loop on his belt, he clasped his hands in front of him. Despite the bloody hole in his robe where Qaliah shot him, he seemed to be in perfect health.

"You're dead! I killed you!" Qaliah held her sword under his chin.

"You're not wrong, but please." He took the tip of her blade with two fingers and moved it away. "Hear me out before you kill me again."

"You're making a habit of this, Minotaur." Edric wiped his axe with a cloak he took from a dead soldier's remains as he approached them. Gisella glared at the dwarf. Of the three of them, he seemed to be the only one not surprised by Pancras's reappearance.

"Everyone be quiet!" Gisella needed to make sense of things before she decided to kill the renegade before her. "Explain yourself, Wizard."

"It is a long story, and until just a few minutes ago, I didn't understand all of it myself." He pressed his palms together. "Perhaps we should see to our horses?"

"No." Gisella raised her blade. "You will tell us, now."

Pancras held up his hands. "Yes, very well. Nearly a year ago now, I was tasked with investigating a ghoul outbreak under Ironkrag. With the assistance of Edric and Kale, we discovered a chaos rift and a shadow demon of some sort. We closed the rift and killed the demon, or so I thought."

He lowered his hands and clasped them behind his back. "The demon survived by binding itself to me. I didn't realize it at first, but when the twins told me I was raising undead in my sleep, I realized something was wrong. It could only act through me when I utilized my magic. The demon manipulated my dreams. In an attempt to stop it, I even changed my arcane focus. It came to a head in Almeria, during which the creature manifested itself. Again, I thought it was defeated. Shortly thereafter, I was killed while defending myself in a petty altercation."

"Petty?" Edric scoffed. "You killed the Prince of Etrunia!"

Gisella had heard of Prince Gavril's death, but no word had reached Muncifer as to the cause of his demise.

Pancras cleared his throat. "Technically, he was no longer prince, nor did I deliver the fatal blow. He lived until after he ran me through." The minotaur rubbed his right horn as he regarded Gisella. "He wanted me to curse his wife. After becoming acquainted with the princess, I could not go through with it. She is a good, honorable leader. Almeria and Etrunia are better off. I died that day."

"Yet, here you stand." Gisella lowered her blade to rest her arm, but did not sheath it.

"Indeed. I saw a terrible visage. Not Aita, but something… someone else. I believe it now to have been the Lich Queen. She was accompanied by the shadow demon. They brought me back, exacting this toll…" Pancras reached up his robe and pulled off the leather sleeve covering his right arm. He clenched his blackened, withered claw into a fist. Though he was glad to be alive, he was disappointed Aita had not deemed it necessary to restore his arm.

"I hoped Aita would fix this when she sent me back once more. But, I digress. I did not know why I was first sent back. Indeed, I was unable to remember any details of my encounter with the Lich Queen. I felt uneasy, tainted, you might say, but for the sake of my companions, I kept my concerns to myself. I eschewed using my magic, as much as possible. A darkness lurked at the edge of my vision, and its intensity increased when I thought too much about magic, or, now that I think on it, when I saw The Golden Slayer for the first time."

"The Lich Queen is dead. Destroyed at the Battle of Badon Hill." Gisella sheathed her sword. Rumors she had heard pointed toward the return of the Lich Queen, but she wanted to determine what this minotaur knew about it.

"So thinks everyone. I do not know the mechanism of her return, only that it is. When I used my magic to fight that cultist in the keep, the shadow demon returned. He took control of me and used me to animate all the dead in the area. Qaliah"—he inclined his head toward the fiendling—"put a stop to that, and for that, I thank you."

"You're thanking me… for putting a crossbow bolt in your chest?" Narrowing her eyes, the fiendling sheathed her sword. She took a step back, and made a warding gesture.

"You killed me. This time, I saw not the Lich Queen, but someone else. A skull. Eyes like an inky-black pond on a star-filled night. The skull became a raven-haired woman. Aita."

Gisella took a step back. "You saw the Princess of the Underworld? The goddess of death?"

"I did. I know it was she. She took the shadow within me and crushed it like an insect. She sent me back, and I understand why. I have been given an opportunity to set things right." The minotaur chuckled. "I no longer feel a compulsion to travel to Vlorey."

Gisella placed her hand on the hilt of her sword. No matter what the minotaur said or was, she was bound to her duty.

He raised his hand. "I no longer have the compulsion, yet I know I must still go there. I have to stop the Lich Queen. It is the reason I have returned."

Edric laughed. "You're mad. Being dead's rotting your brain."

Qaliah cocked her head. "It's doing something to him, all right."

"I will not be alone in this fight. Unlikely as it seems, Aita said that Aurora shamed all the gods when she acted first against the Lich Queen."

A chill passed over Gisella. *He cannot know.*

Pancras stared at her, as if he could read her very thoughts. "I believe she gave me a message for you, Gisella."

The slayer's breath caught in her throat. She gestured to Qaliah and Edric. "Leave us. Check the horses."

"What? Now?" Qaliah took her arm. "This is getting good."

"Go!" Gisella pushed the fiendling toward the horses.

Edric tugged on Qaliah's jerkin. "Let's go. We're not good enough for their serious business. I'll open a bottle of ale with you."

Qaliah watched over her shoulder as Edric led her away. Gisella needed to hear what Pancras had to say in private. She wasn't ready to bare her family secrets to just anyone. Her heart dreaded what he was about to tell her while her mind reconciled he could not possibly possess specific information about her.

"Speak, Minotaur."

"Bekkhildr's blood, blood of Vibeke."

Gisella's stomach churned, and she choked back bile rising into her throat. *He cannot possibly know that!* Her knees weakened, and only through sheer force of will did she not collapse before him. "How do you know that?"

"I told you." Pancras placed his unwithered hand on her shoulder. "Aita herself told me."

"Only one other living person knows what that means."

"I do not know what it means, only that it is significant to one Aita called 'the faithful of Aurora.'"

Gisella turned away from him, covering her mouth with her hand. The minotaur revealed a truth she withheld from her closest friends. Not because she didn't trust them, but because she feared for their safety. All of her adult life, she did her duty while listening. Listening to rumors and stories about the Lich Queen, deciding which tales might contain a kernel of truth and which were wild speculation by the ignorant masses. Most of the people alive today were born after the Lich Queen's final defeat. None of them understood what she truly wanted.

She swallowed and faced Pancras once more. "Vibeke was my mother."

"And Bekkhildr? Your father?"

Gisella shook her head. "Vibeke's mother. My grandmother."

"I see." Pancras pulled the leather sleeve up over his withered hand and arm. "What is their significance?"

"Bekkhildr the Iron Witch was better known as the Lich Queen."

***

Initiates and novices gathered in the practice area. Master Galina, once again, served as proctor, while the Blue and Yellow Wizards observed the proceedings from the reviewing stand. Many of the novices in attendance were initiates the week prior. Except for Katka, Delilah hadn't taken the time to befriend any of the other novices. Her duties with the archmage and her studies with Master Valyrian left little time for socializing.

Unfortunately, that meant Delilah had not free time to help Katka practice her offensive magic. She hoped the girl would execute the shield spell correctly this time. They waited their turn as Master Galina called forth other initiates.

Delilah took Katka's hand when it was the young woman's turn. "Remember, when it's time to hit that target, give it everything you've got. You know what to do. I know you can succeed!"

Nodding, Katka smiled before dashing to present herself to Master Galina and the wizards in the reviewing stand. The challenges, designed to test basic proficiencies rather than challenge the students, were the same as the prior week.

As before, Katka passed the first three parts of the trial with little effort. When it came time to attack the training dummy, the girl took a deep breath, raised her wand, and closed her eyes.

Pausing, she scowled. "*Aktina tees pyrkagias!*" A beam of fire shot from her wand, engulfing the head of the dummy. It erupted in flame, incinerating in an instant.

Delilah grinned and elbowed Conner in the hip. "I taught her that one."

The young man looked impressed. "I'll bet they weren't expecting that."

"Congratulations, Initiate. You may trade in your initiate robes and join the ranks of the novices."

Katka's gait to rejoin her friends was more akin to a bounce than a walk, and her smile widened to the point that it crinkled the skin at the corners of her eyes.

She took Delilah's hands and jumped up and down. "I did it! I did it!"

"That's great—"

"Initiate Delilah!"

"You'll do great!" Katka squeezed her hands.

Yeah, I'd better. I'm too old to be learning how to make light and scrub cauldrons. "I'll show them drak magic."

Delilah bowed before Master Galina. The older woman inclined her head. "Create light."

"*Fos.*" The top of Delilah's staff illuminated.

"Initiate Delilah, I am going to cast a spell at you. If it hits you, it will harm you. Do you understand?"

"Yes." Delilah pulled the strands of magic to her before Master Galina began her spell. The bolt of energy dissipated with a spurt against the shell Delilah's spell formed around her.

"Interesting." Master Galina pointed to the tree behind Delilah. "Get a box from the tree using *your* magic."

"No problem." Delilah faced the tree, scanning the boxes. They were all about the same size. She picked the highest one. "*Dynami antikeimeno kalesei.*" The box flew out of the tree, and Delilah fought to control the energies between her and the it. Although she was not accustomed to exercising this sort of fine manipulation, she managed to slow the momentum of the box by the time it reached her. After hopping up to grab the box, she tucked it under one arm.

Master Galina stepped forward and took the oversized box from Delilah when she saw the diminutive drak struggling to maintain a grip on her staff and it. "Very good. Attack one of the training dummies, please."

Delilah approached the dummies, then raised her staff. "*Dapane phlogone.*" A short stream of fire shot from the eyes of her staff toward the target. She ended the stream as soon as the end licked the dummy, stepping back as flames consumed it.

"That is sufficient, Initiate. You may trade in your initiate's robes for novice's robes and join the ranks of the novices." Master Galina bowed to Delilah. Before Delilah returned to the crowd, the older woman motioned her over. "You'll want to watch how much you show off. Not everyone appreciates it away from the practice field."

"Yes, Master Galina." Delilah kept her voice level and bowed. She returned to Katka and Conner. "Let's celebrate! First round is on me!"

***

"We're never going to remove all the dirt and grime from this place!" Kale stood and arched his back. The kink sent a spasm of pain into his wings.

"At least five years of accumulated crud. It's going to take a while." Kali put down her scrub brush and rubbed Kale's wing joint.

"Maybe I should just burn it away." Kale spat a gout of flame into the hearth, causing the fire to flare for a moment.

Kali wrapped her arms around him and rested her head on his shoulder. "Let me run far, far away before you do that. I like being warm and cozy, but I draw the line at being set on fire."

The two draks spent the last several days doing nothing but cleaning. They started with the living quarters. Once they removed the debris, Kale realized he needed to purchase furniture at some point. Thus far, they continued to use the bedrolls they had slept in on the road. It wasn't horrible, at least they had a roof over their heads, but Kale found himself wanting a real bed. After their personal quarters, Kale insisted they clean up Delilah's room. It was the only other room that could be used for sleeping quarters, and he wanted it to be ready if she arrived.

After they finished uncluttering and cleaning the sleeping chambers, Kale and Kali worked on the rest of the living quarters: the privy, bathing room, and hearth room. Of the furniture they found within the building, they were able to salvage only a copper bathing vessel, one chair, which they cobbled together from three different broken chairs, and the display shelves in the storefront. Kale avoided the bookcases in the stairway leading to the runed circle altogether. After showing the secret area to Kali, he locked the door. He needed neither the distraction of all the books, nor did he trust himself not to search every nook and cranny down there for forgotten trinkets.

They cleaned for a few more hours. The bathing vessel's patina would require some sort of solvent and elbow grease to remove it. Kali wasn't sure removing the verdigris was strictly necessary.

"It doesn't matter. We don't have any way of bringing hot water in there right now anyway." Kale tossed his brush into the tub with a clang.

Kali pointed at the bathing vessel. "You breathe fire. We can start with cold water."

"Good point." Kale craned his neck to look toward the front of the shop, realizing he had lost track of time. The deep shadows revealed the sun was now high in the sky, casting this portion of the undercity into darkness.

"I'm hungry." The minute he mentioned food, his stomach knotted.

Kali nodded her assent, and they dusted themselves off. As Kale strapped on his harness and pouches, he heard someone knocking at their door.

A round young man stood outside, crouching to peer through the drak-sized portal. He flipped back his hood and raised his hand in greeting. "Hello. I'm Clerk Hadeon. I have papers for you."

Kali waved him in. "The ceiling's high enough, I think."

He squeezed through the door. He crouched to avoid a hanging light, the top of his head nearly brushing the ceiling.

"I have deeds and money for you." He withdrew several scrolls from his bag.

"Money?" Kale glanced up from the deed he examined. There were two copies: one for him and Kali and one which was to remain in the Hall of Records. "What money?"

"Oh, Magistrate Yulian said the gem you paid with was too much money. He sent the remainder with me." After fishing in his pouch, the clerk tossed a fat sack filled with coins on the counter.

Smirking at his mate, Kale dumped the money onto the counter. Kali responded by pursing her lips.

Hadeon glanced around the room while Kale and Kali filled out the deeds. "Old family place?"

"No, we just needed a place to call home, and this seemed as good as any." Kale sensed the young man was just making friendly conversation, but he didn't want to reveal any of the secrets he'd found.

"No one will bother you down here. Are you going to open a shop?" He ran his finger along the dusty counter, leaving a clean streak in the wood.

Kale rolled up one of the deeds, then handed it to Hadeon. "I haven't decided yet. We might. It depends on my sister. She's at the Arcane University."

"Oh. I always wanted to be a wizard. Never got the hang of it. Does she have wings, too? I've never seen a winged drak before." He unrolled the deed and examined it before nodding and returning it to his bag.

"No, this was..." Kale wasn't sure how to describe his wings. He decided to lie. "A wizard did it. It was an accident. I've found them too useful to get rid of, you know?"

"Wow, yeah. It'd be great to be able to fly." After closing his pack, he offered Kale his hand. "Everything looks in order. You even look like you've been cleaning, so I'll tell them you're keeping good on your promise."

Kale shook the young man's hand. "You're the inspector, too? Will you be coming back?"

"Maybe in a few weeks, if they don't forget. They usually forget." He cursed when he hit his head on the doorframe. "Good day to you. Hon's blessing to your home and hearth!" Rubbing the top of his head, Hadeon left the shop.

Kale looked at Kali as his mate took his arm. He pointed to the coins on the counter before returning them to the sack and tucking the bag into his pouch. "See? They didn't keep the change."

Kali chewed her lip, nodding. "Well, I guess it's really ours now, huh?"

"Our first home!"

Chapter 14

Processing Gisella's revelation took Pancras a moment. "You're the granddaughter of the Lich Queen?"

"Yes, my sister and me." Gisella glanced behind her, presumably for Edric and Qaliah to ensure the pair weren't eavesdropping. The dwarf and fiendling stood alongside the horses, talking and periodically glancing toward Gisella and Pancras.

"Are you both Aurora's faithful?" Pancras was curious how, exactly, the goddess of beauty and love played into events.

"No. Alysha is devoted to Selene. She's a proper sorceress." Gisella removed her helmet, then flipped matted hair out of her eyes. "That's why she's deep in the Southern Watch. She's far from where the Lich Queen is thought to return."

Pancras thought back to what he learned of resurrection. If that was the method by which the Lich Queen attempted her return, a bit of her body would be required to accomplish the task: a bone, a bit of flesh, or a lock of hair. He was sure it could not be accomplished with the body of a descendant either living or deceased. Unless the issue had been born of incest, there would be too many other influences from other bloodlines.

"Were your parents siblings?"

"What? No." Gisella's curled lips and furrowed brow conveyed her irritation. "What has that to do with anything?"

"I'm trying to determine what her plan is, exactly."

Gisella put one hand on his chest and grabbed his snout with her other, then pulled his head down. Pancras jumped back, but she maintained her grip. "Be still!"

He complied with her order, his nose in her face, until she released him and stepped away. Pancras rubbed his snout and followed after her.

"I needed to be sure you were, in fact, alive. I don't know what is going on, and I don't like it."

"I understand." The first time Pancras returned from the dead, he feared he might have returned as one of the many undead abominations he so fervently fought against. As far as he could ascertain, he was alive. Gisella secured her helmet on Moonsilver's saddle. "As much as I would like to leave this place, we should at least give the soldiers their due. We'll make two pyres: one for the cultists and one for the soldiers and other workers from the keep. They will have peace in death."

"I'm not touching those rotters!" Edric seized Yaffa's reins, then led his pony away from the group.

"Never figured him for squeamish." Qaliah looked Pancras over. "So what are you now, some kind of zombie? A vampire? Are we going to have to put you down?"

Pancras held up his hands and chuckled. "I understand your suspicion. I am quite alive. She checked."

"It's true. He's breathing, he's warm, and his heart beats." Gisella pulled a spare blanket out of her saddlebags, then threw it at Pancras. "Use this for gathering parts. We'll start with the soldiers."

Pancras didn't like working with the rotting dead. Especially those who died violently. It was messy, and he had never become accustomed to the stench.

"I'd give my withered hand for some skellies to do this clean-up for us." He removed his belt, pulled off his robes, and laid them over Stormheart's saddle. He refastened his belt along with his rod and pouches over his loin cloth.

The fiendling pressed the back of her hand against her forehead. "Such a display. I may faint from this shameless show of minotaur flesh."

"Get your clothes bloody if you want. I paid too much for those robes to have them covered in viscera for the next several months." Pancras took the blanket and returned to the courtyard. It was a little chilly to be outside without clothing, even for a minotaur, but he hoped the physical labor would keep him warm.

As he left the two women behind, he heard Qaliah laugh. "You know, the dead guy has a point!"

***

Edric's casual acceptance of Pancras's death and apparent resurrection piqued Gisella's curiosity. In her world, such an event was not only unheard of, but also would be considered either a miracle or an abomination. She pondered in what sort of world the dwarf lived where such an occurrence barely rated a wry quip.

Glad Pancras enlisted Qaliah to gather the bodies of the dead soldiers, Gisella reached for Yaffa's reins. "If you're going to travel with us, you're going to help. Step down and help me gather wood for the pyres."

Edric sighed before dismounting his pony. "Maybe I don't want to travel with you anymore. I'm getting tired of this necromancer and his undead."

Gisella raised an eyebrow but kept her eyes fixed on Yaffa. "Why are you traveling with him, anyway? And what did you mean when you said him returning from death was getting to be a habit?" *Might as well just put it out there.*

"You heard him. He died back in Almeria. I didn't see it, but the draks were there. I saw his body when they laid him out in their undercroft. Stone dead." Edric picked up a branch but he tossed it away when he saw how rotten it was. "At least dwarves have the sense to petrify when we die. You know we're not coming back from that."

Dwarven death rites were foreign to Gisella. She figured Edric must have exaggerated to some extent. "Again, why are you traveling with him?"

"It's a long story I don't care to tell again. I am for now, but I'm not obligated to keep on." After kicking a stick in front of him, he dropped all the wood he'd gathered so far on top of it. "There's a wood pile behind the forge. I don't think there's going to be enough wood for a decent pyre, though."

Gisella spied a wood axe leaning against the forge. "I'll cut the stables apart. Keep gathering as much wood as you can. Bring furniture from the barracks and keep if you have to." She decided to let Edric's motivations lie. If he was in no way bound to the minotaur's service, she wouldn't stop him from leaving.

It took several hours to disassemble the stables with the wood axe. She had no choice but to allow the structure to collapse on top of the horse carcasses within, as she had no means of removing them. While Gisella labored, Pancras and Qaliah gathered all the bodies, including the dismembered corpses lining the road leading to the keep. Then they helped Edric break down the furniture and build pyres using it and the wood Gisella provided.

The sun hung low in the sky and the first stars of night shone bright by the time they completed their tasks. Gisella knelt before the pyre for the soldiers and lit a torch.

"Does anyone have anything to say?"

Edric shook his head. Qaliah shrugged.

Pancras cleared his throat. "We commend these unfortunate souls to Aita's realm. May they find peace there."

"Indeed." Gisella touched her torch to the bottom of the heap. Flames spread like spilled water, licking at the bottom logs before catching the tinder and kindling piled in the middle. She stepped back as roaring flames reached into the sky. Black smoke rolled off the pyre as though even the fire struggled to cleanse the bodies of the evil that had possessed them.

She tossed the torch onto the smaller pyre they made for the cultists. "Maris take you all."

The fires burned long into the night. The four of them made camp outside the walls of the keep, upwind from the choking stench of burning flesh, somber and quiet as they pondered the events of the day. Crickets serenaded them to sleep under the light of the King and Queen.

***

"What do you mean: 'they're not here'?" Delilah surveyed the Granite Anvil's common room, as though her eyes might catch the innkeeper in a lie. "Where did they go?"

"I'm not their keeper. They left. Took everything with them."

"What about my stuff? I had a room here, too!" Delilah fought to keep her heart out of her throat. She never let the pack with her grimoire and lexicon out of sight, but there were a few other trinkets of sentimental value she'd brought from Drak-Anor.

"I checked. Cleaned out. Looks like they nicked your stuff. Want another room?"

Delilah screeched, throwing up her hands. "You're useless!" She turned to Katka and Conner. "My brother ditched me! I can't believe it."

Conner pursed his lips. "Maybe he changed inns. There's places in the undercity run by draks. Probably cheaper, too."

The thought had occurred to Delilah, but she didn't have enough free time to visit every inn in the undercity and inquire if they'd seen her brother. That would take days, if not a week or more.

"What does he look like? You said he has stripes, right?" Katka tapped Delilah's shoulder to gain the drak's attention.

Delilah nodded. "And wings."

"I've lived here all my life, and you're the first striped drak I've seen. I've never seen one with wings. If he went into the undercity, someone is bound to have seen him."

The girl had a point. Delilah squeezed the top of her snout and rubbed her eyes. She took a deep breath and tried to clear her mind. *Of course, Kale will be easy to find. Who else is striped with wings? It's his mate who would be lost in the crowd.* Delilah strapped on her pack. It was filled to the point of bursting since she stuffed her robe into it. Now that she had some free time to roam the city, she didn't want to wear her robes. Conner and Katka both wore the grey of novices, and Katka stopped in front of every darkened window to admire the grey robe Delilah purchased for her.

The two humans led Delilah into the undercity. Merchants hawked their wares, and couriers rushed by, arms laden with deliveries and messages. Draks in the street were immediately drawn to Delilah.

"Another striped drak!"

"Red and black here to deliver us!"

"I'm crimson and ebony, you ignorant git!" Delilah stomped her foot. "Where's the other drak you saw?"

"You can lead us!"

"We must show the humans and minotaurs we're not vermin!"

"Save us! Save us!"

"Hey! I don't think you're vermin!" A lone minotaur loomed above the crowd. "Don't I give you good prices on my potatoes?"

Katka took Delilah's hand. "They're going to mob us. We have to move."

Delilah's mind hatched a different plan. She climbed up on the railing and focused on not looking down into the chasm. When she raised her arms, azure wisps formed at the top of her staff.

"*Fos.*" Her staff burst into light. "Hear me, draks of the undercity!"

"Delilah! What are you doing?" Conner spun, regarding her through widening eyes.

"We hear you!"

"Enlighten us!"

"Not again!" The minotaur hunched his shoulders and pushed his cart away as fast as he was able without bowling over the draks rushing to crowd around Delilah.

"Behold!" Delilah swung her staff in an arc above her head. "A Child of Destiny is amongst you. You shall all have my blessing—"

"Yes, bless us!"

"We are your faithful servants!"

"Can you heal my scale itch?"

"Tell me where I can find the striped drak with wings. Then you may all go with my blessing!" Delilah wagered her words would sway them.

"You're mad, Delilah!" Katka pulled on Delilah's sleeve.

"Down! Down!"

"He vanished at the Shadowbridge!"

"Evil is there! A shop of curses and woe!"

"Woe! Woe!"

Delilah fought to keep dismay from eclipsing her toothy, forced smile. "Go! Go, all of you, with the blessing of Rannos, Hon, and Adranus! May Aurora's love fill your hearts as you go be fruitful. Tinian's ever-watchful eye watch over you… in the winter… the light of Apellon warm you in the summer." Delilah's ad-libs were far from authentic, but they sounded good to her ears.

Apparently, the draks in the crowd agreed. They cheered for Delilah and parted, bowing and uttering blessings and thanks as she waded through them. After nodding and waving, she gestured for Conner and Katka to follow her.

At the bottom of the stairs leading to the next level of the undercity, Delilah lowered her arm and dropped her false smile. "I can't believe that worked."

Conner crossed his arms and frowned. "You're lucky they didn't tear you apart."

"Nah. They think because I was born with stripes, I have a special destiny. They wouldn't dare. I can only imagine what they thought of Kale walking through here with stripes and wings." Delilah giggled. "He probably has an army of them waiting on him hand and foot."

Katka shook her head. "This is unbelievable. Is it like this where you're from, too?"

"No. They wouldn't lift a claw to help us if we were drowning." Delilah noticed their confused looks. "Long story. Do you know where this Shadowbridge is? Or this cursed store?"

Conner led the way. "I don't know anything about a cursed store, but the Shadowbridge is this way. It's the deepest bridge and never gets sunlight. Most of the shops down there closed years ago. It's not cursed, as far as I know, just… abandoned."

Connor's explanation sounded more plausible to Delilah than them finding a shop of damnation and woe. Most cities had areas that fell into disrepair now and again, lying in wait for someone to come along and renovate. Each time they encountered draks, they required Delilah give a "blessing" before they would leave them be. A couple who were particularly persistent confirmed that Kale was seen entering a street near the Shadowbridge, and said the only buildings there were forsaken shops, warehouses, and evil omens.

The street didn't appear deserted to Delilah. A handful of draks crowded around the outside of a shop, peering in through windows so filthy they may as well have been staring at a brick wall.

"Here now!" Delilah decided to exert her authority as a Child of Destiny again. "What are you all looking at?"

"Another stripe!"

"Deliverer!"

Delilah tapped the butt of her staff on the walkway. "Enough of that! What's going on here? You've seen the striped, winged drak?"

"He's inside!"

"He toils without end!"

"*Go away.*" Delilah clenched her jaw and held up her hands. "The blessing of Rannos go with you, but you must give us striped draks time and breathing space." She turned her eyes upward and shook her head as the draks thanked her and scurried off. She felt Katka and Conner's disapproving glances on her back as she banged on the door.

The door cracked open, revealing only an eye that studied her.

"Deli? *Deli!*" Kale flung the door open and tackled his sister. The two draks fell into a heap. Kale laughed, squeezing the breath out of Delilah.

"By Maris's bloody spear, Kale... what are you doing down here?" Delilah pushed her brother off her and stood with Katka's aid. The girl handed Delilah her staff. "This is Katka and Conner, by the way. They're friends from the Arcane University. Good folk, for humans."

"Oh, thanks." Conner's voice dripped with sarcasm. He and Katka crouched to enter the shop, but Katka, at least, was able to stand inside without stooping.

"This is the shop, Deli! The one I wanted to show you. Kali and I bought it."

Delilah was halfway through the door by the time Kale's words penetrated her brain. "You what?" She blinked and stared at her brother. *Surely he didn't just say—*

"We bought it. I didn't want to risk anyone else finding what we found. The city let us have it for cheap, as long as we clean it up—"

"So that's what we've been doing while you've been off playing wizard games." Kali entered from the back room and dusted off her hands.

Delilah glanced around the cobweb-filled, dusty shop. She feared to learn what Kale considered dirty if the state of the front room was what he considered clean. She felt her knees weaken and her brain numb with Kale's revelation. She let Kali's sarcasm go unanswered.

"Let me show you what I found, Deli." Kale took her hand and led her through the shop. The back room appeared cleaner than the front, and a small fire crackled in the hearth. Down a short hallway, she noticed sleeping chambers that were clean by most standards, and she realized that Kale and his mate just hadn't been around to the storefront yet.

"Oh, hey, do you trust these humans? Maybe we shouldn't show them—"

Delilah dismissed his concerns with a wave of her hand. "They're fine." She looked at her friends, "Right? You're not going to go blabbing about this, are you? I guess, technically, this is all my brother's private property."

Shrugging, Katka glanced at Conner before she nodded. Conner raised his hands. "I'll keep my mouth shut, as long as I can talk to your brother about those wings. I've never seen a drak with wings! Can you fly?"

"Oh, sure." Kale's face lit up. "It's a long story, but I don't mind if you don't. It started about a year ago when—"

"Kale!" Delilah punched her brother in the shoulder. "Later! What are you going to show me?"

"Oh, right." Rubbing his shoulder, Kale led them to a locked door at the end of the hallway. He opened it, revealing a staircase that spiraled down into darkness.

Delilah lit her staff. Rows of bookcases bordering the stairwell took away her breath. "What are all these books?" Their musty odor suggested they must be centuries old. She reached for the nearest tome.

Shaking his head, Kale took her hand. "The books are the bonus. I think they're magic. At least, most of them are, but they're really old. What I want to show you is at the bottom."

Kali stuck her head in the stairwell. "I'll make sure no one becomes too curious. Don't be long. I'm hungry."

The stairs descended well below street level. Delilah found the weight of the earth above her comforting, reminiscent of home in Drak-Anor. She tried to scan the books as she descended the stairs, but if there were any titles written on the spines, they were long since lost to the ravages of time.

At the bottom of the stairs, a short corridor led to another door. Conner leaned over Kale's shoulder to examine the intricate clockwork mechanism on the handle. When Kale activated it and it clicked to life, Conner gasped, recoiling.

Delilah entered the chamber beyond the clockwork door. Lights in sconces sprang to life, illuminating the room with glowing gems. Noticing the walls were carved from the rock that surrounded the room, she felt drawn to a stone circle in the center of the chamber.

"Wow, the lights didn't come on when I found this place!" Kale nudged his sister toward the circle. "That's what I wanted to show you." He pointed. "The runes are some form of Ancient Drak, I think. I can't read most of it. I found the sigil of Selene and one for Rannos."

Delilah examined the symbols. She recognized Ancient Drak characters in the language of magic in the runes on the stones. Although she could read the words, she didn't understand their meanings. She found it difficult to focus her eyes on the odd black surface at the center of the circle. When she stared directly at it, it seemed solid, flat, almost like obsidian. From her peripheral vision, though, it appeared to be a roiling liquid, like a lampblack ocean during a storm.

"What is this place?" Katka's voice was filled with wonder, and she spun as she gawked at the room.

Conner's expression was much the same. "I can feel the magic in here. Can't you? It's old. So old."

Delilah nodded. She turned to face her brother and gathered him up in a hug. "This is great! I'm sorry I doubted you!"

"Initiate Drak!" Shuddering with a combination of fear and dread, Delilah recognized the booming voice. She pushed her brother away and spun, pointing her staff in the direction of the voice.

Where Delilah expected to see the archmage, a shimmering image of him hovered before her. "Why are you not at the Arcane University, Initiate Drak? I want you!" The image vanished in a puff of red smoke.

The drak sorceress threw her staff through the mist as the image vanished. It clattered against the floor as she stomped her foot. "I'm a novice now, damn it!"

***

Familiar anxieties about dark, disturbing dreams raced through Pancras's thoughts as he drifted off to sleep. The shadow had spoken to him mostly in his dreams, and even when he was unable to remember details, lingering effects made themselves felt throughout the next day. This night, however, Pancras dreamed of a raven-haired woman, shepherding the souls of the recently departed.

He dreamed of Aita.

When Pancras awoke the next morning, he realized the shadow was well and truly gone. He awoke feeling cleansed, refreshed, and energized. The sun peeked over the eastern horizon. Its brilliant rays pierced the clouds in a phenomenon people called "Apellon's Harp."

Gisella was next to rise. She called to Pancras as he walked toward the fort's main gate. "I'm not sure it's safe to go alone."

"If anything remains, it's just vermin and scavengers. Anything undead was destroyed." Pancras entered the fort. The pyres were reduced to smoldering ash with bits of bone visible where the bonfire collapsed. Pancras hoped to find a weapon in the fort. While he could defend himself with magic alone, especially now that the shadow demon was gone, a Bonelord of Aita was expected to carry some sort of weapon. The bonelord whom Pancras encountered several years prior carried a flanged mace that throbbed with the power of the

Princess of the Underworld. When he called upon his power, the mace's head transformed into a gleaming skull.

Pancras needed such a symbol if he were to carry out Aita's will in this world. His brief communion with the goddess imparted much. It didn't have to be a mace, per se, but his rod or the gilded horn tips he wore were unsuitable.

"What are you doing?" Gisella leaned on one of the smithy's vertical supports. Pancras hadn't realized she followed him. He chuckled; his mind was in the clouds.

"Looking for a weapon." He held up his rod. "I can't bash skeletons apart with this."

Gisella nudged a half-forged sword with her foot. "You might have better luck in the armory. Everything up here appears broken or unfinished."

Together, they entered the keep and stepped down into the armory. For Gisella's benefit, Pancras illuminated his rod. Racks of swords lined the armory walls, and a couple of racks of spears leaned against the back wall. Gisella replaced her spear with one that had a long, flanged tip. Pancras found a rack of maces and flails tucked into one corner, but none of the weapons particularly appealed to him. A weapon hiding in the shadows alongside one of the spear racks caught his eye.

The spiked head sat on the floor; the handle leaned against the spear rack. When Pancras lifted the morning star, a spider at work building its web skittered away. Heavy and brutal, it was forged from steel and possessed spikes as long as Pancras's smallest finger.

"That would certainly bash skeletons to pieces."

Pancras hefted the weapon. It was balanced for someone shorter, but he decided it would be adequate for now. "I'll put it to good use until I can have something more suitable made for me. It's a human's weapon."

"What's wrong with human weapons?" Gisella preceded him up the stairs to the keep's main level.

"Nothing, it's just not weighted right for me. I have a longer reach." He swung it through the air. "It doesn't matter. I doubt I'll have to use it. I don't have a lot of experience with this sort of weaponry."

"Maces and morning stars are easier. You just bash until your adversary stops moving." Gisella patted her scabbard. "They don't require as much finesse as a sword."

Until he saw her after his resurrection, Pancras had never noticed Gisella's sword. It was a handsome blade, with a wire-wrapped ivory handle. "You seem to prefer the spear."

"I prefer to keep my opponents far enough away that they cannot stick their swords into me."

Pancras agreed. They returned to their camp to find Qaliah prodding the fire, trying to coax more life out of the burning embers.

The fiendling glanced up. "Did everything stay dead that was supposed to?"

Pancras slid the handle of his new weapon through the loop on his saddle. "Quite. Wake the dwarf. We'll break our fast and then break camp. We have a long ride ahead of us still." Pancras rummaged through his saddlebag for food.

"Aren't you chipper? Maybe I should try being dead." The fiendling kicked the dwarf's legs. "Get up, Edric!"

Groaning, the dwarf cursed. His desire to leave the keep behind seemed to outweighed his desire to remain asleep, so without much more prodding, he arose. They ate a quick meal and scattered the remaining embers before saddling their horses and mounting up.

A day of fair weather and good spirits helped Pancras sort through the past day's events. Never before had he felt he followed a greater purpose. When he first left Muncifer after becoming a wizard, Pancras escaped sad memories and prejudice against those who didn't conform to expectations. Some of that was his necromancy, the rest was his love for

Thanos. A love that neither his nor Thanos's parents approved. Most of the community frowned upon it as well.

Drak-Anor was better. His job serving the Twilight Overlord allowed him to practice necromancy and alchemy, and most of the Overlords left him alone. When he became involved with Sarvesh and the Twilight Defenders, his life changed again, and he found true friends. Sarvesh's sweeping changes, including the founding of the city of Drak-Anor proper, gave him time to think again. When he questioned the purpose of a necromancer in a city, Sarvesh convinced him to stay as a friend and advisor, and Pancras happily served in that capacity. The more insight and guidance he provided, the less need he found for necromancy.

When he left Drak-Anor to travel to Muncifer, Pancras thought he would travel for months, pay the fine, turn around, and return home. He was prepared to do so, though he was not thrilled about undertaking the journey. Leaving Muncifer a second time filled him with dismay. Teaching had never been on Pancras's list of ambitions, but now, since pledging himself to Aita, he felt renewed vigor. That he would teach students to defend themselves in a city that would likely be the first target of any offensive by the Lich Queen would enable him to serve the Princess of the Underworld much more effectively.

I need a new nickname now, though. Pancras the Putrid just doesn't seem right for a Bonelord of Aita.

Chapter 15

Delilah found Archmage Vilkan in the Court of Wizardry. The Black, Red, and Yellow Wizards sat in the gallery, along with Master Valyrian. The archmage stopped his tirade when he saw the drak.

"Initiate Drak! Where have you been?"

"Novice." Delilah crossed the room. "Novice Delilah."

"That is not your call, Initiate." The archmage glared at her. Delilah felt her face grow hot. "Are you stu—"

"It is indeed not her call, Archmage." Master Valyrian stepped in front of Delilah. "However, she passed her Initiate Trials yesterday. The grey robes are well earned."

"I did not authorize a trial!" The archmage slammed his fist on the arm of his chair.

"The archmage's permission is not necessary for the trials." The Yellow Wizard glanced at his fellow high wizards, though Delilah thought, perhaps, his voice belonged to a female. All the high wizards' voices sounded altered, though, emanating from behind the masks they wore.

"Trials are held once a week."

"The drak passed."

"Thanks to my instruction." Master Valyrian bowed.

Archmage Vilkan's face matched the Red Wizard's robes. "She is my apprentice. It was not your place to instruct her."

"She is not. According to the *Rose Concordat*, initiates and novices are not bound to any one wizard. Only once they pass their Novice Trials may they be assigned primarily to one wizard for the balance of their instruction." Master Valyrian stepped toward Delilah. He placed his hand on her shoulder.

Delilah wondered why he defended her to Archmage Vilkan. She opened her mouth to ask, but closed it when the high wizards continued their inquiries.

"Do you intend to advance her past novice?"

"Justify your actions before the court, Archmage."

"Silence!" Vilkan cut the air with his hand. "Now that the drak shows some measure of skill, it seems our university has a mascot. Everyone is quick to its defense."

Delilah bit her lip. She realized Master Valyrian must have felt her bristle because he squeezed her shoulder.

The archmage gritted his teeth. "Fine. The drak will continue her instruction here as any other student. However, since she came to us as a renegade, I reserve the right to give her special assignments as I see fit."

Delilah slammed the butt of her staff on the floor with a resounding crack. The assembled wizards all turned their heads toward her. "Is that why you called me here? You pulled me away from my brother and his mate in their new home. I hope you didn't call me just to have me listen to you bicker over me."

The drak sorceress, surprised she hadn't been interrupted, regretted implying in front of the archmage and three high wizards she had business more important than the Court of Wizardry.

"Yes, why did you summon the drak?" Master Valyrian squeezed Delilah's shoulder once more before clasping his hands behind his back.

The archmage waved his hand and refused to meet the clf's gaze. "It doesn't matter now. Resume your duties, Init... Novice Drak. I may have something for you in a few days after I speak to the archduke again. You are dismissed."

You don't have to tell me twice. Delilah spun and exited the court. She nodded farewell to Seneschal Lyov as she passed the old man and considered sauntering out of the university compound and back to Kale and Kali's house. Instead, she sought out Katka. The young woman rehearsed her combat spells against the practice dummies.

"*Dynami velos!*" A green bolt of energy shot from Katka's wand, blasting the dummy's head into splinters.

"Hey, you're improving!" Delilah clapped the woman on the back as a show of approval.

"I think I actually am. It's about time. I don't think I'm going to master alchemy, though."

Alchemy was one subject Delilah wanted to practice more, but the petty antics of the archmage had thus far stymied those studies. Katka holstered her wand before approaching a bench near the Blood Oak.

"What do you think that runed circle in your brother's cellar is?"

The circle intrigued Delilah and was at the top of her list of mysteries to solve. She feared it would be a while before she was able to dedicate any significant time to it, though.

"He called it a 'moon gate.' I have no idea what that means, though. If he hadn't seen those runes, he'd be calling it a 'floor circle thing.'" Delilah laughed. Her brother's terrible names for his devices were legendary in Drak-Anor. "Rannos was killed before the Sundering, though, so that thing has to be extremely old."

"I'd forgotten about Rannos." Katka blew an errant strand of hair out of her face. "If it's pre-Sundering, whatever your brother paid for that house was a bargain… and I'll bet no one in the city even knows about it."

Delilah agreed. It was below a part of town that not even the draks consigned to the undercity lived in. "Just keep it to yourself, all right? I don't want the archmage finding out. He's been a pain in my tail."

"What's his deal with you anyway?" Katka's head turned to gaze at a group of young men walking by. One of them winked at her as he passed.

"I wish I knew." Delilah figured it was some sort of deeply-rooted bigotry, or worse. "He says he's going to have some sort of special project for me after he talks to the archduke again. I can't wait."

Katka put her arm around Delilah and hugged her. The drak tried not to show revulsion at the human's affectionate touch.

"Even if the job is horrible, you just need to ask, and I'll help. I owe you!" Katka's face beamed.

Delilah looked up at the young woman and smiled. "Thanks." It was good to have a friend, even if she was human.

***

Acquiring furniture, cleaning the storefront, and making their home livable for three draks took most of Kale and Kali's time over the next several weeks. Not the most exciting time in either of their lives, but they both acknowledged the need to complete the renovations. Kale was eager to be finished so Delilah would have a place to stay when she was done with whatever the Arcane University had in store for her.

Since Delilah's over-the-top appearance in the undercity, the other draks gave Kale a wider berth, although he had to answer the door a few times a day to answer questions about when the shop would be open and what they would sell.

"Perhaps we could do some sort of business out of the storefront." Kali paused her sanding of the counter.

"Like what?"

"Can you make puzzle boxes, or rat traps, or something like that?"

Kale felt a pang of guilt. Since arriving in Muncifer, he'd hardly thought of his puzzle box. He promised himself he would concentrate on unlocking its secrets once they were finished fixing up the shop.

"I suppose so. I'd need a supplier of gears and springs." Kale picked at a rough spot on the floor.

"I've checked out a lot of the shops in town, and there's really no one selling vermin traps. We'd make a killing." Kali returned to sanding the burrs and splinters out of the counter.

"I guess." Kale attacked a rough spot on the floor with his sanding block. He wasn't convinced. Setting up a store seemed like a more permanent solution than he was willing to accept. He didn't mind Muncifer, but he missed Drak-Anor.

A few minutes later, Kali jumped off the counter. "We need to earn money somehow, Kale. The funds Pancras left us won't last forever."

"I know. I just…" Kale stood and stretched. "It seems like committing to a shop says we're going to stay here. I figure once Deli's done, we'll go back to Drak-Anor or go after Pancras."

"We'll need to buy food, pay taxes, pay for stabling, pay for repairs when stuff around here breaks, and it will, and who knows what else." Kali ticked off each item on her fingers. "The last thing we want is to be evicted because we burned through all our money when the tax collectors come by."

Drak-Anor had no tax collectors, so the concept of making citizens pay for non-tangibles after they'd already purchased the building was foreign to Kale. "Maybe we could do odd jobs for people. Maybe we can catch the rats ourselves. I don't know."

"Couriers?"

"What about them?" Kale scratched his head. He didn't need a courier for anything.

"We could be couriers. With your wings, you'd be the fastest drak in the city for delivering things from the upper levels to the lower levels." Kali made a swooping motion with her hand. "You could just glide on down."

Kale liked gliding, but he wasn't sure he had enough muscle control to jump into the chasm on a regular basis. "Nah. Besides, all the draks around here think I'm something special. I can't be running around making deliveries."

Kali cocked her head. "Then you shouldn't go around catching rats for people either."

The two draks brainstormed for the rest of the afternoon but came up with nothing that appealed to both of them. Kale wished he had a reliable means of sending messages to his sister. She always had good ideas.

After dinner, they worked by lamplight for a few more hours before retiring for the night. Kale was pretty proud of what they accomplished. The home he and Kali established was a far cry from the single room with bunks he shared with his sister in Drak-Anor. As he drifted off to sleep, entwined with his mate, Kale found himself redefining home. *Maybe staying here wouldn't be so bad after all.*

***

As Pancras traveled east with the Golden Slayer, Edric, and Qaliah, the days grew longer and warmer. Lush green meadows and fields sprouted with the first crops of the year, nurtured by the showers of spring. Qaliah and Edric passed the time regaling each other with outlandish stories Pancras was certain were mostly lies or embellishments.

For the first few days after leaving the fort, Gisella interrogated him about his death experiences. She wanted to hear the whole story about how the shadow demon bonded with him. Pancras explained what he knew to have happened. As to how the shadow demon bonded with him and the exact nature of their relationship, he could offer only suppositions and speculations.

After hearing the same story for the third time, Gisella seemed satisfied and changed the subject to theology. She was particularly interested in his views on Aita, especially in light of his post-mortem encounter.

"I'm not sure what else I can tell you." Pancras rubbed Stormheart's neck as they strolled alongside their mounts. "Looking back, I see many signs that might lead one to conclude I was supposed to be a bonelord all along."

Nickering and tossing her head, Moonsilver yanked the reins from Gisella's hand. She leapt to retrieve them again before her horse could escape. "Perhaps you're only being made to think that now that you've chosen to devote yourself to her fully."

Pancras conceded the possibility. Having died twice, though, he didn't want to push his luck. "Signs and portents. As reliable as they are unambiguous. And what of the Golden Slayer? Faithful of Aurora? That's not what they call their priests, but it seems quite devout... unusual for a Watchmaiden."

"It's true. Most of my people prefer Hon or Tinian, even Maris for some of the more aggressive settlements." Gisella smiled and fished in her pouch for an apple. "But, I too, had a vision."

"I doubt you had to die to see it." *Twice.* Pancras chuckled. He tightened his grip on Stormheart's reins as his horse snatched at the apple that Gisella offered in her hand to Moonsilver.

"My sister and I were both very popular in our home village. Some might say we were the beauties of the town."

Pancras nodded. There were many features of humans minotaurs found downright unattractive, the lack of fur, flat faces, tiny button noses, but Pancras encountered enough humans during his formative years to understand what they found appealing and agreed Gisella was attractive by human standards.

"Of course, we loved the attention. We were known to use it to our advantage, even. After a particularly passionate evening—" Gisella's face flushed, and she laughed. "Oh, he was so eager to please but so demanding afterwards." She shook her head.

"What happened?"

"Like I said, it was a passionate evening, and we slept in each other's arms, exhausted. Maybe it was the mead and the heat in the sweat lodge, but the dream was more vivid than I'd ever had. Aurora came to me that night. She told me of our grandmother, who she actually was."

"You didn't know before?" Pancras stopped, waiting until after they mounted their horses before he continued.

"I knew she was a sorceress of some renown, but the details? No." Gisella patted Moonsilver's neck as the mare tossed her head and snorted. "Our mother confirmed what Aurora told me. Alysha and I consulted with seers, sages, and as many priests as we could find, and we formulated a plan: I would come north and seek out rumors and signs of our grandmother's intentions while she stayed safe in the south. She was the one with arcane talents. We felt it would be best if she stayed far away from anywhere the Lich Queen was likely to appear."

"She always stayed north of the Celtan Forest, if I recall my histories." It had been years since Pancras read those accounts, and the exploits of a dead conqueror didn't interest him much in those days.

"Yes, her armies made it into Cardoba, almost to the Wizard's Rift, but only as far south as the lake. Anyway, Aurora seemed like she would help us, and since I love the company of men, I figured there were certainly worse gods to whom to devote myself." Gisella laughed. "Aurora doesn't demand sacrifices of blood. Tithes are low, and worship…" She chuckled again. "Well, you can imagine what holy days require."

Pancras felt his face grow warm. Familiar with the sort of ceremonies in which the priests of Aurora engaged during holy days, he couldn't imagine a fierce warrior like the Golden Slayer indulging in that sort of debauchery.

"We make quite a pair, you and I. A minotaur-would-be-Bonelord of Aita and an Aurora-worshipping slayer of the Arcane University, on a gods-given quest to destroy the Lich Queen. Or at least, stop her from returning to this world." He chuckled. "It sounds ludicrous, does it not? I only left Drak-Anor to pay the delinquent dues of my guild membership!"

"We should hire a minstrel to follow us and chronicle our quest." Gisella grinned. "If we've gone mad, their songs will bring laughter to people for generations. If not, then we'll be legends!"

***

Delilah spent her days in lessons with various masters. As a result, her repertoire expanded. She studied with Katka most of the time, though after destroying her third cauldron, Katka was expelled from Alchemy. Fortunately for Delilah, Conner functioned as a suitable replacement, helping the drak retrieve reagents and beakers from upper shelves in Master Agata's laboratory.

In the evenings, Delilah spent half of her time carousing with Katka and Conner and the other half visiting with Kale and Kali when she found time to leave the campus. She carried the grimoire of Gil-Li with her wherever she went as a reminder to study it. It seemed like ages since Delilah had so few responsibilities, though, and the drak sorceress made the most of it. She enjoyed the attention she received whenever she visited the undercity, as well, and bestowed blessings. Regardless of their effect, they seemed to cheer the draks she encountered there.

Each time she visited Kale and Kali, their progress in cleaning up and fixing the old storefront they had purchased surprised her. Because her time there was limited, she was unable to examine in depth the runed circle and the library.

"I hope I'll have more time to visit my brother after my Novice Trials." Delilah pulled a chair up to the table where Katka and Conner were eating. The drak heaped food on her plate, then dug in with relish.

Conner was quick to disabuse that notion. "After the trial, you'll be apprenticed to one of the masters. Everyone seems to think you're the archmage's pet, so it'll probably be him. I'd be shocked if he lets you go off and do research for days at a time."

Delilah shrugged, poking at a sausage on her plate. "Maybe a giant will eat him, and I won't have to worry about it."

Katka swallowed a mouthful of roasted potatoes. "What happened with him and the archduke? Didn't he have a job for you or something?"

"I think he forgot about it. I hope he forgot about it." Delilah stabbed the sausage, squirting hot grease across the table.

"Don't count on it." Conner refilled their mugs with ale.

"He's got something funny going on with the archduke." Delilah took a long drink of her ale. She hated politics. "Have you heard anything?"

"No." Conner looked at Katka and then at Delilah. "Why would we?"

Delilah forgot people in large, human cities like Muncifer didn't have a direct access to the leaders like she did in Drak-Anor. She tried a different tack. "Doesn't matter. What's the deal with the giants in the mountains? I heard the city has some sort of agreement with them?"

Katka laughed. "You think we hear anything about that? My parents have a livery outside of town. We don't hear any news that doesn't come from a traveler buying a horse."

The drak sorceress stared at Conner.

"Don't look at me. My parents might have heard something before they died, but no one tells me anything."

Delilah groaned in frustration. "You guys are useless!" It was obvious her friends were not of the same social status as she enjoyed back home. *Are the draks and minotaurs in Drak-*

Anor just as ignorant about Sarvesh and the council as these two humans are about their leaders?

Conner choked, wolfing down sausage, bread, and ale in succession. After Katka pounded him on the back, he waved his hand, signaling for her to stop.

"What's the hurry?" Delilah wiped up some ale he spewed onto the table.

"I just remembered I'm supposed to meet Marta tonight." He waggled his eyebrows. "She wants to practice with me." He seized another hunk of bread before dashing away from the table.

Katka rolled her eyes. "Marta, Marta, Marta… she's all he talks about ever since he met in her Master Renata's conjuration class."

Delilah heard echoes of her feelings toward Kali. "That reminds me, there's a test in Master Renata's class tomorrow. Are you ready?"

"No. I'm never ready." Katka helped herself to another piece of bread.

"You'll do all right. You just need to believe in your own abilities." The girl memorized the words, but she always doubted herself.

"Easy for you to say." Katka leaned close to Delilah and lowered her voice. "People are saying you're a prodigy."

"I am not. I just have decades more experience than all the other students." Over the last several weeks, Delilah took Master Galina's advice to heart and stopped showing off so much. She reminded herself that the students were all just beginners, and it really wasn't fair to them that she was placed in the same classes with them. Neither she nor the masters chose it; however, the archmage decreed it, and none of the masters felt it was worth fighting him on the matter.

"Most of them don't understand that, though."

"Then they're idiots." Delilah felt a twinge of guilt as soon as the words left her mouth. She glanced around the room to see if anyone had overheard her, although it seemed no one else in the Arcane University's tavern paid her and Katka any mind.

Delilah shook her head. "Let's go, Katka. I'll help you practice for tomorrow."

***

The next morning, Kale and Kali planned to take Taavi and Blackclaw on a ride around Muncifer. They decided to also bring Fang along for some exercise even though Delilah couldn't join them. A trip through the fields and meadows surrounding the city would take most of the morning. The sun shone in a sky dotted with scattered, puffy clouds. As he locked the front door on their way out, Kale noticed a hooded drak standing in the shadows of an alley across the way.

He nudged Kali. "Do you know him?"

"No." Kali drew one of her daggers. She approached the alley. "Don't you have someplace more important to be?"

The drak shook his head as a grin spread across his face. "I'm right where I want to be. You and the winged striper are mates, yeah?"

Already, Kale didn't like where this conversation was headed. Drawing one of his daggers, he stood beside Kali. "I'm Kale, and Kali is my mate. What do you want?"

"Boss Steelhand sent me. He thought you might not know about the rules we have around here." The drak pulled back his cloak and fingered the hilt of a sword. His dark blue scales seemed black in the shadows of the alley.

Kale spread his wings and widened his stance. "What rules? We bought that old shop fair and square."

"Sure you did. From the humans, right? The thing is…" The drak licked his lips. "Down here, we all answer to Boss

Steelhand. You want to have a shop, you have to give the boss his due."

Kali waved her dagger under the drak's chin. "Oh no. We're not paying protection to anyone. We're not even selling anything!"

"Is that so?" He prodded the tip of Kali's dagger with his finger until he drew blood. He licked the bead of red off his finger. "Maybe it doesn't matter. Maybe the boss wants his due from you, no matter what. Your sister comes down here, raising a big stink about how she's going to save all these worthless cretins from their oppression. The boss doesn't like that. You might say he gets nervous when others start moving in on his territory."

"My sister is all talk. She doesn't want his territory. She just wants the crowds out of her way." Kale did not believe this was all about Delilah's little displays.

"Maybe so, maybe no." The drak shrugged. "The boss gets his due, or the boss gets angry. When the boss gets angry, things get ugly. Understand?"

Kale understood the cloaked drak's message. He spat a glob of flame at the drak's feet. Steam hissed where the fire licked a muddy puddle. "We're not giving you anything. The boss wants something, the boss comes to see us himself."

The drak chuckled before pressing his foot into the flame, extinguishing it. "Suit yourself. I'll give him the message."

After he turned away from them, he disappeared into the shadows of the alley. Kali sheathed her dagger. "That must be one of the thieves the magistrate warned us about."

"I'm not paying them a damned thing." Kale turned his back to the alley, taking his mate's hand. "We're not selling anything. They don't have any reason to come after us."

Kali hooked her arm into her mate's. "They think they do. That's all the reason they need. We should probably be sure we're ready to deal with them when they come knocking."

For years, Kale spent his days and nights building traps and weapons to hold back armies. Securing his own home would be child's play compared to that. When they came, he would be ready.

***

Delilah didn't expect to see so many students in Master Renata's classroom. She searched for a vacant seat among the rows that descended toward the stage of the amphitheater. Most of the students she recognized from other classes and from wandering the university, but only a fraction attended the class with her and Katka. Arranged upon the stage were a variety of empty cages with arcane markings on their floors; cages to contain the creatures the students would summon to prove proficiency in conjuration.

"Quiet down!" Master Renata entered, her blue robes swishing about her legs like a frothy sea, her silver hair tied into a tight bun at the back of her head. As she studied the room, her face became drawn and angry.

With many bodies piled into the room in close proximity, the room felt hot and stuffy. Delilah considered giving up her chance at the test would be worth the comfort of the cool breeze outside.

Master Renata's eyes scanned the assembled students. "Where is Novice Delilah? Come down here."

A murmur circulated the room. For a moment, Delilah remained still, not expecting to be called first. The instructors never called on her first. Katka pushed on her arm.

Delilah worked her way through the seats to the aisle and then descended to the stage. "Yes, Master Renata?"

The conjuration master waited until Delilah joined her on the stage. "Now then, I have heard rumors aplenty that you are a prodigy. A student so gifted you put all these others"—

Master Renata gestured to the room above them—"to shame. What say you?"

Delilah felt her mouth become dry, like she'd eaten a dozen cotton balls. "I am not a prodigy. I have decades of experience."

"Exactly!" Master Renata spoke more to the room than to Delilah. "Experience! This student"—she gestured to Delilah—"is here because of the capricious whims of the archmage, not because she's innately superior to you. As an experienced wizard, she could probably teach this class."

Another murmur raced through the room. Delilah felt a knot form in her stomach. She licked her lips with a tongue so dry it felt like sand.

"So"—Master Renata faced Delilah—"you are excused from this test and from further instruction in the basics of conjuration."

Delilah fought to keep from staggering backward. Master Renata's declaration openly defied the archmage's instructions. She bowed to the master.

"However, you are still my student during this time, so you will work for this leniency. Go to the library." Master Renata leaned in close and lowered her voice. "Study the *Rose Concordat*, Novice. You will find answers there you are unaware you seek."

Since her arrival, Delilah wanted to spend time exploring the university library, but until now, she had not been afforded the opportunity. She bit her lip to keep a smile from overtaking her face and bowed again, even though in her heart, she felt she could jump up and fly from the room. She bowed a third time and climbed the stairs of the aisle, nodding to a beaming Katka as she passed.

"Now then, let us continue with today's tests. Novice Aleks, please come down here."

Master Renata's apprentice, a young woman with whom Delilah was not acquainted, though she'd seen the woman within the university, stopped the drak sorceress before she left the hall. "You'll need this"—she handed Delilah a small scroll—"in case anyone asks why you're not in your designated class."

Delilah unrolled the paper. It was a note penned in the precise hand of Master Renata explaining that Novice Delilah was conducting research for her and should be allowed full access to the library and university grounds.

The drak sorceress grinned and nodded in gratitude to the apprentice. *Things are looking up, Deli-girl!*

Chapter 16

Warmer days didn't make riding in the rain any better. Gisella appreciated the rain pinging off her helmet and armor making it almost impossible to hear Edric's complaints about being wet. Distant thunder added to the cacophony.

The rain did little to dampen Qaliah's spirits, but Edric's grumbling and his ignoring her jibes did. The fiendling rode next to Gisella, both of them following Pancras and Edric. Where bare earth was visible, it became redder and redder the farther east they traveled. Soon, they would approach Curton, a town once famous for its copper mines, now barely known for its red-clay mud and pottery.

They approached the spur off the road that led to Curton. Gisella considered diverting there to spend a few days in a proper inn and to give Edric and Qaliah a chance to leave the party. A week's journey would complete the final push to Cliffport, and once there, she and Pancras planned to board the first ship to Vlorey.

With luck, they would arrive in Vlorey before the Dusk of Autumn Festival.

"This damned rain." Qaliah gazed toward the sky and shook her fist at the heavens. "Damn you, Nethuns! You're supposed to keep your water in the oceans and rivers."

"Once we're on the sea heading toward Vlorey, you'd best keep a tight rein on your blasphemies." Gisella chuckled as Qaliah wiped the rainwater out of her eyes.

"The gods aren't going to listen to me." Qaliah pulled her hood up and slumped in her saddle. "We're all thieves and liars, don't you know?"

Gisella was well aware of the reputation fiendlings suffered, particularly in the south. The fewer of them there were in an area, the less people thought of them. Most of the fiendlings Gisella encountered were thieves out of necessity;

stealing was preferable to dying of starvation because no one would hire them.

"You're only saying that because you're wet and miserable." Diverting to Curton sounded better and better the more she thought about it.

"And you're not?" Qaliah's sidelong glance at Gisella revealed her opinion on the matter.

"I didn't say I wasn't. It's coloring your perceptions." Gisella saw hope in the distance, a break in the clouds. Even where they stood, the sky was lighter than it had been all morning. The sun threatened to break through and end the miserable rain.

"My per... ceptions are the same damn color they've been since you kicked my naked ass out of bed back in Rock Ridge."

Gisella cringed. Until now, Qaliah kept any resentment she had about that particular situation well-hidden. "I wish we could move beyond that. While I acknowledge you're very attractive, I prefer more masculine company."

"Yeah, yeah." Qaliah slowed her horse, allowing Edric and Pancras to increase their lead. She maneuvered Comet closer to Moonsilver, then reached over to touch Gisella's arm. "Sorry."

"No need to apologize." Gisella squeezed Qaliah's hand. "You didn't know my preferences until you asked. It was unfortunate everything turned out so awkward."

"Not about that." Qaliah shook her head and moved their horses apart when Moonsilver nipped at Comet. "The outburst. I'm in a bad mood because Edric is so grumpy. There's no hard feelings. You like men? Fine, me too. I have no problem with that. My mouth runs, you know. I'm sorry."

A crack of thunder drowned out Gisella's reply. She waited until the reverberations faded. "Quite all right. Perhaps we'll divert to Curton for a day or two to dry out and enjoy real beds. We should be only a few days out now."

"A bed? What's that?" Qaliah grinned and spurred Comet to catch up to Edric and Pancras. "Hey, this crazy woman is talking about roofs over our head and beds. Do either of you have any idea what she's talking about?"

Gisella laughed. If nothing else, this motley collection of travelers was entertaining.

***

Kale realized something was amiss when he and Kali returned from their ride around the city. The street their home was on was usually deserted, but somehow, it seemed even more so. He drew his daggers as he approached the door and cursed himself for not cleaning the front window better. The encrusted dirt created a diffuse light inside but made viewing what was beyond the glass, in either direction, impossible.

"All right, killer. Put the pig-stickers away, I didn't break into your house."

The drak spun toward the voice. A minotaur stepped out of the shadowed alleyway where Kale and Kali confronted the drak earlier in the day. The sunlight made his black fur appear streaked with grey in spots, and the light reflected off his metallic right hand.

"I'm not a burglar."

"You must be Boss Steelhand." Kale neither lowered his daggers nor relaxed his stance. The minotaur stood at least twice as tall as he, but he wouldn't be the first minotaur Kale fought and beat.

"And you really have stripes. Huh." Boss Steelhand sniffed and nodded in appreciation. "I figured it was war paint or something when they told me. No wonder everyone is up in arms."

"What do you and your thugs want?" Kali stepped across the street, brandishing her dagger. She was careful not to cross directly in front of Kale. If the minotaur decided to attack, he'd have to make a choice.

"Right now? I just want to talk." The minotaur gestured toward Kale and Kali's home. "Why don't we step out of the street and have a civilized conversation, huh? I can see you two aren't stupid, and you've obviously fought at each other's sides before. But I'm not stupid either. You don't think I came alone?"

Kale felt a shiver run down his spine. He saw no one accompanying the minotaur and assumed he actually did come solo. He lowered his weapons. "Fine. You can come in, but just you."

Boss Steelhand held up his hands. "That suits me."

Kali kept her blade at the ready. "Don't get any funny ideas."

"I hear you got a sister, but this one"—Boss Steelhand jerked his head toward Kali—"don't have any stripes, so I'm guessing she's your mate?"

Kale grunted a non-committal reply as he unlocked the door and ushered everyone inside. Boss Steelhand hunched over to avoid gouging the low ceiling with his horns. Kale checked the alley and street, but he did not notice anyone else who appeared to be interested in the events unfolding in their shop. The only person he saw was the potato-pushing minotaur at the far end of the street.

He shut the door behind them and locked it. The storefront still didn't have any furniture, just bare walls, the shop counter, empty shelves, and the hallway leading back to the living quarters. Kali positioned herself between Boss Steelhand and the back of the building.

Boss Steelhand leaned against the counter. "Cleaning this place up must have been a lot of work. I'm impressed."

Kale sheathed one dagger, but he continued to hold the other one. "My mate asked you a question. Time to answer."

"Folks think I run the undercity." Boss Steelhand picked his fingernails. "It's not true. The undercity is part of Muncifer, and the Council of Lords run Muncifer. They make the laws, they control the guards. But, most minotaurs and draks were pushed down here years ago, and someone has to watch out for them."

Kali scoffed. "I suppose that's you?"

"Sometimes." Boss Steelhand shrugged. "I gotta earn a living, you know? I hear about someone setting up shop, claiming to be the savior of the draks, the one who will deliver them, from what? I don't know. I need to check it out."

"I'm not here to deliver anyone from anything!"

"If you're here to set up shop, you gotta give me my due. Plus, a lot of the merchants down here pay good money to make sure they're the only game in town." The minotaur looked around and chuckled. "It looks like you're just selling air though, which any fool can get for free."

Kale paced the floor until the minotaur finished ranting. "I'm killing time until my sister finishes her business with the Arcane University. Then we're leaving. Probably going back home to Drak-Anor." Kale didn't reveal all the details about Pancras and possibly going to Vlorey instead of Drak-Anor.

"Your sister, yeah." Boss Steelhand stroked his chin with his flesh hand. "The one who's been going through the undercity handing out blessings like candy. Telling everyone she's this great and powerful sorceress."

Kale watched a glare flash across Kali's face, but she masked it before Boss Steelhand noticed. He rubbed his snout. "She is a sorceress. She brags. We have stripes, so what? Prophecies aren't real." Kale wanted to throttle his sister. In her absence, he settled for flinging one of the brooms to the floor.

"Everything was going real smooth until you two showed up." Boss Steelhand pointed at Kale. "Now you, I hear you've been trying to lay low. I can appreciate that. Your sister needs to stop riling up the draks. They don't need the agitation."

"Can you blame them?" Kali put her hands on her hips. "Being forced to live down here where all the scum from the upper city washes down whenever it rains."

Boss Steelhand spun on Kali. "You don't know anything about it, sister. The fact is, the draks are down here for their own protection. Out of sight, out of mind and all that."

Kale rubbed his temple. "What are you talking about? Protection from who? You?"

"Ha!" The minotaur threw back his head and laughed. "No. Don't get involved in city politics, little draks. You'll be happier. You just tell your sister to stop stirring the pot."

Kale threw up his hands. "I can't! I can't enter the Arcane University to tell her, and I don't know when she's able to come out for a visit. By the time she arrives here, she's already given out hundreds of her 'blessings.' I don't get what the big deal is; she's just talking. It's not like she's using magic charms"

"Can't get in, eh?" Boss Steelhand stroked his chin as he chewed on his lip. "All right. I believe you. Do you know why?" He didn't wait for Kale to answer. "Because you're going to do some work for me. I can get you in the Arcane University."

Kale ignored Kali's shaking head and sighed. "What do you want me to do?"

"It's a simple job." Boss Steelhand reached across the small room, put his hand on Kale's shoulder, and pulled him close. The steel hand of the minotaur gripped like a vise. "You take a package and deliver it to the Arcane University. You'll receive a pass to go in. Drop it off, and you take your time leaving again. They're not going to worry about a courier wandering around as long as you don't go poking your snout into every laboratory and library."

Boss Steelhand's job did sound easy. *How bad can carrying a package be?* Courier work was one of the jobs he'd discussed with Kali earlier.

"He's not going to smuggle your stolen goods for you!" Kali pulled Kale away from the minotaur. Her dagger was still free of its sheath but not quite pointed at the minotaur.

The minotaur placed his hand on his chest and took a step back. "I have legitimate business with some of the guild mages. We don't smuggle anything into there they don't want."

Kale noticed Boss Steelhand didn't refute the smuggling claim. He glanced at his mate. Her eyes smoldered. He didn't have much of a choice. He didn't want trouble with Boss Steelhand or his thugs, but he didn't want to pay protection money for any reason, and he needed to meet with his sister and convince her to stop her grandstanding.

The drak slumped his shoulders and nodded. "Fine. I'll deliver your package."

***

"What are you doing here? Don't you have classes?" Seneschal Lyov looked up from the tome he was examining.

Delilah handed him the note. "I'm doing a special project for Master Renata."

He glanced at the note before returning it to Delilah. "Fine. Do you see this?" He held up the book sitting on the table in front of him. "This means 'do not disturb.' Understand?"

"Yes." Delilah left him to his studies and gazed in wonder at the floor-to-ceiling shelving filled with books, codices, and scrolls. The ceilings were twice as tall as Pancras, and each row of shelves had a rolling ladder on rails to aid wizards in reaching books on the upper shelves.

The library was arranged in sections by subject matter, each in its own room. Texts dedicated to natural sciences like biology, anatomy, and geology were organized into one area. Metaphysical texts like those concerned with alternate planes of reality, portals to the fae realm, or treatises on the gods could be found in another room. History books, law books, and tomes on magical theory all each occupied separate sections. Delilah even noticed books of poetry and lore.

Where would the Rose Concordat *be?* Delilah started with the law section. The *Rose Concordat* contained the rules by which the Mage's Guild was organized, but she knew little of what else might be contained therein. Engrossed in her search, she nearly stepped on a man flipping through a publication from his seat on the floor.

Novice Ludek glowered for a moment as she stumbled over him, but he reached out to steady her. "I see you passed your Initiate Trials, Drak."

"Weeks ago." She smoothed her robes. Delilah still didn't like wearing them, but at least the new ones didn't irritate her scales.

He pointed toward the shelf behind where he was seated. "Need something from here?"

"I don't know. I'm looking for the *Rose Concordat*."

"Go back out." Ludek pointed to the main hall. "It's on a pedestal in the center of the room. Don't remove it from the pedestal, understand? You'll probably need to stand on a chair to reach it. Sorry."

Delilah thanked Ludek and followed his directions. The pedestal towered over her. *No wonder I didn't see it.* The drak sorceress searched for a chair to drag over. However, the screeching of the legs across the stone floor as she lugged it turned heads. She cringed, cursing to herself and left it to tiptoe back to the pedestal.

She pointed her staff at the chair. *Time to put those classes to work, Deli-girl.* "*Ehpipléon soe'ma.*" Raising her arms, Delilah hissed the incantation through clenched teeth, careful not to raise her voice in the somber confines of the library. She drew on her conjuration skills to do the heavy lifting, albeit, she had not mastered levitation easily. Master Valyrian compared her style to that of a hammer, admitting that sometimes a hammer was the proper tool for a job but also noting that often a fine set of watchmaker's tools was more appropriate. Although the chair wobbled, nearly slamming into the pedestal, she set it down in a spot close to the codex.

As she climbed into the chair, she heard soft applause behind her. Seneschal Lyov clapped and bowed his head in deference. Chuckling, Delilah turned to the *Rose Concordat*. Its binding was thick, rough, primitive even. The codex, bound between two leather-covered planks of wood, predated the Sundering, written in the Age of Legend.

Delilah marveled at how well the *Rose Concordat* weathered the last thousand years. Tomes like the Grimoire of Gil-Li were preserved by the magic contained within them, but the *Rose Concordat* was not enchanted; it was simply a book of rules.

The binding creaked as she opened it, and she realized she knew not what she sought.

***

"Have you gone mad?" Kali slammed the door behind Boss Steelhand after the minotaur exited and then spun on her mate.

At least she waited until he left. Kale took Kali's hands, but she pushed him away.

"I'm making an effort not to become involved in any capers, crimes, or shady activities, and you practically invite them right into our home!"

"Look, Kali, it's the best way to get in to see Deli and get her—"

"I'm your mate, Kale!" Kali pushed past him and stormed into the living quarters. "I'm supposed to rate higher than your sister!"

Kale felt a twinge of guilt at the accusation he favored one over the other. He followed Kali to their bedroom. "It's not about that—"

"Of course it is! It always is! You bought this place so your sister would have a place to stay and for the stuff in the cave below. You made a deal with that minotaur so you could see her again." Kali clenched her fists but trembled as she yelled. "You should have mated with her!"

Kale cringed and scuffed his foot on the floor. She spoke the truth, even if he felt she blew things out of proportion. "I was trying to make things easier for us. I didn't want to pay him anything, and we're not trying to cause trouble. I need Deli to see that she's making our lives harder. Ours, Kali. Not just mine."

Collapsing onto the edge of the bed, Kali grasped her head with both hands. "You don't see it, do you?"

"See what?" Kale sat next to her, spreading his wings and enveloping her within one of them.

"Boss Steelhand warns us not to become involved in local politics, but don't you see? Involving ourselves with him is being involved in local politics. This isn't like me working shady deals to free my people from a salt mine. This city has something going on that we don't need to be involved in." Kali took Kale's hand. "I did my part. I just want a quiet life now. With you. Draklings. Friends and family."

"I want that, too." Kale laid his head on Kali's shoulder. "But the draks here, they're our people, too. If we can help them, shouldn't we?"

"Oh!" Kali grunted in frustration and hung her head. "That's the damnable misery of it, isn't it?"

Kale sympathized with Kali's worries about them getting in over their heads, but he already felt like his head was underwater. "I want to help my sister, but I don't want you mad at me. I don't know what I'm doing, really. What should we do?"

"We'll do it together."

"What?"

Kali pushed Kale's head off her shoulder, then faced him and placed a hand on his cheek. "We'll do this job for Boss Steelhand together. After we've convinced your sister to stop the drak messiah nonsense, we're going to come back here and convince all these draks that we're just plain draks, like them. We are going to gain control of this situation."

It sounded like a good idea, but Kale wasn't just a plain drak, and anyone with eyes could see that. Plain draks possessed neither wings nor stripes, and he had both. It would be difficult to convince the thousands of draks in Muncifer that generations of stories were false. It gave him an idea, though.

"Maybe we should talk to that drak with the broadsheets?" Kale struggled to remember his name. "He can help us spread the word."

"Now that is a good idea." Kali nuzzled him. "We'll talk to him after seeing your sister."

They sat together in silence for a while before Kale decided it was time to meet with Boss Steelhand's contact and fulfill their obligation. "He's had enough time to get to where he was going. Let's do our part."

They made their way to the Stone Maiden where Boss Steelhand stated their contact would be waiting with the package. Characteristic of Muncifer weather, rain clouds from the mountains moved in since they returned from their morning ride. Half of the time, the storms passed over without emptying their clouds. Kale hoped this would be one of those times, though he brought his hat and pulled it down over his head.

Navigating crowds in the upper part of the city was always a tricky affair for the draks. Humans and minotaurs often did not notice those smaller than themselves. For Kale and Kali, today was even worse. They were nervous about their task, and every screech of a child, every dismayed shout, and every whinny of a horse resisting its master seemed extra alarming.

As usual, no one paid the two draks any mind. In front of the statue gracing the Stone Maiden, a man bounced from foot to foot and licked his lips nervously. He held no package visible to Kale.

"Is that our guy?" Kali pointed at the nervous man.

Before Kale could answer, the man met the striped drak's gaze. As he approached, his eyes darted this way and that. "You're the first drak I've seen with wings. Must be the one I'm looking for."

Kale checked the perimeter to confirm no one observing them. "Boss Steel—"

"Yeah, yeah. We all know who we're working for." The man reached into the folds of his cloak and produced a strongbox the size of Kale's fist. "You're taking this to the elf master. Don't know his name, but he's the only elf there."

The box felt light, almost weightless. Kale wondered if there was anything at all within it.

From a pouch hanging from his belt, the man withdrew a brass seal. "Take this. It'll identify you as a proper courier." He licked his lips, before he darted away, disappearing into the crowd.

Kale handed the seal to Kali. "I guess that's it."

She examined the seal before stowing it in her pouch. "What do you think is in it?"

"It feels empty." Kale shook the box. He didn't hear anything rattle or move within. "I have no idea. Let's just find the recipient and hand it off."

They passed half-a-dozen street vendors selling aromatic meats and prepared dishes that made Kale's belly grumble. He wanted to stop off for an ale or mead and answer his stomach's summons for food, but he needed to see this task through. A few merchants called out to him, complimenting his hat, vying for his attention, but Kale ignored them all.

When they arrived at the gates to the Arcane University, two guards stood watch, leaning on their halberds. Kale thought they might be the same guards who were posted the last time he tried to visit.

One held up a hand to stop them. "No visitors. Keep walking, little drak."

Kali held up the seal. "We're couriers. We have a delivery for the elf master."

One guard eyed the other before taking the seal. After examining it, he returned it to Kali. "Fine. Master Valyrian is…" He looked at his counterpart. The other guard shrugged. "No idea. He's the only elf in there. Ask someone in grey or brown robes. Don't bother the other masters."

After the guards opened the gates, the two draks entered the Arcane University. Kale gazed at the variety of buildings surrounding the courtyard. They resembled the buildings in other sections of Muncifer, though perhaps were a bit more colorful. The large tree shading most of the courtyard with its canopy of brilliant crimson leaves reminded him of the World Tree at Drak-Anor, albeit much smaller.

"This is it?" Kale looked at his mate and shrugged. "I don't see what the big deal is."

A group of students rushed past. Kale and Kali jumped backward to avoid being trampled. Certain that finding the elf wizard would be impossible unless he was outside, Kale tried to appear nonchalant. He didn't want to risk too much scrutiny by asking everyone they came across.

One of the novices noticed the two out-of-place draks and approached them. "Are you supposed to be here?"

"We have a delivery for the elf." Kale hoped that was specific enough.

"Oh, Master Valyrian." The novice bit his lip and looked behind him. "I think he's… oh, there he is. Over there by the Initiate Quarters." The novice pointed at a sprawling, half-timbered stone building. It was difficult for Kale to see over the heads of all the students milling about, but he thought he saw a tall, slender person speaking to one of them.

"Thank you." Kale and Kali bowed to the novice, then hurried across the courtyard, keeping the elf in sight. As they hastened closer, Kale was sure the man was the elf whom they sought. His mossy-green hair and nut-brown skin was a sure giveaway, even if the tips of his ears weren't poking through his hair.

"Master Valaran!" Kale cringed as he butchered the name, but it was enough to catch the elf's attention.

"It's Valyrian, yes? Oh!" The elf's eyes widened and his edges of his mouth curled into a smile. "A winged, striped drak! You must be Novice Delilah's brother!" His eyes searched the courtyard a moment before he knelt to meet Kale's gaze. "How did you gain entry? There is a strict no-visitors policy."

Kali held out the seal. "We have a delivery for you."

Kale handed Master Valyrian the box. "I was hoping to run into Deli, but I won't stick around if it will get her in trouble. I have an important message for her, though."

Master Valyrian took the box. "Ah! Yes, I have been waiting for this!" He hid the box away in his robes and pulled out his wand. "*Ageliofedros.*" A glowing, jade-green rabbit coalesced from magical tendrils.

"Fetch Novice Delilah, please. Tell her to meet me in front of the Initiates' Quarters straight away."

The rabbit clicked its teeth and hopped away. After sheathing his wand, Master Valyrian stood. "She should be along presently. Now you won't need to wander around, and if anyone complains, you're still making your delivery."

Kale rocked back on his heels. He had not expected any of the wizards to be helpful. "Thank you!"

The draks watched the novices and initiates in the courtyard as they waited for Delilah. Most were divided into small groups, talking among themselves. A few groups were far separated from the others, practicing illusory magic, and Kale heard periodic cheers erupt from a group firing arcane blasts at practice dummies on the far side of the compound.

They did not have to wait long for Delilah. She strode through the crowds with purpose, moving students aside with her staff when they stepped in front of her without looking. When she saw Kale, she broke into a run and squealed.

"Kale!" She dropped her staff, then wrapped her arms around him. After a moment, Delilah loosened her grip on her brother. After picking up her staff, she smoothed her robes, nodding to Kali.

"Well, now that you're reunited, I'm just going to step over there a moment." Master Valyrian gestured in the direction of the Blood Oak. "You can let yourselves out."

"What are you doing here?" Delilah regarded her brother and then Kali, confusion evident in her furrowed brow. "You're not supposed to be here!"

"We had a delivery for Master Valyrian. I thought I would say 'hi' while I was here."

Delilah's eyes narrowed. "What kind of delivery? From whom?"

"It was for Master Valyrian." Kali pursed her lips. "We didn't ask. It wasn't our business."

"Deli, look. The next time you're in the city—"

"What do you mean, you don't know? Do you know how—?"

"Deli! Let me finish!" Kale seized his sister's arm. "The delivery doesn't matter. He was expecting it, and it got us in. I have to tell you something."

Delilah scowled. "What? What?"

Kale took a deep breath. "You have to stop acting like you're the supreme drak when you come down into the undercity. You have to stop giving out blessings and acting like you're going to save everyone. It's causing us trouble."

"Serious trouble." Kali nodded, crooking her arm into Kale's. "Like gang trouble, okay?"

Delilah scoffed. "You're joking."

"We're serious, Deli." Kale squeezed his sister's arm. "They tried to shake us down and everything."

A dark cloud passed over Delilah's face. Kale needed to head off her temper before it flared. "It's all fine. We talked to them, and everything is fine. As long as you keep a low profile when you come visit. We're going to go talk to some of the draks around town to get them to help us convince everyone you were just putting on a show."

"What's all this about?" Delilah shifted her weight and looked at Kali.

"There's something going on between the draks, humans, and minotaurs in this town." Kali shrugged. "We don't know what it is, but we don't want to be involved. Kale needs to keep that library safe for you, and he can't do that if we're under additional scrutiny because a bunch of thugs think we're plotting to start a revolution."

"All right, all right." Delilah let the matter drop, but only temporarily. She would want solid answers, and at the first opportunity, she planned to push the issue.

Kale hugged his sister. "Everything is fine, honest."

"Yes, we just want to make sure we *stay* out of trouble." Kali patted Delilah on the shoulder.

Delilah nodded and sighed, squeezing Kali's hand. "Okay, fine. You'd better get going before we all end up in trouble."

Chapter 17

Delilah questioned the veracity of her brother and his mate's story. A mysterious delivery just to let them in and news that thugs were harassing them because of her all pointed to the exact opposite. She had more important things to worry about at the moment, though. Her brother and his mate were adults, and Delilah decided they needed to deal with whatever trouble there was on their own.

The *Rose Concordat* was a tough read. She stood upon a chair to view it, since moving it was not permitted. The codex contained several hundred pages of overly complex language, although she was surprised that much of the text was written in Ancient Drak. She found reading the archaic language required more effort and took more time than reading even the common trade language, because some concepts lacked direct translations, and some of the translated words lost their meaning in the Sundering.

That she could read for only an hour at a time and not every day added to her difficulty. Most of the masters did not excuse her from classes, no matter how much proficiency she demonstrated, and she found herself curtailing socialization time with Katka and Conner to make time to look at her grimoire. Thus far, it had yet to reveal anything new to her. *If only I could spend a few days with it.*

A few days of free time were not in her future. The next several weeks her course work required her full attention and concentration. She found her classes on evocation basic and far below her skill level. Alchemy, protective magic, and enchantment classes provided worthwhile instruction, though. Delilah discovered her skill at enchantments and charms lacking, but Katka excelled in those. Each novice helped the other in developing proficiency in deficient or weak areas. She recognized making charms would never come as easily to her as summoning fire or whirling clouds of blades, however.

End-of-spring rainstorms rolled in from the mountains, turning the courtyard into a muddy morass. The days were warmer now, and even in the rain, Delilah felt comfortable. The heat and humidity slowed some of the more manic students, but the drak sorceress enjoyed it. For a brief time, Delilah allowed herself to hope the archmage had forgotten about her.

Her freedom from the archmage was short-lived, however. On the eve of Artume's Feast, an early summer hunter's festival, the archmage summoned her to the Court of Wizardry. When she arrived, she noted, none of the high wizards were in attendance.

Archmage Vilkan sat as straight as a marble column in his chair, drumming his fingers on the armrest as Delilah approached. Dark circles under his eyes made him appear more sinister than usual as he gazed at her from beneath lowered brows.

"Novice Drak, I appreciate your punctuality."

Delilah held her tongue, bowing.

"You will apply for the next Novice Trials scheduled. I have need of your undivided time, and the court won't allow that until you are my apprentice." He scratched a spot on the armrest of his chair, looking past Delilah before returning his gaze to her.

"I have indulged Master Valyrian long enough. You are here at my decree, and your penance for a lifetime of being a renegade is service to the Mage's Guild at my pleasure."

Delilah bit her tongue until she tasted blood. She did not intend to serve at the archmage's pleasure for the rest of his or her life. She noticed the archmage looking behind her again and heard the doors open. A novice holding a scroll trotted past. The archmage gestured at Delilah, and the novice extended the scroll to her. Delilah took it without turning her head toward the novice.

Archmage Vilkan waited until the novice left. "Find out when the next Novice Trials are, put your name on the lists, and then take this scroll to the archduke. Part of your Novice Trials will be dealing with him. Be courteous and give measured responses to his questions. You will be representing the Mage's Guild and the Arcane University in this matter."

"What matter?" Delilah remained silent no longer. *What is he blabbering about now?*

"The archduke will explain what he needs of you. Go now." The archmage dismissed Delilah with a wave of his hand. "Return when you've finished the archduke's task and have completed your Novice Trials."

Delilah left the archmage to his thoughts and searched the courtyard for Master Galina. She, over anyone, would know details about the Novice Trials schedule. She found her working with a group of initiates by the practice dummies. Delilah waited by the reviewing stand until she caught the older woman's eye.

"You need something, Novice?" Master Galina paused her lesson and stepped over to the reviewing stand.

"The archmage wanted me to put my name on the rolls for the very next Novice Trials. When are they?"

Master Galina rubbed her forehead. "He sent you to put your own name in?" She sighed. Delilah noticed her lips moving as the master counted to herself in silence. "It is three days hence. I hope you're not wasting my time."

Delilah placed her hand on her chest and bowed. "I promise you I am not, Master. We all do the archmage's bidding, yes?"

"Yes"—Master Galina pursed her lips, cocking an eyebrow—"so it seems. You may go now, Novice. I have lessons to teach."

After bowing again, the drak sorceress left Master Galina to her students. She shifted her pack as she left the compound and considered if it might be better to leave her grimoire at her brother's. However, the proximity of Grimstone Keep to the Arcane University made a detour to the undercity impractical. Sighing, Delilah girded herself for a hike through the midday crowds.

***

"So? What happened?" Jairo sat on the edge of his chair, listening with rapt attention to Kale's story. Over the past few weeks, Kale had related the story of the foundation of Drak-Anor in exchange for his help in calming the draks in the undercity.

Kale was at the part of his tale where Delilah had just been swallowed whole by the warlock-turned-dragon and he swooped in to save the day on the back of Terrakaptis.

"SPLURCH!"

Jairo recoiled at Kale's exclamation, tumbling backward in his chair. Kali seized his hand just before he fell over, then pulled him upright.

"The warlock exploded! Delilah used her whirling blade spell, I don't know what it's called, while in his stomach, and carved him up from the inside out!"

Kali and Jairo grimaced.

Kale nodded with a grin. "It was nasty. Blood everywhere. I thought she was dead, she thought I was dead, and we almost killed ourselves racing through the gore to get to each other."

"Hey, hey! Maybe you two already fulfilled your destinies as Children of Destiny!" Jairo waved his quill at Kale. He reached over to his desk to dip his quill in the inkwell. Then he scribbled some notes.

"Maybe. Look, Terrakaptis said that prophecies are just stories made up by old men trying to make sense out of the world. Anyway, there isn't a prophecy that says anything about us." Kale wished he could snap his fingers and convince all the draks in the world to stop believing the prophecies about Children of Destiny.

"I've heard the stories, too, Kale." Kali stepped behind her mate's chair to put her arms around his neck. "They're not specific. They all just say striped draks are special and will have great purpose in their lives."

Kale looked up at her. "Yeah, those are the same stories that say draks hatched from the same egg have to be exposed and left to die, right?" If he and Delilah hadn't been hatched with stripes, that would have been their fate. Even with their stripes, their clan exiled them as soon as they were old enough to fend for themselves.

"Well, yes." Kali squeezed him.

"So, how do you decide which parts of those stories you're going to accept as truth and which you're just going to ignore?" Kale held up his hand and looked at Jairo. "You want to say I'm special because of my stripes, but you ignore the same story that says I'm cursed because I was hatched from the same egg as my twin sister. I choose to ignore both parts. My sister and I are muddling through life, doing the best we can. Just like everyone else."

Jairo jotted down a few more notes. "Okay. What happened after that?"

"That's enough for today, Jairo." After stepping around Kale, Kali snatched the grey drak's quill from his hand, then set it on the desk. "I'm hungry. You can hear more stories later."

Kale stood and stretched. Jairo scrambled to secure the papers lying on his desk as the air from Kale's wings stirred the room.

"All right. Thank you." He clasped Kale and Kali's hands. "I've already spread the word, and the next broadsheet is going out tomorrow. Hopefully, they'll start making a difference."

"I hope so." Kale tired of the townsfolk's gawps and murmurs. Not for the first time, he wished he could send a message to Delilah. Her last message to him stated she was scheduled for her Novice Trials, but she didn't expect she would be released from service to the university any time soon.

He and Kali made their way home. They stopped to buy a pair of rabbits from a butcher stall. Though he still heard whispers and felt stares from the other draks, Kale chuckled for a moment. His life was so mundane now compared to how it was in Drak-Anor. While part of him longed for another adventure, part of him was content. He smiled at his mate as they returned home.

"What?"

"A year ago, Deli and I were running around Drak-Anor, fixing defenses and doing other odd jobs for Sarvesh. Now"—he extended his arms—"I have my own home in a city leagues away with a mate. It's surreal."

"Well, don't go wishing for too much. I think we're just enduring a calm before the storm, you know?"

Kale understood what she meant. Even if the draks treated him like one of their own, rather than a fabled outsider with a special destiny, there was still the undercurrent of conspiracy to which Boss Steelhand alluded. Kale decided he had two goals: keep Kali safe, and keep the library and moon gate safe for his sister. *Maris can take all the rest.*

***

The passages of Grimstone Keep were just as cold as Delilah remembered. She considered the possibility that an enchantment made the keep feel cooler than the outside air. However, after passing the third lady garbed in a high collar who pointed her nose upward upon her approach, Delilah decided it was more than the mountain air that kept things chilly.

Archduke Fyodar did not keep Delilah waiting. The drak sorceress was ushered into the room where the archduke sat in a gilded throne. Unlike other royal seats Delilah had encountered, Fyodar's was not raised on a dais but was situated behind a large, polished, cherry wood desk. Guards were stationed throughout the room, and the archduke was attended by a minotaur wearing deep-blue robes.

Delilah waited in front of the desk until the archduke acknowledged her. She stood, eyes level with the top of the desk, wondering if he noticed her presence, until she observed him regularly glance in her direction.

"The archmage sent you, did he?" Archduke Fyodar looked up at last and gestured to the minotaur. "This is my advisor, and Court Wizard, Theros."

The minotaur bowed his head toward Delilah. His black fur was flecked with grey at the tip of his muzzle, and Delilah noticed he wore gloves, unusual for a wizard. He regarded the archduke. "He sends a novice?"

Delilah tossed the scroll she carried onto the archduke's desk. "He bade me deliver this."

"This is the same drak that was with me on the battlements during the last incident with the giants." The archduke unrolled the scroll. "Get her a stool or something."

One of the guards left the room and returned after a few moments with a stool upon which Delilah could stand. It was only one step higher, but now her entire head appeared above the desktop.

Archduke Fyodar handed the scroll to the minotaur. "What's his game, Theros?"

After reading the scroll, the minotaur placed it on the desk. "No idea, Your Grace. Perhaps this little drak can tell us."

Delilah shifted her grip on her staff, wishing people would stop referring to her as "little drak."

The archduke tapped his chin as he regarded Delilah. "I wonder… do you think this novice is privy to the working of the archmage's mind?"

"I can tell you, I am not." Delilah saw no reason to play coy with the archduke.

"He refers to her as his apprentice in the letter." Theros raised his eyebrows. Delilah gritted her teeth.

"Guards, leave us." The archduke stood, gesturing to the door. The guards shuffled out of the throne room, closing the door behind them. The archduke nodded to Theros.

"*Sphraira tees alistheias.*" Azure strands swirled through the air, forming a sphere that started at the wizard's right hand and expanded to encompass the desk, the throne, and all three of them.

Delilah recoiled as arcane energy washed over her. She recognized an enchantment when she felt it, though she did not understand the exact nature of this particular one. Gripping her staff until her knuckles were white, she chewed her bottom lip to keep from retaliating, an act most people would describe as stupid.

"All right." The archduke reclined in his chair. "The three of us stand within an enchantment field created by Theros. Anyone in this field must speak the truth. So, tell me, Novice Drak, what are you feeling right now?"

Despite remembering to use diplomacy and carefully chosen words, she blurted out the direct answer to his question. "Aita take you both for enchanting me with a truth spell. And my name is Delilah, not 'Drak'!"

Theros chuckled. "I'd say it's working."

"Indeed." The archduke steepled his fingers in front of him. "Tell me, Novice Delilah: why does the archmage call you his apprentice in this letter, and what is his plan?"

Delilah desired to tell them both where they could go with their questions, but she was compelled to answer. "He thinks he's going to claim me as his apprentice after my Novice Trial. That's all I know of his plans."

"What makes you so special that the archmage has you all picked out already?" Theros leaned on the desk, bringing his head closer to Delilah. "Besides your stripes."

A flicker of confusion crossed the archduke's face, but it vanished before Delilah answered, "I don't know."

The archduke opened his mouth to comment, but Theros held up his hand to stop him. "Why did you come to Muncifer?"

Delilah twisted her mouth in an effort to keep silent, but she could not resist the enchantment. "To pay my guild dues."

It was not a secret Delilah felt she needed to hide. She was simply determined to fight the enchantment as much as she could, no matter how banal the questions.

"That doesn't make sense." Theros looked at the archduke and then Delilah. "If you're still a student, you don't have guild dues."

The archduke cleared his throat. "If you're a student, why did you come here to pay dues? Where are you student at?"

"I'm not a student; there aren't any Arcane Universities anywhere near Drak-Anor. I was told that I was a renegade, and if I didn't pay my dues, they'd send slayers after me." Delilah scratched the back of her leg with her foot. She wished to be anywhere but here at the moment, but she reflected that this encounter was less painful than the last time the ruler of a city questioned her.

"Indulge me a moment, Your Grace." Theros's mouth twitched into a smirk. "How do you rate your skills compared to your fellow novices?"

Delilah tried to comprehend the reason behind the minotaur's question. Still, instead of laughing at him, as she wanted to, she was compelled to answer, "I have over twenty years of practical and battlefield experience; I could be teaching them."

Theros straightened up. "Yet the archmage wants to claim her as an apprentice and puts her with the rest of the students?"

"This makes no sense." The archduke gestured at Delilah. "What makes this drak special to him? And why in the name of Maris's bloody spear does he want her leading the expedition to the giant's village?"

Delilah failed to conceal her surprise. "He what?"

"I don't know, Your Grace." Theros turned to Delilah and wrung his hands. "What do you know about the giants in the mountains?"

"Nothing. They live there?"

"What are you thinking, Theros?" Stroking his beard, the archduke eyed his advisor.

To Delilah it was obvious as she observed the minotaur clenching his teeth together that he wasn't prepared to answer that question under a truth spell. He fought against the compulsion for a moment before replying, "The archmage has always been interested in what's under the mountains. Perhaps, he thinks these draks are his key to controlling it."

Draks? What draks? Me and who else? Delilah decided to use the truth spell to her advantage. "What other draks are you talking about?"

The minotaur's reaction told Delilah the truth spell again worked against his wishes. She heard him stomp a hoof on the floor. "The other striped drak living in the undercity. Your brother, I believe."

Kale. He knows about Kale.

"So, this drak has a brother?" The archduke held up his hand. "Before we go further, let's make sure we're not being too foolish. Novice Delilah, with whom do your loyalties lie?"

"My brother, as well as Pancras, first Wizard of Drak-Anor, and Sarvesh, Lord of Drak-Anor."

"Admirable." The archduke nodded. "What is your opinion of Archmage Vilkan?"

For once, Delilah chose not to resist the spell. "He's a pompous, arrogant, smooth-skinned waste of flesh."

Theros laughed. "Good enough for me."

"Me as well. Theros, what do you think the archmage is up to, and how does this drak fit into it?"

"I think, he believes Pyraclannaseous slumbers beneath the mountains, and the giants with whom we recently had a treaty are her guardians. He knows draks are dragon kin and will use her and her brother to broker an agreement with the dragon for his own gain."

Delilah stared at Theros. She was certain this was not the conversation the archmage thought would occur after she delivered that note. "Who is Pyraclannaseous?"

"Pyraclannaseous, the Fire Dragon, Firstborne of Rannos Dragonsire and Gaia."

"Pyraclannaseous"—Delilah's heart skipped a beat—"Terrakaptis's sister?"

Theros raised his eyebrows. "You know the lore of the Firstborne? Your progenitors?"

Delilah remained truthful, despite her reluctance to reveal the breadth of her knowledge to Theros and Archduke Fyodar. "Some of it, yes."

Terrakaptis mentioned many times how he intended to seek out and awaken his siblings, but thus far, the Earth Dragon had done nothing but tell stories and sleep.

The archduke leaned forward. "You think the archmage intends to use this drak and her brother to broker a deal with the dragon?"

My brother... Kale has that brand. Delilah decided to keep quiet about her brother's relationship with Terrakaptis. "The archmage does not know about my brother. I think. One of the other masters does, but he doesn't seem to like Manless much."

Theros eyed the archduke. "This could be to our advantage. Novice Delilah's brother is keeping a low-profile deep in the undercity. If the novice here"—Theros nodded at Delilah—"keeps her head down and plays dumb about dragons, we could deal with this situation once and for all."

Delilah fought to keep her expression neutral as she regarded Theros. *How does he know what Kale is doing?*

The archduke cocked his head as he eyed Delilah. "We need to ensure her loyalty. Very well. No threats, Novice Delilah, no bribes, no honeyed words." He nodded to Theros. "Tell her everything."

⋈ ⋈ ⋈

Curton sat nestled in the hills, bisected by a river. Numerous watchtowers dotted the stone wall that surrounded the city. Guards paced the battlements between two cylindrical towers on either side of the road at the city gate. The gate itself, little more than a pair of large, iron-banded wooden doors, was protected by a pair of ballistae on the towers above it.

Apparent from his vantage point on top of a nearby hill, Pancras noted the decay of the city. Parts of the outer wall had crumbled, though the wall's base seemed sturdy enough. The rain that dogged their steps much of the time since leaving the fort behind them had taken its toll on Curton. Wagons and carts traveled the only avenue available to them: a muddy path with ruts deep enough to turn the ankle of the heartiest horse.

"This place is a garden spot, huh?" Qaliah snorted.

"It was once a thriving mining hub. Since the mines dried up, all they have left is mud. Pottery from Curton is very good, though." Gisella spurred her horse and rode through the grass that grew alongside the road.

Pancras followed on Stormheart and heard Qaliah and Edric descend the hill behind him. He agreed with Qaliah's assessment, but any bed they had would be better than yet another night on a bedroll under the stars.

He caught up to Gisella at the bottom of the hill. "What do you know of this city?"

"Just what I've already told you. It is past its glory days."

From where they stood, Pancras noticed the rusted, iron banding on the city gates, which were splintered and peeling. In stark contrast, the guards standing watch wore crisp tabards over their mail. They snapped to attention when a senior guard stepped out of the gatehouse to inspect the wagon of a merchant seeking entrance to the city.

Compared to a merchant's wagon bogged down in the quagmire that served as a road, four travelers on horseback were of little concern to the guards. After cursory questioning, particularly of Qaliah, the four travelers were waved through the gate. One of the guards directed them to The Drunken Horse, the inn and tavern nearest the gates.

To their delight, The Drunken Horse also featured a stable. After unsaddling and securing their mounts, they made their way into the tavern proper. The great room of The Drunken Horse reminded Pancras of The Bloody Spike back in Drak-Anor. A massive bar of warm, polished wood ran the length of the room, and dozens of round tables covered the floor between it and the stage that ran the length of the other side. A grand double staircase dominated the rear of the room, and at its center stood a pass-through hearth.

Behind the bar, doorways led to the kitchens. Two humans, a man and a woman, waited tables in the half-full tavern, while two older women worked behind the bar. Edric and Qaliah claimed an empty table near the door while Gisella arranged for rooms and a delivery of ale and mead to their table.

Pancras did not usually spend much time in taverns, but he found the drone of conversation and aroma of roasting meat wafting from the kitchens comforting after enduring so many uncomfortable weeks on the road. Edric and Qaliah seemed in better spirits once the ale and mead arrived and were soon trading jibes and tall tales again.

Gisella quaffed a mug of mead. "We'll spend a few days here. Wash off the grime of the road, see if there's any news from Cliffport, and relax a bit before striking out again."

"How far is Cliffport?" Pancras sipped from his mug. The mead possessed a floral nose with a hint of spice on the finish.

"Three days, northeast. We'll cut across the hills until the river doubles back. Then we'll follow it to the end."

"Three more days on the road and then the high seas!" Qaliah raised her mug, laughing. Blanching, Edric drained his mug before motioning to a server for a refill.

Pancras felt a flutter of anxiety about boarding a ship to sail up the coast. Edric's pale face betrayed his apprehension about the matter. Pancras didn't fear water, per se, but his knowledge of ships and being on the water was limited to what he heard from stories. *I hope I do not spend the entire voyage ill.*

"Harvest will be upon us by the time we arrive in Vlorey. Perhaps even the start of winter." Gisella leaned back to allow the server to place the meal she ordered on the table. Surrounded by a variety of roasted vegetables, a roasted leg of lamb with crispy golden skin lay in the center of the platter. Pancras's stomach grumbled in anticipation at the aroma of juicy, smoked meat and savory spices.

"I've heard the high seas are fraught with dangers: sea serpents, sea devils, whirlpools, and pirates." Qaliah's eyes sparkled, and the upturned corners of her mouth wrinkled the skin around her eyes.

Pancras's stomach fluttered again. "Then we shall implore the gods for an uneventful voyage."

"Where's your sense of adventure?"

"I'm with the minotaur on this one." Edric stabbed a potato with his fork, then bit into it. "Maybe I'll just stay here. I've already seen more dwarves around here than I have the last several months combined."

Not for the first time, Pancras found himself defending his desire for boredom. "Adventure? Desperation, discomfort, and danger? I never look forward to that. The trip here from Muncifer was adventure enough for me, thank you."

Gisella pointed at Qaliah with her knife. "And no fraternizing with the sailors. If any of them feel slighted or wronged, we're going to be trapped with them for better or for worse."

The fiendling sneered, wrinkling her nose. "Fine." She looked over at the dwarf. "You have to come with us. How are we to pass the time?"

"You're smart. Figure it out. You ain't getting me on the ocean."

"I'm sure we'll figure something out." Gisella sliced a hunk of roast for herself.

Of that, Pancras was certain. Whatever they decided, he hoped it would involve keeping a safe, low profile during the ocean voyage.

***

By the time Delilah returned to the Arcane University from Grimstone Keep, darkness had fallen over the city. Her mind reeled from all that Archduke Fyodar and the minotaur wizard Theros revealed to her. She cursed herself for somehow becoming involved in another dispute between the ruler and those who would be rulers.

"You've done it again, Deli-girl." Delilah paid no heed to passersby who with both concern and bemusement regarded the drak talking to herself. "In over your head, in between two rocks about to smash together."

"Damn it!" She kicked a loose cobblestone, skipping it across the street. The guards at the Arcane University gates nodded in acknowledgement as she passed between them. Despite hunger gnawing at her stomach, Delilah returned to her quarters and opened her grimoire. She had neglected her personal studies in favor of jumping through hoops for everyone else, so to calm her mind, the drak sorceress decided to indulge in a selfish pursuit.

Weeks and weeks of practice amidst the other students of the university enabled her to tune out the others in the area. As a result, coaxing the grimoire to come alive for her once more took less time than she expected. The familiar scenes of Gil-Li the Graven annihilating armies on a devastated battlefield, filled her mind.

Tendrils of aether swirled around Gil-Li like a kaleidoscopic whirlwind of rainbow serpents. The tattoos etched into her scales flared, and fire burst from her body. The flames grew in intensity, swirling until they formed a humanoid shape. Gil-Li pointed toward her enemies, and the furious fire creature dove into the fray, igniting those near it and incinerating those it touched.

The scene shifted. Gil-Li stood at an endless expanse of shore. Waves crashed against the rocks, and Delilah tasted the salt spray of the ocean. Gil-Li's tattoos glowed with arcane energy, shining like a beacon in the night. Ships rocked on the surf in the distance.

Creatures rose up from the water at Gil-Li's bidding and rode the ebb current. The creatures pummeled the ships, their watery fists as battering rams against wooden hulls.

When they were finished, the ships sank, claimed by the sea, and the creatures dissolved, becoming one with the water from which they were formed.

Delilah's mind raced. She'd seen Gil-Li's creature of earth before. Now, she witnessed creatures of fire and water. It nagged at her. Only one element, air, remained. The scene dissolved, scattering like a sand sculpture in a tempest. The drak sorceress heard a snapping noise in front of her, but she saw nothing that would have caused such a noise.

"Delilah!"

The drak sorceress's eyes snapped open. Katka stood beside her, clicking her fingers in the drak's face.

"Wake up!"

Delilah slammed her book shut. "I wasn't asleep! I was concentrating!"

"Oh." Katka stepped back, her face reddening. "I'm sorry."

Delilah's ire faded. The young woman couldn't have known.

"I've never seen someone reading with their eyes closed before."

"This is an arcane grimoire." Delilah traced the pattern on the cover with a clawed finger. "You don't really read it as much as you open yourself up to it and experience it."

She returned the book to her pack. "Anyway, I was just trying to take my mind off some things. The archduke and the archmage have me stuck in the middle of their power plays, and all I want to do is learn some magic and go home."

Delilah pulled the pack onto her lap and wrapped her arms around it. She rested her head on top of the pack, sighing. Not for the first time, she considered fleeing with Kale and Kali. When the challenge was a pack of oroqs charging the city gate, Delilah was prepared and able to act; however, when it involved navigating a political swamp, she feared she would stumble into a sinkhole that would suck her down to oblivion.

"Anyway, what do you need?"

"Master Galina is looking for you." Katka glanced over at a group of initiates who burst into laughter. "Since your Novice Trials are three days from now, she wants to make sure you're not wasting her time."

Delilah clenched her jaw, narrowing her eyes. Katka picked her fingernails and shrugged. "Those were her words."

The drak hopped off the bed. "So much for my free time." She clapped Katka on the shoulder as she passed, then sought out Master Galina in the practice yard. She hoped to spend the next three days deep in her grimoire. At the very least, she expected demands from other wizards to lessen until her test. *Once the archmage apprentices me, I bet they'll all leave me alone.*

Chapter 18

A few days' layover in Curton provided the perfect opportunity for Pancras to search for a suitable weapon. The morning star he found in the fort was adequate, but it was made for a human. A more suitable weapon would be one designed for a minotaur's height and reach.

Most of the smiths in town forged weapons from iron imported from dwarven mines in the mountains south of the city and showcased their wares in stalls in the marketplace. The ringing of hammers on metal mixed with the drone of conversation as Pancras and Gisella walked the cobblestone streets of Curton. The drying mud caking the cobbles diminished the farther from the gates they trudged. Curton was a city of mostly humans, though he spotted more than a few dwarves and draks. He seemed to be the only minotaur, however. To his surprise, his appearance rated only a few cursory glances. The people of Curton seemed to be all about minding their own business.

"Have you decided yet what kind of weapon you seek?" Gisella examined a broadsword while the smith prattled on about the virtues of his dwarven steel.

"I'm getting too old to learn fancy sword play"—Pancras lifted the morning star he brought for comparison—"so something like this, but better built for minotaurs would be ideal."

"Nothing like that here." The smith shook his head, glancing at Pancras. "Piotr likes to make ugly weapons. His shop is behind the sausage tent."

Pancras thanked the smith and left him to his other customers.

"Do you think Edric is serious about staying behind here?" Pancras clasped his hands behind his back as they walked. He towered over most of the people in Curton, a distinct advantage when navigating the crowded market.

"He's made his dislike of water clear. Come to think of it, I have never heard of a dwarven sailor." Gisella pointed at the large tent where ropes of cured meat dangled like curtains. Clanging, which emanated from the building behind the sausage tent, indicated the presence of another smithy.

"Go on ahead; I'm going to see if there are any cured meats to tide us over until we arrive in Vlorey." Gisella entered the sausage-maker's tent, leaving Pancras alone to shop for his weapon.

The smith working behind the sausage tent was a mountain of a man. Muscles like knotted rope flexed as he hammered away at a glowing bar of iron. Sweat poured down his brow, soaking into bushy eyebrows, which matched a salt-and-pepper beard that would do the mightiest dwarf proud. The odor of perspiration mixed with brimstone made Pancras's eyes water.

He glanced up when Pancras cleared his throat. When he frowned, his eyebrows came together in the middle of his forehead like two fuzzy kissing caterpillars. "Whatchoo wont?"

Pancras didn't understand the smith's quick and slurred greeting.

The minotaur held up his morning star. "Are you Piotr? I'm looking for something like this, but more suited to my size."

"I got what you see." The smith gestured to the racks on the walls, then resumed his hammering.

Were he in Drak-Anor, Pancras would commission a weapon, but forging one from scratch would take weeks, more time than they could afford to spend in Curton. Piotr's broad-bladed swords seemed more suited to chopping than for light-footed swordplay. His axe-heads covered with ornate etching and fretwork were equally broad. There was artistry in the brutality of his weapon designs, and Pancras wondered if he'd been trained by a dwarf.

Next to the rack of swords and axes stood a rack of hammers. They didn't look like weapons, per se. They seemed like the types of hammers used by builders and crafters. Above them, on a display set off from the other tools, hung a spike-backed hammer with a head as large as four sledgehammer heads put together. The entire weapon, knobby face and all, appeared to be forged from a single piece of red-tinted steel. Pancras felt a longing well in his heart, a sensation he recognized as coming not from within, but from his connection with Aita.

He reached up and grasped the weapon, lifting it from its mount. It was heavy but felt balanced in his hand. The haft was long enough for him to wield with two hands, yet as he gave it a practice swing, he discovered that one hand would suffice if need be. Pancras noted unfamiliar runes carved into the head of the weapon. He thought they appeared Dwarvish in nature, but he had not previously encountered this particular dialect.

"How much for this one?"

Piotr glanced up from the blade he formed from a bar of iron and grunted. "Shatterskull. Figures. Not for sale."

"Shatterskull." The name could not be more perfect. Pancras would not be deterred by the first refusal. Many merchants intending to haggle would refuse a sale on the first attempt as a matter of course.

"If it is not for sale, why is it with these other weapons? You indicated these were what you had for sale." Shatterskull felt at home in Pancras's hand.

Piotr slammed down his hammer on the blade he was working. "Not for sale to you, minotaur."

Pancras understood. Piotr didn't have a sentimental attachment to the weapon; rather, he just didn't want to sell it to a minotaur. He would not be deterred. "It's a gift. For a friend."

"Ha!" Piotr plunged the glowing steel into the forge and worked the bellows. "Many fine axes here. Pick one of those instead. Make you good deal."

Pancras would not argue the merits of Piotr's fine axes. "Shatterskull calls to me."

"Shatterskull needs someone worthy. Someone with a just cause." Piotr wiped his hands on his apron, leaving the half-formed blade to heat in the forge. He walked over to Pancras and reached out to grab the maul from the minotaur's grasp.

Emerald lighting played over Shatterskull's head when the smith touched it. Pancras felt the power of Aita flow into the weapon, transforming the runic carvings into the relief of a red skull. Piotr recoiled, releasing Shatterskull. The weapon's head reverted to its original appearance.

"Sorcery!" Piotr took up his smith's hammer and held it above his head, poised to strike. "You'll not ensorcell me. Guards! Guards!"

"Aita has made her will known." Pancras regarded Shatterskull in wonder, heedless of Piotr's words. He felt her power infusing the weapon, knowing it pleased her. He heard shouts of alarm from the marketplace outside, but he was too engrossed in the sensation of power coursing through his body to pay it any mind.

Piotr's beard quivered with every shout for the guards. The power coursing through the maul faded. Reluctant to part with Shatterskull, Pancras stood there, shoulders slumped, and waited.

Gisella arrived from the sausage tent at the same time as a dark-skinned woman with hair pulled back in tight braids. She rested her hand on the hilt of her sword, which hung at the hip of her gleaming plate armor. Through scowling eyes and pursed lips, the woman regarded the standoff between the smith and the minotaur.

"What is going on here?" The woman spoke like a native of the area, though her skin color told of more northerly origins.

"I can't leave you alone for five minutes!" Gisella's tone conveyed exasperation and amusement. She hefted a sack full of dried sausages over her shoulder.

"Lady Aveline! This minotaur put a spell on me! He seeks to rob me!" Piotr pointed an accusing finger at Pancras, even as he continued to hold his hammer in an attack-ready position. Pancras marveled that his arm remained steady for the duration.

Lady Aveline closed her eyes and took a deep breath before turning toward Pancras. "In public, no less? A bold move. Foolish, but bold."

Pancras licked his lips. "I did no such thing. I am a Bonelord of Aita, and my goddess made her will known when this man refused to sell me this weapon. I am more than happy to provide fair compensation for his craftsmanship." He raised Shatterskull for her examination.

"A bonelord? Really?" Lady Aveline raised her eyebrows, but she didn't break Pancras's gaze. She stood about the same height as Gisella, and she wore her armor the way a noblewoman at court wore a gown. The clasp of her blue cloak bore the seal of the City Watch of Curton.

"M'lady?" Gisella bowed her head. "I travel with this minotaur and can vouch for his status."

"And she consorts with robbers!" Piotr's voice rose an octave.

"Quiet, Piotr." Lady Aveline rubbed the bridge of her nose with a gloved finger. "Who are you? Both of you."

"Gisella Jorgandottir, the Golden Slayer, from the Arcane University in Muncifer." Gisella placed her free arm across her chest and bowed.

"Pancras, Bonelord of Aita, First Wizard of Drak-Anor." Pancras tilted his head toward Lady Aveline.

"A wizard-cum-bonelord and a slayer." Lady Aveline dropped her hand to her side and sighed. "Why were you trying to enchant poor Piotr?"

"I wasn't." Pancras stared at Shatterskull. No matter how much he concentrated on the maul, he couldn't make it transform again.

"Piotr, tell me what happened."

"I told him he couldn't buy it, and he used his foul magic on me." The smith lowered his hammer at last, backing away from Pancras.

"I need more details than that, Piotr. What sort of magic did he use on you?"

"The maul"—Piotr gestured with his smith's hammer—"He gave it a face! A terrible face… He means to devour my soul with it!" The smith again raised his hammer to strike. Lady Aveline moved to intercept it, then she pushed the smith backward with a hand.

"I do not know what gods you venerate, or even if you believe they can show their will in such direct ways." Pancras rubbed his right horn as he spoke. "The skull our good smith saw was a sign from Aita. I will gladly compensate the smith for this weapon. Fine craftsmanship deserves payment."

Lady Aveline's nostrils flared when she pursed her lips. "Why are the least popular gods always the biggest showoffs?"

Pancras blinked. "What?"

"Piotr, think for a moment." She placed her hand on the smith's shoulder. "If this minotaur truly is a Bonelord of Aita, and the Princess of the Underworld gave a sign, don't you think you should avail yourself of this opportunity?"

Gisella nudged Pancras, and leaned in close, lowering her voice. "You might have some work to do here."

Pancras didn't understand her insinuation. Bonelords sought out and destroyed rampaging undead and death cults. Sometimes they were called upon to help the suffering cross over, but he knew nothing about smithing.

"What do you mean?" The smith's narrowed eyes darted from Lady Aveline to the minotaur and back.

"Your mother, Piotr."

The color drained from the smith's face. He stammered, staring at his feet. Pancras was not sure what the guard intended for him to do with Piotr's mother. He held up his hand. "I don't know that I can do anything. I'm not a healer."

Piotr mumbled something unintelligible. Lady Aveline turned to Pancras. "She's afflicted with an illness Apellon's healers cannot cure. She lingers and suffers. Her mind is gone, yet"—she glanced at the smith—"Piotr and his wife still care for her. It is a most unfortunate situation."

Gisella placed her hand on Pancras's arm. "One for which a bonelord is called."

Pancras gulped. In his heart, he realized he wasn't ready for the most sacred of bonelord responsibilities—ending the suffering of the dying, a fine line between that and murder. He breathed in deeply and did something he had never done before.

He offered a silent prayer to Aita for guidance.

***

An insistent yipping at the foot of his bed awakened Kale. Through bleary eyes, he saw a glowing blue boggin hopping near his feet. When it noticed he saw it, it stood still.

"Mistress Delilah wants me to inform you that her Novice Trials are in two days. She wants you to meet her at The Stone Maiden tomorrow at dusk." The boggin disappeared in a puff of blue smoke.

After rolling over, Kale woke Kali, then exited the bedroom. Stifling a yawn, he poked at the coals in the cooking hearth. After coaxing the fire to life, he threw a couple of bangers into a skillet. The sausages danced in the pan, sizzling and popping, as Kale shook it over the fire.

Banging at the door interrupted the preparation of their meal. Kali shuffled to answer it while Kale finished cooking. A minute or two later, she returned, leading a familiar drak with broken horns and dark blue scales.

"Tell him what you told me." Kali plopped into a chair at the table, then buried her head in her hands and yawned.

"Boss Steelhand wants another meeting." The drak sniffed the air, wrinkling his nose at the sausages Kale was cooking.

"Why? We did his job. He doesn't need anything from us." Kale dumped the sizzling bangers onto a plate, then slid it onto the table.

The drak shrugged, turning his head to glance around the room. "It's not my place to question the boss. He's coming here around midday. You'll be here if you know what's good for you."

"Fine." Kale found he had little patience for Boss Steelhand's thuggery this morning. He spat a ball of fire at the drak's feet. "Get out."

The drak squealed, hopping from foot to foot to avoid the conflagration. He scampered away before the flames flickered out.

Chuckling, Kali picked up a sausage. "You should do that every time one of those creepers comes around."

"I wonder what he wants this time. I don't want to work for some crime boss." Kale's teeth pierced his sausage with a snap as he bit down.

"Tell him no, then. I'll back you up."

"I know you will." Kale thanked Rannos for the fortune of Kali watching his back. He didn't want to wander too far from home while waiting for Boss Steelhand, as midday was not an exact hour. He gave fleeting consideration to run errands and have the minotaur wait outside an empty house, but in the end, Kale chose against antagonizing him.

While they waited, Kale and Kali busied themselves with cleaning decades of dust and grime from the bookshelves and stairs that led to the moon gate chamber. Reluctant to touch any of the tomes for fear of damaging them, he used a small brush he acquired from one of the local merchants to whisk away the dust from the spines of the books.

Together, they finished the top third of the staircase by the time they heard someone knocking on the door. Kale placed his cleaning gear on a nearby shelf. "At least he knocks."

"He's polite for a crime boss." Kali, closer to the top of the stairs than her mate, beat Kale to the door. Boss Steelhand smiled, bowing when the draks opened it.

"You didn't have to clean for me, little draks. I've been in far dirtier places."

Kali stepped aside to let in the hulking minotaur. "We weren't doing it for you."

"How did you hot foot my messenger, by the way?" He leaned against the counter to keep from scraping his horns on the ceiling. "I assume it wasn't magic because that would make you a renegade."

"I can breathe fire, like a dragon. It came with the wings." Kale crossed his arms over his chest. "What do you want?"

"Huh. I want to hear that story someday." He held up his hand to stifle Kale's retort. "That's not why I came here. I have a proposition for you."

"No."

Boss Steelhand laughed. "You haven't even heard it yet."

"We don't need to." Kale looked at his mate for confirmation. Kali hooked her arm in his and nodded in agreement.

The minotaur rubbed his chin. "Won't be any risk to you, and you won't have to do any work to get paid."

No work and get paid? Kale was forced to admit the concept piqued his interest. He glanced at Kali. Her eyes darted under raised brows to meet Kale's.

"All right. I'm curious. What's the proposal?" Kale pointed at the minotaur. "I'm not saying yes!"

Boss Steelhand chuckled. "I know you've been talking to Jairo, so I don't know why he came to me instead of you. His cousin is a limner and needs to set up shop. Jairo doesn't have room, but you"—the minotaur gestured to the empty storefront—"you have plenty of room."

"What's a limner?" At first, Kale thought it must be someone who made or sold lims, but he didn't know what those were, either.

"Have you seen those fancy books with gilded pages and pretty pictures in them?"

Kale shook his head. The lexicon his sister had was little more than a list of words, and her grimoire gave him a headache whenever he looked at it. Books were in short supply in Drak-Anor.

"You mean like nobles and priests are always cooing over?" Kali cocked her head.

"Yeah, well, a limner does all those fancy decorations. They call it 'illuminating.' People pay good money for that. Jairo's cousin does the work here, deals with the customers here, and pays you rent."

The proposition sounded mundane and harmless. Kale narrowed his eyes. "What's the catch?"

Kali grunted. "The catch is Boss Underhand here gets a cut and keeps an eye on us."

Boss Steelhand chuckled. "Underhand... never heard that one before. I do get a cut, from his profits. Not from you. I needed a vacant space, and yours was the first one to come to mind. Of course, if you're planning on actually doing something with this storefront, well, that's another conversation we need to have."

"We need to think about it." Kali nudged Kale before he could respond.

"Fine. Don't take too long. I'll send someone by tonight to get your answer. If you haven't decided by then, I'll find someplace else." Boss Steelhand bowed as low as the cramped storefront allowed and then let himself out.

Kale locked the door behind him. "It sounds too good to be true."

"It's not free money." Kali watched Boss Steelhand stroll away through the cloudy window. "He'll have an inside drak watching us the whole time the shop is open."

Kale didn't understand Boss Steelhand's interest in him. It was yet another item to add to the list of odd occurrences revolving around the draks and minotaurs in Muncifer.

***

Gisella stood watch in the smithy with Lady Aveline while Pancras entered Piotr's home. Like many merchants, Piotr lived in rooms built above his workshop. She heard Pancras's hooves clop on the stairs out back as the minotaur ascended to the living quarters.

Lady Aveline leaned against one of the support columns in the smithy and wiped her brow with a rag from one of her pouches. The air felt as hot as an oven to Gisella.

"What brings a slayer and a bonelord to Curton?" Lady Aveline stuffed the rag into her pouch. "What trouble is brewing in my town that requires the two of you to travel together?"

Gisella shook her head. "We're merely passing through. We have mutual affairs in Vlorey."

"Passing through on the way to Cliffport, then?"

"That's right." Gisella decided to indulge her curiosity. "What leads a northerner to become a guard in Curton?"

"Captain of the City Watch, and that's a long story."

Gisella glanced up at the ceiling. It was quiet in the smith's home, but she supposed that was to be expected. Dignified deaths were often quiet. "We appear to have plenty of time."

The left corner of Lady Aveline's mouth turned upward. "I have no desire to open myself up to a transient. You come, you cause some trouble, and you go, never to be seen in these parts again."

The Golden Slayer regarded Lady Aveline for a moment and clenched her jaw to keep her mouth from falling open. She didn't think of herself as a transient, but the guard captain was right about one thing: it was likely Gisella would never return to Curton. Her reply was cut short by the arrival of another guard.

"Lady Aveline!" The stocky guard panted to catch his breath. Wisps of unruly black hair poked out from under his helm. "Trouble in Danica's Den!"

Lady Aveline pushed herself away from the column and ran her fingers through her hair. "What sort of trouble requires you to race across town to seek me out?"

"Danica says she found a dwarf cheating, and there was something about a fiendling, and the whole place is up in arms. I think they're going to lynch her!"

Gisella felt her heart leap into her throat. "A dwarf and a fiendling?"

"Friends of yours?" Lady Aveline ushered the guard out of the store. Gisella moved to follow, but the guard captain extended her hand to stop her. "We can handle this. I'll be back to check on Piotr, and if I hear anything other than there was a positive outcome here, I will hunt you all down. Understand?"

"Of course." Gisella placed a hand on her chest and bowed. She watched the guard disappear into the marketplace crowd. Her first duty, of course, was to ensure Pancras made it to Vlorey. Running off to check on two people who may or may not be Qaliah and Edric did not further that aim. She passed the time by perusing Piotr's wares and praying to Aurora that the people in trouble were not the dwarf and the fiendling she knew.

With a trembling hand, Piotr pushed open the door to the bedchamber. The acrid tang of urine assaulted Pancras's nose as a breeze passed through the open window. The room was bare, save for a bed pushed against the wall under the window. The bedsheets, whether discolored due to age or by the person under them, stirred. A thin, gnarled hand reached out.

"She likes to look out the window." Piotr stepped into the room and held the door for Pancras.

Pancras held the maul low, at arm's length. Thus far, Piotr had not tried to take it from him again, but he saw no reason to remind the smith that the weapon he held was the one for which he had not paid. The minotaur stooped to keep from brushing his head against the low ceiling and stepped toward the bed. The stench worsened as he came nearer, and he discovered the source peeking out from beneath the bed.

"What's her name?" He pointed to the overflowing vessel. "Is there a reason the chamber pot is overflowing?"

"The boy's supposed to empty it." Piotr slammed the door. The shape in the bed yelped at the loud noise. "Mama's name is Nika."

"What is her affliction?" Pancras reached for the sheet, but a bony hand snatched the edge away from him. He chewed his lip, staring for a moment. Finally, he pushed some dirty rags under the bed with his foot in order to kneel on the floor.

"She complained of her bones hurting. Mama's always been strong, tough. But she's old. Old folks hurt in their bones on cold, wet days. My wife and the boy feed her. Change her bedding. I work. Make money to pay for the food and medicine from the apothecary… for all the good it does."

Pancras felt blessed not to have to live with that sort of pain, but encountered many minotaurs with similar complaints in their advanced years.

Piotr continued. "She got to be hard of hearing. Then she couldn't see. Started getting lumpy and twisted, like old, knotted wood, except hard, like rock. Healer didn't know. Couldn't fix her. Someone cursed her. I know it. It's an evil spell."

Pancras pulled back the sheet. Silvery-grey hair covered the top of the woman's head, thinning around the bulbous growth of the top of her forehead. Additional growths in her cheekbones squeezed her eyes shut, and she breathed through two holes that were once her nostrils. She wheezed a groan of agony through swollen lips. The minotaur shuddered at the grotesque countenance that turned to regard him.

He pulled his rod from his belt. He still needed it to summon arcane power since he had yet to attune himself to the weapon, though he wasn't sure that was necessary now. Tendrils of blue smoke swirled as he tried to sense sorcery at work. There was nothing, although his concentration intensified the sensation of power he felt in the maul.

"I sense no magic at work here, but this is unlike anything I've ever encountered."

"Dwarf magic. She was always fighting with dwarves."

Pancras doubted Piotr's conclusion. He slid his rod into its loop and shifted his grip on the maul. His stomach fluttered and his mind raced. Pancras placed the maul, head down, and gripped the shaft with both hands as he lowered his head. He felt his horns brush against the sheets, eliciting another groan from the woman.

He concentrated on the warmth he felt in the maul, the power of Aita. It felt different than that to which he was accustomed, though intellectually, he reasoned it was the same. *I have no idea what I'm doing here.*

The warmth, the power, flowed into him. He heard Piotr gasp and felt the maul twitch in his hands. A warm, gentle breeze carried the fragrance of honeysuckle. Pancras opened his eyes and found himself standing on a hill overlooking Curton. A woman stood near a row of red-flowered shrubs. He recognized her silvery-grey hair.

"Nika?"

The woman turned to face him. Tears welled in deep-set, piercing, steel-blue eyes that regarded him. "Who are you? Why are you doing this to me?"

"I am Pancras, a Bonelord of Aita." Pancras bowed to her. "Your affliction is nothing I have caused."

"It hurts. I can't move. I can't see. I can't hear. Everything hurts." She buried her face in her hands and wept. Pancras approached her and put his arm around her heaving shoulders.

"Piotr says the healers can do nothing. He hates to see you suffer."

"He's a good boy." Her red-rimmed eyes met his. "Are you here to take my soul now?"

Pancras licked his lips. "I confess, I've never done this before. I think I'm supposed to help you cross over. You're suffering. You'll continue to linger until you can no longer eat, and you'll starve."

Nika pushed him away, then returned her attention to the meadow. "I don't want to go."

"I can't make you. Piotr's wife and son care for you now. They have you by the window so you can experience the change of seasons." Pancras shuffled his feet, sending a puff of white seeds into the air from nearby dandelions. Despite the breeze, the world around them was bereft of sound. No wind rustling the leaves of nearby trees, no insects buzzing. The world was still, yet in motion.

"I'm wasting away. Watching the world pass by with unseeing eyes. You've come to kill me, Bonelord."

The words were knives in Pancras's chest; a sensation he noted with amusement with which he had become all too familiar. He didn't want to kill anyone.

"Why is your goddess doing this to me? I've worked hard; I don't deserve this."

It was a common misconception that Aita not only caused death, but also spread disease and suffering. "Aita does not afflict the innocent with suffering like this."

She spun on him, fists clenched. "Are you saying I deserve this—this—curse?"

Pancras backed away from the woman, holding up his hands. "No. No, diseases are not brought to this world by Aita. She concerns herself with the dead, not the living."

The woman stared at him, her nostrils flaring as her lips trembled. "Then why do you haunt my dreams!"

"This is no dream, Nika. I am kneeling at your bedside, with your son. We want to end your suffering." Pancras wanted to help this woman, but he didn't know what he could say to convince her. *Telling her the world isn't fair seems wrong.*

"Can you cure me? Make me strong again?"

Pancras shook his head.

"Then, get out!"

Pancras flew backward, gasping as he opened his eyes. He stood again in the spartan room with Piotr and the twisted form of Nika. Clutching the maul, he pushed himself to his feet. "Her mind is strong. She's not ready to move on."

"So? What does that mean?"

The minotaur swallowed and rubbed his eyes. "It means I cannot help her. I cannot make her cross over if she doesn't want to go."

"Heal her then!" The smith advanced on him. His eyes were cold, the muscles in his neck stood out like rope.

"I can do nothing. I'm not a healer. She's not ready."

Breathing rapidly, the smith clenched his fists. Pancras noticed the smith's muscles tense before he turned and flung open the door. "Go. Get out."

Pancras didn't wait for Piotr to change his mind. He heard the door slam behind him as he stumbled down the stairs behind the smithy, nearly losing his footing and falling the final third of the way down. Gisella stood inside the shop, still examining weapons on the display racks. He didn't see Lady Aveline.

"Well? Were you able to help him?"

Pancras clenched his jaw. His heart raced, and he took a moment to breathe before shaking his head. "I could not." Thumping from above drew his attention away from Gisella. "I think we should go."

Gisella touched his arm. "I'm sorry."

He lifted the maul. It still felt warm in his hand. Gritting his teeth, he reached into his money pouch. He left a handful of crowns and talons on Piotr's anvil.

"There's a dwarf and a fiendling involved in some trouble at a place called Danica's Den. Loath as I am to know the truth, I think we need to check it out."

Pancras felt his chest tighten. The odds were slim of another dwarf and fiendling pair who were capable of causing trouble. Nodding, he followed Gisella into the crowds.

Chapter 19

Delilah's meeting with Master Galina was not the stress-filled interrogation she expected. The master told Delilah what to expect at her Novice Trials and then sent her on her way. In theory, Delilah's performance in her Novice Trials would be judged by the high wizards, the archmage, and any masters who sought an apprentice. Delilah expected the archmage to claim her as his own, however, as she reflected while strolling back to the library.

It's all busywork and magical theater. A lot of what these wizards do doesn't seem to have a point. About a dozen students moved about the library as they researched various projects. While a few were novices, most appeared to be apprentices. She saw Master Agata at the *Rose Concordat*'s podium. Delilah sat in a nearby chair to wait. Master Agata glanced over her shoulder at the drak sorceress.

"Come to brush up on your guild rules, Novice?"

"Master Renata said I should read the *Rose Concordat*. So, I have been." Delilah swung her feet as they dangled above the floor. Not one chair in the Arcane University was sized to fit draks. She felt like a child among giants.

"There are certainly worse ways to spend your time." Master Agata turned to the codex and flipped forward, stopping about three-quarters of the way to the end.

She stepped aside, then moved a chair in front of the codex. "All yours, Novice."

Delilah hopped off the chair and bowed to the departing master. Right before she flipped the pages back to where she left off, a few words on the current page caught her eye.

Master Gil-Li, former student of Vlad the Iron Justice, was the first to ascend to the position of archmage by Rite of Combat. As enacted by Gerald the Craven in the third series of essays on "Arcane Rules: Civilized Magickry," the Rite of Combat was a formal duel between a ranking wizard and an underling who felt slighted. Prior to the codification of the Rite of Combat, wizard duels were little more than battles of mass destruction. The rules written by Gerald the Craven allow for a formal dueling location designed to minimize collateral damage and allow for an audience of judges to observe the duel from a position of safety.

Delilah's eyes searched the room for Master Agata, but the older woman had gone. She wondered if she turned the book to that page for a reason. It gave the drak a new appreciation for her grimoire; it was the book of an archmage. She must continue to conceal it from Vilkan. So far, he kept his nose out of her personal affairs, but if she became his apprentice, she would be under closer scrutiny.

She continued reading from the dueling section for the rest of the afternoon, committing the words, statutes, and rites to memory. *Gil-li is mentioned in here a lot. Is she why Manless is so interested in me?*

***

Pancras fought to keep his failure with Piotr's mother from affecting him as he and Gisella entered Danica's Den. A row of guards tried to hold back a crowd intent on pushing their way across the gambling floor. A haze of smoke lingered near the ceiling, the air thick with the odor of sweaty bodies and the residue of whatever it was people smoked from the large water pipes set up around the perimeter of the room. Statues of Pacha and Dolios stood on opposite ends of the bar that bisected the room, keeping watch over the proceedings that glorified drinking, gambling, and throwing away ones' money on excess.

Shouts from the crowd calling for violent retribution filled the air. Angry gamblers stood on the gaming tables directing their ire toward the back of the room.

"String 'er up!"

"Get the fiendling!"

"The dwarf, too!"

Part of Pancras hoped there was another dwarf and fiendling in town, but it didn't take more than a cursory glance to determine that the crowd was, indeed, yelling for Qaliah's head. He spotted the fiendling in the center of a group of city guards escorting her through the crowd. Lady Aveline led the procession, shoving people out of the way with her shield.

The minotaur sought a means to intercept Lady Aveline, hoping to smooth things over and release Qaliah and Edric from her custody before things with the townsfolk became ugly. The ice in her glare dissuaded him, along with the way the guards accompanying her half drew their swords whenever anyone came too close. Pancras settled for following them out of the gambling den and into the streets. Shouting obscenities directed at Edric and Qaliah, a crowd of dedicated hecklers followed them.

Gisella pulled him to the side of the street under the awning of a bakery. "Perhaps we should wait until tomorrow. Let the furor die down."

"They appear to be in a lynching mood." Pancras shook his head. "I'd rather deal with this now."

"I have half a mind to leave them." Gisella slammed her hand into the side of the building. "This was supposed to be a quick stop and a chance to sleep in a warm bed, not cause trouble and get arrested."

Pancras motioned for her to follow. "Edric gambled away an entire season in Almeria. I'm surprised he wasn't arrested before now."

Following the mob through city streets, crowded though they were, was easy enough. Pushing their way through the crowd and guards to enter the jail was a different story. The guards turned away anyone not wearing one of their tabards. They met Pancras's pleas with stony-faced stares.

The minotaur threw up his hands. "I guess we wait."

After a few hours of grim glares from rather cross, armed guards, the crowd grew bored and dispersed. Mobs burned hot, but, given sufficient time, the alcohol and fury that fueled them wore off, and the people shambled home angry and hungover.

Pancras approached the guards. "May we go in now? We have business with Lady Aveline." It wasn't strictly true, but he hoped the guards wouldn't know that.

"Fine." The guard held the door for Pancras and Gisella. The interior of the jail appeared more spartan than Pancras expected. The stone walls and stone floor blended together in a depressing expanse of grey. Two desks sat facing each other on opposite sides of the room. Near the back, a large holding cell stood across from the hearth, and stairs led down to, Pancras presumed, the rest of the cells. A long-haired fat man snored in the holding cell, and Lady Aveline sat behind one of the desks, cleaning her sword.

"What do you two want now?" Lady Aveline glanced up from her weapon, but she continued to rub the blade with an oiled cloth.

Gisella pointed to the stairs. "You arrested our friends."

"The dwarf and the fiendling. So? Lord Koloman doesn't tolerate cheaters in the gambling dens. The dens and brothels are the only things keeping the mudders happy since the mines dried up."

Pancras held up his hands. "We're not here to protest their innocence. We want to see about rectifying the situation. We're just passing through on our way to Cliffport to catch a ship to Vlorey. It's been a long journey from Muncifer and more delays are"—Pancras sighed—"difficult."

"Not my problem." Lady Aveline slid her sword into its sheath. Footsteps clomping up the stairs heralded the return of a guard from the jail.

Gisella clasped her hands in front of her. "What exactly is supposed to have happened, Lady Aveline?"

"It's simple: the dwarf was caught cheating, and several eyewitnesses say the fiendling used her demonic powers to help him." She regarded the approaching guard.

Pancras glanced at Gisella. As far as he was aware, Qaliah did not possess arcane skill of any type, whether from her demonic heritage or not. The Golden Slayer's cocked eyebrow revealed she shared his suspicion.

The guard stood at attention. "The fiendling maintains she had nothing to do with the dwarf's cheating. The dwarf continues to berate her for not backing up his story."

Gisella cleared her throat. "With respect, Lady Aveline, I am familiar enough with Qaliah, the fiendling, to know she does not possess any magical skills. Is it not possible the mudders are letting their prejudices against fiendlings shape their stories?"

"It's possible Dolios himself is locked up in our jail in dwarf form, but I find it highly suspect." Lady Aveline pulled a scrap of paper from her desk. She scribbled a note on it, folded the paper, and handed it to the guard. She flicked the end of her quill toward the door. "Go to the apothecary. Tell Tasha I need a favor."

The guard saluted, then quickly exited. Lady Aveline stood, ushering Pancras and Gisella toward the door. "Let me do my job. I will determine who is guilty and who is not. I don't need the help of transients. Where are you staying?"

"The Drunken Horse." Pancras opened the door for Gisella.

"I'll send for you tomorrow, in the afternoon." Lady Aveline closed the jail door behind them. Pancras heard the click of the lock.

"We have to face the possibility that we may be going on without them, you know?" Gisella took Pancras's arm and led him away from the jail.

"I know." Pancras would do what he could to help Edric and Qaliah, but he drew the line at orchestrating an actual jailbreak. If they were guilty of breaking Curton's laws, they would have to face the penalties.

***

"Did they say what he wanted?" Katka wrung her hands as Delilah shoved her grimoire into her pack. The drak sorceress shook her head.

A student interrupted their study session with a summons for Delilah to appear before the headmaster in his office. Delilah assumed the headmaster was Archmage Vilkan. The headmaster's office was located at the top of a tower attached to the main keep in which all the lecture halls and laboratories were located. Katka hurried behind Delilah, asking the drak over and over again what she did to warrant a summons by the headmaster.

"I don't know!" Delilah stopped at the bottom of the stairs leading into the tower and shoved her pack into Katka's arms. She was tired of lugging the thing all over the Arcane University and didn't want the grimoire anywhere near the headmaster. "Guard this pack with your life. I'll be back for it. Wait here, all right?"

Katka nodded, her eyes widening. Part of Delilah felt leaving her grimoire in the human's hands was asking for trouble, but there was another, louder part of her that needed to know if she could trust the girl. After the archduke's revelations, Delilah needed another friend. Kale would always be there for her, but it wasn't fair to Kali for Delilah to continually test her brother's loyalties.

The stairs leading up to the headmaster's office started on the roof of the keep and wound around the outside of the tower. The absence of a railing didn't bother Delilah; none of the precipices in Drak-Anor had handrails. Her legs wearied of the stairs built for humans, however, and she felt as if she'd climbed a mountain by the time she reached the balcony at the top.

Two guards stood watch outside the headmaster's office. One yawned and held the door open for her. Archmage Vilkan sat behind what she assumed was the headmaster's desk. Bookshelves lined the walls of the office itself, stretching from floor to ceiling. Windows and skylights provided bright illumination during the day, and she noticed the dull glow of enchanted gems set in torch scones that provided evening illumination. Smoke from incense rose from a nearby brazier.

"Ah, Novice Drak. Come in. Stand before me." Archmage Vilkan smiled and stood. He gestured to a spot on the bear skin rug in front of his desk. "I understand you've been reading the *Rose Concordat*. I applaud your initiative. I have been brushing up myself."

"You wanted to see me, Arch… Headmaster?" Delilah wasn't sure how to address him now.

"Indeed, indeed. I've been going about things all wrong, you see. As archmage, I'm bound by the rules of the Arcane University, insofar as students like you are concerned. It never occurred to me my authority as headmaster provided an alternative."

Delilah narrowed her eyes. She shifted the grip on her staff as she calculated how quickly she could envelope him in a cloud of swirling blades.

"The headmaster's authority is absolute when it comes to the university, you see; yet I've been so focused on how to accomplish things as head of the guild that I didn't see the obvious solution sitting right in front of me." Laughing, he tapped a piece of paper on his desk.

The drak sorceress craned her neck, but she was too short to see details.

"As headmaster, I can make exceptions of most of the rules here, and I have." He drew his wand and tapped the paper as a blue glow surrounded the tip of his focus. "So, by the power invested in me as headmaster of the Arcane University of Muncifer, I hereby waive the university's requirement to subject you to the Novice Trials and advance you directly to the rank of apprentice, effective immediately."

Delilah squinted as the blue glow flared, searing the paper. The archmage blew away the last remnants of azure smoke and rolled up the paper, holding it out for Delilah. The drak took it with a tentative hand.

"As of now, you are my apprentice, Drak. Even the high wizards cannot dispute the judgement of the headmaster in this matter." He chuckled. "I wish I'd thought of it weeks ago. In this case, the authority of the headmaster supersedes that of archmage. How fortunate I hold both titles. Take that to the seneschal, and he'll see it is entered into the university records." He picked up a brooch and tossed it to Delilah.

After catching it, she examined it. She noted the seal of the Arcane University engraved in the center and "Muncifer" written in the common trade language around the edge.

"You no longer need specific robes. That brooch will identify you as an apprentice. At dusk, report to the Court of Wizardry for your first assignment. Do you understand, my apprentice?"

Delilah, unsure she understood what just transpired, nodded her assent anyway. He dismissed her with a wave of his hand and sat behind his desk. She descended the stairs slowly, reading the scroll he gave her. She didn't understand how his responsibilities as headmaster and archmage intersected, or didn't, in this case. The scroll gave her no new information and failed to alleviate any of her confusion.

Katka still waited for Delilah at the bottom of the stairs, just outside the door that led back into the keep. She sat on the grass with her arms wrapped around Delilah's pack, holding it tightly against her knees. Glancing upward, her eyes caught the afternoon light from beneath black locks.

"What happened? What did he say?"

Delilah handed the scroll to Katka. "The archmage *is* the headmaster. He skipped my Novice Trials and made me his apprentice effective immediately."

"Why didn't he do that before?"

Delilah wished she had the answer to that question. "Maybe he's not as smart as he wants everyone to think. I have to appear before the Court of Wizardry at dusk for my first task as his apprentice."

They descended into the keep. Other novices and initiates greeted them as they passed students in the hall. Outside one of the divination classrooms, the smell of burning incense wafted past them. The pungent odor burned in Delilah's nose and blurred her vision. When they entered the courtyard, she searched for the sun in the sky, gauging, based upon its position, whether she had time to visit her brother before going to the Court of Wizardry. With it over halfway through its descent toward the western horizon and additional crowds in the upper city gathering for the celebration of Anetha's Glory that night, she didn't think she could travel there and back in time.

"It's strange he didn't give the assignment to you when you met with him, don't you think?" Katka stopped underneath the Blood Oak. She returned the scroll to Delilah.

"I assume he wants to show off in front of the high wizards. He was proud that he thought of a way to circumvent their decree." She hoped the archmage would give her an assignment to take her out of the city. Delilah wanted no part of his machinations against the archduke. As far as she was concerned, the two humans could fight it out themselves without her involvement.

"At least you don't have to wear those grey robes anymore, though, right? You draks don't usually wear so much."

"So far, that's the only good thing about it." Delilah suspected the only way she'd obtain the answers she craved was to play their game a little while longer. She hefted her pack and motioned for Katka to follow her. "I'm going to change and then hit the tavern before the meeting. Join me?"

***

The sound of the printing press drowned out the crowds in the street. Kale tapped his foot and stared vacantly at Kali. The note from Boss Steelhand said Jairo's cousin would be in his print shop waiting for them. So far, there was no sign of the other drak. Jairo offered to let them wait while he finished printing broadsheets.

Kali tossed the paper she had been reading onto the counter. "How long are we going to keep waiting? Let's just tell the minotaur 'no deal' and get on with our lives."

"It's a way for us to earn some money without having to work for it." Kale shrugged. He didn't like waiting any more than his mate did. "Maybe it'll pay all our expenses and we can do something fun for a change."

The bell rang as an out-of-breath, blue-scaled drak pushed open the door. He glanced behind him as he closed it, recoiling when he saw Kale and Kali staring at him. "Oh! Sorry I'm late. Where's… Jairo?"

Turning his head, first one way and then the other, his mouth hung agape as he took in the sight of Kale's wings.

"Working." Right after Kali answered, the rhythmic pounding of the printing press stopped. Jairo ran to the front of his shop, wiping ink-stained hands on his equally stained apron.

"Ori!"

"Jairo!"

The two draks embraced. Kale shuffled his feet, clearing his throat. He didn't want to cut short their reunion, but neither did he want to be sidelined all day.

"The note we received said to meet the limner here." Kale fished the scrap of parchment given him by one of Boss Steelhand's thugs from his pouch. He handed it to Ori.

"Oh! You're the draks who own the place I'm setting up shop in?" After examining the paper, Ori handed it to his cousin. He stared again at Kale's wings.

"It's the storefront attached to our *home*." Kale tucked back his wings as far as they would go. Jairo nudged his cousin, then shook his head.

"Oh, well, I'm sure it's very nice. I don't need much space, and I'll be living with Jairo, at least for a while."

"That's right." Jairo put his arm around his cousin. "Are the terms acceptable?"

Kale glanced over to his mate and nodded.

"Boss Steelhand hasn't told us the terms yet." Kali shrugged.

"Oh." Ori fished in his pouch, then withdrew a sheaf of papers. He handed them to Kale. "They're quite simple."

"Simple?" Kale flipped through the pages. Although he could read the Drak words, the terminology was more formal than that to which he was accustomed and appeared to contain doublespeak.

"Just tell us Boss Steelhand's angle here. We know he wants you to spy on us."

"Oh! Spy! Me?" Ori put his hand on his chest, and his eyes widened. "I don't want to spy on anyone!"

Jairo walked to his shop's door and turned the lock. "Why do you think Boss Steelhand wants Ori to spy on you?"

Kali fingered the handle of one of her daggers.

Kale likewise reached up to his bandolier. "What's going on here?"

"Calm down. Calm down." Jairo raised his hands. "I just don't want someone walking in on us while we're having this particular discussion."

Kale narrowed his eyes, watching Jairo lean against the counter after passing behind Ori. The grey drak moved with deliberate action, keeping his hands visible at all times. Kali moved to the door and stood in front of it.

"Oh." Ori's eyes flicked to Kali and then back to Kale. "Boss Steelhand owed me a favor. When I had the opportunity to join Jairo here, I knew his shop would be too small, so I asked the boss to find me someplace to set up shop. That's all. I'm not one of his cronies. I just illuminate manuscripts. That's all."

He reached for the pages in Kale's hand. "I have my own equipment. You just need to provide workspace. In exchange, I pay you thirty percent of my gross income every month, or two crowns, whichever is higher. The contract can be renegotiated after six months."

Kale dropped his hand away from his dagger. "That's a lot of paper just to say that."

"It's a standard Maritropan contract."

Jairo chuckled. "They use a lot of words up in Maritropa."

"Well, we're not from Maritropa, and we're not in Maritropa. What you said sounds fine to me." Kale extended a clawed hand toward Ori. "I'll show you around the place right away, if you like."

He caught a raised eyebrow from Kali, but she, too, dropped her hand away from her dagger before turning to unlock the door. Ori glanced at his cousin, then tossed the stack of papers on the counter before clasping Kale's hand.

"Deal."

***

Gisella observed Pancras staring into his mug of mead. He wore his failure to help the blacksmith's mother as well as their inability to secure Qaliah's and Edric's release from jail like a heavy woolen coat of mourning. The air in The Drunken Horse hung hazy and heavy, laden with clouds of pipe smoke.

The acrid tang of the tobacco the mudders puffed mingled with the aroma of simmering stew from the kitchen.

She sipped her mead. It tasted flat and of clay. *Sweet mud. How delightful.* Grimacing, she set down her mug.

"I've been trying to think of something we can do to assist Qaliah and Edric." Pancras pushed away his mug. "Perhaps if I offer to pay the damages?"

"That's your choice. Making the offer certainly won't hurt." Gisella waved her hand to gain the barmaid's attention. "If they are guilty of breaking the law here, though, I think they should face their punishment."

"What do you need, dearie?" The barmaid, a round-faced woman in a cornflower dress and a white apron, approached the table, the corners of her eyes upturned in a perpetual smile.

"This mead tastes muddy. Do you have any wine or ale? Perhaps something from Ravensforest or Maritropa?"

"Muddy?" The barmaid's grin fell, and she fidgeted with her chignon. She glanced toward the kitchen. "Ivan! We found the contaminated batch of mead!" She gathered up Gisella's and Pancras's mugs. "Sorry about that. One of the boys at the meadery snuck some muddy water into one of the batches. We've spent all summer trying to figure out which barrels were affected. I'll bring fresh drinks straightaway."

"Contaminated?" Pancras stuck out his tongue and scraped it with a fingernail.

The barmaid's hairdo bounced up and down as she bustled away.

Gisella spat on the floor. "I doubt it's poisonous. If you need to burn that taste out of your mouth, have some spirits."

A hush fell over the great room when the front door opened. The sound of armored boots turned Gisella's head. Lady Aveline approached their table, pulled out a chair, and sat down.

"Your dwarf friend must appear before the magistrate to answer charges of cheating the house at Danica's Den." She clasped her fingers together in front of her on the table.

"We figured that." Gisella nodded her thanks to the barmaid as the woman set fresh tankards of ale on the table. Lady Aveline waved away the barmaid's offer of refreshment.

"The fiendling was caught up in trying to defend her friend. I will release her to you on your way out of town. She hasn't broken any laws, but I think she'll be safer in the jail than out on the streets right now. I have a group of mudders camped outside the jail calling for her head."

Pancras raised his eyebrows. "When will Edric appear before the magistrate, and what will the likely penalty be?"

Gisella regarded Lady Aveline. In Muncifer, being caught cheating landed you in stocks for a few days and resulted in banishment from all the city's gambling dens. She was certain the ban wasn't totally enforceable, but the minotaur guards all possessed excellent memories.

"There's a fine; the magistrate will set that. He'll be expected to pay damages to the owners of Danica's Den, and he'll be barred from gambling there." Lady Aveline turned her head to the door slamming open. A couple of mudders stumbled in, laughing. One of the serving maids shook her head before closing the door behind them.

Gisella noticed Pancras fishing in his money pouch. *Counting his coins, no doubt, hoping to pay for Edric's mistake.* "What happens if the dwarf can't pay his debt?"

Lady Aveline raised an eyebrow. "He'll be indentured." She turned to Pancras. "I'm not sure when the magistrate will see the dwarf. He's been dealing with some sick livestock and is reluctant to leave his farm lately. It might be a week or more."

"A week?" Furrowing his brow and rubbing his right horn, Pancras regarded Gisella. "I don't think we can delay that long."

"We shouldn't."

"Perhaps…" Pancras pulled a handful of crowns out of his pouch. "Perhaps I can just pay the damages and take Edric out of town right away? Can we work something out?"

Lady Aveline chuckled. "You're a better friend than he deserves. Were I inclined to make such a deal, I would tell you the damages are at least twenty crowns. I don't have final figures yet."

Pancras swallowed and put away his money. "Twenty? So far?" He sighed before drinking from his tankard.

"I'm also not willing to just let him walk away."

Gisella observed the conflict in Pancras's eyes as he stared into his tankard. He rubbed his right horn again, shaking his head and muttering to himself. She reached over to touch his arm. "We may have to leave him to his fate."

"I'll leave you to your decisions." Lady Aveline stood. "You're welcome to come visit your friends at the jail now."

Abandoning Edric to Curton justice wasn't Gisella's first choice, but neither would she consider planning a jailbreak. Qaliah had potential, however, and that the fiendling would be permitted to go free assuaged some of her guilt at abandoning one member of their fellowship. She hoped Pancras saw reason in leaving Edric behind.

Chapter 20

Surprised by the number of high wizards in attendance, Delilah entered the Court of Wizardry. Whatever the archmage planned for her, he obviously wanted to make a big show of it.

The rainbow of wizards sitting to the left and right of Archmage Vilkan observed Delilah crossing the court chamber. Her clawed feet click-clacked against the stone floor with every step. She adjusted her harness and straightened her apprentice's seal, thankful to be rid of the robes that plagued her since she became involved with the university.

"Ah, Apprentice Drak. Punctual for once."

Delilah resisted the urge to blow him a raspberry. She spent the last hour in the outer chambers waiting for permission to enter the court. "Delilah."

"Excuse me?"

Delilah stopped, then bowed to the assembled wizards. "My name is Delilah, not 'Drak,' Master." She added the last to appease the archmage.

The high wizard garbed in brown robes nodded. "The master should respect the apprentice if he expects the same in return."

"Yes, yes." Archmage Vilkan held up his hand to silence murmurs from the other high wizards. Delilah adjusted her grip on her staff, suppressing a grin. She found it interesting one of the high wizards supported her defiance of the archmage.

"I have informed the court that you are now my apprentice." Glancing to his left and then to his right at the seated high wizards, the archmage drummed his fingers on the arms of his chair.

"His actions are unorthodox but permitted under Arcane University rules."

"Clever separation of guild duties and headmaster responsibilities."

"Surprised it was this long in coming."

Archmage Vilkan glared at the wizard who last spoke. Delilah wasn't sure which one of them said it, and by the archmage's expression, she suspected he could not determine by voice alone which high wizard spoke.

"Yes, I am your apprentice now, Archmage." Delilah tilted her head to hide her sneer. "What would you have me do?"

"My sources report the giants are amassing an army in the mountains." He leaned forward in his chair. "Recent events, however, have given me reason to doubt my sources. I want fresh intelligence. Follow the west road. Two days into the mountains, there is a valley in which the giants make their home. You will be my spy, Apprentice Dra—Delilah. They are rumored to have a dragon pet, as well."

"A dragon?" Delilah made a show of swallowing and shuffling her feet. "I can't take on a dragon alone."

"I understand draks and dragons have a special relationship." A predatory smile overtook his face. "I know you live with one in Drak-Anor."

Archmage Vilkan sat back, sneering at her. "If the dragon is there, you will befriend it. You will convince it that we wizards are its allies, not the giants."

Chuckling, Delilah leaned on her staff. "You want me to sneak into a giant-filled valley and steal their dragon? I don't know where you got your information about draks and dragons—"

He stood, slashing the air with his hand. "This is no laughing matter! Even now, the archduke seeks a truce with those brutes." He pointed behind him, in the general direction of the mountains. "They are treacherous and stupid. They will destroy our crops, and they will ruin our lands! You will pledge yourself to this dragon and poison its mind against the giants. Wipe them out. All of them!"

"A mighty task to entrust to an apprentice."

"Moving so openly against the archduke—"

"A dragon's knowledge and treasure would be most valuable—"

The high wizards spoke over one another. Delilah shook her head. Despite his mania, the archmage was right about the archduke wanting peace with the giants. Sending her to turn their dragon against them seemed like a suicide mission.

"You're cracked. You've turned like milk left in the sun." Delilah wasn't sure what that meant, but she had heard it when Katka insulted an obnoxious novice, and she found it amusing.

"Silence!" Archmage Vilkan's voice reverberated throughout the room. "I have seen our doom. Fiery wings flying above an army of giants. I will not allow it to happen."

After stepping down from the dais, he circled the room, pointing at the high wizards. "I am archmage. The unholy alliance of the giants and their pet dragon must be broken. An army could not do it. I could not do it. None of you could do it. But a drak"—he stopped and pointed a trembling finger at Delilah—"a single drak versed in magic and dragon lore could gain its confidence. Convince it we are no threat. Convince it we will serve in atonement for the slaying of Rannos Dragonsire and the Sundering."

"You seek to control this dragon?"

"You would deceive this dragon?"

"A dangerous game."

"A bold ploy."

The comments from the high wizards flew fast, and Delilah labored to keep up with them. The more she heard of the archmage's plan, the more she became convinced he had gone utterly mad. The archduke sought to live in harmony with the giants, and if they were guardians of a slumbering Firstborne, he wanted peace with her, as well. She couldn't fathom why the archmage would want to destroy the giants. *Even a drakling knows it's best to let sleeping dragons lie.*

The Violet Wizard tapped their staff on the floor, drawing everyone's attention. "Your apprentice should have a say in this. It is a most dangerous assignment."

"She will do as I say."

Delilah cleared her throat. The archmage might silence her, but she anticipated the other high wizards would allow her to speak. "I know nothing about negotiating with dragons. Terrakaptis sleeps most of the time. Muncifer doesn't need a war with these giants. I can spy on them for you. I can deliver a message for you. But I tell you this with all honesty—if there is a dragon in that valley, you have nothing that can tempt it."

She felt the gaze of the high wizards through their masks. Archmage Vilkan clenched his teeth before seating himself. He gripped the arms of his chair with white knuckles. "What, then, do you suggest, Apprentice?"

Delilah's mind raced as she worked through the possibilities. If Terrakaptis's sister lived with the giants, she felt she owed it to the Earth Dragon and her brother to find out. She didn't want to be the instrument by which the archmage incited a war between the giants and Muncifer, though. In all likelihood, the giants would be content to stay in their mountains and trade with Muncifer, just like the archduke wanted.

"I have known a few giants, and I've read more about them than dragons." Delilah hoped no one would see through the lie. She actually hadn't read anything about either one of them; the only giant she'd even known personally was a brutish thug, just like the archmage claimed they all were. "I bet they prefer to be left in peace. I'll deliver a message, a request to meet with them to discuss terms, to clear up recent misunderstandings."

She tapped the butt of her staff on the stone floor. "I'm not stupid enough to mess with a dragon, though. If they have one as an ally, we need to make nice. A dragon half of

Terrakaptis's size could lay waste to this city without breaking a sweat."

The drak sorceress swallowed. Hers wasn't that far from the archmage's plan, but it was a more sensible approach.

The archmage leaned forward, sneering. "This stinks of the archduke."

"The archduke rules Muncifer."

"No wizard has fought a dragon in this age; the drak speaks sense."

"Your apprentice has wis—"

"Silence!" The archmage stood, scowling at the high wizards. "The drak will deliver a message of peace to the giant. We will meet at the Well of the Willow on Midsummer's Day to discuss a truce... and peace." He turned to face Delilah. "You will learn as much as you can about their strengths, their weaknesses, and the truth of this dragon, and you will report back to me."

He flipped his robes, stomping past Delilah. "If they are no threat, so be it. If they do pose a threat, we will wipe them out at the Well of the Willow." He exited the Court of Wizardry, slamming the doors behind him.

The assembled high wizards murmured to themselves and then disappeared in puffs of smoke matching the colors of their robes. All departed, save for the Violet Wizard. He, or she, strode over to Delilah and met her eyes. It felt as if the black eyes of the colorless mask bored into her soul.

"An interesting approach, Apprentice. Take care you do not underestimate your foes."

She eyed the impassive mask. "Usually, it is they who underestimate me."

***

Pancras drained the ale from his tankard. None of the options he considered appealed to him.

"Even if the magistrate is lenient with Edric, I doubt he will avoid paying the fines and damages." Gisella tapped on the table in front of Pancras to gain his attention.

"I know. I'm not paying that for him." His tone conveyed his certainty. Had it been Kale or Delilah, perhaps his feelings would be different.

"Then we have no choice: we must collect Qaliah and leave Edric to his fate. If Dolios intervenes and the dwarf is freed, he can catch up to us, but I tell you now, I will have no part in helping him escape."

Pancras didn't need to meet her eyes to see Gisella's expression. The ice in her voice told him all he needed to know. He shook his head. "The thought never entered my mind. I think it would be best to leave first thing in the morning. It's already too late for us to make any progress toward Cliffport today."

Gisella covered her mouth and nodded. "I expected more of an argument from you."

"I'm nothing if not practical." He tossed a couple of silver talons on the table. "Let's break the news to Qaliah and Edric. Let's be done with this."

The inevitable confrontation with Edric gnawed at Pancras's gut like a boggin. He imagined the verbal abuse the dwarf would hurl at him. Qaliah would likely not be happy either. *Perhaps they will both remain here.*

Pancras felt apathetic about Edric. He didn't mind the dwarf's company, but he hardly considered him a friend. He'd grown fond of the fiendling since they left Muncifer, even though she shot him in the chest and killed him. He rubbed the scar through his robes. In a way, she reminded him of Delilah, and Pancras hoped she would continue to travel with them to Vlorey, for no other reason than that.

The sun hung low in the sky by the time they reached the jail, the fiery orb backlighting wisps of pink and crimson clouds in the western sky. A light breeze blew the earthy odors of nearby pottery kilns through the air. He paused to scrape accumulated mud from his hooves before entering the building. The constant filth served as a bitter reminder of the lack of such in Drak-Anor.

Lady Aveline distributed evening assignments to guardsmen gathered in the front room of the prison. After checking their equipment, they left one by one and headed out to Mudder's Gate, the marketplace, or Vineyard Hill, the district where all the wealthier citizens of Curton lived. Upon noticing Gisella and Pancras standing near the door, she nodded in acknowledgement, then issued orders to the remaining guardsman.

"Patrol the metalworking district. I've heard some grumbling in the drak community about unfair treatment by a few of the smiths. We've had to break up some fights in the square at Copper Street and Iron Way over the last few days. Disperse any unruly crowds, but don't bother arresting anyone until blood is spilled. The draks' grievances are just. All right?"

"Understood, m'lady." The guard saluted Lady Aveline, turned on his heel and left.

"Here to collect your fiendling?"

Pancras crossed his hand over his chest and bowed. "To talk to her at least. We're not resuming our journey until the morning."

"Fine. Follow me." She lifted a ring of keys off a hook on her desk, then led them down the stairs at the back of the jail. Lanterns sputtered in the damp darkness, casting dim, yellow light into the stone corridor. Stopping before the first cell, she unlocked it. She held the door open for Pancras and Gisella. After they entered the cell, she locked it behind them.

"Let me know when you want out. I'll be just down the hall."

Qaliah lay on the cot with her fingers interlaced behind her head. She glanced at Gisella and Pancras as they entered. "I guess you heard the news, huh?"

"Yes. We're leaving tomorrow." Pancras stood at the end of the cot. Gisella offered a hand to Qaliah.

The fiendling ignored the helping hand. "Edric's hearing with the magistrate isn't for a few days."

"That's right. Could be nearly a week, we hear." Gisella nodded. "After which he'll be indentured, and maybe put into stocks."

Qaliah sat upright and slammed her fist into her palm. "The perfect time to spring him and run! Why aren't we waiting around for that?"

Pancras eyed Gisella. "We feel further antagonizing the law and people of Curton will lead nowhere good."

"So you're just going to abandon him?"

"Those Edric wronged deserve justice." Gisella held Qaliah by the shoulders. "We won't force you to leave your friend, but the people of this city view you with suspicion, if not outright contempt. It'll be safer with us."

"I get blondie here." Qaliah glared at Pancras. "But why are you so quick to abandon your friend?

How can I make her understand? Pancras rubbed his horn. "Edric is little more than an acquaintance. I am content to let him travel with me, but I'm not willing to pay for every mistake he makes and become a fugitive myself to ensure he doesn't suffer the consequences of his poor judgement."

"I thought that's what friends do."

"True friends have sense enough to know when to not bring their friends down with them. Besides, he has often spoken of his lack of enthusiasm for our upcoming sea voyage." Gisella turned from Qaliah and rattled the cell doors.

"We'll return for you on our way out of town." Pancras waited alongside Gisella. "You have until then to decide if you're going to burden yourself with Edric's punishment or come with us."

Lady Aveline returned to let them out of the cell. Qaliah lay down again on the cot with her back toward the door.

"Take us to Edric now, if you please." Pancras bowed his head to Lady Aveline. After locking up, she led them to the dwarf's cell, two doors away at the end of the hall.

"You can talk through the bars to this one." She left them, returning to the base of the stairs to afford Pancras, Gisella, and Edric some measure of privacy while she continued to observe them.

The dwarf sat on the edge of his cot, his short legs dangling above the floor. His beard was tangled and knotted, and his eyes were red and bleary from a lack of sleep and what Pancras assumed was a hangover.

"Come to get me out?"

Pancras sighed, grasped one of the bars of the cell, and shook his head. "No. The fines and damages you owe are too great for me to cover."

Laughing, Edric hopped off his cot and approached Pancras and Gisella. "That bad, huh? Ah well, I knew my luck would run out sometime."

Gisella furrowed her brow. "You understand that we're leaving, yes? Tomorrow?"

The dwarf shrugged. "Everyone abandons me at some point." He waved his hand. "I was serious about maybe staying here. I didn't want to get on that ship anyway." He gripped the bars of his cell. "Do you know why dwarves don't like water?"

"You said yourself, dwarves are poor swimmers. It's nothing to be ashamed of." Pancras never felt comfortable in water that was deeper than chest height. "I'm a poor swimmer, too."

"Sure, but at least you float." Edric's eyes widened, flicking to briefly focus on Gisella. "Dwarves sink like stones."

"You'd be on the ship, not on the water." Pancras was certain unfounded fears fueled Edric's exaggerations.

Edric grabbed Pancras's sleeve through the bars. "I don't fancy an ocean voyage. One bad storm, one misstep, and over the side I'll go. Dwarves don't go on the oceans."

"You'd be the first dwarf, then. A pioneer." Pancras wrenched his sleeve from Edric's grasp.

"I'll be the next in a long line of fools at the bottom of the ocean. There aren't any Soul Forges there, and I'll be trapped in a stony corpse for eternity. No thank you."

Pancras heard that dwarves turned to stone after death, but he was not versed in their afterlife. "What are you talking about?"

"We are of the earth. We do not float in water. We sink. A few minutes after going overboard, I'll be dead. I'll become a statue of a drowned dwarf, and no one will take me back to a dwarven city to be consumed in a Soul Forge. My spirit will be trapped at the bottom of the ocean until the world's ending. I. Am. Not. Going."

Edric quivered with every word. Pancras rubbed his right horn and sighed. "Help me understand. What is a Soul Forge?"

"Do you not know anything of dwarven culture?" The dwarf threw up his hands.

"No. I've never lived around dwarves." Pancras glanced at Gisella. Furrowing her brow, she listened to the dwarf. "They didn't exactly leave history books lying around Muncifer when they left after the Sundering."

"I'm not a scholar. Look, our stony corpses fuel the magical furnaces that power our cities. Burning a dead dwarf in a Soul Forge releases his soul to the afterlife." Edric waved his hand. "Maybe I won't fall overboard. Maybe I will. I don't care what debt I owe you or anyone else. I'll risk my life but not my soul."

"Qaliah thinks we should find a way to free you, at any cost." Pancras clasped his hands behind his back.

"It'd be nice to have friends who'd do that for me." Edric regarded them, his hands on his hips. "I ain't foolish enough to think we're that close. It's been interesting, but I think we can agree it's time to part ways."

Pancras took a deep breath. "I confess I'm surprised to hear this from you." Regardless of Edric's feelings on being left behind, the situation still didn't sit well with the minotaur.

"I know if I was one of those draks, you'd burn this town to help them, but I'm just a dwarf, and you're a minotaur." Edric nodded at Gisella. "Me and her don't have enough history to ruin our lives for each other. So, go. Take the fiendling and try not to get killed."

"And what will you do?" Gisella knelt so she was eye level with Edric.

"What I always do. Pay my debts. Then find someplace else to live. There's a dwarven city in the mountains south of here. They haven't heard of me, so maybe I can go there and stay a while." Edric shooed them away. "It ain't the first time I've been in jail. It won't be the last. I don't expect you to do nothing for me, and like I said, I ain't gettin' on no ship." He glanced over his shoulder at them. "If what you got to do in Vlorey saves the world, then all I ask is you don't fail. I like not being undead."

The dwarf climbed up on his cot, then lay down. Closing his eyes, he crossed his hands over his chest. Pancras watched him for a moment. In Drak-Anor, most folk watched out for one another and would not lightly abandon a friend in need. Edric was a dwarf, however, and Pancras spent many years helping the city defend against them until Delilah helped bridge the gap that divided them. *He accepts his fate. Who am I to argue otherwise, when he clearly deserves to face justice, no matter how petty his crimes may seem?* Pancras squeezed his eyes shut and took a deep breath. He nodded once before turning and clomping down the hallway toward Qaliah's cell and Lady Aveline. He heard Gisella follow after him.

As he passed the fiendling's cell, he paused and turned his head. "We'll be back in the morning. Think of where you'd rather be: in a city full of people who want to hang you because of what you are, or with us, going to Vlorey."

***

Kale held the door open for Ori and Kali. "So this is the storefront. We've cleaned it up but haven't done anything with it. The hallway leads back to a storage room and our living quarters."

"Those are off limits." Kali stood at the end of the counter as Ori glanced down the hallway.

"Both or just your living quarters?" The blue drak knelt, disappearing behind the counter. He stood up and took stock of the store, nodding.

"The living quarters."

Kale stepped over to his mate. "We've just been storing food in the other room but not enough to fill it."

Ori ran his hand along one of the shelves behind the counter. "If I wanted to make some changes up here, you know, make the space more suited to my needs, would you object?"

Kale turned to Kali. She shook her head. His eyes returned to Ori. "I guess not. You'll have to pay for it yourself."

"Of course!"

Kali touched Kale's shoulder. Turning, she returned to the living quarters. Ori dropped his pack on the floor behind the counter and stepped around to the other side.

"I'll start immediately." The blue drak stopped when he reached Kale. "You have every right to think I'm working for Boss Steelhand, but I'm not. I just want to make an honest living. You'll see."

"We'll see." Kale, still unsure if he should trust anyone associated with the minotaur, nodded. "We're not planning to go anywhere today, so come and go as you need."

He waited until Ori left the shop before joining Kali in the hearth room. She was cutting up dried meat and vegetables and throwing them in a kettle suspended over the fire.

"What do you think?"

Kali laid down her knife. "I'm not convinced he's on the up-and-up, but if he is, this could be lucrative for us."

"I guess I'll work on a better lock for the basement door. Those books and stuff are probably worth a fortune to the right people." Kale didn't want to risk Boss discovering what was under the store, assuming the minotaur wasn't already aware.

"Shout if you need anything."

Kale returned to the storefront to find Delilah waiting for him. He embraced his sister and shouted for Kali.

"I can't stay long, Kale." Delilah nodded her greetings to Kali. "I wanted to see you before—"

"What's going on?" Kali took Kale's arm in hers.

"It's long and complicated." Delilah's eyes narrowed as she gave them a sidelong glance. "I'm not sure I understand it all myself. The short of it is: I'm heading west into the mountains to search for a dragon."

Kale's jaw dropped. "A dragon? What dragon?"

"The archduke's court wizard, Theros, thinks it's one of the Firstborne. Pyraclannaseous. She's his sister, Kale."

Kali scratched her head. "The court wizard's sister is a dragon?"

"No! Terrakaptis, the dragon who lives in Drak-Anor. Pyraclannaseous is his sister."

Kale rubbed the mark on his chest. "I have to go with you."

"You're not leaving me behind!" Kali squeezed his arm.

Delilah paced in circles and held her head. "Ugh, this is such a mess! The archduke wants me to find the dragon and convince her and the giants to be friends. The archmage wants me to find the dragon and convince her to kill the giants. The high wizards just want me to bring back as much information as possible, not kill the giants, and avoid the dragon."

"Why you?" Kali held her hand out and shrugged.

"Drak." Delilah pointed at herself. "Stripes." She pointed outside. "Dragon."

Kale understood. "They all think because you're a Child of Destiny, you can make nice with the dragon and solve all their problems for them."

"But you're just a novice, right?" Kali shook her head and glanced at Kale. "This is insane!"

"The humans believe it worse than the draks around here do." Kale chuckled. The absurdity of it all might be funny if their quest weren't so dangerous.

"The archmage made me his apprentice officially so he can boss me around without the other masters interfering." Delilah threw her staff to the floor and stomped her foot. "We should have run away with Pancras, Kale!"

"And that slayer would have hauled you right back here"—Kale pulled his sister into a hug—"or killed you."

Delilah pushed him away. "We could have taken her." She wiped her nose. "Life was easier when we were just hexing oroqs and fighting off the dwarves."

The door creaked open as Ori returned, carrying a crate of supplies.

"Oh no." Kale slapped his forehead. "What are we going to do about Ori and Boss Steelhand?"

Delilah eyed the newcomer. "Who's this? Who's Boss Steelhand?"

Kale explained the situation to her, careful to avoid mentioning his concerns about the minotaur finding out about the library on the stairs and the moon gate while Ori was in the room.

Ori grinned and bowed to Delilah. He placed his crate on top of the counter and then took her clawed hand in his and brought it to his lips. "What a vision! I am most honored to meet you. I assume you're Kale's kin?"

Scowling, Delilah snatched back her hand. "He's my brother." She leaned in close to Ori, baring her teeth. "My twin brother. Better wash those lips before the curse consumes you."

Ori rubbed his mouth and then laughed. "Oh, I like her. Curse? Because you're hatched from the same egg, right?" He stepped over to the door and held it open. The stream of draks who carried in crates stacked them in front of the counter.

Kale rested his head on Kali's shoulder as he glanced at his sister. "Your complications are even more complicated now, Deli."

Chapter 21

Gisella stood in the doorway of Pancras's room while he sorted through his pack. "I didn't expect Edric to accept his fate so calmly."

"Nor did I. It makes sense, I suppose." Pancras pulled a black leather belt out of his pack, then shook his head and shoved it in again.

"How so?" Gisella cocked her head. She hadn't become well acquainted with the dwarf during their journey from Muncifer. Edric spent most of his time over the past few months harassing or being harassed by Qaliah. She had assumed he was close friends with the minotaur. She was, apparently, mistaken.

"He joined up with the draks and me after being banished from Ironkrag. He didn't say for what, exactly." Pancras closed his pack and set it in one of the chairs. "I assumed it was for shaming his house with excessive gambling debt or some such. He didn't offer, and I didn't ask. Frankly, I'm surprised he stayed with us this long.

"Qaliah will take it hard. She developed quite a rapport with the dwarf. Edric entertained her during the long journey because he tolerated and participated in her manic fun." Gisella doubted the minotaur would do the same. *Perhaps this will be a good opportunity to train her as a sparring partner.*

"She may choose to remain behind."

Gisella considered it. She scratched her head. "I think I would prefer her to come along."

"Oh?" Pancras rubbed his chin. "Well, she's welcome, of course."

"I don't know what we're going to find in Vlorey. She might come in very handy up there. I hear fiendlings aren't uncommon in the city." Gisella suspected Qaliah would be more than happy to act as a spy on their behalf, should such services be required.

"Have you been there before?" Pancras locked the door behind him before the two of them made their way to the common area for the evening meal.

"Vlorey? No. I've heard stories, of course. It's the biggest city on Andelosia. I expect any elements you disliked in Muncifer or Almeria will be at least twice as bad there." Gisella offered a smile of reassurance to the wide-eyed minotaur.

"Fantastic. I miss Drak-Anor more and more every day."

"What's it like?" Gisella hadn't even heard of Drak-Anor until two or three years earlier.

"Underground, pretty comfortable most of the time. Now that we've run out the goblins and the oroqs, it's quite a nice place to live. We trade with Ironkrag and Celtangate now. It's far better than when I first arrived. We fought off invaders almost every day."

"People who thought it was a den of monsters to be killed for treasure?" Gisella had encountered the type. Self-righteous wanderers with little to do but stick their noses in other people's business. They called themselves adventurers and thought of themselves as heroes. Most of the people left cleaning up their messes had less charitable names for them: murderers, vagrants, and gallivanting swaggies.

"Mostly. To be fair, it did seem to attract a certain demonic element. The Twilight Throne was an artifact of immense power that drew in the worst type. Sarvesh destroyed it, though. Things have been better since." Pancras claimed a table near the hearth and ordered mead, but then stopped the barmaid and changed his order to wine.

"I'll risk the mead." Gisella nodded to the barmaid. "Hopefully, they've tapped a good keg this time."

***

Kale waited until the nebbish blue drak and his workers left and then explained his arrangement with Boss Steelhand to Delilah.

As he finished, her chest tightened, and it seemed tiny hammers rang repeatedly on anvils at the base of her skull. Holding her head, Delilah groaned and leaned against the counter. "Just once, I wish something would be easy. I should be going."

Kale touched his sister's shoulder. "I'm sorry. I didn't know any of this was going down. We needed some way of earning money."

"What are we going to do?" Kali chewed her lip. "We can't just leave the library and cavern unguarded while this strange drak has the run of the shop."

"The door is locked as best as I can." Kale paced, clasping his hands behind his back. "I can build a few more traps on it, maybe one or two at the base of the stairs, too."

Delilah perked up. Kale triggered an idea; her assignment could wait. "I could rig up some magical traps, too. The kind we used to put in the lightning canons in Drak-Anor. That won't take long at all." Her mind raced as she mentally listed the parts she needed. A cursory glance around the empty shop revealed she could scrounge almost everything from there.

"Crystals. I need some high-quality crystals."

Kali snapped her fingers. "Kale, do we have any gems left in that money Pancras left us?"

Kale shook his head. "Yes, but those aren't the kinds she needs. Big quartz crystals will work if they're clear enough."

Delilah smiled. Her brother knew exactly what she needed, just like old times.

"I think I saw a place selling things like that. Some mystic's shop a few levels up across the gorge."

Kale ran to their living quarters and returned clutching a small money pouch. He shook it to jingle the coins within.

"Kali and I will go get what you need. Can you watch the place, Deli? Or… do you want to come with me and Kali can watch the place?"

Before Kali retorted, Delilah nodded and shooed them out of the shop. "I'll watch things. I'll make sure that other drak knows not to mess with our stuff."

"So much for a quick visit." Delilah pulled over a chair from near the hearth so she could see the front door while she studied. She pulled her grimoire from her pack, opening it to the last page she remembered reading. The grimoire seemed to show her what it wanted her to see, so Delilah doubted whether or not it actually mattered to what page she opened the book.

Gil-Li's grimoire pulled Delilah in faster than it had in the past. Within moments, she viewed a scene of Gil-Li standing on a promontory overlooking a city under siege. Clouds pregnant with unfallen rain hung low over the battlefield, and below them drifted thick clouds of smoke from burning buildings. An army pounded the gates and attempted to scale the city's walls while a fleet of ships launched balls of flaming pitch into the docks and buildings surrounding the harbor.

The drak archmage held her arms high and swayed. Her movements flowed in a complex rhythm, not dissimilar from that of dance. A flash of lightning split the sky, and Delilah felt the thunder rumble deep within her chest. Gil-Li's tattoos blazed like sapphires shining in sunlight, searing the movements of the elder sorceress into Delilah's mind.

Clouds swirled above, faster and faster, until vortices formed, and tornadoes descended from the heavens into the midst of armies attacking the city. Clouds of clay and dust swirled up into the cyclones, obscuring the battlefield beneath a storm of soil and debris. Gil-Li directed the tornadoes through the troops and flung men, beasts, and siege weapons high into the air. When half their number was devastated by the unrelenting fury of nature, the rest fled.

Gil-Li changed her movements, spinning to face the sea. The tornadoes changed direction, skipping over the city. When they reached the harbor, they drank in the bay and blasted through ships, turning stout sides of oak and teak into splinters. Blasting powder exploded on the deck of one of the ships, and the fireball flowed upward in a spiral, becoming one with the waterspout.

When the fury of the storm was spent, the winds calmed, and the tornadoes released all the debris, water, and bodies they carried into the ocean. The harbor was filled with the smoldering wreckage of the attacking ships, yet the city itself was untouched by Gil-Li's power. The drak's shoulders slumped.

She turned yet again to face Delilah.

Gil-Li's eyes, flaring with a golden light, connected with those of the drak sorceress. Delilah sat rigid, unable to close her eyes against the blinding radiance. Tears welled in her eyes and spilled down her cheeks. Gil-Li reached out and took Delilah's head in her hands, pulling her close until their foreheads rested against one another.

"You have seen my battles. You have seen my victories and my failures. You have learned much from me. Use what you have learned wisely, and beware the lure of blood. There is much yet to learn."

Delilah wanted to reply, but she was unable to either speak or move. Gil-Li reached out, touching her mind through the vast gulf of years that separated them.

"I bequeath you my legacy, Child of Destiny, child of the Windsinger clan. Show our kin they are not the least of the peoples of Calliome."

A golden light enveloped Delilah. Its warmth saturated her body. It drowned out all other sensation and grew in intensity until she felt as though she would explode from it.

With a cry that was equal parts pain and ecstasy, Delilah dropped the grimoire and fell from her chair onto her side, pinning her tail underneath her and slamming her head against the wall.

The pain in her tail and head returned her to the real world. Delilah opened her eyes to meet the blue drak's stare, his mouth agape. He extended a shaking hand to her and helped her to her feet.

"Oh! That was amazing! I've never seen anything like it!"

Delilah pushed her knuckles into her eyes and staggered across the room. She shook her head to clear it and saw faint wisps of golden mist rising from every surface. When she blinked again, they were gone.

"Oh, are you all right? You seemed to be in a trance. I didn't want to bother you; I don't know much about magic, but then you cried out." Ori held her arm, steadying her as she stretched her legs.

"I'm fine. It's a magic thing. You wouldn't understand." Delilah decided to use Ori's self-professed ignorance of all matters arcane to her advantage.

"Oh. Wow. Okay. You're all right, though?" Ori stepped back when Delilah shook off his grip. He wrung his hands, watching her. "I wouldn't want the other draks to be mad at me because something happened to you while you were here alone with me."

"I can handle my brother. He knows I can become very involved in my books." She pointed at him. "Speaking of which, they have to go away with me for a few days. You can't stay here."

Ori held up his hands. "Oh! I would never go into their personal quarters! I just need a place to do my work."

"You can start after we return. Would you trust someone you barely knew to watch all your worldly possessions while you were away?"

The blue drak clicked his teeth together, looking around the crate-filled room. "Oh, who would want my stuff? Most draks I know can't read Elven and Etrunian."

"What is it you do, anyway?"

"I'm— I'm—" Ori panted, closed his eyes, and swallowed. "I'm a limner."

Delilah pushed out her bottom lip. "What's that?"

"Oh! I illuminate manuscripts." He withdrew a book from one of the myriad crates stacked by the counter, then opened it to a page full of text with half-inked drawings covering the margins.

"So… you put light on these pages?" Delilah's confusion revealed itself on her face. Her ignorance further relaxed Ori, and he grinned.

"Oh, no." He shook his head. "I embellish the pages to make them beautiful. It's art! I can gild the edges of the pages, too." He flipped to a completed page. A complex pattern of green, blue, and gold leaf knotwork covered the margins and surrounded the text in an ornamental frame. "Normally, these things are planned from the outset, but you'd be amazed what people will pay to have it done after the fact."

He returned the book to its crate and gestured to the rest of the stack. "I have three books I'm working to embellish, plus two more commissions to do from scratch. They take a long time, so I do other smaller work on commission to pay the bills."

Delilah understood better now. "So you need a workspace and an indoor storefront."

"Oh, yes. This space is perfect. People don't pay for illumination on a whim nor for the other gilding and painting I do, so I don't need to be in a high-traffic area. Jairo is going to help send customers my way."

"I see." Delilah picked up her grimoire. She felt his eyes on her and turned to meet his gaze.

"Oh! I'm sorry. I tend to stare… it's just… I've never seen such brilliant crimson scales before." He shook his head. "And the rich, ebony stripes…"

Delilah felt warmth blossom in her heart and heat rush to her face. No one had ever identified her scales as crimson before. They always assumed she was red and black. The difference was subtle, and until now, Delilah thought she was the only person gifted enough to know the difference.

"That's right…" Delilah's voice was a whisper. "Crimson and ebony. You see it."

"Oh. Others don't? Red and black, right?" Ori licked his lips and nodded.

"Even my brother thinks he's black with red stripes. I stopped correcting him when we were still hatchlings."

Delilah wanted to trust this drak, who was clearly more educated than most she encountered. It would look bad for Kale to evict his tenant the same day he set up shop just because he had to leave. *Maybe the traps will be enough.*

She approached him, then took his hands in hers. Concentrating, she pulled together just enough energy to cause swirling blue and golden tendrils to dance around their hands. "There's a locked door, just down the hall. That's where my stuff is. Guard it with your life if need be."

Ori's eyes widened while they stared at the rope-like wisps enveloping their hands. His mouth moved, but no words escaped. Then he gulped and nodded. Delilah allowed the tendrils to fade away. She hadn't placed a geas on him, the display was just for show, but she counted on the fact that he didn't know that.

Delilah slapped him on the shoulder. "Relax! No one except my brother and his mate even know I have anything valuable stored in their home. Well, no one except them and you." She offered him a smile.

Ori giggled. "Oh. Why don't you have wings, too? Stripes are pretty special, don't get me wrong, but—"

"That's a long story. He wasn't born with them. What do you know about the chaos from which the world formed?"

"Oh! Chaos! Umm… nothing, actually. I've heard the word, that's all."

Delilah parted her lips to tell the story just as the door opened. Kale and Kali entered, each carrying bulging sacks.

"We're back! We have everything you need, Deli!"

"You didn't frighten poor Ori too badly, did you?" Kali winked at Delilah as she walked past.

"Oh! No, she didn't. I think she's amazing."

Delilah grunted and regarded the ceiling. Her brother elbowed her, jerked his head toward Ori, and grinned. Delilah snatched the sack from Kale's claws and shoved him.

"I don't need your help, Kale. Thanks for the rocks." She left her brother to deal with Ori and followed Kali to the door that led downstairs.

Kali handed her the key. "Hopefully, your brother knows what he's doing. We haven't tested this."

"Gee, thanks." Delilah wasn't too worried. If her brother knew anything, it was about locks and traps. Delilah's only concern was that he was too distracted by his mate to do his job properly. She turned the key in the lock. An impressive number of tumblers and latches released, far more than were indicated by the deceptively primitive lock on the front of the door.

She pulled the door open. A complex lock mechanism covered the back side. "I am officially impressed. He's never done work this intricate before."

"I think that puzzle box is affecting him. We can't figure out any more of it, but he often watches those clockwork mechanisms before we go to sleep." Kali held up her sack of crystals. "Need this?"

"Yes. I could use a hand, if you don't mind."

Kali recoiled in surprise. "Me? Sure! Leave the boys to their business." When she pulled the door closed behind them, the latches clicked, engaging the lock.

Delilah examined the key in her hand. "I hope this opens it both ways."

"It will." Kali led the way down the stairs. "It's the only key, too, so we're safe from them for a while."

When they reached the bottom, the gems in torch sconces burst into golden light. Kali gasped. "That's different! They weren't that color before."

Delilah had a suspicion their appearance was connected with her earlier encounter with Gil-Li. "Maybe they needed to warm up some. The last time we were here was probably the first time they lit up in centuries."

"You think?"

Delilah spread out the crystals Kale and Kali acquired for her. They brought hammers, pitons, and sufficient twine for Delilah to rig the place to fend off an army of curious treasure seekers.

She cracked her knuckles and smiled. "This will be just like old times in Drak-Anor. Let's get to work!"

***

Pancras swung his leg over the saddle horn, mounting Stormheart. His steed nickered and stomped his feet, eager to run in the open country once more. Pancras patted the horse's muscular neck, clucking his tongue to calm him. Gisella rode ahead on Moonsilver to scout the countryside while Pancras waited for Qaliah. He suspected the fiendling dawdled as a protest of sorts against leaving Edric to the whim of Curton's magistrate.

Earlier that morning, after Gisella proceeded to the jail to determine if Qaliah had decided to join them or remain behind with Edric, she returned with a sour-faced fiendling in tow. Finally, Qaliah exited The Drunken Horse carrying her saddlebags. Lady Aveline approached from behind him.

"Good thing you're leaving, Bonelord." Lady Aveline held Stormheart's reins. After fishing in her pouch, she produced a treat for the horse. Nickering, he flapped his lips over her fingers to reach it.

"Trouble?" Pancras never liked to hear someone was glad he was leaving, even if he, himself, was happy to depart.

"Piotr the smith was arrested last night. It appears he did what you could not: he smothered his mother with a pillow. They brought him in ranting about a Bonelord's Curse." She cocked an eyebrow, glancing up at him.

"I"—Pancras's mouth felt as dry as a desert in drought— "I had nothing to do—" His heart pounded in his chest, and a dark cloud passed over his thoughts. He wanted to help that woman, but despite his pleas, she would have nothing to do with him. Now her light was extinguished, taken by her very son.

"I realize that. Long has Piotr been tormented by his mother's affliction. Still"—Lady Aveline observed Qaliah retrieving and saddling her mount—"enough people overheard that, and there'll be talk. Best if you make yourself scarce."

"We're heading to Cliffport and then Vlorey, so I doubt I'll be back this way. Ever."

At the mention of her homeland, Lady Aveline stared skyward, and she sighed. "I haven't been to Vlorey since my parents and I left when I was a little girl. I wonder what it's like now. Probably different, yet the same."

Pancras fished around in his pouch and pulled out a gold crown. He offered it to Lady Aveline. "Edric has a pony stabled. Yaffa. This should cover her stall and care for a couple more weeks."

Blinking, she shook her head. "Look at me, becoming nostalgic. Thanks for trying to help the smith, Bonelord. Sorry your visit to Curton wasn't less eventful." She took the coin from him. "I'll see to it the livery gets this."

Qaliah rode Comet alongside Pancras and Stormheart. "It seems everywhere this minotaur goes, something bad happens."

Pancras felt a shiver run down his spine. Instinct told him to protest Qaliah's words, but his heart felt the truth. First, he was killed in Almeria. Then separated from his friends in Muncifer. Then killed again at the fort. Once again, he separated from a companion in Curton. Finally, his inability to help Nika burned like salt poured into an open wound.

"Dolios watch over your journey. Be vigilant near Dawnwatch Keep. It's abandoned and crumbling. Might not be safe." Lady Aveline released Stormheart's reins and waved them off.

Qaliah rode ahead of Pancras, spurring Comet whenever he started to catch up. After the third time, the minotaur realized she purposefully evaded him and contented himself with following behind. Stewing in his dark thoughts, he wondered how often he would be called upon to exercise his new power as a bonelord and how often he would fail. When all he did was brew potions and create undead, he didn't have to worry about failure. He was well-trained and practiced in all the proper techniques.

Life was simpler. Regimented. Easy, even.

Now, his burden was to help people. Not just friends, but strangers who would see him as a bonelord first and minotaur second. Some would be suspicious of him, of course, but others wouldn't care; the reputation of a bonelord would precede him, and they would have certain expectations.

How many more people are there like Piotr the smith? People who expected help from a bonelord. People he would disappoint, because not everyone was as ready as their families were to have them cross over.

A flash of light in the distance caught his attention. He spotted Gisella's armor glinting with the light of the rising sun when she waved to them from the crest of a hill. After returning the wave, Qaliah spurred Comet into a gallop, pulling farther away from Pancras. With the two women riding ahead, Pancras trailed behind.

They rode in that manner most of the morning, following the road that led east out of Curton. Near midday, Gisella steered them off the road and over the rolling hills of the countryside. Technically, although these lands were part of Etrunia, this far south and east people remained ignorant of the Almerian political situation, even before the prince's recent death. Mostly, the towns and villages fended for themselves, protected themselves, and turned to Curton or Cliffport for assistance only when situations became grave.

When they made camp that night, Curton was well behind them, past the horizon. A clear sky allowed the summer constellations to fill the sky in all their celestial glory, and the King and Queen made their way through the houses of the gods. By their light, Pancras noticed the dark shapes of a farm in the distance.

Qaliah approached him as he groomed Stormheart. "Do you have a minute?"

"Certainly." Pancras worked to loosen a knot in his horse's mane. He had not expected the fiendling to approach him after she spent most of the day avoiding him.

"I heard what Edric said last night."

"Did you now?"

The fiendling nodded. "Even whispers can echo off stone jail walls. Blondie told me about your history with him. I thought you were closer than that." She rubbed the velvet on the end of Stormheart's nose. "I may have been hasty in my judgement of you."

Pancras ran his brush along his steed's muscular neck. "He was your friend. I understand."

"I spoke to him briefly, last night." Qaliah rested her head against Stormheart's flank. "He's an outcast like me. I think he feels like if he's indentured, he'll at least have someplace to stay for a while."

"Is that why you played the fool in Muncifer?"

The fiendling straightened, nodding. "Being indentured was better than rotting in jail. Playing the fool fed me, kept me clothed, and sheltered at a time when turning tricks and robbery were the only things between living and being face-down in a dark alley's gutter."

"Life is cruel towards those of us who don't fit in with what most people consider normal." Pancras felt a twitch in his gut at the memory of his own tribulations. "I'm sorry about Edric, but I suppose being indentured is preferable to living a life on the run. Maybe he'll find a home in Curton. The mudders seem to be the type of people who could understand him."

"I guess we all just want to be accepted." She chewed on her lip for a moment. "I'm told I can be capricious." She ran her hand through her hair, brushing it out of her face. "Like the fires in which my forebears spawned, I suppose."

"It's in your nature." Pancras's experience with the fiendlings in Drak-Anor told him Qaliah's behavior, her fickle, hedonistic personality, were normal.

Qaliah frowned and huffed, then shook her head.

Pancras paused a moment as the meaning of what he just said dawned upon him. "My apologies, Qaliah. I, of all people should know better. My subconscious biases got the best of me. I'll try to be better."

"I just want you to know, even if I get angry or annoyed with you and Blondie, I'm with you." Qaliah inhaled. "This quest… thing you're doing… it's… it's my chance to do something good, something worthwhile with my life. I want to help. I want to be a part of it."

Pancras stopped untangling Stormheart's mane and met her eyes.

She reached out and touched his arm, her grip heated, on the verge of causing discomfort. "I don't want my legacy to be nothing more than that of a prancing fool forced to debase herself to keep from starving. I want my life to have meant something in the end."

"I can understand that." He placed his good hand on top of hers. "The quality of our legacy is measured by the lives we touch. The older I become, and now, especially, after what I've been through, I realize that making a difference in someone's life is the best good we can do."

Chapter 22

"I don't expect us to be gone for more than a week." Kale handed Ori a box of brushes from the crate they unloaded. "I guess you can use the hearth room if you want."

"Oh, you don't have to worry about me. I intend to use this shop to do my work and ignore all the rest of the building." Ori placed the brushes behind the counter, then reached into the crate to retrieve a tray of inks.

"That's probably wise. Even I don't mess with my sister's stuff. Wizards are dangerous, you know."

"Oh, I know. Speaking of your sister," Ori bit his lip and glanced up at Kale, "I don't suppose she has a mate back where you come from or at the Arcane University?"

Kale fought to keep a smile from crossing his face. He thought briefly about Zarach, but since Delilah hadn't spoken of him since they left Drak-Anor last year, he shook his head. "No one I know of. Of course, I don't know what she does all day at the Arcane University."

"Wizard business." Ori spoke the words as a solemn vow. He glanced down the hallway toward the door leading to the cellar stairs. "Maybe you can put in a good word for me during your journey? I'm a hard worker, loyal. I would never do anything to harm her in any way."

Kale chuckled. "You've only just met. We've only just met. I don't know a thing about you." He poked Ori in the chest. "You could be a spy for Boss Steelhand for all we know."

Ori's face dropped, and his shoulders slumped. He shuffled to the next crate, nodding. "Oh. You have no reason to trust me. I understand."

"I just don't want you to get your hopes up. I'll talk to her, sure. She's always busy though, doing things, wizard things. You know."

"Oh. Okay." Kale's promise seemed to lift Ori's spirits a bit.

They spent the next few hours unpacking and sorting through Ori's tools and supplies. By the time Kali and Delilah returned from the cavern, Ori declared the work done. "Good enough for now. I'll likely rearrange as I work out my routine."

The once-empty storefront resembled an artist's studio. Even to Kale's untrained eye, he noticed improvements in the working conditions could be had by making minor adjustments in the shop's furniture and layout. He planned to leave that to Ori, though.

"So, are we leaving right away? Kali and I still need to pack our gear."

Delilah chewed one of her claws. "I'd like to leave today, if possible. Gather your gear, and meet me at the Arcane University gates. I have a few things I need to pick up from there before we leave."

"Sounds good." Kale and Kali left Ori to fidget with his supplies while they packed. Kale liked to travel light, but he packed his puzzle box and a handful of dried, cured meat. He checked his daggers and helped Kali buckle on her daggers and harness.

"Think I'll need a cloak?"

Kale eyed his. "I won't. The mountain might be chilly, but it's still summer."

After rolling one up, Kali shoved it into her pack. She tossed Kale's hat at him. "Don't forget this. My mate must be rakish and handsome if we're going to meet a dragon."

Ori was in the midst of sorting through brushes and vials of ink when they left.

"We'll be back. We're trusting you, Ori."

The blue drak glanced up and placed his hand across his chest. "I won't let you down. You'll return to find everything exactly as you left it. I promise."

Kale hoped the drak was as good as his word. As they made their way through the markets of the undercity, Kale noticed the other draks still stared, though they made far less of a commotion this time. The potato-cart-pushing minotaur braced himself when he noticed them, but when no other draks rushed them, he relaxed a little, grunting an acknowledgement as Kale and Kali passed by him.

Before leaving the undercity, Kali stopped at a weaponsmith. She browsed through the selection of drak-forged swords. "If there's a chance we'll have to fight giants, I want something with a bigger bite than a dagger."

Kale sympathized, but he decided to stick with the daggers in his bandolier. He never trained with any other weapon and didn't want to be responsible for injuring one of his friends or his mate in the heat of battle. He pulled his cloak over his head, wrapping it tight around him, while his mate selected a single-edged sword whose blade pitched forward toward the tip and whose stylized grip resembled a nailtooth head.

The drak weaponsmith, a lanky fellow with midnight-blue scales, rubbed his black-clawed hands together. "Ah, my finest falcata. Note the grip: the finest oil-rubbed walnut, and the spine reinforcement is forged brass."

Kali swung the weapon through the air a few times. The grip fit her hand perfectly. "How much?"

"Ten crowns."

"Ten?" Kali sheathed the blade, before thrusting it at him. "Nonsense. Keep it, you swindler!"

"Ten is a bargain! I sold the last one to a stupid human for fifteen crowns." He made no move to take the weapon from her.

Kali examined the grip closely. "It's not worth more than six. There's pitting on these rivets."

"Oh, you wound me!" The weaponsmith clutched his chest, then staggered backward. "I have a mate and three hatchlings to feed. You would see them starve tonight?" Upon recovering from the feigned injury, he snatched the weapon from her. Peering at the rivets on the hilt, he snorted. "These aren't pits! They're depictions of The Bear!"

The constellation associated with Adranus, god of craftsmen, The Bear was often depicted in subtle ways by smiths to honor him. Kale put his hand on the weapon. "Look, we're in a rush. We'll give you seven crowns. You wouldn't want her to go into giant territory with just those puny daggers, would you?"

"The Striped One!" The weaponsmith's eyes widened in awe. Kale caught him before he dropped to his knees.

"None of that. I'm just a regular drak, like you."

"You are He with Wings, the Striped One! You will deliver us from our oppressors!"

For a moment, Kale was tempted to ask for the weapon for no charge. Instead, he shook his head. "No, no, no. Those are just stories. Look, we just want to buy the sword, and we'll be on our way. Six crowns is too much, but my mate is offering seven."

The weaponsmith chomped his teeth together and grumbled. "I'll give it to you for eight."

Kali took the falcata from the weaponsmith. "Eight, plus you throw in a whetstone."

"Deal!"

The two draks paid the weaponsmith, gathered their purchases, and rushed to make up lost time, weaving in, out, and around the legs of humans and minotaurs alike as they dashed to the upper city. They found Delilah and a human girl who played with the hem of her grey robe waiting for them by the university gates.

"You're bringing a human?" Kale spoke in Drak. He was sure that wasn't what his sister meant when she told him she had a few things to pick up.

"The archmage said I could take some resources from the university to help me, so Katka is going as my assistant."

"She's still wearing novice robes." Kali cocked her head.

"I understand some Drak, you know." Katka crossed her arms over her chest.

Kale felt heat rush into his face. "Sorry. It's just… it's going to be dangerous."

"And you want to make sure I'm not a liability, right?"

Delilah patted Katka on the shoulder. "Kali, don't worry about her. I wouldn't bring her along if I thought she wasn't ready. Two wizards are better than one, and there's no one else I trust."

Kale shrugged. "Fine with me, really. I'm thrilled she doesn't tower over us to be honest. It's always hard to sneak around when there's someone twice your size hanging over you." He wasn't sure if Katka was short or if she was so young that she had not finished growing. He hoped it was the former. Hatchlings had no business trekking into the mountains in search of a dragon. Although Katka stood taller than a drak, she was nowhere near as tall as the university guards or even Pancras.

Shielding her eyes with her hand, Delilah checked the sky. "Let's get moving. If we hurry, we might be able to reach the base of the mountain trail before dusk."

They stopped at the stables on their way out of Muncifer to pick up their mounts. Katka marveled at the sight of Fang, Blackclaw, and Taavi. Nailtooth lizards were a rare sight in Muncifer. Eager to stretch their legs, the lizards bounced from foot to foot, hissing, while the draks saddled them and mounted up.

"My family's farm is just outside of town." Katka pointed to the northwest. "I'll go retrieve my horse and catch up with you tonight. They won't eat him, will they?"

Delilah patted Fang's neck and shook her head. "I've been conjuring boggins for them to eat, so they should leave your horse alone.

"You're pretty small for a human." Kali fought to keep her mount from rearing. "I'll bet Taavi can carry us both. It'll be faster, and we won't have to worry about keeping the lizards from having a horse snack."

Katka wrapped her arms around herself , furrowing her brow. "I've never ridden double on a lizard before."

"Me neither." Kali reached behind to her saddle bag. After withdrawing a blanket, she held it out to Katka. The novice folded it, tucked the edge underneath the back of the saddle, then settled in behind Kali. The three draks spurred their mounts into a run. Despite the extra weight, Taavi kept up with Fang and Blackclaw. After a few hours, they increased their pace across the rolling farmland west of Muncifer.

Kale felt energized to be out of the city and on the move again. Invigorated by the possibilities the wider world offered, part of him was tempted to engaged in endless exploration; he wanted to keep riding and never turn back. The thought was fleeting, however, as he enjoyed the comforts of home more than his bedroll.

As dusk fell, the city became a dot on the western horizon, and snow-capped mountains filled the view ahead. The deeply rutted dirt road servicing nearby farms gave way to a trail few wagons or carts traveled. The trail cut an irregular, dirty scar through a sea of green grasses and brush of the foothills and overlooked a creek that carried cool, mountain snowmelt down to the Icymist River.

They made camp on the banks of the creek in a hollow carved out of a hill by a flood many years earlier. Clicking their claws on the rocks, the lizards shuffled, awaiting their evening feeding. Delilah and Katka took care of the nailtooths while Kale and Kali set up camp. By the time the wizards returned, Kale tended a roaring fire while Kali skinned a pair of rabbits she'd hunted. Fatigue and full bellies ushered them to sleep under constellations wheeling above in the night sky.

***

They rode another day and a half before they saw the ruins of what Gisella assumed was Dawnwatch Keep. They passed to the north of the keep, its crumbling walls marking what was once the eastern edge of Etrunia. The furthest outpost from the throne in Almeria, it appeared not to have been occupied for some time. A tower stood at each of the four corners of the outer wall, monuments to Etrunia's negligence of the far reaches of her realm.

A chestnut tree protruded through the keep's roof, its canopy providing shade to at least a third of the structure. Two squirrels chased each other up the trunk, disappearing into the leaves.

"Is this the place Lady Aveline told us to avoid?" Pancras halted Stormheart next to Gisella and Moonsilver.

"Dawnwatch." Qaliah trotted up on Comet. "It doesn't look so bad." She spun her horse around. "Run down, but not dangerous."

"It must have been abandoned for decades." Moonsilver stomped her feet and whinnied while Gisella stroked the mare's neck.

"With the tree taking over part of the keep, and those crumbling walls"—Pancras shook his head—"the whole thing could come down at any time."

Gisella glanced upward toward the sun. "We still have several hours of daylight, so there's no need to stop here anyway. If we push hard, we can probably reach Cliffport by tomorrow evening."

They spurred their horses, continuing on. The lands between Dawnwatch and Cliffport were not officially claimed by anyone, though most assumed they belonged to Etrunia. Cliffport itself was a free city, unbeholden to any crown, save for that of its Merchant-Prince. Gisella visited once, years ago while she tracked a rogue wizard.

She found Cliffport to be unremarkable and dull. A massive temple to Nethuns and a few shrines to other gods dotted the city's center, but the harbor defined it. Surrounded by cliffs and protected by watchtowers carved into those same cliffs, the city lived and died by its maritime trade. Almost everyone who lived there supported themselves by providing services to the sailors and traders who passed through.

Despite its singular focus, Cliffport, more cosmopolitan than Curton, hosted traders of all the sea-faring nations of the world, and more. Gisella recalled seeing a handful of cathar, bird-folk from the Western Wastes, on her last visit. Far from home, they were eager to bring back all manner of goods from more fertile lands.

Qaliah bounced in her saddle like a boggin at a roast, excited at the prospect of visiting a new city. Gisella hoped the lure of decadence there did not land the fiendling in trouble. Once they paid their way on a ship and boarded, they would be months without landfall. If they were being chased by the law, there would be nowhere to run.

**

The nailtooths' sharp claws, ill-suited for the trail through the foothills, slipped on the smooth, sheer stone. The jagged peaks of the Iron Gate Mountains lay ahead, but the road was already treacherous and rocky. Delilah feared they would be forced to turn their mounts loose and proceed on foot.

They continued onward, albeit slowly. By midmorning, Katka lost her grip on a scrabbling Taavi and fell. Kali maintained her death-grip hold as the lizard leaped and scratched at the stones. When Taavi finally found her footing, Kali slid out of the saddle and helped Katka to her feet.

"They're having a hard time, Deli." Kale hopped off Blackclaw and helped Kali steady her mount.

Delilah dismounted Fang. "Turn them loose." She rubbed Fang's neck as she unbuckled the lizard's harness.

"Only take what you need off of them; leave the tack and saddles." Katka drew her wand. "I have an idea. Kale, Kali, gather our things from the lizards. Delilah, do you have any parchment and ink? I'll write a note explaining that we're all right and need someone to tend our mounts."

Delilah rummaged through her saddle bag for a piece of parchment and found a stick of charcoal. She handed the implements to Katka. The young woman scribbled the message. When she finished, Katka pulled the three nailtooths together at the edge of the trail. She rolled up the note and secured it on the pommel horn of one of the lizards.

Green tendrils formed at the tip of her wand. She tapped each lizard in turn with the glowing tip. "*Zoe'oh goe'tia.*" Wisps of emerald aether swirled around each nailtooth's head. "Go to the Cervenak farm. They will feed and care for you. Run swiftly!"

The three lizards hissed and chirped before bounding down the mountain. Katka put away her wand. "My parents have space at their farm. We'll probably need to pay them something for boarding and feeding them when we return, but it's better than setting three nailtooth lizards loose in the western farmlands."

Nodding in appreciation, Delilah squeezed Katka's arm. "Good thinking." A flash of light near the bottom of the trail caught her eye. "Did you see that?"

"What?" Katka peered in the direction where Delilah pointed.

"I thought I saw a flicker or a flash. Down there, at the bottom of the trail."

Kale and Kali joined Katka, but also saw nothing. After searching every nook and cranny visible from their vantage point, Delilah was forced to admit it was likely a trick of the light.

"Keep your eyes open, though, all right? There's something funny about this whole business. It wouldn't surprise me one bit if we're being followed."

"By who?" Katka brushed her hair out of her eyes. "The archduke or the archmage?"

"Either. Both." Delilah shrugged. The archmage certainly did not have her best interests in mind, and she remained unsure how much she should trust the archduke and that minotaur lacky of his. "Who knows? Let's get going."

***

The wind howled, whipping Kali's cloak into Kale's face. Grunting, he pushed it away before glancing over his shoulder at his sister. His fingers ached from gripping the rocks as he climbed. "Maybe the archduke and the archmage are just trying to get rid of us."

"I don't know about the archduke, but I could believe that of the archmage. I'm glad to be away from him, though, so I don't really care." Delilah pulled herself up onto a ledge alongside her brother. "After this is done, I plan to spend as much time as I can decoding those runes on that moon gate thing we found. It's important, Kale. I know it."

Kale held his sister's shoulder. "No, I mean, they're trying to get us killed. These giants aren't going to listen to us." He regarded Kali and Katka below them. "Three draks and a human? I've been thinking about it, Deli. They're going to smash us to pulp and grind our bones to dust."

Kale learned everything he knew about giants from listening to minotaurs and oroqs trade stories in Drak-Anor. Kazi and Meriz could tell him nothing about their own kin; the two-headed giant cared only for three things: smashing, sleeping, and eating. Nothing in the stories led him to believe any giant would look upon a drak more charitably than it would a human. If these giants behaved like the ones in the stories or Kazi and Meriz, they would be eager to dispose of any draks who invaded their homes.

He clambered up onto the ledge, offered his sister a hand up, and then waited for Kali and Katka. Titan's Staircase was a winding series of cut-rock ledges leading away from the main trail. According to Delilah's information, it led directly to the giant's valley.

"We should cut and run while we have the chance." Kale didn't want to risk antagonizing a city full of draks, minotaurs, and humans if something went horribly wrong with their visit to the giants. *Pancras should be here. He should be doing this.*

Katka huffed and puffed upon the ledge where she sat. "Can we take a breather? I'm not used to this much climbing." She shaded her eyes, then gazed at the mountains behind them near Muncifer. "Wow, I've never been this high up."

Kale stood next to her, placing his hands on his hips. "Quite a view up here. Are these the Iron Gate Mountains? Or are we still in the Dragon Spines? Reminds me of home, anyway. It almost makes you forget why we came up here, huh?" He always enjoyed the view overlooking the Celtan Forest from his vantage point in Drak-Anor. The Iron Gate mountains, a younger range, featured rockier, jaggeder peaks. This close to the region where the two met, he found it difficult to tell one from the other.

"Do you really think there's a dragon sleeping under these mountains?" Kale rubbed the mark on his chest left by Terrakaptis. It had mostly faded, but the edges still felt raised under his fingers. He figured dragons would sense it, regardless. If what Delilah told him was true, the mark would prove beneficial.

The young woman faced him. "I'd love to see a real dragon up close."

"Too bad Terrakaptis couldn't bring us, huh, Kale?" Delilah sat next to Katka. "We'd be finished with all of this business and back home by now."

"Who's Terrakaptis?" Katka flicked a pebble off the edge of the cliff and watched it fall. "Another wizard from Drak-Anor?"

"Do you want to tell her, Kale?" Delilah grinned at her brother.

"You two are awful!" Kali paced behind them.

"Terrakaptis is a Firstborne, the Earth Dragon, son of Rannos and Gaia." Kale put his arm around Katka's shoulders and swept his free hand across the horizon, as if to show the young woman the world for the very first time. "His lair is at the base of the world tree at Drak-Anor."

Katka's eyes widened, and she covered her mouth with her hands, gasping. Kali smacked Kale on the top of his head. "Don't tease her."

"What? It's true!" Kale rubbed the top of his head as he regarded his mate.

After scooting away from the edge, Delilah stood. "All right, let's go. We have to be nearing the trail by now. This mountain isn't going to climb itself."

Kale wished his wings were strong enough to fly them all up to the next ledge. For a giant, these were little more than steep stairs. He supposed they did a fine job keeping all the shorter peoples of Calliome away from their village, though. Upon reflection, his sister's decision to send their mounts away was the correct one. The nailtooth lizards would never have been able to climb here.

The setting sun warmed their backs as they reached the top of Titan's Staircase. A short trail led to the crevasse marked on their map. Deep shadows gave the area a cave-like feeling, despite the clear sky above. Strange markings on the walls of the fissure seemed familiar to Kale, like the idle scratchings Terrakaptis made pacing while he regaled Kale with stories of ages past. In the distance, he heard a faint roar, like water cascading down a steep course of rocks.

Delilah and Katka gasped. Before them the crevasse gave way to a valley, at the far end of which water plummeted from a series of falls into a lake. A group of skin-and-stone huts at one end of the lake matched the location of the village on the map. From their position, the huts appeared to be typical dwellings. Smoke drifted upward in lazy ribbons from the chimneys, and people scurried about, visible from across the valley. Carved out of one of the cliff walls near the lake stood a citadel, a stone fortification that, even at this distance, dwarfed the monolithic structures of the giants.

From the overlook, they took a moment to gaze across the top of a pine forest and contemplate a scene as far removed from the politics of Muncifer as the moons were removed from Calliome. The trumpeting bellow of an animal drew their attention to the trail before them. A long-necked creature, its legs themselves the diameter of trees, emerged from the forest . Upon the giant, grey-skinned creature, sat an equally giant humanoid. He held a spear aloft, ready to hurl it at the first sign of aggression from the invaders to his home.

The giant wore leather and furs, with plates of stone serving as greaves and pauldrons. Kale glanced at his bandolier of daggers and realized if there was a fight, fleeing would be his only option. *Their skin is probably thicker than the blades of any of my daggers!*

"Draks! Human! You will come no farther. This place is forbidden to you!"

Delilah motioned for everyone else to remain still and stepped forward. She crossed her arm over her chest and bowed. "Our mission is one of peace. Archduke Fyodar of Muncifer wishes to clear up the recent misunderstandings."

The giant flicked the top of Delilah's staff with the tip of his spear, sending her focus clattering across the path. "You come bearing magic. The archduke has a strange idea of peace. We know what the archmage did to our envoys."

"But the archduke does not agree with the archmage. He sent us to speak to you about Pyraclannaseous." She peeked over her shoulder at her brother and waved him forward. The giant's spear swung around to point at Kale.

"I come bearing a message from Terrakaptis, the Earth Dragon, for Pyraclannaseous." Kale stepped forward, pulling down his bandolier to give the giant an unobstructed view of the markings seared into his chest. He hoped Delilah's plan worked. The giant's spear was long enough to skewer him before he'd have a chance of dodging it.

He considered Kale and Delilah's words before withdrawing his weapon. "You will wait here. I will return." The giant coaxed his mount to turn, then stomped off into the forest.

Delilah's shoulders slumped as she released her breath. She sat down on a nearby boulder. "Now we wait."

***

Mist kissed the tops of the trees as dawn broke over the valley. Throughout the night, Delilah neither saw nor heard any sign of the giants, though the firelight from their village winked across the valley. She was tempted to ignore the giant's warning and proceed into the valley on her own. Surely, three draks and a small human would pass unnoticed in the dense forest.

Readying her pack, Delilah prepared to lead her friends to the giants' village. A distant stomping noise, growing closer with each impact, alerted her to the giant's return. The giant who visited them the previous day emerged from the trees riding his massive, long-necked beast.

"I am to take you to the Citadel of Fire and Stone." He pulled on a rope behind him, unfurling a ladder from the basket behind his saddle. "You will ride with me."

Gawking at the giant, Katka whimpered. Delilah touched her arm, reassuring her as she passed the human girl, then climbed the ladder. The beast's skin felt leathery and cool to the touch. Its texture felt like pebbles on the shore of a lake.

Delilah gripped the rim of the basket, peering over the side. "Well, come on up. Best to get this over with."

Kale climbed up next, followed by his mate and Katka in the rear. Delilah helped the human girl over the edge. They fell into a pile, gasping, when the giant clicked his tongue and the beast lurched forward. It lumbered in a circle before it headed toward the forested valley. They watched the giant's massive hands reeling up the ladder, then securing it behind him. The basket pitched, bouncing them with each of the creature's steps, abating only after they reached the relatively level floor of the valley.

The canopy of the forest, lush and thick, shrouded the valley floor in darkness, allowing only scant rays of light to pass through. In the distance, Delilah heard a wolf howl, and as the giant creature tromped through the forest, the swaying basket lulled her to sleep, despite her efforts to remain awake and remember their path.

Delilah awoke to her brother kicking her leg from across the basket. "Wake up, Deli! We've arrived."

The giant lowered the ladder once more and pointed to the citadel across the lake. "Morlon will ferry you across."

Katka was first to descend, jumping off the ladder before she reached the bottom and landing in a crumpled pile of her own arms and legs. After standing and brushing the dirt off her robes, she steadied the ladder for Kali, Kale, and Delilah as they each descended. Her skin appeared paler than Delilah remembered.

"Are you all right?"

The human girl nodded, swallowing. "The swaying motion made me sick. I'll be all right now that I'm on my feet again."

"Don't get too used to it." Kali pointed to the boat on the shore of the lake. "Looks like we've some more riding to do."

Katka's pallor turned green just before she raced into the scrub at the edge of the forest. Delilah heard some of the giants in attendance snickering at the girl's discomfort. Like the one who brought them through the forest to the village, the giants, attired in leathers and furs, resembled tall, massive humans. Most chopped wood or chiseled stone, but a few leaned on weapons and regarded the draks, sneering down their bulbous noses at the strangers in their midst.

The village resembled those in stories of human settlements Delilah heard about from traders in Drak-Anor, albeit on a larger scale. Round and square huts with thatched rooves were clustered around a central bonfire. Children ran and played, laughing and shrieking. Others pointed at the draks and clutched at their mother's legs, fearful of the newcomers.

"These hardly seem like the sort of people to send emissaries back in pieces, eh?"

Kale shrugged. "The guards might."

On her way to the edge of the lake, Delilah ignored the staring child chewing on his finger who shuffled along behind them, taking note that the top of her head reached only his waist. She approached the giant standing knee-deep in the water alongside the boat. She waved her hand in greeting, allowing the cool waters of the valley lake to lap over her feet.

"Are you Morlon?"

The giant pointed at himself. "Morlon vosta ka nook. Bala fu kanoo pok turock." He pointed at the citadel.

Delilah had never before heard the giants' language. She waved Kale and Kali over, peering into the forest in the direction Katka ran to empty her stomach. The human girl emerged, wiping her mouth on her sleeve, then trotted to the shore.

"Sorry. The thought of getting in a boat at that moment was too much. I'm better now."

"Are you sure?" Delilah brushed Katka's arm "You can stay here."

The color drained from Katka's face again as she glanced at all the giants watching them. She shook her head. "No. No, I don't think I can do that."

"Let's go then." Kali climbed into the boat and helped Kale over the side. The draks, dangling their feet, held onto the planks that served as seats. Katka's toes, barely touching the bottom of the boat, provided more stability, but she still held onto the plank for support. Morlon grunted, pulling the rope. The ferry lurched forward before gliding across the water.

Chapter 23

Leaving Dawnwatch Keep behind them as dusk fell, Gisella led Pancras and Qaliah to the road. Her overland route shaved days off their journey, and it was a simple matter of following the road and river past the southern edge of Raven's Forest to Cliffport.

Pancras recalled rumors that told of the elves of Raven's Forest watching the banks of the river day and night, jealously guarding their border. Lush with thick, deciduous growth, shrubs, and bushes, both the northern and southern sides of the Copper Run River could easily conceal elven archers. The river's edge, however, left travelers exposed with nowhere to hide in the event of an attack.

From his seat atop Stormheart, Pancras saw no signs of watchful elves. He found most rumors were merely stories concocted by bored folk trying to one-up each other while sharing ales at the tavern. Concluding the stories were fabrications, he decided it was highly unlikely they were being watched.

Qaliah rode next to Pancras. "The Icymist always looks so inviting. Even if you know it's too cold to go swimming, you want to. This thing looks like it would drown you in mud."

The minotaur nodded, curling his lip at the thought of taking a dip in the uniform-brown sludge of the Copper Run rushing downhill in an attempt to escape itself.

"It runs downstream from the industry of Curton, where the mudders churn up clay and gods know what else." Pancras steadied Stormheart as the horse tossed his head, snorting. "You couldn't pay me to go swimming in that."

"I bet the elves love it." Gisella gestured to the forest on the opposite bank.

"No doubt." Pancras scratched his chin. "I wonder if the roots of Syl'drasil reach this far."

"What's that?" Qaliah regarded the river as they rode.

"The World Tree of Raven's Forest. Said to be at least a mile tall. It would have very far-reaching roots." Its location was a closely guarded secret, and though the city of Raven's Forest was built on and around the World Tree, its occupants welcomed no visitors.

"It's hundreds of miles away. I doubt its roots run this far." Gisella spurred Moonsilver into a trot, calling to them as she pulled away, "Let's stretch their legs some. We're losing daylight." They pressed on, running their mounts for a while before slowing to a lazy canter. They passed a caravan of tinkers and traders around midday and another as the afternoon hours waned. At night, after dining on crusty bread and dried meat procured from the traders, Gisella offered to spar with Qaliah. The two women possessed different fighting styles but fell into a rhythm that, to Pancras's untrained eye, seemed to benefit them both.

Meanwhile, Pancras communed with Aita and performed the rituals needed to attune himself to his maul. He felt a twinge of guilt, like a rock in the pit of his stomach, for how he acquired the weapon. His inability to help the blacksmith's mother weighed on him. Pancras realized only through the success of his future acts could he atone for his failure in Curton. For a moment, his thoughts turned to Edric. The dwarf was rude and gruff, but was, after a fashion, a friend.

Pancras reviewed escape scenarios in his head. *Was there anything we could have done?* Every permutation he considered ended with the rest of them imprisoned or dead and depended upon the assumption Edric would have left with them willingly; he seemed adamant in his vow to avoid sailing. The minotaur pushed the thoughts aside, cradled his weapon in his lap, and then closed his eyes, concentrating on the warmth he felt from it.

As the power of Aita flowed into him, a suffuse glow surrounded him. He sensed the life all around him: the worms in the earth, the grass and trees, an insect alight on a nearby shrub, the fiendling and the human as they practiced their swordplay. He felt not the strength of their life force but its ebbs. Around him, all life was dying, some more quickly than others. Combined with the universal constant of the slow turn of time, each breath a living creature drew brought them closer to death, closer to the realm of Aita.

Pancras felt the presence of his goddess as she affected all living things. His consciousness expanded as he fell deeper into his trance. The world itself was dying on a timescale beyond his comprehension, but he felt it ebb, nonetheless. Calliome and Gaia were one, still healing from the Sundering.

In the distance, on the far side of the continent of Andelosia, Pancras's mind touched another: a dark, dead presence. A hole in the life force of the world. The presence was old, but not ancient, powerful, yet without form or substance. It was cold, yet infused with a hellish heat.

The presence was aware of him. He knew it perceived him. For an instant, their minds touched, and he learned more than he wanted to know. Fearing the exchange was reciprocal, Pancras opened his eyes.

He could see nothing but darkness.

The minotaur's mind was still connected to that of the Lich Queen. Deep within her bower at the northern edge of the Celtan Forest, she gathered strength. She sought out willing servants and champions to lead her armies.

I feel the Princess of the Underworld in your touch. How fortunate for you that she saved you from my shadow. Now she uses you in a feeble, misguided attempt to destroy me. You will fail. My purpose, my nature, is beyond your comprehension. Pledge yourself to me, and I will spare you. I will give you dominion over this world.

Pancras pulled away, recoiling like a sapling's branch after one plucks a fruit from it. His mind would not allow him to construct a reply, and after the brief brush with the Lich Queen's consciousness, a disjointed, kaleidoscopic flash of whirling shapes and colors formed the chaotic image in his mind

Your path will lead you to me, just as it has since you took my shadow from the chaos. You will serve me, or you will die. In death, you will serve me. It is inevitable. It is your destiny. Your fate and that of this world lie with me.

Pancras cried out, falling backward before he opened his eyes. The glare of dawn blinded him for a moment. Blinking to clear the tears created by the light of the sun, he rolled over. Gisella helped him to his feet.

"You were deep in that trance. We were afraid to disturb you."

Qaliah brought Pancras a steaming mug of mulled wine. "You glowed all night. I wanted to throw a blanket over you to save our eyes, but Blondie here wouldn't let me."

Pancras accepted the mug with shaking hands. He tried to speak but could only open and close his mouth; no sound issued forth. He fought to control his ragged breath and allowed the warm wine to fill his belly instead. By the time he emptied the mug, his hands had steadied once again.

"Thanks for watching over me." He poured himself some more wine from the pot sitting at the edge of the fire.

"Didn't have a choice. It was like sleeping with twin full moons shining in our eyes." Qaliah tossed him a hunk of dried meat.

"It wasn't as bad as all that." After pulling the pots away from the fire, Gisella scattered the embers. "I am curious what was happening with you, though. Are you all right?"

"It began as… I was just attuning myself and the maul to Aita's power." Pancras lifted the weapon. It felt more connected to him and the goddess of death's power than ever before. *At least that part worked.* "I'm not certain I understand all that transpired. I felt the life force of the world, all that which Aita touches and affects as goddess of death, and then something intruded. It was like a hole in the world. Intelligent, malevolent. I believe it was the Lich Queen."

Gisella stopped scattering ashes and turned toward him. "Are you sure?"

"No. The entity did not identify herself." Pancras held his head. "Perhaps I fell asleep. Perhaps it was just a dream."

Qaliah poured herself more mulled wine. "I wonder if your devotion to your gods is worth the risk. It seems like they take perverse delight in messing with you and your friends." After draining her mug, she lifted the pot. She shook out as much of the residue as possible before shoving it in her saddlebag.

Pancras kept silent. Many people felt as Qaliah did, that the gods were little better than meddlesome nuisances. Pancras hoped with his newfound faith and his more intimate connection with Aita, he would be able to answer such challenges.

Thus far, however, each encounter provided more questions than answers.

***

The Citadel of Fire and Stone loomed over them, the carvings on its face unfamiliar to Delilah. She noticed the windows on the watchtowers flanking the approach resembled eyes. Attached to a pulley mechanism on the inside of the citadel, the rope guided the ferry. She felt as if the cliff swallowed them when the ferry slid through the entrance. It bumped to a stop into the interior dock.

She lent a hand to Kale to steady him. After her brother exited the ferry, he helped her, Kali, and finally Katka disembark.

The air within the citadel smelled of mold and decay. Darkness shrouded the interior dock, save for a bit of sunlight reflecting off the water and shining through the entryway.

Apart from their breathing, water lapping at the stones and wood planks of the pier was the only audible sound.

Katka held aloft her wand. "*Fos.*" The tip glowed.

Delilah angled her staff forward. "*Fos.*"

Their arcane foci provided more than sufficient illumination to guide them. The dock led to a stone ramp. At the top of the ramp, a doorway opened deeper into the citadel. Delilah took the lead, checking her footing, careful to avoid slick spots on the damp stone.

"It's warmer in here than I expected." Katka wiped her brow. Now that the human girl mentioned it, Delilah noticed the heat, as well.

"Stone and fire, just like the giant said, I suppose." The drak sorceress came to a door, but the handle lay above her head, just out of her reach.

Katka jumped up, but she failed to grab the handle. She pointed her wand at the door. "*Dynami antikeimeno kalesei.*" After the light at the tip of her wand winked out, the door handle jerked downward. Katka guided the door open with her wand.

"Good work." Delilah stepped through the doorway into a vast room, its vaulted ceiling supported by columns thick enough for draks to build homes within them. The light from her staff illuminated only a fraction of the cavernous space.

The air in the room felt thick and heavy. It stank of sulfur and soot, yet Delilah observed no source of the odor. She noted the dark grey dust that covered the floor, except for a well-worn path wandering through the columns. Gesturing to the others, she followed the path across the room. The clicking of her claws against the stone floor echoed in Delilah's ears, and for the first time in her life, she found herself envying the coverings humans wore on their feet.

"Ba lor, kon… forgive me. It has been too long since I have had such small visitors."

Stopping, Delilah searched for the source of the voice. It came from within the darkness ahead.

"Please, continue. I dwell in darkness but do not mind the light." The voice sounded raspy and breathless, as though its owner was unused to speaking.

Delilah led her friends forward. At the far end of the room, she noticed a throne. Upon it sat a wizened giant. His snowy white beard spilled over his knees and covered his feet like a blanket. A crown of disheveled white hair covered his head, hanging down over his drooping face. Even though he was seated, Delilah stood only as high as his mid-calf.

"Welcome, draks. You'll forgive me if I don't stand. I am so very old, you see." He coughed. "I'm told one of you bears the mark of a draevyehfehdin. Your purpose here confuses me."

"We come on behalf of the Archduke of Muncifer." Delilah stepped forward, noting the giant's eyes were hidden behind his snowy mane.

"Yet, there is a human of the archmage with you. He has proven himself to be no friend of my people."

Delilah glanced back at Katka before bowing to the giant. "She is here as my friend and assistant. The archduke and the archmage are at odds with regard to your people."

"I would speak with the draevyehfehdin."

Kale gulped audibly and stepped forward. "That would be me. Kale of Clan Windsinger."

"Who marked you thus?"

"Terrakaptis, the Earth Dragon—"

"Firstborne of Rannos Dragonsire and Gaia the Earth Mother." The giant nodded, reclining in his throne and tilting back his head. "Yes, I knew him once." Delilah heard his elbow joints crackle when he extended his arms, but she attributed the sound to his advanced age.

The giant sighed before folding his hands in his lap. "It was so very long ago. An age has passed, and what we were has long since been forgotten. I am Ragnok the Younger, King Under the Mountain, ruler of the Iron Giants."

Delilah's mind reeled. She had heard of the Iron Giants, but everything she had read, everything anyone ever told her about them, suggested they all died during the Sundering.

She cleared her throat. "Am I to understand that you were born before the Sundering?"

"Yes." Ragnok chuckled before his face settled into a slanted grin. "As I said, a long time ago. Why has Terrakaptis sent a draevyehfehdin to me?"

Delilah nudged her brother. Kale frowned at her and slapped at her hand. "I heard his sister is here. Nearby? Pyraclannaseous?"

"The Fire Dragon." Ragnok gripped the arms of his throne. "The Iron Giants guard her slumber."

Kale licked his lips. "Terrakaptis thinks it's time for his siblings to wake up."

Delilah shone her staff around the room. The King Under the Mountain was not attended. No guards, no servants, just him, alone. It struck her as odd. "Kale should see her. In the meantime, you and I can speak of Muncifer and your agreement with the Archduke."

"There is nothing for you here, draks." Ragnok coughed and wheezed. "I know what the archduke desires. I know what the archmage desires."

Kale seized his sister's arm, but Delilah shook him off. "What they want are complete opposites, it seems."

"Delilah!" Katka tapped her arm. Delilah shook her head, keeping her eyes on the giant king.

"Kale, grab her!"

Delilah willed Kali and all the rest to shut up while she tried to be diplomatic. Her brother forcefully spun her around. Her profanity-filled tirade caught in her throat as her eyes focused on the skeletal giants advancing from the darkness.

The wheezes of Ragnok faded, and he chuckled. "Like those who have come before you, you will find only death here."

***

"Do you think he's gone mad?" Qaliah glanced over her shoulder at Pancras as they rode. Gisella guided Moonsilver around a soft patch of earth. Encounters with deities often drove folks mad, but she hoped that was not the case with Pancras. The minotaur remained quiet most of the morning, responding to questions directed to him but offering no conversation without first being prompted.

"Much has happened to him since we left Muncifer. Perhaps he is reflecting." Gisella considered if she had died, met her goddess in a near-death experience, and then encountered her grandmother's disembodied spirit while trying to commune with Aurora, she would have many things to think over.

"I think he's cracked and he's having vivid dreams he thinks are real." Qaliah withdrew a stick of dried meat from her pack.

"You killing him was no dream. Clearly, something greater is at work here." There was a time when Gisella indulged in skepticism as the fiendling did. Since her own encounter with Aurora, however, she learned the gods of Calliome interfered in the world, albeit rarely. She couldn't blame Qaliah for her doubts, though. To anyone who had not experienced the touch of a god themselves, it might seem like madness.

"Well, hopefully, he'll keep those mad dreams to himself while we're on the ship. How long will the journey to Vlorey take?"

"A few months, I expect." Gisella wasn't sure herself but had heard stories.

"Joy." Qaliah spurred Comet and ran ahead of Gisella, who slowed Moonsilver to allow Pancras to catch up. His eyes stared off into the distance, so she let him ride in peace. He appeared to her to be lost in thought as opposed to having gone mad.

They rode without conversation the rest of the afternoon. Qaliah eventually circled back to them. When they were all three together, walking alongside their horses on the banks of the river, Pancras broke his silence.

"If what I encountered was the Lich Queen's consciousness, then what she told me was troubling." As they strode, their horses' hooves crunched through the pebbles of the riverbank. Chirping, a pair of thrushes fled a nearby bush, and a light breeze carried the aroma of honeysuckle.

"Care to elaborate, big guy?" Qaliah kicked a rock into the river.

"She said we could not comprehend her nature, her purpose. She offered me dominion over this world if I pledged myself to her." He stopped for a moment to pluck a stone from the bottom of his hoof.

"Power-hungry maniacs often attempt to tempt others with promises of power." Gisella heard enough stories from her mother to recognize Pancras's account as one of her grandmother's favorite tactics.

"It didn't sound like her goal was to return to this world in a physical form." Pancras rubbed his right horn as he shook his head. "And what's so special about me that I'm a prize for her?"

Gisella had an answer for that. "You have been touched by Aita. People make an effort not to think of her. Contemplating death is unpleasant, but, in the end, none of us are out of her reach. Beggar and king, warrior and scribe, weak, powerful, it doesn't matter. Each of our final destinies lies with the goddess of death. We cannot escape it."

"I'm glad we can have such cheerful conversations." Qaliah snorted, patting Comet on the neck.

"She's right. It is part of life." Sighing, Pancras leaned on Stormheart as he gazed across the river. "The end of the circle is also a beginning. What lies beyond the veil is the last great mystery any of us will ever confront."

Gisella ran her fingers through Moonsilver's mane. "A bonelord would be a valuable resource for one hoping to defeat death itself. The Lich Queen's quest for immortality is part of our history. Why would the destruction of her physical body hinder that quest?"

"Wait, wait, wait." Qaliah held up her hands. "Are you saying that this moldy, old dead bitch is still trying to figure out a way to not be dead? And she's willing to destroy the world to do it?"

The minotaur scratched his chin. "I am not certain she wishes to destroy the world, but yes, I think she is so obsessed with her quest for immortality that the last two times she was defeated merely delayed her."

Gisella yearned to discuss the situation with her sister. Alysha was more learned in Lich Queen lore than anyone else Gisella knew. The blood ties she and her sister shared with the Lich Queen undoubtedly played into her plan, though Gisella was at a loss to explain why. Her sister was so sure of it, she warded herself against magical scrying and communication; hence the letter she sent with Grímar. For now, all she could do was join with the minotaur's speculations and hope the Lich Queen's plan became clear, before it was too late to act.

***

Kale pulled his sister out of the reach of a skeleton's oncoming bony arm. With its attempt to scoop up the drak thwarted, it gripped its club with both hands and swung it in a powerful overhead blow. Kale jumped backward as the club smashed the floor where he stood previously. Bits of broken stone peppered Kale, stinging where they pierced his scales. Grabbing the end of the club, he rode its ascent until he could jump onto the giant's shoulders as the goliath prepared his next swing.

Delilah scrambled to avoid another bony giant's attack, her claws slipping on the smooth stone floor. Katka blasted another, sending chips of bone flying through the air, but causing no real damage. Kale watched his sister conjure a protective shield to protect the human from a blow from the giant and then drew his dagger. He plunged it into the giant's head, but its skull was too thick, and he succeeded only in chipping bone. As the undead creature ignored the drak on its back and turned its attention to Kali, Kale found himself wishing he'd purchased a heavier weapon when he had the opportunity.

The one Kale stabbed in the head swung its club at Kali as she dodged an attack by a third skeletal giant. Her falcata whirled and flew, hacking its shins. Flakes of bone flew from her opponent's legs, each blow from her blade carving new notches. Kale yanked his dagger out of the giant skeleton's skull. The giant spun, and Kale felt himself slip. Despite spreading his wings to maintain balance, he fell off the giant's shoulders. Gliding in an arc around its head, he breathed fire.

The giant's head erupted in crimson flames. The bone turned black as it burned, but the undead giant continued attacking the area underneath itself, trying to smash the small annoying creatures below .

Delilah conjured a magical ball of fire and hurled it at another giant, engulfing it. It, too, pressed its attack and ignored the flames that charred its bones.

"Great, now we're fighting flaming giant skeletons!" Kale landed next to his sister. Katka slid across the floor after dodging a blow from a giant's club.

She rolled to her feet, pointing her wand at their advancing foe. "*K'teep'ma tis astrapis!*" A bolt of lightning shot forth, coursing through the skeleton.

"Nothing is working!" The human grunted as a swing of the giant's club caught her arm and sent her spinning. She collapsed onto the floor, cradling her arm.

"The king! Get the king!" Delilah pulled her brother's arm and spun him, pointing him toward Ragnok.

The elderly giant grinned, his crooked, rotting, yellow teeth visible behind the sea of white covering his head and face. Kale ducked under the legs of one of the skeletons, drawing another dagger as he ran. He stopped to throw both of them toward the giant king.

Kale's blades sank into his chest. The king's hands snapped up, clutching at the protruding hilts. His grin faded as he wheezed, and flecks of blood colored his lips.

A burnt-orange flash passed him as Kali rushed toward the king with her sword raised. She cried out and swung, sinking the blade into his leg. He grimaced and swatted at her, knocking her aside.

From the corner of his eye, he saw Katka point her wand at the king. She loosed another bolt of lightning. It struck his temple, snapping back his head. Arcs of electricity danced across his features as he screamed.

Kale felt the whoosh of air and dove forward a split second before one of the skeleton's clubs came crashing down. He felt it brush his heels and tucked into a roll that brought him to the base of the throne's dais. When he came to his feet, he unleashed a gout of fire at the giant king.

The king's robe and beard erupted in flames. His screams rose in pitch as he burned. Kale felt the ground rumble and turned to search for his sister.

Delilah darted back and forth, avoiding the blows of the giant skeletons whose attention she held, weaving her staff in an intricate pattern. Kale heard her chanting. Pebbles and dust fell from the ceiling in a steady rain.

Spikes of stone burst from the floor. One upended a skeleton, sending it falling toward Kale. He ran toward Kali and spread his wings to protect them as he crouched over her. The giant hit the dais, cracking ribs on impact. Its head popped off its neck, crashing into the lap of the giant king. Both tumbled to the floor, the latter still ablaze.

Another spike impaled one of the giant skeletons, splitting it and sending chunks of bone flying. More dirt and rocks fell from the ceiling, and Kale pulled his wings closer, hugging Kali nearer to him.

The screams of the burning giant king subsided, and the rumbling earth slowed and stopped. When the dust cleared, Kale dared to pull back his wings and open one eye.

Delilah climbed on top of a pile of rocks and bones. When she reached the top, she offered a helping hand to Katka as the human girl joined her.

Kali pushed Kale off her. "Tinian himself would have a hard time topping that!"

The corpse of the giant king smoldered, his head smashed by a block of stone from the ceiling. Shards of giant skeletons littered the chamber the way leaves clutter the forest floor. Everyone and everything was covered in a layer of dust and caked with blood.

Delilah peered at her brother from the top of the pile. "Well, that worked."

"I don't think our negotiations were successful, Deli."

Chapter 24

"He didn't even give us a chance to negotiate. What's going on, Delilah?" Katka picked her way down the side of the pile of bones and rocks. She leaned on the drak sorceress for support, keeping her broken arm tight against her stomach.

"Something's not right." Delilah rubbed the back of her neck, picking flakes of stone from her scales. "I'm sure someone would have told me if these giants were being ruled by a lunatic with monstrous skeletons."

"He certainly seems like the type who would want to attack Muncifer instead of trade. But why now? What changed this year?" Katka hopped down to the floor and rubbed her arm.

Delilah had an idea about that. "The archduke said something about some tremors this past spring, during the archmage's visit with the giants."

Katka shook her head, wincing in pain as she touched her wounded arm. "I don't know anything about that. There were some tremors, yes, but they happen every couple of years."

"Did he think the archmage caused the tremors?" Kale struggled to roll the giant king's charred body over. Kali crouched down to help him.

"They accused each other of all sorts of things, but he said he didn't know any earth magic." Delilah considered that the archmage may have lied.

"Earth magic is unheard of at the Arcane University." Katka pulled out her wand and levitated the giant king's body enough for the draks to shove it out of the way. Kale retrieved his daggers, wiping them clean on an unburnt remnant of the king's clothes.

"In fact, they teach us in History of the Arcane Arts that earth and water magic was lost during the Sundering. I've never seen anyone do what you just did, Delilah."

"Deli's always surprising people." Kale put his arm around his mate.

"I learned it from Gil-Li's grimoire."

"Gil-Li?" Katka's jaw dropped. "The drak archmage? That book you have was hers?"

Delilah rubbed her snout. "Yes. Terrakaptis gave it to me."

Katka's eyes grew wide, and she stepped backward until she stumbled and fell onto the dais. She steadied herself with her good hand and stared at Delilah. "Does the archmage know you have it?"

"No." Delilah scoffed at the thought. She knew better than to tell Archmage Vilkan anything about any of her prized possessions. "Are you going to tell him?"

Katka huffed. "Certainly not! You're my friend. He's an oaf! You should know better than that!"

Kali cleared her throat. "These magic lessons are probably fascinating, but we shouldn't linger."

"You're right. Sorry, Kali." Delilah smiled when she realized she didn't feel a twinge of irritation admitting that to her brother's mate. She produced a light from her staff, then stepped to the back of the room, near the dais. The wall loomed over her, the ceiling far out of range of her staff's light.

The others followed behind her as she traced along the edges of the room, seeking a passageway or some exit apart from the one through which they entered.

"Here, here!" Katka found the passage they sought, a crumbling tunnel which, to the giants, probably resembled a mouse hole.

Delilah saw a faint orange glow at the far end of the tunnel and smelled the strong odor of brimstone. She extinguished her light and followed the winding path, careful to avoid loose rocks. The ceiling was low enough for her to touch with an outstretched hand, and some narrow passages required Katka to crouch to squeeze through.

"Where ever this goes, Deli, is not a place the giants visit."

"Thanks, Kale. I figured that out for myself." As soon as she uttered the words, Delilah felt the sting of their harshness. Her stomach growled, and her muscles ached from dodging the attacks of the giant skeletons.

The glow grew ever brighter as they descended deeper and deeper. Soon the odor of decay overtook that of brimstone. The stench grew stronger the closer they grew to the end of the tunnel.

"Oh, that's rank." Kale waved his hand in front of his nose as the tunnel emptied into a vast cavern. A chasm split the cavern in two, with a river of lava at the bottom providing a hellish glow that illuminated even the ceiling far above. Drak-sized crystals protruding in every direction from the walls and ceiling added to the radiant glow.

Delilah felt as though she'd stepped into the middle of a giant geode. Many draks kept fist-sized geodes as decorations in their homes in Drak-Anor, but she doubted any of them imagined standing inside one the size of a small village. She took a moment to absorb it all: the way the vermilion light from the magma reflected in the faces of the crystals, the echoes of her friends' footsteps as they found secure footing inside, and the distortion caused by the rising heat from the lava river.

Through the heat distortion, Delilah saw a sinuous, elongated shape lying on the opposite side of the chasm. Using her staff for support, she climbed down the smooth crystalline faces, making her way to the crack in the geode's floor. Multiple reflections from the crystals surrounding the shape, distorted by rising heat, made it impossible to clearly identify it.

When she reached the edge, Delilah teetered for a moment before stepping back. The reptilian shape, covered in cracked, black scales and obscured by crystalline pillars and clusters, wound around crystal formations as large as houses.

Kale landed next to her, flapping his wings for stability. "Is that Pyraclannaseous?"

"It looks like a dragon, doesn't it?" Delilah squinted, hoping to see more clearly through the sulfurous haze rising from the chasm. "It's not moving though."

The haze and the heat shimmer made it difficult to determine if the dragon was motionless or merely sleeping. She watched its limbs for a moment to see if they twitched. Her breath caught as she heard the squeak of leather on the crystal behind her.

"What is that?" Katka helped Kali climb down to the large crystal on which they now all stood.

"Let's have a look, Deli."

As she cried out in protest, Kale grabbed Delilah under her arms and pushed off the crystal. For a dizzying moment, Delilah saw nothing below her except a river of lava and then felt an updraft catch in Kale's outstretched wings. The heat from below felt as if it would roast the scales off her body, and for a moment, she couldn't feel her brother's hands under her arms. She drew a ragged breath and clenched her jaw to keep from screaming. The updraft lifted them over the chasm, and the two draks landed next to the unmoving tail.

Katka and Kali seemed so far away as they stood on the other side of the chasm. After catching her breath, Delilah waved at them. "Stay there! We won't be long."

She heard Kali's faint, but clear warning. "Be careful!"

Delilah jammed an elbow into her brother's ribs. "Hear that? Your mate says 'be careful.' That means no more flying over lava without warning, got it?"

"I knew the updraft would carry me over, Deli." Kale jumped. He grabbed onto a crystal ledge, pulled himself up, and then offered his sister a hand.

"But both of us?"

Kale's silence as they climbed was telling. Delilah chose to let the matter drop, since they were both alive and well for the moment. As they worked their way through the crystals, following the dragon's body, she was struck by the extent of its emaciation. The stench of decay grew stronger as they covered its length, and after climbing up on a monolithic crystal, she saw why: a massive crystal lay shattered amongst the ruined remnants of the dragon's head.

Blood stained nearby crystals. Ragged, blackened flesh lay shriveled. Long exposure to the heat of the lava dried and withered the flesh and exposed tissue.

Kale took his sister's hand as the draks surveyed the grim scene. Pyraclannaseous, the Fire Dragon, was dead.

***

Unlike other cities Pancras visited, no walls, guard towers, or fortifications guarded Cliffport's entrance. Only the Copper Run River itself formed any sort of barrier between Cliffport and the surrounding lands. The arched, stone bridge that crossed the river served to funnel travelers into the city. Even on the far side, enough shops and stables surrounded the road, that Pancras wasn't sure where the official city boundary lay.

Qaliah patted Comet's neck as she dismounted. "I hope you're not thinking we'll need to sell our horses to get on a ship."

Stormheart whinnied as if protesting the idea. Pancras swung his leg over the horse's neck and slid from his saddle. "Hopefully that won't be necessary."

"It will cost more to find a ship willing to accommodate them." Gisella remained mounted, gazing at the surrounding buildings from atop her saddle. An ox-pulled wagon passed them, the bells around the oxen's neck ringing in time with its steps as the wheels of the wagon clattered on the cobblestones.

Pancras led Stormheart by his reins across the bridge. "I think we should head to the port first. Perhaps the tides are rising, and we can board a ship sooner, rather than later."

"It can't hurt to investigate, I suppose." Gisella dismounted Moonsilver when they reached the far side of the bridge. Cliffport was built on the downslope of the granite cliffs which flanked the river. They followed the road to a square by the entrance before it turned parallel to the Copper Run. The river plunged through the middle of the city before it emptied into the back of the harbor.

The streets of Cliffport were less congested and straighter than those of Muncifer and Almeria. Pancras found it easy to maintain his bearings as they made their way through the Market District, through several residential districts, and to the Trade District, which reached to the very edge of the cliffs. A series of carved steps and lifts scaled the final hundred feet down from the edge of the city into the Docks District.

Apart from a few taverns, most of the buildings in the Trade District functioned as warehouses and stored the various goods arriving or waiting to depart by sea. Some operated lifts by which travelers could lower their mounts to the docks for a few coins.

Pancras held his breath as he took in the view overlooking the harbor. Twin promontories surrounded the harbor, offshoots of the cliffs upon which the city was built. Gulls flew at the end of the docks, squawking at anyone who ventured too close. Like corks in a basin, moored ships bobbed under a stark white arch that spanned the harbor entrance from the end of each promontory.

After dismounting, the three companions led their horses onto the lift.

"Nethun's Arch." Gisella rubbed Moonsilver's nose and appreciated the surroundings with Pancras. "The Archway to Andelosia."

"Or the exit." Qaliah stood with her arms wrapped around Comet's neck, standing as far away from the edge of the lift as possible. A gust of wind rocked the platform, and she gasped before burying her face in her horse's neck.

Pancras steadied himself with a hand on Stormheart's withers. He'd never seen the sea before. Beyond the arch, a vast expanse of brownish-green water awaited. Dark clouds touched the ocean on the horizon, a wall to meet the edge of the world.

"They say the sea is cold. Capricious. Unforgiving. It's difficult to comprehend the extent of the thing." The minotaur shivered, though the breeze was warm. He inhaled the salt air, wrinkling his nose at the stench of dead fish wafting up from the docks.

"Who says that?" Qaliah's voice sounded muffled as she spoke through Comet's mane.

"Sailors I've met."

They lost sight of the archway when the lift passed behind some warehouses. Jerking to a halt, the platform reached the end of its journey, and Pancras stumbled. A grubby man with a bandana tied around his head opened the gate. "Get a move on. We've cargo to lift."

Pancras, Gisella, and Qaliah led their horses onto the docks. Unlike the stone streets of the upper city, the Docks District was built entirely upon the silty shore at the bottom of the cliffs. Supported by thick wooden beams, wood planks set atop the silt formed streets and boarded walkways over the shallow tide pools.

"We should find the harbormaster's office." Gisella stopped at an intersection to make way for a team of sailors pushing a cart laden with crab baskets. "They should have a listing of ships and departures."

"What's that building over there?" Qaliah pointed toward a square tower rising above the warehouses near the piers.

"Probably the harbormaster's office." Gisella squeezed Qaliah's arm, passing her. The clopping of their horses hooves on the wooden planks joined the cacophony of commerce on the docks, making conversation nearly impossible.

A mixed group of sailors and laborers leaning against the wall in a line, complained about the humid air, their back-breaking labor, and poor pay. Their eyes followed the three travelers approaching the entrance to the building.

Gisella took Stormheart's reins. "I'll watch the horses with Qaliah. Leaving her out here alone doesn't seem safe."

"I can handle myself." The fiendling tried to take the reins from Gisella, but the slayer refused to relinquish them.

"Indeed you can, but we don't have time to deal with magistrates and misunderstandings. There's safety in numbers here."

Pancras removed his hammer from his saddle. "I'll be fast."

The harbormaster's office sat perched atop a staircase that zig-zagged up the center of the warehouse. From his seat behind a stained, cracked desk, a grey-furred minotaur with upswept, black-flecked, tawny horns wiped a glistening nose on his sleeve when Pancras entered.

"Looking for work? That's the line outside. Got a complaint? Not my problem." The harbormaster's voice was as salty as the air.

"Seeking a ship to take us and our horses to Vlorey, as a matter of fact. Myself, a human, and a fiendling." He shook his money pouch. "A good, comfortable ship."

The harbormaster reached under his desk to scratch himself. "There aren't any ships for just passengers. What can you do?"

"I'm a wizard and a Bonelord of Aita." Pancras laid his maul on the desk so the relief skull faced up, visible to the harbormaster. "My companions can fight with blades, maybe bows."

Wiping his nose again, the harbormaster sniffed. "Wizard, huh? Well, that's not useless." He grunted, pushed himself away from the desk, and clomped over to a shelf in front of the window that overlooked the docks.

"Had an elf mystic come through here a few months back. He could talk to trees and sing to birds. Wanted to hire on a ship to see the sea." The harbormaster flipped open one of the books sitting on the shelf and ran his finger across the lines.

"Here she is: the *Maiden of the High Seas.* Selene's Pier up at the north end of the harbor." The harbormaster pointed out the window to a ship mostly obscured by warehouses. "The captain's a Watchman called Eingvar Salt-Wind."

"Thank you, Harbormaster."

Grunting, the minotaur flipped shut his book. He stared out the window, offering nothing further. Pancras descended the stairs and found Gisella and Qaliah across the street waiting with the horses, ignoring the sailors' catcalls and off-color comments .

"Found a ship. The *Maiden of the High Seas* at Selene's Pier at the north end."

Qaliah regarded Pancras with wide eyes. "That was easier than I expected."

Pancras took Stormheart's reins from Gisella. "It's a possibility. We haven't booked passage yet."

With a bit of Dolios's luck and a few coins, perhaps we can depart this place sooner, rather than later. "Have you heard of Eingvar Salt-Wind?"

"Who's that?" Gisella shook her head.

"The captain. He's a Watchman."

"Many people live in the Four Watches. I know only a handful. Many of my people on the coasts have ships."

"Yes, of course. I hoped, perhaps, you'd heard of him by reputation. No matter." As they reached the road that ran along the docks, Pancras noticed the statue of the god at each intersection matched the name of the pier. The sun hung low on the horizon by the time they led their horses across the Docks District to Selene's Pier.

The *Maiden of the High Seas* bobbed up and down without regard for the sailors carrying cargo across her gangplanks. A three-masted sailing vessel, she was fit for a voyage from the south to the northern ports of Vlorey and beyond. The captain stood on her poop deck, shouting orders to the rabble hustling about on the main deck. He was a stout man with a wild mane of blonde hair and a braided beard, which hung down to his chest.

Pancras stopped one of the sailors loading cargo and inquired how they could book their passage. The sailor pointed to a wiry man standing at the top of the gangplank.

"The quartermaster handles that." The sailor returned to his work. Pancras handed his reins to Qaliah. Gisella did the same, and together they walked up the gangplank. It creaked, bowing under their weight.

The quartermaster pointed at them when they neared the top. "Here now! What's this about?"

"We're looking to buy passage." Pancras stopped at the top of the plank. "Permission to come aboard?"

"Yes, yes. Get out of the way." The quartermaster waved them on board. Pancras gripped the rail to steady himself as the deck heaved under a wave.

"Now then, we're not going to Vlorey. Nearest we go is Port-of-Dogs. It's about a week overland to Vlorey from there."

"I don't understand. Isn't Vlorey a port?" Gisella clung to the rigging to maintain her balance. "The harbormaster said this ship goes to Vlorey."

"Yeah, but to make it to Vlorey, we got to sail up and around Verdant Point and back down the length of it." The quartermaster raised his eyebrows. His tone and cadence sounded similar to that of a parent speaking to a willful child. "Takes near a month sailing against the wind. It's much faster for all to unload at Port-of-Dogs. Only ships from the Elven Empire or from the west sail into the Bay of Vlorey."

"Fine then. There are three of us and our horses." Pancras gestured down the gangplank at Qaliah.

The quartermaster pursed his lips. "Livestock is extra. If the womenfolk want privacy, they'll have to negotiate with one of the officers for their cabin. One of the women officers might let them stay with her, but it's up to you to find a berth."

He reached over and squeezed Pancras's arm. "Minotaurs have strong backs. What work do you do?" He nodded at Gisella. "And you? The other woman?"

Pancras rubbed his arm where the quartermaster touched him. The man's grip felt like an iron vise. "I'm Bonelord of Aita and a wizard."

"Yeah?" The quartermaster raised his eyebrows. "Can you control the winds?"

"No." Pancras shook his head. One downside of spending most of his life practicing necromancy was that he had little opportunity to study any sort of elemental magic.

"What about you, girly?"

Gisella pursed her lips. "I am a slayer of the Arcane University."

"She fights," Pancras added in reply to the quartermaster's blank stare. "So does the fiendling."

The quartermaster peered over the rail at Qaliah and the horses. He grunted. "A hundred and fifty crowns, for the lot of you. Sleep where you find space, unless you can negotiate something better and"—he punctuated his statement by poking Pancras in the chest—"expect to work. This ain't a pleasure cruise."

Pancras and Gisella returned to the dock where Qaliah waited for them. They explained the arrangement to her.

"That seems expensive." The fiendling shielded her eyes with her hand and squinted at the heaving ship. The seas became rougher as the tides rose and storm clouds moved in.

"No more than I expected." Pancras glanced into his money pouch. "It shouldn't be a problem. I might be able to help with your negotiations for private quarters. How are your funds?"

"Not enough for private quarters." Qaliah bit her lip and glanced at Gisella. "Blondie might want to pony up for some privacy though."

Gisella frowned. "I wish you'd stop calling me that."

"Fine."

After they pooled their coin, Pancras returned to the quartermaster and paid their fare. The quartermaster instructed him where he should take their horses to be loaded. The minotaur returned to his companions. Within the hour, they were aboard the *Maiden*, peering over the rails on the forecastle.

Aware it was likely the last time he'd step foot on dry land for several months, Pancras turned to gaze at Cliffport. The sailors scurried over the *Maiden*'s decks like insects, responding to overlapping, shouted instructions from the deck officers and prepared the ship for launch.

From his vantage point on deck, Pancras hardly noticed the rising tide against the Docks District, which had been built to withstand the highest tides of a double full moon. At present, the King waxed while the Queen waned, although the heavy, grey clouds that moved in over the last few hours obscured them from view.

Enchanted lanterns illuminated the sea in front of the *Maiden* as she cleared her moorings and navigated the harbor. The buildings and the land shrank into the distance, and once the *Maiden* passed underneath Nethun's Arch, Pancras turned to gaze at the sea once more.

The minotaur thought of his friends, half a continent away in Muncifer and Drak-Anor, and hoped they were well. Aita was with him, and though he feared he would never see them again, he acknowledged he was about to embark on a new segment of his life. *A new life. A new purpose. Onward to Vlorey.*

***

Kale knelt by the ruined head of the dragon. He found the odor almost unbearable, but he forced himself to tolerate it. His sister stood behind him, hugging herself. The light from her staff cast long shadows over the carcass.

"What do we do now, Deli?" Kale stood and wiped his hands on his legs. "I didn't even know a Firstborne could die."

Delilah rested her hand on her brother's shoulder. "She's too big for us to bury, but we might as well search around. Maybe there's something we can take back with us, you know, to settle this business with the archmage and archduke?"

After sending a boggin message to Kali and Katka explaining the situation, Delilah and Kale picked their way through the rubble. This side of the chasm was littered with more fallen and shattered crystals than the other side.

Kale thought, perhaps, it was from the earthquake Delilah told them about earlier. He didn't understand how a mighty Firstborne dragon, a literal child of a god, could be brought low by something as mundane as a blow to the head, but he supposed if a crystal the size of a building landed on Terrakaptis, it would injure him.

"Kale, over here!" Delilah increased her pace, jumping over a fallen monolith. She skidded to a halt, flailing her arms at the edge of an area that resembled a crystal eruption. Small crystals of every shape and color jutted from a larger crystal in a circular pattern. The crystals formed a ring around a flat, textured area.

The two draks climbed over the outer ring. The surface of the crystals below them felt almost like pebbles beneath their feet. Kale found the texture less slick than the smooth areas of the geode chamber. The surface was still slanted, however, and Kale flapped his wings to aid his balance.

"Watch out over there." Delilah pointed to a dip in the surface of the textured area. After Kale shuffled toward it, he noticed it appeared to have been scooped out. The smooth, concave surface of the depression sloped toward one of the cracks that opened over the lava river. He saw an oblong object perched at the edge of the crack.

"Hold my hand, Deli." Kale stretched toward the object. "Don't let me fall!"

Upon discovering he could not reach the object from his position, he lay prone and extended his arms. When his fingers brushed the surface of the leathery object, the sigil on his chest burned. With a final lunge, he snatched the object, then he scooted away from the edge.

"What is it? Treasure?"

Kale rotated the object in his hands. It was almost as large as he was, albeit minus arms and legs. It's pebbly surface appeared almost translucent. It seemed to glow from within, but Kale supposed it might be a trick of the light. The closer he held it to him, the more the sigil on his chest burned. His own body remained unchanged.

"I think… I think it's an egg, Deli."

His sister whistled. "A dragon egg."

He glanced at the scooped area. "She must have been trying to save it and nearly knocked it into the crack when she died."

"We can't let the archmage know about this, Kale." Delilah crouched down, placing a hand on the egg. Kale felt movement within. He ran his hand along the egg's surface. Terrakaptis wanted to wake his siblings and trusted Kale to help with that task, but the Earth Dragon's sister was now dead.

"This egg is all that's left of Pyraclannaseous." Furrowing his brow, he clenched his jaw. "We need to bring it to Terrakaptis."

Delilah placed her hand on top of his. "We will. We have to deal with Manless, first, and keep this secret."

Kale nodded. His sister was right. If they fled for Drak-Anor with the egg, they still needed to worry about Katka, and if the human returned to Muncifer without them, eventually Boss Steelhand, the archduke, and Archmage Vilkan would discover that the draks fled. He pulled the egg close to his chest. The burning was a steady heat, but not painful. He swore he would guard the egg with his life and find a way to reunite the life within with its kin.

Heraldy of Andelosia

Free City of Celtangate

Free City of Ironkrag

Principality of Etrunia

Heraldy of Andelosia

Duchy of Muncifer

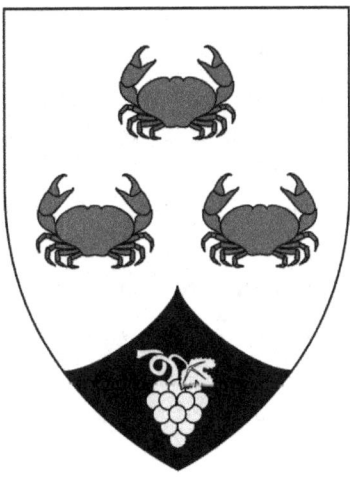

Free City of Vlorey

Arcane University

Hans Cummings
Author/Publisher

Author of the fantasy duology: The Foundation of Drak-Anor: *Wings of Twilight* and *Iron Fist of the Oroqs* as well as the Zack Jackson science fiction series, Hans Cummings published his first novel in 2011. Two of his short stories appear in Fear the Boot's Sojourn speculative fiction anthologies. He was Nuvo's Best of Indy — Best Local Author 3rd place Honoree for 2014 and 2015.

Hans is a voice over atist and gamer, and has appeared in "Great Voice No Training," "I Should Roll," Faerie's Tales," and more.

Hans earned a Bachelor of Arts degree in English from Indiana University in 2006. He grew up in Indiana, Germany, and Virginia and returned to Indiana when he was 21. He currently lives in Indianapolis with his wife. Hans's hobbies include tabletop and computer gaming, cooking and smoking meat, and igniting young people's curiosity and passion for science and exploration.

Learn more about this and other works by the author at:
http://vffpublishing.com/

Use Twitter? Follow the author @hccummings